Emily Maguire was born in Canberra in 1976, but has spent most of her life in Sydney. She has worked in a variety of occupations, read a lot of books and travelled to many countries. When she is not writing, Emily studies Literature at the University of New England and tutors English. She was awarded an Australian Society of Authors' Mentorship for 2003 with Liam Davison. *Taming the Beast* is her first novel and she is currently working on her second novel and writing feature articles for newspapers. She is married and lives in Sydney.

Taming the Beast

Emily Maguire

First published in Australia by Brandl & Schlesinger Pty Ltd in 2004

First published in the UK in 2005 by Serpent's Tail,
4 Blackstock Mews, London N4 2BT
website: www.serpentstail.com

Printed by Mackays of Chatham, plc

10 9 8 7 6 5 4 3 2 1

Part One

1

Sarah Clark felt like a freak for two and a half years. It started when she received a leather-bound copy of *Othello* for her twelfth birthday and ended when her English teacher showed her exactly what was meant by *the beast with two backs*.

In between, she read every one of Shakespeare's plays and then moved on to his sonnets, before discovering Marlowe, Donne, Pope and Marvell. With peers who read nothing but *TV Week* and parents who were inclined towards the *Financial Review*, Sarah was forced to conceal her literary leanings. She hid poetry anthologies under her bed and read *Emma* by torchlight, the way boys her age read *Playboy*. For the first two years of high school, she came top of her English class without opening a single school book. It wasn't necessary since the curriculum consisted of a few familiar texts, plus comic strips and newspaper clippings.

Then on the first day of the third year of high school, Sarah met Mr Carr. He was unlike any teacher she had ever encountered. For the entire forty minutes of his first class he spoke about why Yeats was relevant to Australian teenagers in the year 1995. In the second class, Sarah put up her hand to make a comment on something he had said about *Hamlet*. When he called on her to speak, she started and could not stop. She stayed in his classroom all through lunch, and when she re-emerged into the sunlight and the condescending stares of the schoolyard cliques, she was utterly changed.

Mr Carr began an active campaign to keep Sarah's love of learning alive. To prevent boredom, he brought her books of his own from home and gave her a note that allowed her to access the senior section of the library. Every novel and play and poem was discussed in depth. She had never received a better compliment than when he told her that he knew she would love a particular piece because it was his favourite too.

While Mr Carr was shaping Sarah's mind, her body was changing of its own accord. Small, painful breasts appeared overnight, as did ridiculously placed hair. She kept waking up in the middle of the night to find her blankets tossed to the floor and her hands tangled up in her pyjamas. Whenever the School Captain, a lanky blond boy named Alex, walked past, Sarah had an inexplicable urge to press her thighs together. She started to daydream about how to become more beautiful.

One day in June, Mr Carr asked Sarah's advice on how to make Shakespeare more exciting for the class. The sonnets studied so far had failed to ignite a spark of enthusiasm in anyone except Sarah, and he thought she could help identify where he was going wrong. The problem, as Mr Carr saw it, was that many of the sonnets dealt with themes that couldn't be understood by your average fourteen year old kid. Sarah told him that the average fourteen year old understood plenty about love and lust and longing; it was the language that put them off. After all, she said, every second song on the radio dealt with the same themes as old William, albeit with more grunting and less wit.

He laughed a throaty laugh and reached across the space that separated them. His hot, damp hand settled on her bare knee. Sarah noticed, all at once, that his forehead was shiny and the blinds were lowered and the door was closed and her heart was racing. She didn't move or speak. Breathing was all she could manage.

Mr Carr leant forward in his chair and moved his hand to Sarah's shoulder, then let it slide until it rested on one of her never before touched, brand new breasts. She felt like she might cry, but she also felt a sick kind of excitement. She sat very still with her arms at her sides and watched as he stroked and kneaded her breasts through the cheap polyester. His gold wedding band caught the light, and she wanted to reach out and touch it, but didn't. He was saying her name over and over, so that it no longer sounded like her name at all, but like one those mantras that Buddhists used to go into a trance.

Sarahohsarahohsarahohsarhohsarah.

One of his hands slipped inside her shirt, under her bra, and she was shocked by the thrill she got when his fingers caught hold of her left nipple and squeezed. *Ohsarah.* He moved forward, right to the edge of the chair, his head lowered to her chest, his shins pressed hard against hers. She had to bite down on her lip to stop herself from laughing. How strange that a smart and accomplished man could be reduced to such an undignified state just by touching her breasts!

Mr Carr stopped chanting her name, and the room was silent except for his rasping breath and the rustle of her shirt as he unbuttoned it. Then Sarah felt his tongue sweep across her nipple; she let out a surprised gasp. This excited Mr Carr even more, and his head all but disappeared into her half open shirt as he fell to his knees in front of her. A giggle escaped her, which Mr Carr obviously interpreted as encouragement. *OhSarahohSarahohohohohsobeautifulSarahoh.*

He pushed her legs open and knelt between them, his head still buried in her chest but his hands pushing up her scratchy pleated skirt. Sarah tried to remember which underpants she had put on that morning. She hoped it was not the pair with little ducks. If Mr Carr saw little ducks on her underwear he would think she was a child, and then he would stop. But he couldn't see her underwear anyway, because his mouth was still latched onto her nipple as if he was a hungry baby and she was a mother with heavy, milk filled breasts, instead of a girl with hardly enough to fill a training bra.

She liked the way it felt, the sucking. It was gentler and more rhythmic than she had expected. In the movies it all looked so frantic and out of control. Not that Sarah had anything to compare it to, but he seemed good at what he was doing: sucking her nipple and stroking her through her underwear in perfect time. Stroke and suck, stroke and suck.

The tempo changed when he plunged his hot, unexpected hand into her underpants. He seemed to be searching for something, his hands moving quickly, stroking and pressing one hidden spot after another and then moving on. Sarah thought she knew what he was trying to find and wondered why he was having so much trouble. She considered telling him that he had missed it, but found that she did not have any words to describe what it was he had passed over, or what it was that she expected him to do when he found it.

But then a flash of heat shot through her body, and she cried out in surprise as her hips bucked upwards. She felt the flash of heat again, followed by another and another as he continued pressing the secret spot, and she could not stop the noise that rose in her throat from escaping as she felt herself dissolving into his hand.

Mr Carr pulled away abruptly, gasping for air. *OhSarah wrong this is so wrong oh Sarah ohsarahsowrongohsarahoh.*

This was the best Sarah had ever felt. Ever. She wondered what to do to make him keep going. Then she realised her hands had been by her sides the whole time. She placed them on his stooped shoulders, holding him back, and he looked up, his face creased with need and guilt at that need. She slid from her chair, so she was on her knees in front of him, and slowly unzipped his trousers. She felt removed from herself, watching these stranger's hands reach in and take hold of this odd, hard, hot *thing*. It was as if all reason had left her and the part of her that was just instinct and heat had taken over.

Mr Carr groaned and his chant became frenzied and fast, not even distinguishable as language anymore, just a low desperate growl. He pushed her hand away, and for a second she thought he was angry, but then he said *OhGodohGodohGod* and fell on her. The pain tore through her, and she had to shove her fist into her mouth to stop from crying out. Then the pain stopped, and she felt warm and calm. Mr Carr was looking into her eyes, grunting at her. She touched his face and hair; he grimaced and moved faster. Then with one last, louder grunt, he rolled off her, leaving a warm, sticky mess.

The entire incident had taken less than ten minutes. As she buttoned her shirt, she could hear kids yelling outside the window, the sound of a netball whistle, a car engine turning over. She took a tissue from the box on his desk and wiped away the stuff trickling down her thighs. Mr Carr watched her while fat tears slid down his red cheeks. Sarah finished her clean up, and then she went to him and wiped his face.

'It's okay,' she told him. 'You don't have to feel bad.'

'I don't feel bad, Sarah. That's the tragedy.'

2

Because he was older and her teacher and married with children, Mr Carr could absolutely not allow a repeat of yesterday's incident. 'Oh,' said Sarah, who had thought the point of her staying back after school again was so that yesterday's incident could be repeated. The way he had kissed her as soon as the door was locked, the way he had run his fingers through her hair while he asked her how she was, the way he had begun to stroke her thigh as soon as they sat down, all seemed to confirm her initial assumption.

'I don't care about that stuff. I just feel happy being with you.'

'Oh, Sarah…' He squeezed her thigh. 'I wish being happy with each other was enough, but it isn't. I would lose my job, my kids. I could go to jail. The law doesn't care how happy we feel. You're fourteen years old, and according to the law you aren't capable of recognising what makes you happy.'

'Well, the law is wrong.' Sarah did what she had been thinking of doing ever since they sat down: she leant forward and kissed the crease between his eyebrows. 'It's insulting to assume I don't know what I want. You know for most of history girls my age were expected to be married and popping out babies. It's ridiculous to think that five hundred years ago I would be considered capable of raising a family, but now I'm not even allowed to decide if I like a guy or not.'

'It seems silly, I know.'

'It *is* silly. I wish I lived in the middle ages. I'd have my own damn village by now.'

Mr Carr laughed. 'Yes, and except for the leprosy and bad breath and illiteracy I'm sure you'd be very happy.'

Sarah felt herself growing hot. Hot because she was embarrassed by his laughing at her. Also, hot because of the way he was touching her thigh. His hand was as big as two of hers; it covered a lot of skin with every stroke. She kissed his wrinkle again, then his forehead, then his lips.

'Sarah…'

'So society doesn't approve. We won't tell them.'

'Sarah…'

'Yesterday was the best day of my whole life. I felt like Pip does after he first goes to Miss Havisham's house. Yesterday made great changes in me; it forged the first link in the chain which will bind me. I need to find out what my chain will be. Thorns or flowers. Iron or gold.'

Mr Carr withdrew his hand from her thighs and stood up. He went to the window and opened the blind. He looked out on the empty quadrangle, shaking his head. 'In sixteen years of teaching I have never come across a student even half as clever as you. And only rarely have I seen one as beautiful.' He snapped the blind shut and turned back to face her. 'No one can know.'

'I know. That's okay.'

'No one can even suspect.'

She couldn't stop smiling. She went to him and pressed her face to his chest. 'We'll be careful.' She ran her hands over his back, feeling how big he was, how solid. 'Careful and happy.'

He hugged her hard, as though he was afraid, as though he thought clinging to her would save him. She reached up and stroked his face. She kissed the curly blonde hair at the V of his shirt, and he moaned and said her name *ohSarah*.

'What do I call you?' She asked his collarbone. 'Can I call you Daniel?'

'No. You can't get in the habit. If you call me that in class…'

'Okay, that's okay.' She untucked his shirt and ran her hand across his belly. The skin there was so soft; if it wasn't for the coarse hair down the centre, it could have been the belly of a child. His skin was so soft it could almost have been her own.

Mr Carr and Sarah arranged to meet after school at the petrol station around the corner. From there he drove to Toongabbie Creek, keeping both hands on the wheel, both eyes on the road, talking about poetry in such a way that she wished they would never reach their destination. But then when the car was parked beside the creek, hidden from the road by paperbarks and scrub, Mr Carr did things to her that made words superfluous. Fucking was poetry unbound.

At sunset, he drove her home, stopping at the end of her street and warning her not to kiss him, just in case.

'I don't want to go,' Sarah said.

He patted her hand. 'It's after six. Your mother will be worried.'

Sarah snorted. Her mother, who spent seventy hours a week at the university and the rest of the time in her home office, would not notice if Sarah stayed out all night. Sarah's father worked even longer hours than his wife and barely knew he had a second daughter. Her sister, though, had no life and so noticed everything.

Sure enough, Kelly, who at seventeen was already middle-aged, pounced as soon as Sarah walked through the front door.

'I was studying,' Sarah said, because if there was one thing Kelly enjoyed more than nagging Sarah about her whereabouts, it was nagging Sarah about studying. But then Kelly wanted to know what she was studying and where she was doing it and with whom and why couldn't it be done in Sarah's room which their parents had equipped with a corner desk, a study lamp, an ergonomic chair, a computer and well-stocked bookshelves?

'Mind your own beeswax,' Sarah said, pushing past her sister.

'You know you're not allowed to have a boyfriend.'

'So?'

Kelly rolled her eyes. 'So, if you're meeting a boy after school and Mum finds out–'

'How would Mum find out unless someone tells her?'

'So there is something to tell?'

'Like I'd tell you.'

Kelly looked hurt. 'I'd tell you.'

'Like you'd have anything to tell.'

'You're such a bitch.'

'Takes one to know one,' Sarah said, and went to her room to think about Mr Carr until dinner time.

Sarah and Kelly were not allowed to have boyfriends because it would interfere with their academic development. When they started university they would be allowed to date, but nothing serious, nothing too time consuming. Women could not afford to be distracted by romance until they had established themselves in their careers. This did not bother Kelly, who was going to be a lawyer in a few years, and marry another lawyer when she was thirty and give birth to two future lawyers when she was thirty-two and thirty-five. She would not put herself in a position which could lead anyone to accuse her of depending on a man. Like their mother, Kelly would marry based on compatibility of life goals, which all intelligent people understood was the only way to ensure a marriage lasted beyond the honeymoon.

Sarah did not see what any of this had to do with her. She was fourteen years old with clear skin and shiny brown hair down to the middle of her back. She had read more books than anyone she had ever met, could speak French fluently and Japanese haltingly.

She had had sexual intercourse three times, had experienced orgasm twice, and was so in love and loved that her head swam whenever she tried to think about anything else. That was okay; she didn't need to think about anything else anyway. Average thoughts were for average people. Which she was not. Which she would never be.

3

They quickly grew frustrated with the cramped back seat of Mr Carr's Falcon and with the time wasted in driving and parking, and so met instead at the school. The classroom was too risky, Mr Carr said, but he had scoped out the school and come up with a number of alternative meeting places.

There was the English department book room, which was never used after hours and could be locked, but which was on the same floor as the staff room, so lovemaking had to be silent. The Agricultural storeroom was a safer bet, since it was a tin shed separated from the permanent school buildings by the student vegetable plots, but it was airless and filled with fertiliser, and the stink clung to their bodies for hours afterwards. The boy's P.E. locker room was perfect – set well apart from the main buildings, lockable and with tiled floors which would announce any intruders early enough for Sarah and Mr Carr to flee through the back exit – but it was in use for after school sport every day except Monday. There was also the canteen (empty every afternoon but difficult to get to without being seen by half a dozen teachers and students) and the auditorium (as long as they were gone before five-thirty when dance classes were held).

Each day as they were parting, Mr Carr would tell Sarah where to be the next afternoon. Some days he was in a rush because he had a meeting, often he was late and twice he did not turn up at all. He left his phone turned on so he would know if someone was looking for him, and several times he had to leave half-way through fucking her, because another teacher rang and said they were on their way to the library or staffroom or wherever it was he said he was.

Some days, the door was locked and Mr Carr's trousers off before Sarah had even put down her school bag. Other days he kept her sitting at his feet for hours while he lectured her on poetry, not touching her at all until it was time for her to leave, when he would beg her for five more minutes. If she agreed, which she almost always did, he would kiss her tenderly and make love to her. The one time she said no, that she had to get home, he looked at her with wet, wide eyes as though she had hit him. Then he slapped her, hard, and called her a tease and a time waster. He pushed her to her knees, unzipped his pants and with one hand on the back of her head and the other up against the locker room wall, he fucked her mouth until he came.

She slumped against the cold tiles, eyes and scalp stinging, trying not to choke or vomit. He zipped up his trousers and nudged her with his foot. 'Well, off you go, Sarah. I know you're in a big hurry to get home. Run along, now.'

Sarah grabbed his legs and pulled herself to a standing position. She removed a checked handkerchief from his shirt pocket, unfolded it, raised it to her lips, spat out the sour stuff in her mouth, refolded the handkerchief and replaced it in his pocket.

'Disgusting,' she told him, because it was, but she couldn't sleep that night with wishing she had kept the handkerchief.

For two hours each weekday, Sarah Clark ceased to exist. Afterwards, she could never identify the exact moment it happened, but always there was the crossing over, the melting, the absorption. There was no border where her body ended and Mr Carr's began. Mr Carr explained that this was what Shakespeare meant by 'the beast with two backs.' When two people were completely bound in the expression of love, they ceased to be separate individuals and became one creature. The act of passion, when properly performed, created an organism larger than the sum of its parts; it created a beast with two backs, but one soul. Sarah knew it was no metaphor: if anyone were to stumble across their secret meeting place between three and five each day, they would not see a girl and her teacher making illegal, impossible love. They would see only a bucking, screaming two-headed monster. A dumb creature with no awareness of a world outside of itself. With no desire except to become more itself and less everything else.

For the other twenty-two hours a day, and through the interminable, school-less weekends, Sarah felt more separate than ever, as if the edges of her body were thicker than they had been previously, as if she disturbed the air when she moved through it. When she ran barefoot to the bathroom each morning, she felt every fibre of the carpet as it was flattened under her feet. Biting into her morning toast, she could feel the tiny grooves on the thin edge of each tooth as they serrated the bread. She could feel every individual taste bud being awakened by the strawberry jam. The stimulation was so intense that she couldn't eat more than half a slice.

Brushing her hair, cleaning her teeth, washing herself in the shower – everything felt like masturbation. She fastened her bra thinking *the skin on my back is smoother than my face.* She poked at herself saying *this is my finger, these are my ribs.* She woke in the night because someone was touching the inside of her thighs; a stranger's fingers were pulling on her nipples. An old man touched the small of her back when she was getting onto the bus and she shuddered as though he had stuck his whole hand inside her, as though he had taken a piece of her soul.

Her body was always hot. Her underpants always damp. Every night, her hair needed washing and her legs needed shaving. Her knees were sore more often than not, and small bruises appeared, faded, reappeared on the insides of her thighs and wrists. Sometimes, there were bite marks on her buttocks or the back of her neck. She felt taller and stronger and walked with longer strides. She glowed and could not believe that everyone who looked at her didn't *know*.

'No one can know,' Mr Carr said every day, before, after, sometimes during, their love making. Sometimes he softened the message, saying he wished he could tell the world how happy he was, what bliss he had found, and that he dreamed of a world where true passion would be celebrated not punished; other times he was stern, threatening even, telling her that if anyone found out, he would lose his job and maybe even go to jail. 'Just think about that next time you get the urge to gossip to your friends.'

'I don't gossip,' Sarah told him, which was true, but it was also true that she was driven to tell someone about what was happening. She was compelled to say it aloud – *I love him* – and have someone hear it and know it was true.

She thought about telling Jess, whom she had known longer than anyone else in the world outside of her family. Jess had lived in the two-story mock Tudor house next door to Sarah's two-story mock Tudor house since the girls were four years old. Their parents played tennis together and went to all the same dinner parties. Sarah and Jess were friends not because they liked each other excessively, but because the circumstances of their lives meant that to *not* be friends would require a pointed decision which neither of them had ever felt enough dislike of the other to make. But even if they'd known each other a hundred years, Sarah would not tell Jess about Mr Carr. Jess giggled when she heard the word 'penis' and screwed up her face on 'vagina'. She was bored by poetry and thought Mr Carr was a drag for making them learn it.

Jess was Sarah's oldest friend, but her best friend was Jamie Wilkes whom she had only known for two and a half years. They met on the first day of high school, in the first class of the day, which was Geography. The students were seated alphabetically in a classroom laid out like a horseshoe, which meant that Clark was directly opposite Wilkes, both of them second from the front of the room, with only Burton and Yates ahead of them. The teacher told them to stare straight ahead while the assignments for the year were distributed. So for ten minutes, Jamie and Sarah had to look across the classroom at each other. Jamie kept looking away – down at his desk or over his shoulder – but his gaze always returned to Sarah's. She smiled at him; he looked down, then up, and smiled back. When the assignments had been distributed, the teacher told them they would work in pairs to complete the first task. Knowing no one, Sarah raised her eyebrows at Jamie, who turned red and nodded. They found they worked well together and had the same sense of humour. Also, being short, skinny and asthmatic, Jamie was a natural ally to undeveloped, bookish Sarah. They hung out together on the fringes of their class and were happy there.

Jamie was sensitive to the sun, the wind, pollen and grass. The other thing he was sensitive to was Sarah. He monitored her every breath and mood, and so now that all her breaths and moods were for and about Mr Carr, Jamie knew something was up with her.

'Are you sick?' he asked her when she got to school on the Tuesday of the sixth week of her affair with Mr Carr.

'Never better.' It was true. Yesterday afternoon Mr Carr had read to her from Donne's *Songs and Sonnets*. He told her that Donne's love poems were inspired by his teenaged student whom he later eloped with. 'Imagine,' he said to Sarah, unbuttoning her shirt, 'if Donne had not loved his young student.' He removed her shirt and bra and covered both her breasts with his hands. 'What a loss to Western culture. What a tragic, tragic loss that would have been.'

'You're all flushed,' Jamie said. 'Like when you had that fever at camp last year. Your eyes are all bloodshot too. I really think you should go—'

'I'm fine!' Sarah laughed. 'You're such a nana.'

'Jess said you haven't been walking home with her lately. She thinks you're pissed off at her.'

'She's such a drama queen. I've been staying back a bit. Studying in the library.'

'Why don't you just go home and study?'

Sarah ignored him. She mentally rehearsed the Thomas Carew poem she had memorised last night. She was going to recite it to Mr Carr this afternoon. It was called *The Rapture*, and she hoped it would send him into one. There was a bit in it she was sure was talking about a clitoris, and a whole lot of stuff about fluids and elixirs which made her think about the mess her underwear was in when she got home each day.

'I think you're hiding something, Miss Clark.' Jamie used the fake-confident voice that he used to tell his older brother to get out of his room or he'd kick his head in. 'I think maybe you're staying back after school to meet up with someone.'

Her heart beat faster. 'Why would you think that?'

'I don't know. Maybe because you spend the last hour of every day playing with your hair. And you check your watch every twenty seconds and then bolt for the door as soon as the bell rings.'

'I do not.'

He raised his eyebrows. 'You retied your plait four times in half an hour yesterday afternoon.'

Mr Carr liked to play with her hair. He sometimes used her ponytail as a sort of lead, pulling her head where he wanted it to go, or if she had plaits either side he used them like reins. Yesterday he had wrapped her single plait around his cock, then released her hair and had her drag its length over his body.

'Ha! You're blushing. Why won't you tell me? I thought we were friends?'

'Jamie, we are, it's just…' She checked to make sure no one was in earshot. 'No one can know, okay?'

'Okay.'

'I'm serious. There will be major, major trouble if anyone finds out. Going to gaol kind of trouble.'

Jamie laughed. 'You call Jess a drama queen! Why would anyone go to gaol for–' He blinked. 'I don't get it.'

'Because I'm underage and he's a teacher.' Her smile was unstoppable, even though she knew this moment should be a serious one.

'What? You're kidding?' He blinked fast. 'You are kidding?'

'No. I've been meeting Mr Carr every day after school. I'm having an affair with him.'

Jamie blinked at her for a few more seconds. Then he shook his head and punched her shoulder. 'Bitch,' he said. 'You had me going there for a second.'

4

While Mr Carr continued to warn Sarah against revealing their secret, he flirted – thrillingly! – with self-exposure. One time, he had the office messenger deliver an envelope to her during second period Maths. On the outside it said: *Public Speaking Competition Entry Form*. Inside, the note said: *Your face, contorted in agonising pleasure, just appeared in my mind unbidden. I am trapped behind my desk, burning*. Another note, dropped onto her desk during English class, while she was deep in thought, her pen hanging from between her lips, said *O, how I wish I was that ballpoint pen*. Sometimes, passing her in the hallways, he brushed her arse or breasts or mouthed words obscene or romantic or both.

When their affair was two months old, Sarah gave a presentation to the class about Emily Dickinson: a poet whom she knew Mr Carr believed should be expunged from the canon. Sarah took this as a personal insult and was determined to change his mind. While her classmates dozed up the back of the room, passed notes or covertly listened to the Walkmans hidden in their pencil cases, Sarah passionately argued Emily Dickinson's significance. Mr Carr listened intently, interrupting now and then to clarify a point or ask a question. 'I'm not sure about your claim that Dickinson was comical. Can we have an example?'

'Of course.' Sarah looked him in the eye and recited Poem XI:

'*Much madness is divinest sense*
To a discerning eye;
Much sense the starkest madness
'*T is the majority*

> *In this, as all, prevails*
> *Assent and you are sane;*
> *Demur, – you're straightway dangerous*
> *And handled with a chain.'*

He slow-clapped her, smiling. 'Very impressive, but perhaps *wry* would be a better word than comical?' He leant forward in his chair. 'And I hope you understand how provocative you're being. Chains as a penalty for dissent? My, my, Sarah.'

Sarah felt her face growing hot. She looked away from him, out at the class, but no one – except Jamie, who was staring wide-eyed and open-mouthed at an unseeing Mr Carr – seemed to have noticed his comment. They were not listening to nerdy Sarah Clark and boring Mr Carr debating some dead chick's poetry; they didn't realise they were witnessing foreplay.

Sarah finished her presentation with an anecdote: 'Emily Dickinson once had her work rejected by an editor who criticised her unconventional use of punctuation, specifically her overuse of dashes. Her reply was to the point: "I am in danger, Sir." Reading her poems today we can feel her racing heart, her quick breath, the hot blood rushing through her veins. We feel her urgency and it becomes ours.'

Mr Carr thanked her for her work and called on the next student to come forward, but after class he whispered for her to meet him at the petrol station *now*, and though they both had half a day of classes remaining, they fled to their old parking spot by the creek and Mr Carr told her that her speech had filled him with unbearable longing.

'I never realised Emily Dickinson could be erotic,' he said and Sarah told him that nothing had ever seemed erotic until he showed her that everything was.

The next afternoon in the canteen, Mr Carr was in a foul temper. He accused Sarah of purposely provoking him into the sort of risky behaviour which would get him fired. He called her manipulative and vicious, which made her cry. He told her she was ugly when she cried, and so she held her breath until she had control of herself. Feeling dizzy and ashamed, she pressed her ugly face into his chest and was weak with relief when he stroked her hair and told her he was sorry and that she was so beautiful he could hardly stand it.

'It's my wife,' he said. 'She called the office yesterday afternoon, and they told her I'd gone home sick. She cried half the night. I didn't know what to say to her.'

Sarah lifted her head, stood on her toes and kissed his lips. She rubbed his back and kissed him behind his ears. 'Yeah, I nearly got busted too. My stupid sister's stupid friend saw me walking across the car park. I said I was going to get something out of Miss Wright's car for her. Don't think she believed me…' Sarah kissed his Adam's apple. 'We better not leave like that again.'

'Sooner or later, we will be found out.'

'Maybe by then it won't matter.'

He stepped back and looked down into her face. 'How could it ever not matter? I love my wife, Sarah. I love my kids. Do you have any idea what knowing about us would do to them?'

Sarah froze. It had never occurred to her that he didn't want what she did. She had thought of his family as an obstacle, like her parents and her age. She had assumed all obstacles would be overcome, that love was *an ever fixed mark, that looks on tempests and is not shaken.* But if love was what he had for his wife, then Sarah was the tempest. She was the impediment which would not be admitted.

'Are you dumping me?'

'Am I *dumping you*?' Mr Carr laughed. 'God, what an expression.'

Sarah couldn't help it; she began to cry again. 'Why are you being so mean?'

'Oh, precious.' He folded her up in his arms. 'It's ridiculous to think of this, us, as the kind of adolescent romance that could be ended by *dumping*. As if we could stop this just by speaking a few little words. I wish it was that easy, truly. I wish I could say "it's over" and it would be. You and I won't stop needing each other until we're both dead and buried.'

'Until *my quaint honour turns to dust*?'

'My God, you are remarkable.' Mr Carr lifted her easily and sat her on the preparation bench. He parted her legs and stood between them, his hands and hers working together to undo his zipper, remove her underpants, push his trousers and jocks to his knees. 'How is it possible that you always know exactly what to say? I've been such a grumpy, mean man and you, oh!' He pushed inside her. 'Oh, Sarah, I fear I'm going to wear your *quaint honour* into dust before your fifteenth birthday. Your poor little, oh, God, am I hurting you?'

'No,' she said, although he was.

'I am, aren't I?' He moved faster. 'Tell me, Sarah, please. I'm hurting you, yes?'

'Yes, it hurts. But I like it, Mr Carr, really.'

He groaned. He was finished. 'Oh, my little Sarah. You always know what to say.'

'Sarah?' Jamie asked. It was Friday night and they were sprawled on Jamie's living room couch. MTV was on, but neither of them was watching it. Sarah was reading *Madame Bovary* and Jamie was flicking through *Rolling Stone*.

'Mmm?' She did not look up. Jamie hadn't said more than two words to her since the Emily Dickinson presentation yesterday. She wondered if he was finally going to ask her about it.

'Wanna drink?'

She sighed. 'Nah.'

Jamie left the room and came back with a can of coke and a bag of Doritos. He sat on the floor, opened his drink and took a swig, then opened his chips and crunched through a handful. 'So,' he said.

'What?'

'You and Mr Carr are really…'

Sarah's heart skipped. She closed her book and sat up. 'Yeah. I told you.'

He nodded. 'I thought… Um, so you… you kiss and stuff?'

'Yeah.'

Jamie took another drink. 'Have you done it with him?'

She nodded.

'Fuck.' Jamie stood up and kicked a bean bag. 'Fuck, Sarah, this is… he must be forty!'

'No. He's only thirty-eight.'

'He's a teacher!'

'We're in love.'

Jamie sat down and picked up his magazine. After a while, Sarah returned to her novel. She felt let down by him, but wasn't sure why. What did she expect? Congratulations? She tried to imagine how she would have felt if the situation was reversed, but the thought of Jamie doing to a woman the things that Mr Carr did to Sarah was just too bizarre. She would be surprised if Jamie had even heard of some of the stuff she did with Mr Carr. But then, she had never known about any of it before Mr Carr had taught her. A couple of months ago she was as innocent as Jamie; now she doubted that anything about sex could shock her.

'Are you angry?' she asked Jamie when she was leaving.

He shrugged. 'Who else knows?'

'Just you. You won't tell anyone will you?'

He shook his head. Sarah thought she saw a tear forming in his left eye but he turned away before she could be sure. 'Goodnight,' he said, and closed the door, not offering to walk her home for the first time ever.

5

Sometimes he was so much the English teacher that it drove her crazy. While he was locking the change room door, she let slip that she had finished *Madame Bovary* last night, and now he wanted to waste precious alone time talking about it.

'We can talk after.'

He smiled. 'Anxious, aren't you?'

Sarah shrugged her school bag off her shoulders. 'The weekends are so long. By Monday afternoon I'm just so—'

'Horny?'

She felt herself blush. It was the sort of word the girls who shared smokes in the toilet block used to describe the boys they drove around with on Saturday nights. Sarah did not think it was the proper word for what she felt.

'It's not that. I just miss you.'

'So hurry up and sit down.' He pointed to the stainless steel bench that ran through the centre of the room. 'Talk to me.' He sat himself at her feet, looking up at her. 'I want to know what you thought of Emma Bovary.'

Sarah sighed. 'I don't know. I sort of hated her, especially how she treated her kid, but I felt sorry for her, too.'

'Tell me why.'

'Well, because she was searching for something amazing, for ecstasy. But her husband's such a plodder, so she falls for the first guy who offers her a bit of excitement and he turns out to be a pig and then the next guy is this awful coward and it just seems the more she searches, the worse things get for her.'

'And this makes her deserving of our sympathy?'

'I just think it's sad she never found what she was looking for.'

'Do you think what she was looking for even exists?'

Sarah nudged him with her shoe. 'Yes.'

He took hold of her foot. 'And what makes you think you're not as deluded as poor Emma?'

'You do.'

Mr Carr frowned up at her. 'Ah, Sarah,' he said, and started to untie her shoelace.

'You didn't say if you missed me on the weekend.'

'Didn't I?' He continued untying her shoelaces.

'No.'

'Do you want me to say it?' Mr Carr slipped off her shoes and placed them on the floor beside him.

'Only if it's true.'

He removed her socks slowly, using both hands for each foot, then laid the socks on top of her shoes. 'Of course I missed you, you silly little thing.' He raised her left foot to his mouth and kissed each toe in turn. 'It's intolerable to be away from you for so long.' He kissed the top of her foot and her ankle. 'Excruciating.'

'I don't see why we can't meet on the weekends. I'm sure I could–'

He stopped kissing his way up her shin. 'I'm sure you could, Sarah, but I could not. I live in the grown-up world and grown-ups have responsibilities. Obligations to other people. I can't just turn my back on my family because you're having *urges*.'

Sarah bit her lip. She hated it when he used his teacher's voice on her. More than that, she hated it when he talked about his family. She knew they were out there – sleeping in his bed, eating at his table, laughing at his sticking up hair first thing in the morning – but it made her chest hurt to think about them. She wished she'd never brought up the damn weekend.

'I'm sorry.' She reached for his face and ran her palm over his smooth forehead, then the invisible, scratchy hairs on his cheek and jaw. 'I forget there are other people who need you. When I'm with you, I forget that there's anything else in the world. Please don't stop kissing my leg. I like that so much.'

'*She is all States, and all Princes, I. Nothing else is.*' He smiled without teeth and lowered his head. His lips touched down on her knee for the briefest moment and then he looked up again. 'Source?'

'Donne. Um, *Sunne Rising*?'

'Good girl.' He began to lick the inside of her thighs, pushing her skirt up little by little. He moved slowly. Unbearably so. She was almost in tears by the time he reached the top. He groaned into her crotch, pressing his face into her underwear for a moment, before pulling back.

'Take your pants off. And your skirt.'

She stood and did as he asked, while he sat below her looking up between her legs.

'Now lie on the bench. On your back with your–' He pushed at the inside of her knees. 'A leg on either side. Yes. Good girl.'

The steel was cold beneath her, but she didn't complain. In a few minutes he would be inside her and she could be lying on broken glass for all she'd care.

He knelt at her left side and took her hands. 'I'm going to show you something, Sarah, and I want you to pay attention. When you're feeling lonely–' He took her left hand and placed it firmly between her legs. 'When you're missing me–' He took up her right hand and positioned it over her clitoris. 'This is what I want you to do.'

Sarah closed her eyes and let him move her. It was her hands, her fingers, but it was Mr Carr making her moan and shake. He kept control, nudging her to go further, move faster, make smaller circles. 'You're nearly there, darling,' he told her and she started to tell him she wasn't, but he shushed her. 'I want you to clench your muscles really tight. Try and squash your fingers.' Almost right away, she was coming, the clenching bringing on the waves, which made her muscles contract, which brought on more waves.

She sat up, and the blood returning to her head made the room spin. She closed her eyes until the dizziness stopped. When she opened them, she saw that Mr Carr was looking up at her with a toothless smile.

'Well, I'd say that was a success.'

She touched his lips with her fingers. 'What?'

'You did a fine job. You don't need me anymore.'

'No.' She rubbed her hands over his face and lips. She slid to the floor, kissed his lips and tasted herself. 'I do need you. I need you. I need you.'

'You managed pretty well with your own–'

'Shut up! You think you're so smart, but I know what you're trying to do. It won't work.' Sarah was kissing him, wrestling with his trousers, pulling off her own sweaty shirt. 'You can't make me not miss you. Having a stupid orgasm is nothing. Okay? Nothing. God, you're so stupid! I'm always, always on my own. I could have a thousand stupid orgasms a day if I wanted. But it would just make me more alone. Can't you understand that? If I touch myself it reminds me that I'm not touching you. I don't want to touch or be touched by anyone else. I need you. You! Okay, do you get it, you stupid old man?'

There was so much blood pounding in her head it was clouding her vision. She couldn't see the expression on his face when he knocked her over, but the sound he made as he drove into her was frightening. Then there was no question of them not needing each other; they couldn't seem to disentangle, couldn't stop clutching and clawing, couldn't not be one. By the time Mr Carr rolled off her, panting and gasping so badly that Sarah's own heart began to flutter in fear for his, it was dark inside and out.

Sarah's mother was in the front room when Sarah got home. 'Where have you been?' she asked, without looking up from her book.

'Jamie's.'

'Don't lie to me, Sarah. Jamie called for you over an hour ago.'

Sarah's legs and back ached. She needed a hot shower and a soft bed. She leant against the wall, as far away from her mother's chair as she could get without leaving the room. 'I was just hanging out with some friends. I lost track of the time. I'm sorry.'

'Your sister tells me you've been coming home late for weeks.'

Sarah closed her eyes. Why the hell did her mother suddenly care what she was doing? Sarah would have killed for this much attention a year ago, but now she wanted to melt into the wall. She wanted to be invisible to everyone except *him*.

'I'm sorry, Mum, but I don't have anything else to tell you. I was with friends and I lost track of time. It won't happen again.'

Her mother put down her book. 'I know what's happening here. You're fourteen; you're trying to assert your independence. You're testing the limits of your personhood. That's a perfectly healthy, natural impulse for someone in your age group.'

'I'm not an age group, Mum.'

'Of course you're not. You're Sarah Jane Clark. An individual. I see you.' She smiled. 'You're an individual who needs to know where her boundaries are. So, let's negotiate.'

She wished her mother could be normal, just yell for a couple of minutes and cut off her pocket money or something. Instead everything had to be done according to how The Research said it had to be done. Every parenting decision was made in line with Expert Opinion. The book her mother was reading was probably called 'Professional Parenting.' It probably instructed her to *Empower your child by Negotiating rather than Demanding. Allow your child to own his or her behaviour.*

It would go faster if she played along. 'Okay, I would like to be allowed out until nine on week nights and twelve on weekends.'

A laugh. 'The first rule of negotiating: Always ask for more than you expect. Right, I refuse that offer and propose that you come straight home from school every day. Weekends will be negotiated on a case by case basis depending on where you are going and with whom.'

'I can't come straight home every day. My English teacher is tutoring me after class.'

'Why?'

'I'm struggling a bit. I only got a B for my last assignment.'

Her mother nodded. 'Fine. Study with your teacher, but be home by six-thirty.'

'Can I go to bed now?'

'In a minute. We need to decide on your punishment. Something commensurate. What's fair, do you think?'

'I thought negotiating boundaries *was* my punishment.'

'How droll.' She sighed. 'Fine, I'll decide. You're grounded for a month. You'll go to school and you'll come home. For one month. Okay?'

'Marvellous. I don't want to go anywhere but school anyway.'

'Yes, Sarah, I'm sure. Good night.'

Sarah began to move away, taking care to walk normally and to stay to the shadows. If her mother noticed her limping or, worse, the scratches on her throat, her life would be over. When she got to the doorway she snuck a peak at her mother, just to make sure she hadn't noticed anything. She needn't have worried; her mother was already reabsorbed in her book.

6

Sarah smiled when Mr Carr walked into the classroom. He hadn't shaved this morning, and the tiny hairs she often felt on his face at the end of the day were visible. She might ask if she could pluck a hair out with her teeth, or maybe he would let her shave him.

She wasn't only smiling at the stubble; his whole appearance was funny today. Usually he wore his hair spiked up with a little gel, but today it lay flat against his skull. His nose was red, as though he'd spent the previous day at the beach, and there were dark circles under his eyes. He looked old and like he would smell of cough medicine and mothballs if you got up close. She could hardly wait to tease him about looking like a bum. He would tease her back, because she too looked like hell. Their mutual raggedness was a consequence of what took place in the boy's locker room last night, and knowing that made her hot all over. She was busting with joy just from looking at how changed he was. Look at what my love has done to him, she thought. My love is so strong you can see it.

She made herself look away from him, gazing down at her book so it would appear she was smiling at something written there. Not that anyone would be watching her, except Jamie who would know who her smile was for anyway. She glanced up again, looking straight into Mr Carr's eyes. Oh! How could eyes be so green? She had seen every inch of his body and been surprised and delighted by what certain parts of it could do, but his eyes were far and away her favourite part. His eyes stripped her completely; under his gaze she was naked in a way that had nothing to do with lacking clothes.

He cleared his throat. 'Before we start, I have an announcement to make.'

Oh, she loved his voice, too. Maybe even more than she loved his eyes. It was so hard to look at him and not be able to touch him. She clenched her thighs and stared at the top of her desk.

'As I'm sure you're all aware, we have just under three weeks left of this term.' He waited for the cheers to die down before continuing. 'Which means you only have to put up with me for another fourteen periods.'

Sarah looked at him. He was looking at the back wall, not smiling.

'When you get back from the break you'll have a new teacher, who I know will enjoy teaching this class as much as I have.'

Sarah willed him to look at her. She needed to know what this meant. She had to see his eyes.

'Did you get sacked?' Jerry Gleason called out. Everybody laughed, except Sarah who was now certain that this was exactly what had happened.

'Incredibly, enough, no.' He smiled, but it wasn't real. 'I'm transferring to Brisbane.'

Still he wouldn't look at her. Brisbane? It couldn't be true. She tried to take a deep breath but there was no air. A hand closed over her arm. 'You okay?' Jamie whispered. She shook her head no.

'Why the sudden move?' Jamie asked.

'It's not sudden at all.' Mr Carr addressed his answer to the back wall. 'My wife's family is in Brisbane. We've been planning the move for some time. I confirmed my new position with the department this morning.'

Sarah's stomach contracted, and her throat filled with bile. Covering her mouth with her hand, she pushed her chair back and ran from the room. She heard Jamie say her name, then Mr Carr said 'What's the mat–' Then Jamie said, 'You fucking creep.' She made it to the garbage bin in the hallway just before her breakfast came up. When she finished vomiting, she found that Jamie was standing beside her and the classroom door was closed.

'Fucking creep,' Jamie repeated.

'Go fuck yourself, Jamie.' Sarah wiped her mouth and headed back to Mr Carr's classroom.

One day, for pleasure simply, we were reading
Of Lancelot, and how love overpowered him;
Alone we were, and free from all suspicions.

Often that reading caused our eyes to meet,
And often the colour from our faces went,
But it was a single passage that overcame us:

When we read how the desired smile was
Kissed by one so true a lover, then this one,
Who from me never will be taken,

Kissed me, his body all trembling, on the mouth.
…And no more did we read that day.

Sarah handed the slip of paper back to him. 'What the fuck is this?'

'Dante Alighieri. It's from *Inferno*, Sarah. You haven't read it yet, I know, but you will. You'll read it after I'm gone and you'll think of me. You see Francesca and Paolo–'

'I won't read it.' She tore the paper from his hand, ripped it in two, then in four. 'I can't believe you're doing this.'

'Sarah, last night was insanity. You know that don't you?'

'I thought it was… I was happy.'

He stood up and ran his hands through his hair. 'Try and understand… I walk in the door at nine-thirty when my family have been expecting me since six. My shirt is ripped. I have bite marks on my chest. I have blasted scratches all over my back. My wife starts crying and I can't get her to stop. Then my…' He took three deep breaths. 'The girls were still awake. They were crying too. It was…' Mr Carr pressed his forehead against the blackboard. 'I had to make a choice, Sarah.'

'What about me? Do I get a choice?'

He was quiet for too long.

'So that's it?' Panic was rising in her. Her mind scrambled for something – anything – that would change his mind. 'All that– everything you, we, did and all those things you said to me. I don't believe you didn't mean it. I know you did. Our souls are joined! I know they are. I feel it every time we, God, I don't even know what to call it. But we are one in it. You know this is true.'

Mr Carr knelt at her feet. He buried his face in her lap. She wanted to hurt him, to knee him in the jaw, punch him in the face, kick his disgusting balls. No, she wanted to *want* that. She wished she could hate him.

'What can I do to make you stay?'

His words were muffled by her skirt, but clear enough. 'Nothing. I'm sorry.'

She could not believe him. He was upset by the scene with his stupid family. He would calm down, if she helped him. She stroked his greasy hair, wishing she could wash it for him. 'How long do we have then?'

He looked up at her. 'You still want to be with me?'

'Duh.' She forced a smile.

'I leave in a month.'

A month was long enough for him to change his mind. More than enough. Sarah held her hope inside. She nodded bravely. 'Okay. So let's not waste it with fighting and crying.'

He sobbed and buried his face in her lap again, this time pushing her skirt up first. His stubble scratched her thighs and his tears wet them. 'Thank you, Sarah, oh my Sarah, thank you.' She stroked his head and felt strong.

7

For all of August, Sarah remained sure that Mr Carr would stay in Sydney. Their afternoon trysts were more passionate than ever, and many, many times he told her they would be together forever. It wasn't a question of believing him or not: she felt the truth of it deep, deep inside her. Being with him was like breathing, and everything else was like running under water.

Jamie said she was deluded, but he was too jealous to be objective. Besides, he didn't know Mr Carr the way she did. He didn't understand that what Mr Carr said to the class, to his family, to the principal, was just what he had to say to get by. They were public words that went with his public face and his public personality. Only Sarah saw his true self and heard his true thoughts, so only she could know that nothing in the world would keep him away from her.

And then on the last day of school, there was an assembly and he was presented with a farewell gift – a leather briefcase with his initials engraved in the handles – and he made a speech in which he named the school he would be teaching in and the Brisbane suburb where it was located and it all seemed so *concrete*. For the first time she thought that Jamie might be right. Maybe the reason Mr Carr never talked about any of the details of his move was that it would upset her and therefore ruin their time together. 'Stop you from putting out,' was what Jamie said.

But then Mr Carr told her he had a surprise for her, and she felt stupid for doubting him. The surprise wouldn't be a surprise at all; it would be the announcement that he was only leaving the school, not the state. It would be the declaration that of course he could never leave her.

'Tomorrow morning,' he said, squeezing her hands so hard she had to concentrate to stop from wincing. 'I'll pick you up at the top of your street at eight.'

'I get to see you on a Saturday?' Sarah kissed him. 'That is a treat. Where are we going? What should I wear?'

'Where we're going is the surprise. Wear something pretty. And tell your Mum not to expect you back until late.'

The early morning of Saturday, August 28, 1995 was cold enough to call for jeans, but he had told Sarah to wear something pretty and so she put on a white cotton sundress with butterflies embroidered on the bodice and hem. Mr Carr loved it; he kissed all of the little butterflies and gave her his leather jacket to wear in the car. He didn't talk while he drove. The radio was on – some adult contemporary easy listening station – and he hummed along to the songs, glancing over to Sarah with a smile every so often.

The drive was short. 'Surprise,' he said, pulling up outside the Parramatta Motor Lodge.

'We're going to the motel?'

'Wait here while I check in.' He jogged across the car park, coming back after a minute with a key attached to a block of wood in his fist. 'Come on, Sarah, time's a wasting. Get a move on.'

It was the first time Sarah had ever been in a motel room, but she barely noticed her surroundings. Orange curtains, a chipped mirror and a general dankness were the only lasting memories of the room itself. As soon as she had stepped inside, he ordered her to take off her clothes and then he pushed her to the floor. 'Today,' he said. 'You're mine.' She realised that he really was moving to Brisbane.

He spent the first hour biting her legs. He started on her left ankle, moved up to her shin, her calf, her knee, her thigh and then across to her right thigh then back down to the ankle. She cried and kicked him in the face until there was no way to tell which blood was coming from her legs and which from his nose and mouth.

'I hate you,' she said, when he was inside her, his legs chafing against the thousand bites on her own.

'No, you don't.' He pulled out of her with a groan, coming all over her thighs. He rubbed it into her skin, mixing it with her blood. He licked her clean and then kissed her so tenderly she started to cry again. He nuzzled her breasts, sucking on her nipples gently. He called her angel, princess, *ohsarahoh*. She begged him not to leave her.

'I have to, but it will be okay.' He kissed her face all over. *'If they be two, they are two so As stiff twin encompasses are two, Thy soul the fixt foot, makes no show To move, but doth, if th'other doe.'*

'What a load of shit,' Sarah sobbed. 'What total and utter bull-shit.'

'Sarah, you have to–'

She slapped his face, hard, one, two, three times. 'Just shut up,' she said. 'You didn't bring me here to talk, and I don't want to hear anything you have to say, anyway.'

He took her at her word. There was nothing resembling speech for the rest of the day. There was nothing resembling anything she had ever experienced. The earlier leg biting was nothing. It was like holding hands. She thought she would die and did not care. The beast was fighting for its life and she wanted it to win.

At the end of the day, Sarah could hardly sit up. Mr Carr carried her to the shower and washed her. He cried a lot, but he didn't talk and neither did she. After all, what was there to talk about after the biting and tearing stopped and the screaming died down? He drove her to the bus stop in silence, and remained silent while she sobbed and dug her fingernails into his unyielding arm. Eventually, too exhausted to go on, Sarah got out of the car and he drove away.

Part Two

1

Jamie made his way through the party, scanning the clumps of people, searching out Sarah. Jess had just returned from a six-month jaunt in Europe with a new boyfriend in tow, and Sarah had promised she would be here. But Jamie had searched the front hallway, the living room, the poolroom and the kitchen and it was too early, even for Sarah, to be locked in one of the bedrooms. He should have insisted on picking her up and bringing her himself; that was the only way he could ever be sure she'd be where she was supposed to be.

Through the kitchen window, he noticed that there were twice as many people outside as there were in. Of course that's where she'd be. Sarah had a theory that smokers were the most interesting bunch of people at any given function, and since these days smokers were always outside, that is where Sarah always wanted to be. She said that smokers were the coolest because of their blatant disregard for their own health and the middle finger raised to political correctness. Especially at this age. Older smokers at least had the excuse that *we didn't know back then* or *stoppin' at this age would kill me*. But people of Sarah and Jamie's generation had no defence. They had endured years of health education and government-funded advertising showing black tar pouring from cut open lungs. From the moment they lit their first cigarette and raised it hesitantly to their lips, the Generation Y smoker knew they were sucking in a lungful of overpriced black death. Sarah had memorised a list of chemicals found in cigarettes so she could recite them to people who told her that smoking was harmful: acrolein, benzene, formaldehyde, nitrosamines, polycyclic aromatic hydrocarbons, urethan, arsenic, nickel, chromium and cadmium. On the last syllable she would press her lips together and hum: *cadmiummm*. Then she would inhale deeply and say *yum*. Disregard for personal welfare was very cool. Smokers were very cool. And you could tax them into bankruptcy and send them outside to cower around doorways and they were still way cooler than the pink lunged, fresh smelling, goody-two shoes scrunching up their faces inside. Not you though Jamie, she would say, I know you have asthma and stuff, you'd smoke if you could, right?

But although smoke – of several varieties – choked the back-yard, Sarah was not there enjoying it. Jamie checked his watch: 8:49. It was possible she was running late. Likely even. He couldn't remember an occasion when she had been less than twenty-minutes late. Usually it was more like an hour.

Jamie spotted Shelley and Jess standing with a tall blond bloke by the pool. He got to them just in time to hear the man finish what was evidently a riotous story. Shelley and Jess clutched each other, laughing and shaking their heads. Jamie stood behind Shelley and slid his arms around her waist. She continued shaking with laughter, turning slightly to kiss his cheek.

Through increasingly irritating laughter, Jess introduced Jamie to Mike, and Shelley tried to recount the story Mike had just finished telling them. It was to do with a local TV personality and a vacuum cleaner and a casualty ward, but the cause of the nearing-hysterical laughter was unclear. Jamie knew that if Sarah was here she would roll her eyes at him, and he would feel brave enough to say he didn't think it was funny. But she was not here, so he just smiled and waited for the laughing to stop.

But as soon as the girls calmed down, Mike started in with another outrageous story, and soon they were gasping and holding their sides again. Despite hearing the whole story this time, Jamie still did not find it particularly funny. He suspected that if he himself had told the same story, Shelley and Jess would have barely cracked a smile. The fun they were having was clearly due to the man rather than his message. Mike had the weathered skin and sun-bleached hair of a surfer and a voice which would be easily heard over the roar of the waves. He wasn't a surfer though, not professionally anyway; he worked as a profile writer for a national men's magazine, which meant he got paid to have lunch with porn stars and drink cocktails with supermodels. It was the 'off-the-record' part of these interviews that had provided him with the endlessly uproarious anecdotes.

'Is Sarah with you?' Jess asked when Mike stopped talking for a moment in order to light a cigarette.

Shelley visibly tensed at the mention of Sarah. She stepped out of Jamie's reach and looked sideways at him. 'Nah, haven't seen her,' Jamie told Jess, careful to sound unconcerned.

'Yes, where is the famous Sarah Clark?' Mike asked Jamie, who shrugged and wondered why this man he had never met would ask Jamie – who was very much involved with Shelley – about Sarah's whereabouts.

'I suppose the *famous* Sarah Clark is off doing what she's *famous* for,' Shelley said.

It was Jamie's turn to tense up. 'What does that mean?'

Jess laughed and punched Mike's arm. 'Now you've done it. I told you Jamie was Sarah's White Knight.'

'I've missed something. What are you all talking about?'

Mike slapped Jamie's back. He bit down on the impulse to slap back. 'Jess and Shelley were telling me tall tales about your friend Sarah. They warned me not to repeat any of it to you, *allegedly* because you'd get shitty, but I know it's really because they've been pulling my leg and you'll ruin the fun by setting me straight.'

Jamie raised his eyebrows at Shelley. She looked at the ground.

'Every word was true,' said Jess.

'We'll see.' Mike rubbed his chin. 'True or False: Sarah lives in a filthy flat with no furniture or food but with piles of books everywhere and an esky full of beer.'

Jamie laughed. 'That's about fifty percent true.'

'Fine,' Jess said. 'So maybe she's got a bed and, like, one chair. I was right about the dirt and the books though.'

'So I'm guessing the stuff about her working full-time in a restaurant during high school and still topping the state in English is only about half-true also?'

Ridiculously, Jamie felt a rush of pride. 'Actually, that's one hundred percent true. She came third in French, too.'

'Someone owes us an apology, I think,' Jess said, touching Shelley's arm. Shelley looked at Jamie and gave him a small, guilty smile.

'Ah, but I haven't even got to the interesting stuff yet.' Mike leant in close to Jamie and dropped his voice. 'Tell me it's true that this girl seduces men by reciting poetry?'

Jamie tried to minimise his cringe. 'She has been known to.'

'Although usually she just comes right out and tells the bloke she's taking him home with her,' Jess added.

That was also true, but Jamie chose not to confirm it.

'And the French rugby team?'

Jamie glared at Shelley; she had *sworn* not to tell. 'It wasn't the whole–'

Mike clapped his hands. 'I *have* to meet this girl.'

'I don't think you're getting a proper image of Sarah from these stories.'

'But they are true?'

Jamie shrugged. There was not much point defending Sarah's honour when she herself would be telling these stories – and worse

– if she had bothered to show up. It was just if she was here – if Mike could see her little bones and hear her rounded vowels and her deep, low laugh – he would understand that you could hear any number of scandalous stories about Sarah, could spend a day and a half listening to them, but you wouldn't come close to knowing her. Sarah Clark was not translatable.

'See? Told you so! I expect a full apology, mister.' Jess tickled Mike's stomach and he swatted at her hands then grabbed her around the waist and kissed her. Jess giggled and pressed into Mike, and then it was like they'd forgotten they were in the middle of a conversation.

'Ah, new love,' Shelley said. 'I remember when we were like that, back in the olden days.'

Jamie forced a laugh. He and Shelley had been together six months; Jess and Mike almost three.

'Oh, I *want* to be punctuating every sentence by pushing my tongue down your throat, it's just I know if I start kissing you here, I may not be able to stop.'

Shelley took his hand. 'I may not want you to.'

Jamie could not help noticing that Mike had pushed Jess up against the pool fence and that both her hands were on his backside. God, Sarah would love this. She would be kicking herself when he told her she'd missed seeing Jess finally abandon her primness.

Jamie kissed Shelley, because he knew she expected him to, and then he kept kissing her because – as always – he found that kissing Shelley was much nicer than he had remembered. She really was a great girl, and they did make an excellent couple. Shelley liked it that he was studious and softly spoken; she said she couldn't wait to see him finish uni and set up in his own accountancy business, that she dreamed about being his office manager and also his lunch lady and personal masseuse. She cut his hair for him because she said she couldn't bear the thought of another stylist getting her scissors on his precious sandy locks, and he didn't want anyone else doing it because Shelley pressed her breasts into the back of his neck while she was cutting and told him funny stories about all the filthy haired, lecherous men she usually had to cut for.

'Okay, stop.' Shelley smiled up at him. 'No, not stop, pause. To be continued in the near future in a more suitable location.'

He nuzzled her neck. Over her shoulder he saw that Mike and Jess had disappeared. 'We could go inside. Find a nice, private room.'

Shelley giggled. 'Or we could go back to my place. Mum and Dad won't be home till after midnight.'

Jamie hesitated for too long. Her smile faded. She stepped out of his embrace. 'You don't want to come to my place?'

'No, I do. Of course I do.' He tried to pull her closer, but she resisted. 'I was just thinking that I don't want to wait that long. If we went inside–'

'You could screw me and then come back out and moon around waiting for Sarah to arrive.'

'That is so fucking unfair.' He couldn't believe how unfair it was. For once – yes, he admitted, it was only for once – he had not been thinking about Sarah at all; he genuinely had been thinking that he'd like to have sex with his girlfriend in one of the unfamiliar rooms of this unfamiliar house whose owners he did not know.

'This jealousy thing is getting old, Shell.'

'What's getting old, Jamie, is you acting like you're just killing time with me until your precious Sarah comes to her senses and gives up her mega-slut life to settle down with you.'

'I'm not going to listen to this shit again.' He started to walk away, stopped and turned back. 'Sarah is my friend. When you disrespect her, you disrespect me.'

Shelley laughed, shrill and loud. 'Oh, please, as if it's offensive to call Sarah Clark a slut. It's practically her official title.'

Jamie walked inside. He checked the living room, kitchen, lounge room, hallway. He went back outside and shuffled around the perimeter of the yard. She definitely wasn't here. And Shelley was right about Sarah. So right that it felt like she had crept inside his head and walked around and taken notes.

Mike reappeared, looking dishevelled and happy. He told Jamie that he and Jess had seen Shelley crying in the hallway and that Jess was in there now, comforting her. 'You're in the shit, heh?'

'Yeah. I guess I better go and make it up to her.'

'Sometimes it's better to let them cry themselves out.'

Jamie nodded and took a sip of his beer. He was exceptionally bad at small talk. Before Mike had come along he had been lurking on the edges of a group of people he vaguely knew from uni, pretending to be listening to the conversation. But by holding his shoulder and talking fast, Mike had drawn Jamie away from the group, and here he stood face-to-face with this bloke he barely knew who had very recently had sex with one of Jamie's oldest friends. A different kind of bloke would say something like *so how does old Jess shape up in the sack*. Jamie didn't know why he could think these things and not say them, but it explained why his friends were all girls.

'The legendary Sarah hasn't shown up then?'

Jamie shrugged. 'I haven't seen her. She might be around somewhere.'

'Sounds like the kind of girl a bloke would notice though.'

'True.'

Mike nodded and lit a cigarette. 'Notice in a look-at-that-ugly-crack-whore-throwing-herself-at-everything-in-pants way?'

'No! Did Jess tell you she looked like that?'

Mike laughed and held up his palms. 'Jess didn't say anything about how she looked. I just assumed from all those stories that she...' He bit his lip, looking off into the distance. 'So what *does* she look like?'

Jamie stalled by tossing his almost-full beer into a nearby cardboard box, then taking another from a slightly further away box, opening it, drinking from it. He had no idea how to describe Sarah's looks. She was not ugly. She did not look like a crack whore or any kind of whore or any kind of addict. She did not look old enough to be in university or to live alone or to drink alcohol, smoke cigarettes and have sex. She did not look as though her voice would be as deep as it was.

She looked like – she was – the daughter of suburban, upper middle-class professionals. She was what a lot of people called short and skinny, but what Jamie called average. Her skin was so pale she could be mistaken for an English tourist. She was the only person Jamie had ever seen who could have hair down to her arse without looking like a religious freak. It was shiny and not quite black, and when she tied it back, her ponytail was thicker than Jamie's wrist. Her eyes were fucking terrifying.

Of course he didn't say any of this to Mike. He just shrugged and said, 'She's okay,' and went to find Shelley.

2

Most kids Sarah knew applied for their Learner's Permits on their sixteenth birthday, spent a year of Saturdays learning to drive, received their Driver's Licence on their seventeenth birthday, and on turning eighteen, a brand new car from Mum and Dad. Sarah managed the first step okay; at sixteen she was still – barely – living up to her parents' expectations. But then everything went to hell, and she spent most of that year struggling to keep herself fed and clothed and in school, and so had neither the time nor the money to take driving lessons. Her seventeenth birthday was a blur of drinking, smoking and fucking, followed by another year of bare-knuckled survival, and by her eighteenth she had decided it was better she didn't have a licence because she was quite often either drunk or high, and besides, getting lifts from men was the easiest way to get them into her flat.

The downside to her non-driver status was that she was reliant on the local private bus company to get her to and from work each night. As the only bus service in the district, it had no competition, and thus its drivers were careless about sticking to the timetable, sometimes ignoring it altogether and ending their shift an hour or two early. On these occasions – and after freezing her arse off at the bus stop for twenty-minutes, Sarah realised tonight was just such an occasion – she was forced to either walk, hitch or call Jamie. She had promised Jamie she would never, ever hitch, and she had promised herself she would only ever do it in daylight.

'Shit.' She stamped her feet against the cold, but her legs were tired after her double shift and the stamping hurt, so she stopped. She looked back at the steakhouse; she would have to go back in there to use the phone. She really didn't want to do that: the drunks started to get nasty after eleven and she was still in uniform which meant she couldn't kick them in the nuts or tell them to go fuck themselves. Not without losing her job, anyway.

'Shit. Shit. Shit.' Her leather jacket was warm enough, but the wind whipped against her bare legs. Her sore, tired, cold, bare legs. She swore again, stepped to the edge of the footpath and stuck out her thumb.

It didn't take long – three or four minutes, seven or eight cars – before a late model Commodore station wagon pulled up alongside her. 'Where you going?' the driver called out. He was fortyish, dark, thinning hair, wire-rimmed glasses. Sarah peeked into the car: a child safety seat and a couple of picture books on the back seat; an empty diet coke can on the floor in the front; a blue bear with a polka-dot bowtie hanging from the rear-vision mirror.

'North Parramatta. Just past the gaol. Is that out of your way?'

'Not at all. Hop in.'

The car smelt like the bottom of Sarah's fridge, but it was warm and she was off her feet so she was happy. He drove like a man used to chauffeuring small children around. Slow, but with frequent, fast glances to the side, over his shoulder and into the rear-vision mirror.

'Just got off work?' he asked, glancing sideways and down at her legs.

'Yeah. I normally catch the bus but it didn't show up.'

'Still though, you really shouldn't get into cars with strange men.'

Sarah looked at him. He had a lot of wrinkles around his eyes, and his nose was the tiniest bit crooked. From the front it probably wouldn't even be noticeable, but Sarah was looking at him side on, and so she could see the kink that was probably from football or maybe squash. Not from a bar fight though: he was too clean cut.

He was about three years away from being past it. He had nice ears. Small, neat ears.

'I mean…' he glanced at her legs again, 'I could be an axe murderer, or a serial killer.'

'You could be, but you're not, are you?'

He chuckled, revealing a double chin. 'Well, I'd hardly tell you if I was, would I?'

Sarah smiled. 'You wouldn't need to. I have an inbuilt psychopath sensor.' She touched the top of his arm, briefly, as a test. He gasped, then tried to cover it by clearing his throat. She touched him again, this time letting her hand rest on his forearm. 'I'm perfectly safe with you, I can tell.'

He looked at her face for the first time. 'How old are you?'

She skimmed her palm along the soft fur of his arm. 'Old enough.'

The man frowned at the windscreen. 'Where do I turn off?'

'Left at the next lights.'

He drove on in silence. Sarah wondered what he had been doing, driving this family wagon around the suburbs so late on a weeknight. She suspected he had been heading for one of the Sorrel Street brothels. Either that or he actually was a psychopath looking for his next victim.

'So where are you off to tonight? After you drop me off, I mean.'

He licked his lips. 'Oh… nowhere.'

They were nearly at her place. She was so tired; she really should just go to bed. The man was biting his lip, concentrating way too hard on his driving.

'Pull up in front of that truck.'

He did as she asked. Leaving his hands firmly at ten and two o'clock, staring straight ahead. She was tired, yes, but that was the least of what she was feeling. Waitressing robbed her of herself; she became a girl in a uniform who would smile perkily at the twenty-something blokes who asked her if hospitality was a fulfilling career; a cookie-cutter waitress who would not pour beer over the head of the old man who pinched her arse every time she walked by his table; a sturdy competent pair of hands moving from wiping to stacking to scribbling order codes to scrubbing. Fourteen hours of being closed to the world left her bursting to be opened.

'I'm going to have a beer before bed. You want one?'

The man gripped the steering wheel with shaking hands. 'I do, yes.'

He babbled while she unlocked her door – he had been to a work function, couldn't stay long, his wife was expecting him home – but once inside he fell silent.

Sarah watched his face; she could always tell how a man would fuck by the way he reacted to her flat. Raised eyebrows and a turned-up nose meant the bloke would go on to screw her like he was the prince and she the scullery maid; sad eyes and pitying sighs meant she would be the little lost girl getting fucked by her kind protector; open disapproval at her housekeeping skills warned her she would be the naughty daughter getting punished by Daddy; and hesitation, fear even, meant she would be driving the action, showing the poor fellow that everything was okay. Her favourites – and the rarest by far – were the ones who didn't react at all, didn't even look around. The blokes who had her on her back as soon as the door was closed, who could spend a day and night in her slum and never discover the colour of her walls or the layout of her kitchen.

'Is this...' The man squinted at her. 'You live alone?'

'Yep.' Sarah walked past him, reaching her arm to the right to turn on her bedroom light, then to the left to light up the bathroom. The one in the combined hallway/kitchen/living room was already on. The man continued to squint through the gloom. She really should get a lamp. A tall, bright lamp to stand next to the sofa. But then what was the point? All she did here was sleep, screw and study, so as long as she could see her books, she didn't need much light at all.

'Have you lived here long?'

Sarah handed him a beer and opened one for herself. 'Forever,' she told him, which felt true. It had been five years, which was almost a quarter of her whole life.

The man sipped his beer, staring intently at the nicotine yellow wall in front of him. 'How old did you say you were?'

'I didn't.' Sarah peeled off her jacket and kicked off her shoes, sighing at the immediate relief this gave her feet. 'Smoke?' she offered.

'No, I don't–' He nodded at the pile of textbooks on her fold-out card table. 'You're a student.'

'When I'm not a waitress.' Sarah sank into one of the five-dollar chairs, indicating to the man that he should sit in the other. He hesitated, perhaps wondering if the rickety old thing would hold him, then lowered himself until he was perched on the edge of the seat.

'What do you study?'

'Arts.' Sarah stubbed out her half-smoked cigarette. At first she had thought he was the nervous type, but it was clear now he was a protector. She could see the cogs turning behind his small black eyes: how it would only take a little money to get her some decent furniture, how the least he could do was pay her uni fees, how he could make sure he always picked her up when she worked late, so she wouldn't have to come back alone to this grim little flat.

'Hey, you haven't seen the view.' Sarah stood and walked the three steps to her bedroom and then the two to her bedroom window. She knew without checking that he was right behind her.

'It's an alley.' There was an angry edge to his voice. 'A garbage filled alley.'

'What a pessimist. You're looking at a treasure trove. Look, we've got a couple of mattresses, some car tyres, and that cane chair would be lovely if only the seat wasn't punched out.' Sarah felt his breath on the back of her neck. 'That TV out in the kitchen came from that alley. It doesn't have colour, but it works well enough otherwise. I like to watch the late news when I get home from work. It keeps me company.'

'Don't you have parents?'

'Everyone has parents, silly.'

'Where are they? Why do you live like this?'

Sarah loved that he wanted to understand her. There was not a chance in hell he ever would, but she loved that he wanted to. She reached behind her, catching his hands, drawing his arms around her waist. He made a small noise of pleasure and nuzzled the back of her neck.

'Have you read *Jane Eyre*?' she asked.

'Have I…' He was audibly surprised, but recovered quickly. 'Ah, yes, yes, I think so, at school. A long time ago.'

'Do you remember why Jane leaves the comfort of Thornfield Hall even though she will be homeless and poverty stricken? Why she voluntarily reduces her station in life from governess to beggar?'

'I don't…' He chuckled into her hair. 'I wasn't expecting a test. I haven't studied.'

'She left because her dignity was worth more to her than physical comfort.' Sarah turned around and looked up into his face. 'And that's why I live like this.'

Oh, the pity in his eyes! Sarah took off his glasses so she could see it without interference, and the pure, wet, sincerity of it made her ache. With a burst of passion she kissed him, tugged at his shirt, his belt, his fly. She grabbed a handful of the delicious soft flesh around his middle and pulled him to her bed which squealed in protest. She knew she stank of lard and stale smoke and beer, but the man did not seem to care. 'Oh, Jesus,' he said, repeatedly.

His efficiency at undressing her – the ease with which he lifted her dress over her head without catching the zip on her ponytail, his practised way of loosing her hair from its elastic – impressed her. He must have a daughter, she thought. Men with daughters knew how to painlessly undress a girl.

Sarah had her own much practiced actions to impress with: the condom plucked seemingly from thin air, opened with one hand, rolled on before he had a chance to tell her he would rather not wear it. And then, with the smallest movement of her hips, the barely noticeable tilting of her pelvis, he was inside her. His face changed instantly, transformed by that expression which made Sarah briefly love every man she fucked: shock that he was inside her, mixed with gratitude that she was allowing him to be. With most men the expression appeared at the moment of penetration and then morphed into a look of triumph or resolve. But this lovely, soft bellied, father of daughters remained shocked and grateful almost to the end. Then, in the final moments, he was, as they all were, overtaken by the need for it to be finished, and his face turned ugly in its greed.

Sarah came, as she usually did, because she knew how her body worked, how to position herself, how to tense and relax, clench and release, how to keep a man from coming until she was done with him. Mr Carr – another man who had learnt from his daughters how to undress a girl without messing up her hair – had taught her all these things, and she was grateful for this every day of her life. But he also taught her that an orgasm was nothing; it was a sneeze or a good cry. So although she sought out sex like the drug it was, and although she came and came and came and came, what she hoped for was always the other thing: the merging into one, the making of the beast with two backs. Every man, every time, she waited for that moment of transcendence, the melting of self which allowed the absorption of another's melted self; she wanted so much for Mr Carr to not be the only one who could reduce her like that. But after seven years of determined fucking she was beginning to lose her faith. Sweating and gasping beside her was another man who had been tried and enjoyed but who, in the end, had failed to be anything but a good fuck.

After the man left, Sarah smoked her last three cigarettes and drank the two flat beers she had opened earlier. She pushed aside an overdue electricity notice to get to *The House of Mirth*, which she carried into the bedroom. She was more than halfway through; hopefully sleep would come early tonight. But less than an hour into her reading, the light bulb blew. She thought about getting up and changing it, but decided it was too much effort. The last line she had read echoed in her mind: *There had never been a time when she had had any real relation to life*. She lay awake most of the night listening to the rats squealing and scratching in the alley below her window.

On the previous Saturday night, when she was supposed to be at a party with her old school friends, Sarah had stayed up all night fucking an eighteen-year-old professional dancer. On Sunday, she slept and studied and took her phone off the hook. Yesterday, Monday, she went to uni and then to work and then had sex with the man who'd driven her home. So it wasn't until Tuesday morning that she answered her phone and was screamed at by Jess for missing the party on Saturday night. Sarah had a headache and was running late for uni, so to shut Jess up, she promised to meet them at the pub after she finished work.

She spent the rest of the day regretting her promise and arrived in a bad mood, expecting to be bored, and without bothering to change out of her stinky work clothes. She was relieved to find that Jamie was there, less happy that Shelley was with him, and astounded that Jess' boyfriend was hot. She wished she had taken the time to change.

'Finally we meet,' Mike said, taking her hand and kissing it.

'Finally? I've only known you existed for three days.'

He held onto her hand. 'But I've known about you for months. Jess talks about you all the time.'

Sarah raised her eyebrows at Jess, who was glowing. Well good for her. She turned back to Mike. 'So I suppose you think I'm a nerdy slut with terrible housekeeping skills.'

He laughed. 'You're not?'

'Occasionally. But sometimes…' She pulled her hand free and twirled around. '…I'm just a simple, hard-working waitress in desperate need of a cold glass of beer.'

Mike went to get her a drink. Sarah took the opportunity to tell Jess how hot her new catch was. 'I really like this guy,' Jess said. 'I really, really like him, you know?'

'That's great,' Sarah said. 'Good for you.'

Jamie pulled Sarah aside and leant in close. 'Don't even think about it,' he whispered.

'Don't know what you're talking about.'

'Sarah, I mean it. Look how happy Jess is. Just keep your hands – your *everything* – to yourself with this one. '

'But he's so irresistible. How ever will I control myself?'

'I'm not joking.' Jamie narrowed his eyes the way he did when he wanted to appear serious and severe. Sarah had never told him how cute that look was, because then he would stop doing it. 'You can have any bloke you want. Except this one.'

'Can I have that one?' She pointed to a random table-slouching drunk.

Finally, a smile. 'Yes, Sarah.'

'Thanks, Mum.' Sarah kissed his cheek. She considered sitting down and drinking the beer Mike had put on the table for her, but she didn't know how to sit across from a hot stranger and not flirt.

She picked up the beer. 'Thanks. Now, I'd love to stay and chat but Jamie told me I can have that man over there.'

'Sarah! That's not what I–'

'You said I could, Jamie-boy, and I'm going to. Just watch me.'

There was a stunned silence. She felt a surge of pride at her ability to render them all speechless, followed by a bigger surge of fear at what she was about to do. She turned and began walking to the table she had indicated. The man was staring into his almost empty glass. He had greasy black hair, a crooked nose and a salt-and-pepper stubbled face. Why, oh why, Sarah thought, do I do these things? Why can't I just sit down with my friends and have a drink and go home and clean my teeth and go to bed? Why do I always have to–

'She won't will she?' Mike's voice behind her.

'No way,' Shelley said. 'That man is so *ugly*.'

And then Sarah had no choice, because the man *was* ugly and the world being what it was, he probably never had women wanting to sleep with him. Sarah knew she was pretty, and she knew she hadn't done any more to deserve her beauty than that man had to deserve his ugliness. It wasn't fair that he had to go through life being unwanted and untouched when Sarah had all the wanting and touching she could handle. And besides, *Love looks not with the eyes, but with the mind, And therefore is winged Cupid painted blind*. This man had as much chance as any other of being the man who would split her soul wide open.

3

Every weekday morning, Sarah argued with herself about whether she could afford to miss just one day of uni. She had worked till late, partied until later, was too tired, too hungover, needed to clean her flat, wash her clothes, get stuck into the next due paper. But she knew that even one day would hurt her, because it would not seem to hurt her at all and she would be tempted to repeat the exercise until it did. So every day she dragged her tired, aching, hungover carcass out of bed, threw on her least dirty clothes, stumbled through the wreckage of last night's beer cans and walked the two blocks to the bus stop. She always sat up the back of the bus, her head against the window, her legs up on the seat to prevent anyone from sitting close to her. The journey took twelve minutes and every second of it was spent wondering how the hell she was going to make it through another day. She knew she would be sick as soon as she smelt the blood and bones fertiliser on the lawn. She would fall asleep in Gender Studies for sure. If she made it to lunch without passing out, it would be a miracle.

And every day, the miracle occurred. No matter how wrecked Sarah felt when she staggered off the bus, she was instantly refreshed by the sight of the Miles Franklin Building up ahead. It wasn't a beautiful building; it was standard seventies red brick, four floors, reflective glass and iron bars on the windows. But it was Sarah's true home, her spiritual home. If she could afford to not work, she would spend every moment here. She loved the student lounge with its threadbare orange and green sofas, its chipped formica tables and wobbly chairs. She loved the ancient silver urn which only the second and third year students knew how to operate without scalding themselves. She loved the squeak of her sneakers on the linoleum floors, the persistent knocking of the front door against its frame on windy days, the nook under the stairs between the third and fourth floor where you could always find Joe D, buy some pot, pinch a smoke. She loved the old stoners who took a decade to complete their Bachelors', and she loved the shiny new first years who could be overheard earnestly discussing the theories of Barthes and Lacan as though they too were shiny and new. Most of all, she loved the classes, where she vacillated between being sure of her wisdom and insight and being convinced of her impossible ignorance.

The other students adored Sarah, because she gladly shared her always precise and coherent notes and was generous with praise and encouragement. She was humble but enthusiastic, easy to talk to but undeniably clever. Sometimes she slept with her classmates, sometimes with her lecturers and tutors, but this made her neither more nor less popular. Here at least, fucking for stress release, for celebration, or to relieve boredom was commonplace. That was another reason Sarah loved it.

She wished she could stay at university forever. Learning, teaching, thinking, talking, fucking. Sleeping under the gum tree behind the science block in summer, and on the squishy green Arts lounge sofa in winter. Drinking bad coffee and half-price beer, eating peanuts and Joe D's chocolate-chip hash cookies. She had another six months of her undergrad degree, and then her honours year, and after that, she did not know. Although almost everybody she knew said she was bound to do great things, nobody, including Sarah, seemed to know what this meant.

Whatever she did, she was determined to not live up to anyone else's expectations. These expectations were, depending who you asked, that she would fall pregnant and live off welfare; that she would become the pampered mistress of some old but rich businessman; that her heavy drinking would tip into full blown alcoholism and she would die in a gutter clutching an empty metho bottle; that her occasional dabbling with illegal substances would become less occasional until she reached the point where she was turning tricks to pay for her next hit; or, that she would get tired of fending for herself all the time and return to her parents, happily copping their shit as long as they cleared her university debt and gifted her with the traditional Antipodean post-uni tour of Europe. The first and last of these were laughable; the others she had flirted with throughout the years. She had to remain on guard to ensure these flirtations did not become love affairs. She had to work hard at being something more than a living cliché.

Jamie was waiting for Sarah at their usual table in the uni pub. They met here at lunch each day, because Sarah would only go to the Economics building if she was in the mood to pick up a virgin, and Jamie refused to go to the Arts lounge because he believed that everyone there thought that Commerce majors were soulless subliterates.

She bought a beer and a packet of cigarettes and headed over to Jamie who was sipping a coke and picking at a basket of fries.

'I called you when I got home last night,' he said. 'It was after two. Where were you?

'I was running amok with Andy the alcho.' Sarah kissed his cheek and sat down. 'Say what you want about middle-aged unemployed drunks, but *shit* do they know how to party. I don't think there's a pub in all of Sydney I didn't drink in or a street I didn't vomit or piss in last night. Plus you've got to love a bloke who doesn't let go of his bottle even while he's fucking a girl.'

'Jesus, Sarah!' Jamie looked like he was going to cry. 'Why do you do these things?'

She shrugged. '*Nostalgie de la boue.*'

'I'm not even going to ask what that means, because I don't care. You know it's only a matter of time before one of these blokes cuts your throat.'

Sarah rolled her eyes. Jamie gave her the same lecture at least once a week, although sometimes he predicted a bullet to the head or a stocking around the neck, rather than a cut throat. She knew he was right, but she also knew he would never understand that it was necessary. To reach ultimate bliss, one must face grave danger.

'I wish you would at least get a mobile phone. That would be some security.'

'Good idea. Excuse me while I pluck some spare cash out of my arse.'

'Well if you didn't spend all your money on booze and cigarettes.'

Sarah sipped her beer and then lit a smoke, ignoring Jamie's glare. 'Seriously, I've been doing extra shifts all week, and I'm still fifty short for the electricity bill. I'll have it by next week, but if I get cut off I'll have to pay for the reconnect–'

Jamie put a fifty-dollar bill on the table in front of her. 'Are you sticking to your budget?'

Sarah shrugged. Jamie wrote her a new budget at least every six months, and every time she told him there was no point because she would never stick to it, but he was in serious denial.

'Something must be wrong there... Has your study allowance decreased again or something?'

'I don't know. It's always going down. It's way less than what I got back at high school, and I was barely making rent then. If it wasn't for all the overtime I would be totally screwed.'

'You know, Sar, Mum's offer is still open.'

Ever since Sarah and her parents had parted ways, Mrs Wilkes had been auditioning for the role of Sarah's mother. And although the Wilkes family were the most generous people she knew, and the spare room in their house was bigger than Sarah's whole flat, she had never been seriously tempted to join their family. For one thing, Jamie and Brett were both ex-lovers of hers and the idea of them being her de-facto brothers was too creepy. Also, she needed emotional space more than physical, and the Wilkes were the kind of people who had deep, touching conversations over dinner and told each other they *cared*. Having these people prodding at her brain, trying to get into her psychic pants, put her off her food, and if she didn't eat, they all started thinking she was anorexic and wanted to mindfuck her body image. And she couldn't tell Jamie any of this because he would want her to talk about why she felt threatened by emotional intimacy.

'Thanks, Jamie-boy, but living with your family would totally kill my sex life.'

Jamie smiled, but in the tight, tense way that he did when he was frustrated. 'Do you ever wonder if maybe your priorities are out of whack? I mean, really, Sarah, it's just sex.'

That's what Jamie didn't understand: it was never *just sex*. Even the fastest, dirtiest, most impersonal screw was about more than sex. It was about connection. It was about looking at another human being and seeing your own loneliness and neediness reflected back. It was recognising that together you had the power to temporarily banish that sense of isolation. It was about experiencing what it was to be human at the basest, most instinctive level. How could that be described as *just* anything?

And aside from all that there was the possibility that maybe, *maybe* she would find another man like *him*. The other half of the beast that scratched up her insides, kicking and roaring.

Sarah finished her beer and stubbed out her cigarette. 'Haven't we had this conversation before?'

'Yep. Every time you need to ask me for money because you can't afford your lifestyle.'

Sarah flicked the fifty at Jamie's lap. 'You can keep your money and your judgements thank you very much.'

'Sarah, come on.'

She jumped off her stool. 'I'm library bound.'

He held out his hand, his face an illustration of regret. 'Take the money, Sarah, please.'

'I don't need it. I just remembered I had some money stashed somewhere.'

Jamie came towards her, the note waving in front of him. 'Bullshit.'

'No, really. It's true,' she said, running out of the bar, and if it wasn't true at that moment, it would be.

★

Jamie arrived at Sarah's door just as it opened. A grey haired man in a pinstripe suit stood in the doorway.

'What?' The man touched his chest. 'Why are you lurking out here?'

'I'm not– Um, is Sarah–'

'Yes. Excuse me,' the man said, stepping past Jamie. 'I'm in a hurry.'

'Sarah?' Jamie stepped inside, locking the door behind him. 'You decent?'

'Yeah. In here.'

He stepped into her bedroom and immediately gagged as he inhaled a lungful of semen and sweat. He concentrated on taking shallow breaths to minimise the amount of sexual waste product breathed in. Sarah was lying on her side, her glorious, messy hair covering half her face and all of the arm which held her up. She was wrapped in a burgundy sheet, which clung to her jutting hipbones and emphasised rather than concealed her round little breasts.

Jamie looked away from the terrifying magnificence of post-coital Sarah only to be confronted with something far more awful. On the floor beside her bed lay a shrivelled, cloudy condom, a pile of scrunched up tissues and – Jamie felt like his lungs were going to explode – a neat pile of twenty-dollar bills.

Jamie stared at her. 'Is this the spare money you had stashed away?'

'Yeah, it was stashed in Joe's trousers.' She laughed, showing Jamie the shiny wet inside of her mouth.

Jamie had long ago stopped reacting outwardly when Sarah did something like this. Inwardly, it was like a tiny shard of glass stabbing him in the heart. So small that it didn't really hurt at all, except that there were now so many tiny shards that his heart kind of ached all the time, and every little new one made it that tiny bit worse.

He forced his face into what he hoped was an expression of exaggerated shock. 'You robbed that poor old man I saw hobbling out of your apartment?'

'You're hilarious, really. Joe happens to be a genuine old-fashioned gentleman. More than happy to help out a financially needy young girl, asking nothing in return.'

'What a saint.'

'You don't know the half of it. Not only did the darling man give me enough money to pay all this month's bills, but then he let me fuck him for, like, three hours.'

Feeling very, very sick, Jamie grinned at her. 'The selflessness!'

'I know.' She yawned, looking small and young and in need of a mother's goodnight kiss. 'I'm a lucky girl.'

4

'I have big, big news.' Jess twisted her plait around her finger, smiling coyly at the table top.

Shelley put down her diet coke and leant forward. 'So? Tell, tell.'

Sarah watched the couple at the next table, trying to ascertain their relationship. The man was easily thirty years older than his companion and their matching red hair and pale skin allowed the possibility of shared genes. But the girl was mesmerised, smiling and shaking her head at the bloke as though she'd never seen anything like him outside of her dreams.

'Sarah? Are you paying attention? This is important.'

Sarah nodded at Jess. 'Yes. Absolutely. Full attention.'

'Okay, well…' Jess smiled, looking from Shelley to Sarah and back again. 'I'm getting married!'

Shelley screamed, throwing herself half across the table and catching Jess in an awkward embrace. 'Congratulations! Oh, that's so wonderful!'

'I know, I know! He asked me last night, and of course I said yes right away, and I don't have the ring yet because we're going to pick it together this afternoon but I couldn't wait to tell you both the news. Ah!'

'Ah!' Shelley squealed back.

People were staring at them because of the screaming and hugging and knocking of salt and peppershakers from the table. Of everyone in the café only Miss May and Mr December were oblivious to Shelley and Jess's squawking. The man continued to talk in a voice far too low for Sarah to hear, and the girl continued to stare up at him as though he was not old and ugly and wearing a dreadful Snoopy tie. Sarah felt a tiny stab of jealousy, but mostly she was happy to have discovered evidence that true love did exist. She smiled at them, knowing they would not see her even if she went and lay naked across their table.

'Well, Sarah?'

'I'm speechless.' Which was not true. She had plenty to say but most of it involved calling Jess a stupid fucking idiot, and she at least had enough sensitivity to hold back from insulting the girl in her moment of frothy princess joy.

'Oooh, I could scratch your eyes out I'm so jealous.' Shelley squeezed Jess' hand. 'Well, maybe this news will give Jamie the push he needs to finally pop the question.'

Sarah almost swallowed the cigarette she was about to light. 'You want Jamie to propose? As in marriage? *Jamie?*'

'What? You don't think we're good together?'

'God, I don't know about that.' Sarah paused to light her cigarette. 'But Jamie and *marriage*? He's such a sheltered little mummy's boy.'

Shelley snorted. 'So why the hell do *you* spend so much time with him?'

Sarah thought about it, but not for too long, because Shelley's eyes were narrowed. Also, Sarah and Jamie's friendship was, like all long-term relationships, complicated. Her throw-away bitchy comment was coming back to bite her, because Jamie was way, way better than any man she knew; it was just that he was so *fragile*. But here and now was not the time or place to be going in-depth about what Jamie meant to her.

'I just meant that he doesn't strike me as ideal husband mate-rial. If there is such a thing, which for the record, I don't believe there is.'

'Well, he's perfect for me anyway,' Shelley said. 'And he was *so* right about you. You are such a cynic.'

Sarah's skin prickled. Later she would deal with Jamie, for the moment she shrugged and sucked back on her cigarette like she didn't care at all.

Later that night, after many celebratory drinks at the pub, Mike drove everyone home, dropping off Jamie, then Shelley, then Jess. 'Hey,' he said when only Sarah was left. 'Jump in the front. I feel like a fucking chauffeur up here.'

Mike drove with one hand on the wheel and the other on Sarah's thigh, using every gear change as an opportunity to replace his hand closer to her crotch. She laughed at him when he told her how he had wanted her since the first moment he'd laid eyes on her, and she laughed even harder when he called her a fucking bitch. When they were parked in front of her building, he grabbed her and stopped her laughter by shoving his tongue in her mouth.

'You're a nice kisser,' he said, when she pulled back.

Sarah kissed him again, to thank him for the compliment. He was not such a nice kisser. His tongue was sloppy and his jaw was slack. His hands were a different matter; one held her thigh firmly, while the other drew zigzag lines across her spine. After a couple of minutes, he started to fiddle with her fly.

'Stop,' Sarah said.

'No.' Mike moved his hand around to the side of her waist. His forceful tone was a point in his favour, as was the very sexy way he was nuzzling the side of her neck.

'You don't feel bad about this?'

'You're pretending that you do?'

'I'm not pretending anything. I feel fine. I'm just wondering why *you* don't feel bad.'

'I love Jess. She's an incredible girl. But she's not like you and me. She isn't relaxed about sex. Every time it's got to be a whole big production.' He took Sarah's hand and placed it on his groin. 'I'm busting, Sarah. Be a sport, heh?'

Sarah took her hand away, and then she peeled his hands off her. She would not *be a sport*. If they were going to fuck each other then it would be because it felt like a good thing to do; it would not be because he'd pleaded with her like a john with no cash.

'Goodnight, Mike.'

'What? No!'

'Drive safely now.'

Later that night, in bed alone, Sarah considered Mike's proposition. Not so much what he had said, but the way he had said it. Like he was certain she wouldn't say no. Like she was a sure thing. Like she was breaking some law by not fucking him. It was an attitude she was used to, but which still got on her nerves. People didn't understand the difference between being easy in the sense of fucking anyone who asked, and being easy in the sense of not making a bloke wait six months before deciding to fuck him. Sarah was easy in the second sense and resented people thinking otherwise. Her version of easy meant not wasting time playing games; the other version meant being a desperate sad case who lay down and waited to be used by whoever was passing by.

She knew she shouldn't have been surprised at Mike's attitude. She had been relieving sexual frustration for men who were in love with frigid princesses for her entire sexually active life. After Mr Carr left she threw herself at a romantically attached but desperately horny man and had been screwing grateful boyfriends and husbands ever since. The first was Alex Knight – school captain, exceptional student, keen athlete, church youth group leader – and she fell hard for him. He had a girlfriend named Laura who refused to have sex until she had a ring on her finger. Alex was happy to wait for Laura, but not for sex. That's where Sarah came in.

Sarah learnt a lot from Alex. Like the way men could say one thing, then another, then act in a way inconsistent with both positions and somehow still be convinced of their own integrity. Alex used to talk about how much he loved Laura and how he was going to marry her after he had his degree. Then he'd turn to Sarah and lecture her on how she was too young to be parking down at Toongabbie Creek with men, too young to be mucking around with blokes at all, and that she should have more respect for herself. After he'd gotten all that off his chest, he'd bang the hell out of her.

Alex was always sorry. His face grew darker with guilt as the frequency and heat of their couplings increased. He felt guilty about betraying Laura and guilty about using an infatuated fourteen-year old girl for his own pleasure and guilty about turning from his God. But still he did not stop. At the end of the year, Alex told Sarah that Saint Laura had gotten smashed at the end-of-year party and surrendered her precious virginity. It had been worth the wait, and they were more in love than ever, and... At the age of fourteen years and eleven months, Sarah was already over this romance bullshit.

She decided that she would abide by the rule her mother had made and not have a boyfriend. It amused her to tell men who propositioned her that she couldn't go out with them, because her mother believed that involvement in romantic relationships impeded academic development. Would it be alright, she would say, if we just fucked?

By the time she was sixteen the word was out. Sarah Clark did the things that nice girls didn't do, she did them skilfully, and she did them enthusiastically. And she was hot, which was something worth commenting on, because most girls who fucked around were desperately ugly. The local rumour mill churned out a never ending stream of Sarah Clark sex scandals, only about half of which were true, but all of which helped cement her reputation as the best way to spend a Saturday night in the north-western suburbs of Sydney.

Sarah acknowledged the labels given to her and continued to do as she pleased, thereby both confirming and subverting those labels. She had a near perfect academic record, she was beautiful, and she fucked like a porn star. If the occasional arsehole thought that easy meant 'indiscriminate' or that enjoying sex was equal to 'asking for it', then that was something she had to live with, much like the fact that her parents were as emotionally retarded as they were intellectually brilliant. Other people's deficiencies could not affect Sarah's life unless she allowed them to. And she didn't.

Mike was no exception. There was no point worrying that he thought she was a sure thing; she wasn't, and he had discovered that tonight. Next time he slobbered all over her face and zigzagged his hands along her spine, she might decide to fuck him, or she might not. Either way it would be totally about how Sarah felt, and not at all to do with what he was or wasn't getting from the blushing princess he was in love with.

*

Jamie thought that since he had watched Sarah enter rooms at least two thousand times over the last ten years, he should be used to it by now. Should be. Wasn't. Even when he was expecting to see her, when he was sitting at a sticky table at the back of the pub, sipping a beer he didn't want, wondering why she had asked to meet on a

Sunday morning, trying to guess what was wrong this time, staring at the door, fuming that she had told him ten o'clock and here it was five to eleven with no sign of her, even *then* seeing her walk through the door struck him as something fantastic.

Every time, he was jolted. That such a person could exist – could be walking toward him – could want to speak with him – was always a fresh and wonderful realisation.

She kissed his cheek, lit a cigarette, sank into the chair across from him, took a swig of his beer, screwed up her face at its flatness and warmth and exhaled loudly. 'Jamie, listen: I need you to promise me something.'

'Only if you apologise first for demanding my presence here at an ungodly hour and then keeping me waiting for fifty-six minutes.'

'You should be thanking me.' She blew smoke in his face. 'This is for your own good.'

'Thank you. What is?'

'Me warning you that Shelley is desperate to get married.'

'Piss off.'

'Jamie, promise me you are not going to marry her.'

'As if.' He laughed. Married! It was okay for Mike who was nearing thirty and owned his own house, but Jamie and Shelley were only twenty-two. They weren't even all that serious about each other. Except... The other night, Shelley cried when he was leaving her house. She said that he used her, and that he didn't even bother talking to her or being nice to her unless they were in the bedroom. This was not true; Jamie was never anything *but* nice to her. Unless her idea of nice was different to his. Unless she spent all their time together waiting for Jamie to do something which had never, until this moment, occurred to him.

'She said she wants to get married?'

Sarah nodded. 'Just tell me you won't let this happen.'

'Of course not. I don't want to… I mean, I do want to one day, but not now and not… I don't even know if I even… I do love her I think but…'

'Just promise me.'

He met her eyes. 'I promise I'm not going to marry Shelley.'

She nodded. 'Good boy.'

5

Five and a half years ago, when Sarah was still living under her parents' roof, she received a card in the mail. It was the first post day after the Christmas public holidays, which also happened to be two days before Sarah's sixteenth birthday, and so there were several cards addressed to Sarah in the letter box that day.

The first was from Sarah's grandmother on her mother's side. It had a bouquet of pink and yellow flowers on the front, and inside was a poem about blossoming womanhood. The second card was from her Aunty Glad and Uncle Rick. It had flowers on it too, but thankfully no poem. It just said *Happy Sweet Sixteenth*. Third, she had a card from her grandparents on her father's side. They lived in Tasmania and Sarah had never met them, but every year she received a birthday card and twenty dollars. This year, to her surprise, there was an extra five dollar note.

'Hey, Mum. Grandma and Grandpa Clark sent me twenty-five bucks this year. They obviously understand that I need more money now I'm an adult.

Her mother looked up from her book. 'Sixteen is not adult, Sarah, and if this is leading into another discussion about you getting a job you can stop right now.'

'I just want to have a bit of spending money. You're always saying we have to learn responsibility and independence.' Truth was that Sarah needed money for grog and pot and clothes that weren't chosen by her mum.

'I'm not going through all this again, Sarah. When you finish university you will get a job, not before. End of discussion.' Her mother went back to reading.

Sulking, Sarah ripped open the final envelope. The card was white, with a single long stemmed gold rose on the cover. Inside, neat, slanting, black words said *Sweet Sixteen and never been... forgotten*.

Sarah stopped breathing. Although there was no signature, and – she checked the envelope – no return address, Sarah knew that handwriting as well as she knew her own. It was the same hand-writing that had once told her *You're a Star* and *Great work, but don't forget to credit your source*. Later, the handwriting would be cramped up on slips of paper saying *Distracted by your kneecaps. Car 3:30?* And, *Skip soccer practice, need to kiss your shoulder blades one more time...*

She told him once, during a post-sex confessional cuddle, that she used to fear remaining un-kissed at sixteen. She told him that she had feared no man would ever want her, that she would be a brilliant but lonely academic. She would have several degrees and lots of cats. He said that by the time she was sixteen she would've been kissed so much she would laugh that she ever thought otherwise. He said by the time she was sixteen she would've forgotten all about him. She said never and meant it.

The memory of him made her face hot and her eyes fog up. She sat very still, willing the shaking in her legs to stop before her mother looked up from her book and noticed. She stared at the card until she couldn't make out the words. So few words! Couldn't he have spared her a few more? Couldn't he, at the very least, have signed his name? Not because she needed him identified, but because it was his name. Couldn't he have given her that?

Sarah stood up, gathering her birthday cards and her twenty-five dollars.

'Can I go to Jamie's?'

Her mother glanced up, frowned, looked back at her book. 'You spend a lot of time with him lately. Is he a boyfriend now?'

Sarah pulled a face at her mother's bowed head. 'I'm not allowed to have a boyfriend.'

'Exactly.'

Sarah ran her finger over the gold rose. 'Exactly. So can I go?'

'Yes, Sarah. But please get changed. An outfit like that, and Jamie might think you don't take the no boyfriend rule seriously.'

Sarah wondered how her mother even knew what she was wearing since she never looked at her. Plus, Jamie didn't look at Sarah in that way. She could turn up in her underwear and he would just ask her if she wanted to play Nintendo. Whatever, she wasn't going to Jamie's anyway. She was going to sneak into the Leagues Club and find someone to have sex with. Someone old. It would be her birthday present to herself, inspired by Mr Carr.

Sarah never heard from him again. Her sixteenth was the last birthday she spent at her parents' home, and so she could never be sure if he didn't write again, or if he did but the cards ended up in her mother's stainless steel kitchen bin.

Then on a cold July night, almost seven years since he'd left her, Sarah saw Mr Carr. Her bus was stopped at a set of lights three blocks from the restaurant, when she glanced out the window and saw him flashing past. It was less than a second, just a glimpse of thick blonde hair and black clad shoulders, but she knew. She turned in her seat, trying to get another look, but the car had disappeared around a corner. She was certain though. She'd know him anywhere.

'Uhuh, sure.' Jamie said, when she told him the next day. He was pretending to read *Sense and Sensibility*. Jamie hated Mr Carr. Jamie hated all the blokes Sarah had been with, but he hated Mr Carr the most, because he was the first. She wondered if fourteen-year-old Jamie had hopes of being her first. She knew now that he used to have a crush on her, but that ended after she had sex with him. Not because of the sex, which was fine, but because of what happened afterward. She did not like to think about that, so didn't.

'So anyway, there are eighteen D. Carrs in the directory, if you can believe that. I called them all. Nothing. He mustn't be listed.'

'You need help. You're delusional.'

Sarah poked him with her pen. Jamie poked back. Sarah took his pen away and wrestled him onto his back. He went down easily, barely struggling as she pinned his wrists to the floor. She pressed her face right up to his, nose to nose. If he was another man, any other man, she would open her mouth, suck on his pale bottom lip and press down with her body. He flexed the small, tight muscles of his trapped arms and pressed the inside of his thighs against the outsides of hers. If he was any other man she would've pressed back.

'Apologise,' she demanded.

'No way.'

'I'm not delusional. It was him.'

'Has it occurred to you that your obsession with someone you haven't seen for seven years is slightly unhealthy?'

'No.' Sarah rolled off him and noted that his face fell. He was maybe not getting enough. That was typical of girls like Shelley Rodgers; all shiny lips and colourful hair clips to suck a guy in, and then once they've got them, they turn grey and sexless.

'I went back to the school this morning,' she said, lighting a smoke.

'Oh, my *God*, you are insane.'

'I only wanted to know if anyone had heard from him. I thought he might have been in touch if he was back. I thought he might even have…' Sarah sighed. She knew Jamie was right. It had been crazy to think she could just walk into the old red brick English block and find him sitting behind his desk waiting for her.

'So anyway, I was all worked up and angry and disappointed, and as I was leaving I saw this kid hiding in the bus shelter smoking–'

'Shit, Sarah, please tell me you didn't–'

'I did. I went up to him and said "All they that love not tobacco and boys are fools." And he was like, "What the fuck?" And I said, "It's Marlowe." And the boy says, "Huh?" So I told him about Marlowe and how he got knifed in a bar fight and he was sort of interested, and I told him how that line was what popped into my head when I saw him – a beautiful boy – standing there sucking back on beautiful tobacco. He offered me a cigarette – a durry, he called it – and we smoked together, and then I told him how nicotine is a biphasic drug. And he knew that; they learnt it in science. He said, "It both relaxes and invigorates." And then I said, "Like orgasm." And he blushed like mad and then I–'

'Stop! God, that's disgusting, Sarah. And probably illegal!'

Sarah laughed. 'Chill out. He was sixteen. Totally legal and totally delicious.' The boy had been truly lovely: a Greek god in training with a baby smooth chest and a recovery speed and enthusiasm which made up for his clumsiness. He hadn't been what she was looking for, but then no one was. They were all mere consolation.

Jamie took hold of her shoulders. 'You have a problem, Sarah. You're like a sex addict or something.'

'Get out. You usually laugh when I tell you this stuff. What's wrong with you today?'

He let go of her shoulders but picked up one of her hands and turned it over. He traced circles on her palm without speaking. He had been weird all afternoon. Needy. He kept touching her and looking at her out of the corner of his eyes. He seemed to be on the verge of telling her something, and then he would change his mind and look away.

'Jamie, what?'

He dropped her hand and picked up the book. 'What am I supposed to be doing with this book again?'

'Identifying sexual allusions.'

'In Jane Austen?'

'Don't scoff.' She picked up *Pride and Prejudice* and turned to the first of several marked pages. 'For example: Caroline offers to mend Mr Darcy's pen for him, telling him that "I mend pens remarkably well." And then Darcy says: "Thank you – but I always mend my own."'

'Yeah, and?'

'God, you finance types are thick! Mr Darcy is telling Caroline that he'd rather masturbate than let her touch his "pen."'

Jamie tossed his book to the floor. 'Not everything is about sex, Sarah. In fact, *most* things aren't. The fact that you manage to find a sexual subtext in what is a completely innocent book is yet more evidence – as if I needed it – that you have a serious problem.'

Sarah closed her book and placed it on top of the one he had thrown. 'And whatever it is that's making you such delightful company today – is that one of the many, many things which is absolutely, positively not about sex?'

'Are you going to work or am I wasting my time?'

'Talk to me.'

'About what?' He rubbed his eyes. Cigarette smoke irritated him but he never complained. Sarah knew though, and she liked him more for it.

'You tell me.'

Jamie bit his bottom lip. His forehead creased up, and he looked to Sarah like he was going to cry. Shit. She hated it when he cried. It was impossible to know what to do. Shit.

'Shelley's pregnant.'

Sarah stared, laughed, realised it wasn't funny, swore, laughed again, and then stood up and kicked the sofa. 'Fuck.'

Jamie grabbed her leg and pulled her down. She put her arm over his shoulder and he rested his head against her. Sarah stated what she dearly hoped was the obvious. 'She'll get rid of it.'

'No.' It was more a sigh than a word.

'Fuck. What then?'

'We're getting married. Her dad's giving us the deposit on a unit.' Jamie pressed his face into Sarah's arm. She felt his tears through the flannelette of her pyjamas. Damn Shelley. Sarah wanted to go around and sort the bitch out. Give her a good kick to the stomach or push her down some stairs. She kept waiting for Jamie to leap up and say he was kidding, but he just cried until the top of her pants was soaked.

'I've always wanted kids,' Jamie whispered. 'You know that, Sarah, I've always said it, haven't I? It's what I wanted, just sooner. It'll be good, I reckon. Just need to get used to the idea.'

Sarah stroked the back of his head and swore to herself that she would rip out Shelley's heart with her bare hands. She would rip it out and throw it to the ground and jump up and down on it until it was a pile of bloody mush.

In the first week of August, Shelley and Jamie held a small dinner party in their unit to celebrate the apparently wonderful trifecta of mortgage, engagement and pregnancy. The party consisted of two blondes, their freshly caught men and Sarah.

Jamie showed Sarah around the flat, which was almost as small as her own but much newer. She tried to make appreciative noises and pretend to be happy for him, but she was seething inside. Jamie had dropped out of uni for *this*. He was selling financial services over the phone for *this*. He had dark circles under his eyes for *this*.

'You hate it don't you?' he asked after she had failed to muster the required enthusiasm for the way the bedroom windows looked out over the council reserve.

'No. I like it. I'm jealous. It's much nicer than mine. But then you get what you pay for don't you? This place is beyond the reach of a poverty stricken student.'

'You think I should have stayed at uni?'

'It just seems a waste.'

Jamie pulled the blinds closed and sat down on the edge of the bed. Sarah could hear Shelley giggling from somewhere down the hallway.

'I've got responsibilities. I can't be a student while I have all these responsibilities. Later, when things settle down, I can go back.' Jamie sounded as though he had rehearsed the words.

Sarah shook her head. 'Jamie, don't pretend that you want this. You've been tricked and–'

'I want it. Be supportive.'

Sarah sat beside him and put her hand on his knee. 'Fine. If you're happy, I'm happy.'

'That was convincing.'

'I'm trying.'

Jamie patted her hand and smiled, and Sarah wanted to kiss him. It was a purely platonic urge, or mostly platonic. Kissing Jamie was natural and comforting. It was a way of saying *You're okay, I'm okay* whenever their differences came between them. But maybe now the differences were too large. If she kissed him on the bed he shared with Shelley, would that be crossing some line? A line that had always been soft and ever shifting but now seemed hard and restrictive.

Sarah hated hard lines. She hated Shelley. She hated Venetian blinds and council parks and the smell of fried onions. She kissed him. For a little too long. With open lips. With just a touch of tongue.

'What was that?'

'A kiss. So you know that I am genuinely happy for you.' Sarah watched his face carefully. Had he felt anything? He must have felt *something*. Personally, she felt quite warm.

'Shelley made punch. Come and have some.' Jamie walked out of the room, and Sarah felt the unfamiliar cold wind of rejection.

Sarah drank a glass of Shelley's punch. It was too sweet and the pineapple pieces were too big and kept getting stuck to the bottom of her glass. She said something polite about it and then went for the bottle of Jim Beam.

'Ah. A girl after my own heart.' Mike winked at her, and Sarah poured him a glass.

'Ooh, on to the strong stuff this early?' Shelley said, with raised eyebrows and a darting glance at Jess.

'Oh, it's never too early for bourbon.' Sarah downed the entire glass in one go. She had not planned on drinking at such a pace, but then she had not planned on kissing Jamie or on wanting him to kiss her back or being winked at and condescended too. She poured another glass and smiled at Mike, 'Ready for another?' she asked, gesturing to his still full glass.

He raised his glass and drank the lot, not taking his eyes off her.

'Come see the new car, Mike. Shell's brother got it for us wholesale,' said Jamie.

Sarah said that she would like to see the new car too, but Jamie ignored her and led Mike away. That hurt. Jamie never ignored her. He couldn't be pissed off by the kiss. It was a damn good kiss.

As soon as the men were gone, Jess and Shelley started gushing. Look at the diamond ring, and wasn't it fun to have your own place, and the flat was *sooo* beautiful. And the furnishings! Oh, there was so much to talk about with furnishings. Sarah was not interested in hearing about the various trials and tribulations of sofa shopping; she'd picked hers up at a garage sale for twenty-five dollars.

Sarah wished that Jamie and Mike would come back before she died of boredom. She tried hard not to be a sexist since she would hate to discriminate against herself, but the truth was that ninety percent of women her age were boring as shit. As compared to men her age, of whom only about seventy percent were coma inducing. Add ten years and remove clothing and there was barely a man alive that Sarah couldn't find something interesting about.

'I'll tell you one thing I didn't expect,' Shelley was saying, 'the constant pressure to *do it*. Like, he was satisfied with once or twice a week when he was at home and now he's nudging me every bloody night!'

'Don't you like doing it with him?' asked Sarah.

Shelley and Jess looked at each other and rolled their eyes. 'That's not the point, Sarah. It's *exhausting* doing it every night. Sometimes I would just like to cuddle up and go to sleep.'

The one time Sarah had done it with Jamie, he had been careful but fast. That was a long time ago, but even allowing for less caution and longer duration, she couldn't see how screwing Jamie could be *exhausting*. Anyway, the stupid bitch had ruined his life; the least she could do was have it off with him without complaining.

'So what do you do then?' Sarah asked Shelley. 'Just leave him to look after himself?'

Shelley's face was white as she picked at her cuticles. 'Jamie doesn't do that.'

'I'm quite sure he does.'

'I think Shelley would know better than you,' Jess said. 'She lives with him after all.'

'Right,' said Sarah. 'She does.'

★

Jamie was pissed off. Correction. Jamie had been pissed off at seven o'clock when Sarah had kissed him, now at seven forty-five he was nothing more than a concentrated mass of rage in the form of a human being. Sarah was so infuriating, such an unashamed bitch, that it was all he could manage not to grab her by the ponytail and toss her out on the street.

First, there had been that kiss. He thought he had handled that quite well. He had kissed her back, which probably wasn't the right thing to do as far as Shelley was concerned, but he would challenge any straight man with a pulse to not respond to Sarah for at least that first thoughtless second. Then he had walked away. That had definitely been the right thing to do. God knows what would have happened if he hadn't.

But Sarah being the vain, selfish little cow she was, could not leave well enough alone. She started flirting with Mike so blatantly that Jamie was embarrassed for Jess. He managed to get Mike outside, away from her brushing fingertips and suggestive smiles, but they had to go back in eventually and when they did she started in straight away.

'Hey, boys, settle something for us will you?' she said, and Jamie knew it was trouble because Jess and Shelley both said *Shut Up!* She ignored them of course, stood up and leant forward with her palms on the table so that her T-shirt stretched and a patch of pale skin on her lower back was revealed. Jamie knew that if she leant forward a little more, he would see the thin, pink scar that trickled across her spine.

'How often would you say that a normal, healthy, Aussie bloke flogs his log?'

Jamie looked at Shelley and saw that her face was red. He would be getting it later tonight. She had not wanted to invite Sarah. She said that it would be nicer to just have Mike and Jess over. Calmer. She felt threatened by single women now that she was not one. Actually, that wasn't true; she had heaps of single friends. She felt threatened by Sarah and why shouldn't she?

'Do you keep statistics on that? For the magazine?' Jamie asked Mike. It was important not to let Sarah see she had got him flustered. She could smell fear.

Mike laughed and looked at Sarah in a way that turned Jamie's stomach. 'Not official statistics, no.' He took the cigarette Sarah was offering, his fingertips brushing her wrist.

'An educated guess though,' Sarah said, lighting Mike's smoke, 'Based on personal experience and a livelihood based on writing about men and their penises.'

Jamie tried to glare at her, but she only had eyes for Mike. Which really pissed him off, because what was with that kiss if she was angling for Mike? Was this an attempt to make him jealous, or was that wishful thinking? Was it more that the kiss had been nothing to her and the effects or consequences, or lack of both, were already gone from her frivolous and fickle little mind?

'Bare minimum would be three times a week.'

'Dinner ready yet, Shell?' Jamie asked.

'Yeah, should be. I'll check.' She smiled at him and he was relieved. She didn't blame him for Sarah's crudity; she thought they were in this together. He realised that they were, or that they should be, and felt horribly guilty.

'What about married men? Men in steady, committed relationships? Do they still do it?'

'Shit, yeah. Any man who reckons he doesn't is lying through his teeth.'

'I rest my case.' Sarah nodded at Jess who smiled tightly.

'And you, Sarah?' Mike said.

Jamie almost whimpered as the picture of Sarah touching herself appeared in his mind. It wasn't a new picture; it was an old favourite. It was just that he normally had control over it, making it appear only when he was locked in the bathroom with the water running.

'Well, you tell me,' she said. 'If you could have intense, bone shaking orgasms over and over and over with no time out to recover, how often would you be doing it?'

Jamie walked out of the room. He stood in the hallway, his forehead against the wall, until his pulse slowed, his body relaxed. Then he went into the kitchen and asked Shelley if she needed any help.

'Nope. All good here. I think you should stick close to Sarah. Stop her from embarrassing herself.'

'She's alright.'

'According to you.'

Jamie checked out in the hallway to make sure no one was around. He could hear Mike's raucous laugh over the top of Sarah's low one. 'What does that mean?'

'I don't know, Jamie. You tell me how smart she is, how interesting or whatever, but I just... I don't *get* her. She's like a bloke.'

Jamie smiled, thinking of Sarah's hair, her laugh, the delicate feet which could fit in his hand. 'How is she like a bloke?'

'She's... distant. She doesn't reveal herself, you know? She just gets drunk and talks about sex. She doesn't let anyone know her.'

'When she gets drunk and talks about sex, she *is* revealing herself. That is her.'

Shelley sighed. 'That's so sad.'

Jamie wanted to argue, but he wasn't sure he disagreed. He shrugged, grabbed another beer from the fridge and returned to the dining room, where Sarah was pouring another glass of bourbon and talking about sex.

Sarah's behaviour throughout dinner was above reproach. When Jess went on about the difficulties of keeping deli meats fresh in the storefront window, Sarah appeared to be listening to every word. She even asked questions, without a trace of sarcasm. Then Shelley talked about the savings plan they had started and how by the end of the year they would have a deposit on a proper house. Jamie cringed, expecting Sarah to be scathing, but she nodded seriously and discussed the benefits of fixed-term verus variable and whether it was better to buy new or to get a fixer-upper as long as it was in a nice suburb.

After dinner they sat around the table drinking until all the punch was gone. Shelley offered to drive them all home since she was the only one who hadn't been drinking. Mike and Jess agreed, but Sarah refused to take the hint, saying she would stay and finish off the bourbon. Shelley rolled her eyes for only Jamie to see but did not argue.

'Are you still mad at me, Jamie-boy?' Sarah said as soon as they were alone.

'No.' He resisted the urge to brush away the hair that was hanging over her left eye. 'You are very hard to stay mad at. I think I lasted all of half an hour.'

'Ah… he loves me!' She squeezed his arm. Her hand was hot and moist. Her breathing was heavy. An involuntary glance at her chest revealed stiff nipples poking through white cotton. An image of Sarah – damp, naked, writhing underneath him – flitted across his mind. He pushed it away, but it was too late. Sarah could sense lust the way she could smell fear, and both excited her to the same degree.

'That kiss was pretty hot, huh?'

'God, it's hard to be your friend sometimes.'

'Because you want to fuck me, right?' She put her hand on the bulge in his jeans. Ashamed, he stood up and moved away, but she followed. She stood in front of him and took his hands. 'It's okay. I want it too. I want it so much.'

'What? Sarah, I–' Her kiss cut him off. He knew this was impossible, a dream, a joke. But her kiss felt genuine. 'Sarah, wait a second, I–'

'You don't want to fuck me?' She was unbuttoning his jeans.

'No, I do, but–'

'Jamie, listen to me. I have never been so wet in my entire life. I had no idea it was even possible to be this wet. You understand me? I need you to fuck me right fucking now.'

And he could not believe how much he wanted to do that. They started for the bedroom but it was so far away. The hall carpet was soft. She was softer. They were both fully clothed. Jeans pulled down just far enough and underwear pushed to the side. He wanted to keep touching her because she was so soft and open and wet but she was pushing his hand away and guiding him into her. *We don't have much time.* It didn't matter because he was already coming. There was no condom, and Jamie was pleased because it meant he could feel her properly. Feel himself pumping into her, filling her up. His precious, precious Sarah.

Shelley returned as they were sitting back down at the table. While Shelley hung the keys on the hook near the door, Sarah emptied the bourbon bottle down her throat. She lit a cigarette, and Jamie noticed her hands were shaking.

'Booze is all gone,' she said. 'Guess I'll be off.'

'I'll drive you,' he said, meaning *I love you*.

'You're too drunk. I'll walk.'

Shelley sighed. 'I'll take you. Come on.'

Sarah stood. 'No, really. I'll walk.' She kissed Jamie on the forehead, cradling the back of his head in her hand for just a moment. Then she thanked Shelley for dinner and was gone.

7

Mike stood in the doorway, jiggling his car keys, hopping from one foot to the other. 'Jamie, mate, come to the pub?'

Jamie emphatically did not want to go to the pub with Mike. He had to wait at home until Sarah called; he couldn't call her, because Shelley would want to know why he was calling Sarah only twelve hours after he'd last seen her.

'Please, Mike, get him out of here.' Shelley handed Jamie his wallet. 'He's got ants in his pants this morning. Driving me insane.'

'I need to–'

'Have a nice time.' Shelley kissed his forehead, gave him a shove and the door was closed behind him.

They sat in the beer garden, which was empty at this time of the morning, and Mike spent ten or so minutes tearing his coaster into tiny pieces while Jamie cursed himself for not grabbing his mobile phone on the way out. He tried to remember where the nearest public phone was.

'So, ah…' Mike stared off into the distance behind Jamie's left ear. 'About Sarah. Did you and her used to go out or what?'

Jamie's gut twisted. 'No, we never… We've always been mates.'

'Yeah, but… You've had a go at her?'

'Whatever that means.'

Mike gave him a contemptuous look. 'You've screwed her?'

Jamie took a gulp of beer, which seemed to solidify in his throat. With effort, he swallowed it. 'Just the…' He cleared his throat. 'Just the once. We were sixteen. Pissed.'

'Yeah, and? She's a firecracker, right?'

'Yeah, I suppose.'

'Ah, mate, I am hanging out for some of that.'

Jamie sat silently for another minute. He was no good at talking to men about intimate things; he was missing the instinct that seemed to tell other blokes how sincere they could be without crossing the line into effeminacy. But the thought of slick, shallow Mike grunting all over Sarah made his already upset stomach churn.

'You're not thinking of going after Sarah, are you?'

Mike looked surprised. 'Going after her? Mate, I thought you and her were tight. Doesn't she tell you anything?'

Jamie had thought she did, right up until about three seconds ago. He shrugged, waited.

'She has been working on me for months. I can't believe she hasn't said anything to you.'

'Working on you?' Jamie battled to keep the rising panic from his voice.

'Yeah, you know. A kiss here, a grope there. Teasing. Working me up.'

Jamie sipped his beer. He would not let Mike see how shaken up he was. Probably Mike was full of shit anyway.

'I'm helpless to tell you the truth. She's just...' Mike mimed casting a fishing rod and reeling it back in, '...got me hooked, my friend. I'm at her mercy. Whenever she wants she'll reel me in and then I'll do whatever the hell she tells me. And she knows it too, the sly bitch.'

Jamie felt like vomiting. It really was inconvenient the way that Sarah made him want to throw up. 'Do you feel bad about Jess?'

'Yeah.' Mike rubbed his forehead. 'Kind of. I mean, Jess is a sweetheart, but Sarah, man. Fucking Sarah Clark! You don't turn your back on an opportunity like that for anything.'

'Got any smokes?' Jamie said, and Mike handed him a pack. Jamie lit one, ignoring the immediate tightness in his chest.

Mike lit himself a cigarette and inhaled deeply. 'So here's what I wanted to tell you. Last night, at your place, we got so dirty, right in front of everyone. No one had a clue!'

'At my place?' Jamie's face flushed. 'What are you on about?'

'Me and Sarah were going for it, right there at dinner.'

Dinner. Jamie ran the tape over in his mind. Nothing had happened at dinner. Before dinner Sarah had kissed Jamie and flirted with Mike. After dinner, Shelley had driven Mike and Jess home and Sarah had… *God!* What was Mike talking about?

'There I am, eating the delicious meal your lovely lady cooked up, and suddenly my pants are open and there's a hand on my knob.' Mike shook his head as if he couldn't quite believe it. 'There's Sarah, chatting away about variable loans or some shit, and all the time she's pulling me off under the table. I returned the favour though. When I licked my fingers after the meal, it wasn't just the chicken I was lickin' if you get what I mean.'

'Sorry, I have to–' Jamie bolted for the toilets and made it inside just in time to vomit up what felt like everything he had ever eaten and drunk in his entire life. After a couple of minutes, he stopped and rocked back on his heels to catch his breath. Then he remembered her saying *I've never been so wet in my life*, and his stomach heaved again.

When Jamie was sixteen, he wanted nothing more than to wake up one morning and discover that he had magically become his brother. Brett was everything Jamie wasn't. Strong and muscular, while Jamie was weak and prone to broken bones. Tanned and rugged, while Jamie was pale and freckled with mousy hair that stuck straight up no matter how much gunk he used in it. Brett was a star athlete, while Jamie had been excused from PE all his life because of his asthma. And Brett had girls falling over themselves to get to him. He knew how to talk to them without stuttering and staring at his feet, and what clever things to say to make them laugh and look up at him with starry eyes. The only way girls looked at Jamie was with pity. Sometimes they called him cute and such a nice guy, words that were the kiss of death for an Aussie bloke who was meant to be rough, tough, rugged.

It was Brett who told Jamie about the secret life of Sarah Clark. He said it was time Jamie knew that his little friend was the best fuck in Sydney. He said it was pathetic the way Jamie mooned around like a lovesick puppy dog while Sarah was giving it to every bloke who looked at her twice. Brett confessed, with a wide grin, that he had personally got his end wet three times in one night with her. Sarah Clark was, he said, a wild thing. A totally uninhibited, sexy as hell, wild-thing. Didn't go on with that talking, commitment, take me out to dinner crap that other girls ask for. She just wanted dick.

Jamie refused to believe it at first. He knew Sarah better than anyone – she'd said so herself. So many nights she had sat on his bed and talked until her voice was croaky and his neck was stiff from looking up at her from his position on the floor. She told him about Nietzsche and William Blake. She told him about her affair with Mr Carr, about how her parents ignored her, about the way she never slept more than two hours without waking. All night she'd talk, wild eyed and wired and brilliant, making him feel like nothing he'd ever thought about before was important. It was never until the sunlight came streaming through the window that she would stop. Then she'd look around as though just noticing where she was, laugh in an embarrassed way and slink off into the breaking day to be home before her parents woke up.

Surely she would've told him if she'd slept with his brother. And surely he was close enough to know if she really was sleeping around. Surely. But Brett had no reason to lie. Brett was, in fact, the only person who ever talked to Jamie on the level. He treated him like a man, unlike their parents who treated Jamie as though he was five-years-old and made of glass.

Jamie asked around and found that he had spent the last couple of years with his head up his arse. Every bloke he broached the subject with knew about Sarah, and many of them knew about her from personal experience. Jamie got to thinking that it really wasn't fair that he was missing out. Why were his balls permanently blue while she was off doing every bloke and his dog?

His opportunity to correct the injustice came the following week when his parents went to Melbourne for the weekend. Brett, always the party animal, invited half the university over to get smashed. Jamie invited Sarah, and she laughed and told him he was the tenth person who'd asked her.

She arrived late, alone and drunk. She was wearing perfume and lipstick and a skin tone skirt that kept riding up her thighs. Jamie steered her away from the salivating hordes and told her she looked beautiful. She said *oh my*, wrapped her arms around his neck, pressed her whole body up against his and began to sway to the music. Jamie stroked her hair and pressed the small of her back, then after a minute he dared to brush his sweaty palm over her backside. She said *oh my* again, and he said *Sarah, I really…* and then she kissed him hard on the lips and said *Wanna go upstairs?*

Jamie's only sexual experience to that point had been with a girl he'd met the previous summer when his family rented a holiday house at Pearl Beach. She was seventeen with spiky blonde hair, calves the size of his thighs and a tendency to snort when she laughed, which was often. Jamie didn't like anything about her at all, but she wanted to practice having sex for when someone she liked came along, and Jamie thought that was a damn good idea. At the end of three weeks she shook his hand, told him he wasn't too awful and wished him luck.

What Jamie and Sarah did in his bedroom bore no resemblance to what he did with the girl at the holiday house. What he did with Sarah was so far removed from that dry, determined rutting that he was amazed it could be considered the same act at all. What he felt could only be described as bliss, and incredibly, Sarah seemed to feel the same way. She pressed her face into his chest and said *who would have thought?* And sixteen-year-old Jamie had thought that was that, but sixteen-year-old Jamie had been an idiot.

And, as it turned out, so was twenty-two-year-old Jamie.

While he was washing his face, it occurred to him that he should actually speak to Sarah rather than unquestioningly accept everything Mike had said. A phone call wouldn't cut it; he needed to see her face.

Her door was unlocked. He pushed it open and stepped inside, turning cold at the thought that *anyone* could push this door open and step inside. 'Sarah?'

'Bedroom.'

She was sitting on the windowsill, smoking, a paperback opened across her knees. She looked small and forlorn, so much like the abused and abandoned child he knew her to be. He wanted so much to touch her, to be touched by her, to feel again the tiny weight of her hand on his cock. He wanted to be close enough to smell the smoke in her hair, to taste the sweat trickling down the back of her neck. But how could he touch her when she had not even turned to look at him, had not acknowledged his presence in the room at all? He leant against the wall, as close to her as he dared. Still she did not move except to lift her cigarette to her lips, inhale, lower her hand, exhale.

'You shouldn't leave the door unlocked.'

'No, I probably shouldn't.' She blew smoke out the window.

'It's dangerous.'

'I suppose.'

'Anyone could walk in. You'd be trapped.'

She shrugged.

'Jesus, Sarah! Do you want to have your throat cut?'

'Stop being such a fucking nana. Why are you here?'

He had never wanted to hit a person so much in his life. He took a deep breath and plunged ahead. 'What happened last night, Sarah?'

'You don't remember? You must have been drunker than I thought.' She threw the cigarette butt out the window, and they both watched it sail down and land in the alley, still trailing smoke.

'You'll start a fire doing that. You should put it out first.'

'Yeah, guess I should.'

'You don't think much about the consequences of your actions do you?'

'I don't think about the consequences of where I throw my ciggie butts, no.'

'Must be nice to not care about anything or anyone else.'

Sarah was quiet for a very long time. No matter how long it took, how sweaty and shaky and sick it made him, Jamie would not leave this room until she faced him. He watched her hands as she lit another cigarette. Her stubby little girl's fingers topped with a serious young woman's neat, rounded nails.

He couldn't help touching her, just resting his palm on the top of her arm. 'Sarah? Please?'

She looked up at him and her face was unutterably sad. 'I'm sorry,' she said, touching a fingertip to his chin. 'I don't know what to say.'

Jamie steeled himself. 'Was it no good?'

'Oh, *God*.'

'Was it that bad? Was *I* that bad?'

She stood up, still holding his chin. For a second he thought she was going to kiss him. His stomach lurched. But no.

'It was *wonderful*. But it shouldn't have happened. You're having a baby, for God's sake.'

'I know, it's just–'

'Shit, Jamie.' Sarah stroked his face. 'I'm such a selfish cow. I felt as though… it's hard seeing what's happening to your life. I needed to be with you, to be close to you. I didn't think about what would happen afterwards, I just… Can you forgive me?'

'Nothing to forgive,' Jamie said, with bitter acid bubbling in his throat.

Relief washed over her face. Or it could have been exhaustion. 'I love you, you know that?'

'Sure.' *And Mike?* He couldn't make himself say it. Her arms were around him, her head on his shoulder. He had her spine under his palm. How could he ask her if… ugh, he didn't even want to think about it. But he knew he would think about nothing else unless he knew for sure.

'Sarah? Um, I saw Mike this morning and he said–'

'Mike. Oh dear.' She held Jamie tighter. 'He'll be here soon.'

'Sarah, no, please tell me you haven't…'

'Not yet.'

'But you're–'

Sarah broke out of the embrace. 'Jamie, *don't*.'

She was too much. Just too fucking much. He started to cry, which he could tell pissed her off, but… God, she was too much. Fuck.

'Go home, Jamie.'

'Sarah, how can you–'

'Go home.'

8

The last few months of the year were always busy for Sarah. There were final papers to hand in, exams to prepare and sit for, and as many extra hours at the steakhouse as she could handle. Her only relaxation was having sex with Mike, who turned up at her house every couple of nights whether she asked him to or not. She didn't complain; he suited her. She didn't have the time or energy to pick up men; Mike got into it, got her off, and got gone. The perfect man for the moment.

Jamie, on the other hand, seemed determined to punish her for the huge mistake of fucking him. He spoke to her only if she called him, and even then he was cold and distant. When they saw each other in the company of others he was his old friendly self, but the minute they were alone together he found somewhere else to be. If she let herself think about it, she felt unbearably sad at the damage she had done to Jamie and at the damage he seemed determined to inflict upon the friendship. Fortunately, she had little time to think these days, and so the pain, although gut wrenching, was infrequent and fleeting.

On Christmas Eve she went to the Leagues Club after work to find some young stallion to ride, but then she got talking to a bouncer named Bob who revealed that he volunteered to work right through the Christmas period because it was better than being alone. Sarah was flattened with empathy and self-disgust. She spent all night hanging in the doorway talking to him, ignoring the disfiguring acne that covered his face and thick neck. When he knocked off work at three o'clock on Christmas morning, Sarah gave him a blowjob in the front seat of his car and he cried.

The restaurant was closed until the New Year, there was a month and a half until uni started again, and everybody she knew spent the week between Christmas and New Year's with their families. She would have gone out clubbing but she was broke, and also, now that she had slowed down enough to notice it, remarkably tired. So she slept twelve, thirteen, fourteen hours a day, and missed Jamie, and wondered if she would ever get out of Sydney, and re-read all of her books, which didn't take that long because she only owned the twenty-three she had had when she moved out of home.

And reading this way – with no deadline, no agenda – she remembered why she loved literature so much. It was like fucking a new man and knowing that he had made other women come, but that when she came it would be an unshareable, untranslatable pleasure. She opened herself up to her books, and the words got inside her and fucked her senseless.

When she read how Emma Bovary believed 'she was entering into something marvellous where all would be passion, ecstasy, delirium…' Sarah remembered her own hopes of escaping her existence through sexual passion, and in her mind she saw Mr Carr throwing her across that dingy hotel room. She felt as though a layer of skin had been ripped from her body, and so pulled off her pyjama pants and fucked the corner of the hardcover book until she felt better.

For light relief she read Huckleberry Finn but the image of the pubescent white boy and the rugged black slave, naked and drifting on their raft, had her on all fours, rubbing her book-battered clitoris with her palm. Then Donne's *Songs and Sonnets* was so unbearably erotic she had to put it aside before she did herself real damage. Next, she chose *Jane Eyre* and got through comfortably until the last few pages, which made her squirm. If there was anything in the history of literature more erotic than the moment when Jane kisses Rochester's blinded eyes, she had yet to come across it.

Then while reading the scene in *Richard III* where Richard seduces the newly widowed Anne, Sarah became so frenzied she fell of the sofa, overturning the ashtray and hitting her head, hard, on the floorboards. As she sat amongst the scattered ash, rubbing her forehead, she wondered whether Jamie was right. Maybe her interest in sex was abnormal, her hunger excessive. Maybe falling off the furniture while reading Shakespeare was perverse. She read the passage over:

Your beauty was the cause of that effect—
Your beauty did haunt me in my sleep
To undertake the death of all the world
So I might live one hour in your sweet bosom.

No, her reaction was entirely appropriate. Anyone who read that scene and was not aroused must be dead from the waist down. Still, she wished Jamie was around to contradict her. She wished he was around.

New Year's Eve also happened to be Sarah's twenty-second birthday and the occasion of a party at Mike and Jess' new place. Sarah would have skipped the party altogether and spent the night in the city with the rest of Sydney's drunk and horny singles, but Jamie would be at the party and so she had to go. She would get him someplace he couldn't get away from her, and she would make him be her friend again.

But before she could think of a way to separate Jamie from the swollen thing at his side, Mike whisked Sarah upstairs and into the spare room. He had spent the last week with his family and was, he said, 'about to pop.' Sarah was going to tell him that this was not her problem, but then he pushed her back on to the bed and tore her underpants right through the crotch, and she was about ready to pop herself.

'Guess what happened at Jess' parents' place on Christmas Day?' Mike said after they were done.

Sarah was brushing her hair. She looked at him in the mirror and smiled. 'Mmm?'

'I met the lovely Jocelyn Clark.' Mike came up behind her and kissed her neck. Sarah stared straight ahead. 'Had a chat with her over lunch.'

Sarah kept her face blank. She wondered how long it would take her to get the money together to disappear. Probably not long if she put her mind to it. She could go to London or France or New Zealand. Anywhere would do, as long as no one knew her.

'How come you don't see your mum anymore?'

She smiled at his reflection. 'I like your shirt. Blue suits you.'

'Because I thought she was really nice. She asked about you.'

'You should wear blue more often, it brings out your eyes.'

'She looks a bit like you. You have her eyes and her chin. The nose must come from your dad. I didn't get to meet him. He was working apparently.'

'Did Jess buy it for you? She has good taste in clothes, I'll say that much for her.'

'He must be a really hard worker. Imagine going to work on Christmas Day! He's an accountant or something isn't he?'

'An actuary. To the best of my knowledge he has never taken a single day off in his life. Maybe his wedding day, I'm not sure.' Sarah stepped away from Mike. 'If I ever find out you have been talking to my parents about me, that will be the end. Not just of this sleazy little affair, but of any contact between us at all.'

Mike reached for her. 'Sarah, they're your parents, you–'

'Stop!' Sarah took several deep breaths, holding her arms out in front of her with the palms out. 'If you ever want to even *speak* to me again, you will shut up about them immediately.'

'Christ, Sarah, calm down. I'm sorry. Come here.' Mike looked contrite, and Sarah allowed his arms to go around her.

'I was just curious,' he said into her ear. 'Jess said they kicked you out over some scandal? Some sex thing? I was thinking maybe enough time's passed. Maybe you could have some kind of reconciliation?'

Sarah pressed her head into his shoulder, clinging to his body. The surge of adrenalin and the violent tensing of her muscles had caused the blood to rush away from her head and she was afraid of fainting. He misinterpreted her tension and began to stroke her head. 'It's okay,' he said. 'It's okay, babe.' Again and again he said it, while Sarah seethed and tried to regain her composure enough to stand independently.

Finally, her pulse slowed to something approaching normal. 'You don't know anything about me,' she said, calmly stepping away from him.

'Sarah?' He reached for her. She jumped back, holding her hands out in front of her.

'Don't touch me. Not ever again.'

His hands flew up to his head. He gaped at her for several seconds, dropped his hands, began to reach out, then returned to combing his hair with his fingers. 'Sarah, I–'

She dismissed him with a flick of the wrist and walked away with her head held high. She would not cry. It was beneath her.

★

Jamie saw Sarah and Mike sneak inside together, and twenty-two minutes later he saw Sarah approach a big black man with a shaved head, and press her giggly, wriggly body up against him. Three minutes after that, Sarah and the man were kissing each other against the fence. Jamie tried to take courage from the spectacle, to let the sight of her throwing herself around so glibly harden him further. He reminded himself that he was much better off now that he knew she saw him as just another expendable dick in a never-ending line of expendable dicks.

It hurt so much he wanted to rip his fucking heart out of his chest.

But that was good. Sarah meant pain; Shelley meant comfort. As long as he remembered that, he would be able to keep away from *her* and concentrate on being the kind of father his child deserved. And his child *did* deserve a good father – every child did. Sarah was evidence of how fucked up a person could get from having shitty parents.

'Jamie, got a second?' Mike slapped his back.

Jamie looked at Mike, took in the sweaty face and messed up hair, and quickly looked away again. 'What's up?'

'Sarah's pissed off at me, big time.'

'Why?' Jamie asked, trying to not care about the obscene performance at the fence.

'Fucked if I know. Typical bloody irrational woman. Maybe she's about to get her period.'

'Sarah doesn't get her period.' As the words came out of his mouth he realised what a freak he was for saying them. Sure enough, Mike was looking at him as though he'd spoken the entire sentence in Greek. Jamie thought he might as well explain. 'She manipulates her pill. She doesn't believe in wasting five days out of every month feeling like crap.'

Mike pulled a face at Jamie and shook his head. 'I knew you were close but I didn't know you talked about that kind of stuff. That's fucking disgusting, man.'

'The point is that whatever's upsetting her it isn't that, okay?' Jamie barely cared what Mike thought of him. Sarah was clearly about to leave with her new friend, and Jamie hadn't even wished her a happy birthday yet. He had never missed wishing her a happy birthday, not since her thirteenth when he gave her a book about Medieval Europe and she kissed his cheek for the first time.

'Since you know every last detail of her existence, maybe you can offer some insight into what the fuck is wrong with her.'

Jamie sighed. What was wrong with Sarah was that she had some kind of personality disorder where she wasn't happy unless she was causing pain and discomfort to herself and everyone around her.

'What happened?' he asked, knowing he would regret it.

'I just tried to talk to her about why she doesn't see her oldies, and she went schizo and stormed out of the room.'

This caught Jamie's full attention. 'What did you say to her?'

Mike raised his chin defiantly. 'I told her it was silly to hold a grudge against her family just because she got busted fucking a couple of blokes–'

'Shit, Mike. You said that to her?'

'Not in those words.' Mike kicked the dirt. 'I was *trying* to be nice.'

'Maybe, but you got it wrong. Way wrong.'

'Well, what then? Why doesn't she see them?'

'That's Sarah's business. If she wanted you to know, you would.' Jamie was glad to have a noble excuse to keep his mouth shut. It was not a story he wanted to ever, ever have to tell.

'I just want to understand why she's so… why she's the way she is.'

That was the question which kept Jamie awake at night. Every time he thought he'd figured out the answer, he remembered something else, or she said something which changed his mind and he was left with the same old pile of *maybes* and *possiblys* and a large number of *if onlys*.

'Sarah's made some dumb choices in the past – she still does sometimes – but she… she's been treated badly, had some shitty things done to her. Just believe her when she says there are things she can't talk about. Just let her be for once.' He didn't want to talk anymore and it appeared he didn't need to. Mike was visibly remorseful, staring at the ground with a face drained of colour.

'I'll apologise.'

'Not tonight, okay? She's had enough drama I reckon.' Jamie swiped the start of a tear from his left eye. Caught it just in time. 'Let her salvage the last couple of hours of her birthday, heh?'

Mike opened his eyes wide. 'It's her *birthday*?'

Jamie watched Sarah over Mike's shoulder, watched her kissing, and laughing, and standing on her toes, and spinning around, and walking out. Every man wanting her, and trying to be near her, or talking about her, and wondering about her, and there probably wasn't a single person in the world who had wished her a happy birthday.

9

At ten o'clock at night on the first day of the year, Jamie was curled up on the sofa with Shelley when Sarah called. She was hysterical. *Please, come over,* she sobbed. *I really, really need you.* He looked at Shelley curled up on the lounge. She was wearing white and yellow sunflower pyjamas that didn't quite cover her belly, and her hair was all mussed up. Until the moment the phone rang, they'd had a remarkably pleasant evening. Snuggling in front of the television, kissing and making up silly names for the baby. He couldn't remember enjoying her company so much since they'd first started going out. New year, fresh start, he'd thought.

Sarah sounded really distressed. He said he'd be right over.

'Please don't tell me you're going to Sarah's,' Shelley said when he'd hung up.

'Something's wrong. I have to go.'

Shelley groaned. 'Something's wrong all right. Something's wrong with you leaving me at ten o'clock at night to go to *her.*'

'Come on, Shell. She doesn't have anyone else.'

Shelley stuck out her bottom lip. 'We were having such a nice night. Can't she wait until tomorrow?'

Jamie leant forward and sucked on the pouty lip until she giggled. 'That's better,' he said, smoothing down her fuzzy hair. 'I'll just make sure she's okay, then I'll be back. Promise.'

'You're too bloody nice, Jamie Wilkes,' Shelley said, but she smiled and blew him a kiss as he left.

Sarah met him at the door wearing only her underwear and holding a beer in one hand and a cigarette in the other. Within sixty seconds, he was sitting on her bed and rubbing her back. Through drunken tears she told Jamie what had happened.

Mike had dropped in unannounced at around eight and found her in bed with Charles, the man from last night. Well, no, he didn't *exactly* find them in bed. More like, Mike knocked on the door and was greeted by an enormous naked black man, holding a giggling naked Sarah over his shoulder. Mike let fly with a torrent of abuse. Charles took exception to the language that Mike was using and proceeded to punch him in the face without putting Sarah down. Mike retreated with a busted nose. Charles asked Sarah if there were any other ex-lovers he should know about before they got any more involved. Sarah kicked Charles in the kidneys and told him to fuck-off, and then he dropped her on her head, called her all the names Mike had called her and broke one of her chairs.

'I'm sick of it all,' she sobbed into the pillow. She was wearing a pale blue g-string and matching bra. Jamie couldn't remember Shelley ever wearing a g-string. Or matching underwear of any kind. She used to wear plain coloured cotton undies with a mismatched black polyester bra, but these days she wore maternity underwear, which he understood was necessary from a comfort point of view, but it was obscenely ugly. After the baby was born he would buy her a cute little matching set like this one.

'Sick of what?' Jamie had read in Mike's magazine that men who got turned on by damsel in distress types had power issues. Jamie wondered if he was a misogynist or if he had a suppressed hatred towards women, because Sarah was more attractive to him than she had ever been before. Which was saying a lot.

'I'm sick of the way men claim ownership of me just because they've had an orgasm in my body.' Sarah took a heaving breath after every third word.

Jamie was undoubtedly turned on, but he thought maybe it was because of the underwear and not the weakness or despair. If she would put some clothes on he would be able to tell. Or if she stayed in her underwear but stopped crying. Either way would tell him what he wanted to know.

'I hate men. *Hate* them. They think they know everything. Men! They know nothing. Good for one bloody thing and most of them aren't even good at that.'

'If you hate them so much, why do you spend every waking hour with them?' Jamie forced himself to stare at the picture of the Eiffel Tower over her bed. It was a horrible shiny poster with *I Love Paris* written across the top in red, blue and white. She had bought it for fifty cents at a school fete a few years ago. She said it reminded her that all she would have of the world was cheesy mass produced tourist shots unless she got off her arse and saw it for herself.

'I *don't* spend every waking hour with them and that's the problem. You know what Mike said to me? He said I didn't have a heart! Can you believe that?'

Jamie had never heard Sarah talk like this. She went through men like she went through underwear. Itsy, bitsy, teeny, weeny pale blue underwear. *Stop.*

'He doesn't know you, Sar.' Jamie patted her smooth, pale back. 'Do you think it might help to get out here? I'll take you out for a drink to get your mind off it all.' Jamie was proud of himself. She would have to get dressed if they went to the pub.

'You're too bloody nice to me, Jamie. Such a goddamn *nice* guy.'

Well, Shelley and Sarah agreed on that one. But would they still think he was a nice guy if they knew he was imagining grabbing Sarah's arse with both hands, pulling it towards him, pressing his face into the firm cheeks, slipping his index finger under the thong and running his tongue along the crack? Would

Sarah and Shelley say he was *too nice* if they knew he had an enormous boner from comforting a drunk, confused, parentless girl?

He had to put the brakes on this before it was too late. 'Sarah, can you get up?'

'Why?'

'So I can talk to you. Sit up for me, will you?'

Sarah rolled over onto her back. 'You can talk to me when I'm lying down.'

This was worse. She looked so open, arms at her side, legs slightly spread and bent at the knees. Her ribs jutted up and so did her hipbones. The urge to feel the curve of her waist was strong. She was so perfect, it was hard to look at her and impossible to look away.

'Why are you staring at me?'

Jamie looked up at the Eiffel Tower. 'Can you put some clothes on?'

'Why?'

'Because it's hard to talk to you when you're nearly naked.'

'Why?'

'Do you have a dressing gown or something I can get you?'

'A dressing gown? Is that something that dumpy pregnant ladies wear because they don't want anyone to see how fat and awful they look?'

Jamie stood up. 'I'm leaving.'

She reached for his arm and pulled him back down. 'No.'

'I know you're upset, but don't be mean about Shelley.'

'Sorry. Do you love me?'

'Yes.'

'Not as much as you love her though?'

'It's different.'

She flopped over onto her stomach and buried her face in the pillow again. He allowed himself another good look at her. Her skin was so smooth and pale. Cadaver pale. Bloodless.

'Rub my back,' she said. 'You sound like Mike.'

'How do I sound like Mike?

'Mike always says it's *different* with Jess. Rub harder. I'm not going to break.'

Jamie rubbed harder. 'I'm probably not as good at this as he is.'

'He never gives me back rubs. He gives Jess back rubs I think, probably he does, I don't know, I might ask him. Do you give Shelley back rubs?'

'Sometimes. Belly rubs lately.' A wave of guilt at how hurt Shelley would be if she knew what he was doing engulfed him. Just comforting an old friend. On her bed. While she's in her underwear. Drunk and vulnerable. Nothing wrong with that, Shell.

'Will you rub my belly?' Sarah rolled over abruptly so he had no time to move. He had one hand on her stomach and the other landed on her left breast. He was certain now that his arousal had nothing to do with her being distressed, and everything to do with the fact that she was intentionally seducing him.

He held his hands in the air. 'No.'

She reached for him and placed his hands back where they were. Funny that she looked so cold, as if there was no blood to warm her at all, yet her skin was burning and he could feel her heart pumping forcefully under her breast.

He pulled away from her. 'I'm going to go home to Shelley. She's pregnant you know?'

'I know. Don't leave.' Sarah sat up and took off her bra in one smooth, practised movement.

Jamie refused to look at her breasts. He looked instead at her tear-stained, blank face. It was the only part of her skin with any colour and that was all concentrated around her eyes, which were so red and squinty that they were barely recognisable. In fact, her whole head looked odd, too big and strangely coloured, like one of those dodgy internet photos of a soap star's head pasted onto a centrefold's body.

'Did you ask me to come here for this?'

'Maybe.'

Jamie wished he didn't love her so much. He wished he could turn her down flat and walk away. But he wanted her to understand what she was doing to him. He needed her to know that she was killing him, and then he needed to see how she reacted, whether it mattered to her at all.

'How can you think it's okay to use me whenever you need to get off? Mike told me that the night you and I… he told me that he was… you were touching each other at dinner.' A sob broke free and the tears began to stream out. He didn't care. 'He said you were excited. He said you were all… All that desire, Sarah, God! I thought it was for *me!*'

Sarah took a tissue from the box next to her knee and wiped Jamie's face. 'It was, Jamie. I swear. You shouldn't listen to him. He's jealous of you.'

Jamie pushed her hand away. 'I was so happy that night. I thought you really wanted me.'

'I did. And I want you now.' Sarah grabbed his hand and forced it between her legs. 'Feel that? That's for my Jamie-boy.'

He felt it. Felt the damp heat coming through the too thin fabric. The damp heat that her body had made just for him. There was no one else here; it had to be for him. *Oh God.* He closed his eyes and focussed on an image of Shelley; she was exactly the wife he should want. Think about the baby. Think about how you'll feel tomorrow when Sarah pretends this never happened.

119

'I need to go home,' he said, without removing his hand.

'You need to stay with me.'

She kissed him again, and he lost himself for a second. Then he remembered that she had done this with at least two other men in the last thirty-six hours. He was nothing to her and everything to Shelley. He pulled back. 'Last time we... you said you did it because you were upset about me and Shelley and the baby and everything. And you still are. You don't really want me but you can't fucking stand it that someone else does.'

'Maybe that was it at first but, now–' She kissed his closed mouth wetly. 'Just looking at you makes me want to fuck you.'

He was kissing her without meaning to. Her breasts were under his hands, feeling hotter than he remembered but otherwise the same. She said his name and grabbed the front of his shorts, and he sobbed and pulled away.

'Why now? All these years, Sarah, and when I finally have– Why are you doing this *now*?' His voice sounded all broken, which made sense because Sarah was pulling him apart. Soon it would be too late; much more of this and he would never be able to put himself together again.

'We can't know why.' Sarah pushed him on to his back and straddled him. He let her. 'It's like a volcano. The damn thing lies dormant for years. People build their houses right around the base.' She was unbuttoning his shirt, tugging at his shorts. 'Then one day *boom*! That harmless old mountain erupts and there's suddenly molten magna over all those cute little hotels and theme restaurants and quaint log cabins. And then, *then*, everybody says that it was a disaster waiting to happen. It was fucking inevitable. It was always a volcano; never a mountain.'

She stood up with one leg either side of him and leant forward to place one hand on the wall over his head. With her other hand, she slid her pants down to her knees, then lifted each leg in turn, finally kicking the damp scrap of cotton off the side of the bed. She squatted over him, her arms holding his down. 'I know I hurt you, and I know you're scared I'm going to do it again, and I can't promise you I won't. Sometimes I think I hurt you just by existing. But I can promise you that I will not pretend this didn't happen, and I will not pretend it didn't mean anything.' She shifted position, and the wet lips of her cunt brushed his cock. He raised his hips, straining to be inside her, but she hovered just out of his reach. 'Ask me to fuck you.'

'Fuck me, Sarah. Please.'

She smiled and lowered herself onto him. Jamie closed his eyes at the sensation of being inside her, then opened them again because Sarah was making love to him and he didn't want to miss it.

'You are so fucking beautiful,' Sarah said, pulling on his sparse chest hair. 'You are a beautiful, wonderful, incredible man and I am so proud of you.' She spoke softly, touching his chest and stomach, sliding up and down his cock at a gentle pace. 'I don't think I ever told you that I'm proud of you, but I am. You're going to be the best daddy—'

'Sssh. Please, Sar, don't talk about—'

'Deal with the reality of this, Jamie.' She smiled and picked up her speed. 'We've been friends for a long time, and knowing how it feels to have your cock inside me has never changed that, and it won't change it now. In a few months time, you will be a married man with a kid, and I will still be your best friend, and I will still want to fuck you and maybe you'll still want to fuck me. That's the reality.'

'I will always, always want you, Sarah. This is… ah!' He had been going to tell her that this was everything he'd ever wanted, but she reached back and cupped his balls in her hand and he couldn't speak.

'See, I've always known that one day you would have a family of your own. I was shocked – and yes, pissed off – that it happened so soon, but it was always going to happen. You're a nurturer, Jamie. Fatherhood is what you were built for.' This while she was massaging his balls and bouncing on his cock. Her breath was getting ragged. 'I, on the other hand, was built for *this*.'

Jamie understood that she was telling him that she would never be his wife or have his child. She was offering him the opportunity to have the family he had always wanted and the girl he had always wanted, but not in the same house, not from the same source. And that was really, really okay.

But now he wanted her to shut up, because however much he loved to hear the sound of her voice, he had never in his whole life needed so desperately to *come*. 'Sarah,' he said, and that was all. He said her name and then everything he'd ever wanted to say to her coursed through his groin; he shuddered, sobbed and then lay still.

10

Throughout January and February, Jamie and Sarah saw each other as much as they ever had, but instead of watching movies or getting drunk or going out for lunch, they climbed into Sarah's bed and stayed there until it was time for Jamie to go home. Sarah was surprised by how much she liked fucking him, but more than that, she was surprised at how easily she fell asleep when he was by her side. His breath in her ear, his hand on her waist, the scent and sound of him, tranquillised her. Many times he had to wake her to tell her it was time for him to go, and she would spend the night trying without success to recapture the serenity he took with him.

Mike came knocking at the end of January. His nose had healed and his tail was between his legs. He told Sarah that he missed her and that sex with Jess reminded him of when he was thirteen and he used to get off by humping a pile of pillows. Sarah couldn't think of any good reason to not sleep with him, and so their affair resumed. Within a month she was sick to death of him again. She looked forward to his wedding in July. Not so much the wedding, but the honeymoon which would give her a full three weeks break from him.

On the third of March, Shelley gave birth to a baby girl named Bianca. Sarah went to the hospital, took yellow roses for Shelley, a cigar for Jamie and a tiny white bonnet for the child. She held the pink and white bundle Jamie thrust at her, and tried to feel something other than impatience. Jamie walked her to the bus stop, talking the whole time about contractions and epidurals, feedings and bathings. He did not kiss her goodbye, but instead squeezed her hand and thanked her for coming to see his *girls*. On the way home she tried not to think about the hot, squirmy little bundle, but she felt the weight of it in her empty arms, heard its gurgling sigh above the noise of the bus. She felt injured and confused. Shocked that a heat-emitting, smell-making creature had been produced by Jamie, that it could make her arms ache and her nose twitch, that it could make Jamie blind to her, cold to her desire.

Sarah did bad things that night. Dangerous, painful, unclean things. She did not go home until her body's memory of the child was all gone. Until her skin was red raw and she stank like a person without a home, without sense.

In the weeks after Bianca's birth, Jamie stayed away from Sarah. He phoned her nightly, apologising for yet another missed appointment. The baby was unpredictable, demanding, impossible to leave. Shelley was exhausted, sick, impossible to refuse. Plus, there was work and housework and wedding arrangements to make. He would come see her the first chance he had.

Sarah told him that she was busy anyway. The honours program was more demanding than she had expected, and she found her old study routine was inadequate. Now she was in the Arts lounge by seven each morning, drinking coffee, tapping her feet and clicking her pen, with the rest of the black-eyed, black-clad diehards. From seven until nine they argued over whether Slessor was really a modernist and whether Hope was a genius or a bore. Sometimes they helped each other draft papers or formulate discussion points. They ate chocolate biscuits, hash cookies or peanuts stolen from behind the uni bar. At nine o'clock, they wished each other luck, kissed each other, lightly or seriously, and headed off to their classes or meetings. At lunchtime, they would regroup, eat whatever was leftover from the morning's session and argue some more. Afternoon was more classes, early evening meant study in the library or typing up a paper in the computer lab, after which Sarah would catch the bus directly to work, where she would wait tables until ten o'clock. Jamie called at eleven o'clock each night, without fail. They would talk for a few minutes, and then Sarah would study some more. Most nights she got to bed around three, and would fall asleep around dawn. On weekends, she slept and studied and saw no one.

So she did not really have time to spend with Jamie, but she was annoyed and distracted by his continued absence anyway. By the third week she was losing the place in her reading and getting caught daydreaming in lectures. She figured she was losing more time to the *idea* of him than she would if she could just *see* him for an hour or so. Not that she could say that to him; he'd go all mushy on her. Instead, she did not answer the phone for three nights running and on the third night, at fourteen minutes past midnight, he turned up at her door dressed in shirt and tie and stinking of baby powder.

Sarah had not been touched for weeks. That was why she felt like weeping when Jamie kissed her neck, why she found the sex painful in its intensity, why she had to bite her tongue to stop from saying something stupid while she lay in his arms afterward. 'I think you actually missed me,' he said. 'Well, duh,' she said.

When Bianca was a month old, Jamie and Shelley got married. It was not the flashy affair originally planned, since money was tight and the happy couple were shockingly exhausted. Shelley wore a pale pink silk dress and flowers in her hair. Sarah thought that she looked quite pretty. Jamie smiled a lot, but mostly at his daughter who slept in her mother's arms for the whole ceremony. The reception was held in the church hall, with finger food and cask wine supplied by the bride's parents and a jukebox hired by the groom's.

During the reception, when Shelley went to feed Bianca, Jamie pulled Sarah into the supply cupboard. 'For you,' he said, handing her a small black box. Inside was a gold band. Sarah stared at it blankly. Jamie took the ring from the box, lifted Sarah's right hand, and slid the ring over her finger. 'There, it looks beautiful.'

'Did you get two for the price of one or something?' Sarah said, and felt bad straight away. She fingered the thick gold band. 'What's this for?'

'I wanted to show you that me being married doesn't change how I feel about you.'

Sarah felt like she was suffocating. 'I know that. You don't have to give me a wedding ring. People will notice.'

Jamie kissed her hand. 'No one will notice if it's on the right hand. And it isn't a wedding ring, anyway, it's a…' He smiled at her, and kissed her ring finger again. 'It doesn't have a label, Sarah. It's like us, like this thing we have. Beautiful and strong and nameless.'

Sarah nearly lost the six glasses of moselle she'd drunk. Jamie was such a soppy pain in the arse sometimes. But though his sentimentality made her sick, his eyes made her sad and she couldn't be cruel or sarcastic.

'Come here.' She caught him around the waist and pulled him to her. 'Have I told you how good you look in that suit?' She kissed his throat above his collar.

'No. Sarah, I have to go back–'

'In a minute.' Sarah unzipped his pants. 'I want you.'

'How can you be so fucking insensitive? I can't do this on, oh, Sarah, don't.'

'Sssh.' She took out his already hard cock and worked it with her hands, while he kissed her neck and lifted her skirt. From the other side of the door she could hear *Only You* and the sound of high heels on tile and the white noise of forty people having twenty conversations.

'Sarah, this is really wrong,' Jamie said into her ear, as he pushed her underpants aside and drove into her. She fell back onto a box of toilet paper rolls, and for a moment he was apart from her. Then he reclaimed her and fucked her like that, both of them fully clothed, both of them wearing plain gold bands, both of them biting down on their own lips to stop from crying out. A fast song started playing and the noise from the hall increased as the high heels and the heavy leather dress shoes pounded the dance floor and a few beered up men attempted to sing along.

The airless closet stank of bleach. Sarah's vision – already slightly shaky from the wine – began to blur. She closed her eyes, but that made her feel like she was falling fast, so she opened them. Jamie's face was red; sweat dripped from his temples and down onto her dress. He smiled, or grimaced really, and touched her face with a hot, wet hand and she felt his cold ring against her cheek and she bit down hard, hard, hard to stop from howling as the orgasm slammed through her.

He left first, after she had checked him for lipstick or wet spots or other telltale marks. She sat on the box and licked the blood from the inside of her lip. She was more shaken than she had been in a very long time. Certainly more shaken than she had ever been after fucking Jamie. An unfamiliar feeling, something true and bright and deep, had hijacked her. It wasn't love, but it was damn close. Something that looked a bit like love if it was dark enough and you turned your head to the side and squinted. She felt it and knew she was in trouble.

Fucking for pleasure was a difficult, dangerous game. Especially for women, whose bodies were specifically designed to trick them into attachment. Sarah knew how it worked: the surging adrenalin and testosterone creating the desire; the gentle buzz of dopamine, reliably kicking in just as it did after every cigarette; and then all that lovely serotonin. Then while she was on this glorious natural high, the primal, three-billion year old instinct took over and she became nothing but a grasping, sucking mating machine. The delicious spasms of her orgasm were just her body's way of getting her to contract her cervix and suck that sperm up like a vacuum.

And in the blissful moments after the shaking stopped, the oxytocin came flooding in, poisoning her blood with the same chemical that caused mothers to bond with their babies. The more frequent the exposure, the more intense the bond. It was a biological ploy to ensure the survival of the species and it had worked brilliantly in Sarah. This was what she felt now for Jamie. Not love, just a chemical addiction developed after months of recreational use. She vowed to cut down.

11

Due to a hangover which prevented her from getting out of bed until well after four o'clock in the afternoon, Sarah was late for Jamie's birthday celebration at the pub. By the time she arrived, Mike and Jamie were half full already, their beer garden table cluttered with empty glasses and full ashtrays. Jamie looked like shit, and Sarah told him so.

'You try getting half an hour of sleep a night, then we'll see who looks like shit. You should hear how loud my kid can yell. Thank God, Mum agreed to take her for the day. Shell and I are exhausted.'

'Poor boy.' Sarah kissed his forehead and resisted the urge to move down and kiss his lips. She straightened and patted his shoulder. 'You can always stay at my place if you need a break.'

'Nah, don't do it, man,' Mike said. 'Whenever I've spent the night with Sarah I've had no sleep at all.' He grabbed Sarah by the waist and pulled her down onto his lap. She swatted at him with both arms and slid off his lap onto the seat.

'What? The girls are in the wine bar, relax.'

Jamie cleared his throat. 'Yeah, but I'm right here.'

'You know that me and Sarah can't keep our hands off each other.' Mike lunged at her, taking her face in both hands and kissing her on the lips.

'God, I think you two might need a moment alone.' Jamie stood up. 'Drinks?'

Sarah and Mike gave him their orders, and when he was gone Sarah slapped Mike's hand, which was creeping up her leg. 'What's wrong with you? Are you suddenly single and forgot to tell me?'

'It's only Jamie.'

'And anyone else who decides to walk through this public drinking area on the busiest day of the week. You're so dumb sometimes.'

Mike put his hand back onto her thigh. 'It's been ages, Sarah. I'm ready to burst.'

'Do you *ever* have sex with Jess?'

'Rarely. And besides, it isn't the same. She doesn't do the things you do; she doesn't know what I like.'

Sarah rolled her eyes. 'Why don't you tell her then? Or should I? I'll have a nice girly talk with her and give her some advice on how to suck your dick in such a way that you won't grope her friends in public.'

'What the fuck is wrong with you?'

Sarah didn't answer him. She had just realised that Mike and Jamie represented her entire intimate world. The last time she'd fucked anyone else was almost four months ago, on her birthday. And Mike she hadn't seen for over a month, which meant that she had been having sex with Jamie and no one else for all that time. How the hell had that happened?

'Is this because I'm getting married?' Mike's tone was so patronising that Sarah wanted to slap him.

'You know I don't care about that.'

'Right, but...' Mike stroked the inside of Sarah's leg. 'It's only a couple of months away. Are you maybe freaking out a bit? Maybe even feeling jealous?'

'No.'

'So what? You got a boyfriend or something?'

'No.'

'Why are you being so cold then?'

'I'm not. I've been busy. If I have time this week, we'll get together and fuck. Okay?'

'Jesus, you're so fucking–'

'Drinks. Thank God!' Sarah turned her back on Mike and helped Jamie with the glasses he was juggling. Then she drank both her own and Mike's drink in two large gulps. 'Oops!' she said to Mike. 'Guess you'll have to go and get some more.'

'Fucking bitch,' he said, but he stood up and headed for the bar.

'What was that all about?' Jamie said.

'He's pissed off because we haven't done it in a while.'

'Oh.' Jamie sipped his beer. 'Um, how long since you've…?'

Sarah looked at him; he was staring a hole into the tabletop. She worried about how tired he looked, and how stressful his life had become. She wanted to kiss him – properly, on the lips – but settled for another pat on the shoulder. 'Long enough that he suspects I've got a boyfriend hidden away.'

Jamie looked up at her with a worried smile. 'Do you?'

'Well, you're a boy. And you're my friend.'

'Yes, I am. Which isn't the same as a *boyfriend*.'

'Except when it is,' Sarah said, surprising herself with her words, and with the lump that had appeared in her throat.

'Oh.' He smiled, blushed, looked over her shoulder then back into her eyes, smiled again, then frowned. 'I'm your boyfriend?'

'No. Absolutely not. Don't know where you got that idea.'

'Sarah!' Jamie punched her in the arm. Sarah punched him back and noticed that he leant into her. She liked it that he did that, and that he didn't linger, pressing against her arm, but pulled back and looked at her and brushed a stray strand of hair from her face.

'I don't understand what you're saying,' he said.

'Me neither.'

'I like it though.'

'Me too.' The lump in her throat swelled. She wished Mike would hurry back because she needed another drink, but she wished he would stay away because… God, that was it! She wished Mike would stay away because she *wanted to be alone with Jamie*. She was going all soft and unintentionally monogamous over *Jamie*. After nine years of almost daily contact, she was suddenly hungry for more.

'I'm drunk you know,' she said.

'You're not.'

'Yes, I am. I'm shattered. You shouldn't listen to anything I say when I'm this drunk.'

'I don't listen to anything you say anyway. I'm just using you for sex.'

Sarah was so overwhelmed by his smile that she grabbed him by the collar, pulled him close and kissed him on the lips.

'Sarah!' He pulled away and looked over his shoulder, then over Sarah's shoulder, then back at her face. 'Didn't you just have a go at Mike for doing that?'

'Yes. Shit. Yes, I did. I'm sorry. I don't know what's wrong with me.'

He looked at her for several seconds. His squint emphasised the bags under his eyes, making him look thirty. 'Something's changed, hasn't it? Between us?'

'I don't know. I… Yes, I think so. Maybe. I feel–' Sarah noticed that Mike was heading back with their drinks. She sighed and leant in closer to Jamie. 'We'll finish this later. Promise.'

Mike sat down beside Sarah, placing a tray with four glasses of bourbon in front of her and promptly sticking his hand up her skirt. 'Get those into you.'

Sarah drank, and talked to Jamie about nothing that mattered and let Mike put his hand inside her underwear. She remembered that she used to enjoy this kind of thing, but she couldn't remember why. Mike's finger was rough and insistent; he made no allowance for her lack of arousal, or for the fact that Jamie was sitting right beside her. She wondered how it made Jamie feel to know that his friend's index finger was dragging at her flesh, and she wondered if he knew that she wanted it to stop but couldn't seem to raise the energy to end it.

At some stage Shelley and Jess joined them. Sarah was glad because it meant Mike removed his finger from her body. Shelley started talking about the problems she'd been having getting Bianca to feed properly. Sarah was disgusted by the discussion, what with the cracked nipples and infected milk ducts, but Jamie reached across the table and patted Shelley's arm and said, *you're doing a great job, Shell*, and Shelley smiled and leant across and kissed him. An open mouthed, wet kiss. Sarah couldn't help noticing how big Shelley's breasts were, and how pretty she looked now that the last of the pregnancy weight had dropped off.

Sarah felt like the bad girl in an eighties teen flick. The girl with big hair and a tight shirt who seduces the nice girl's boyfriend but loses him in the end, because she's shallow and tacky and no match for a sweet girl with good morals and freshly scrubbed skin.

She touched Jamie's arm, looked him in the eye. 'Come play the pokies?'

He nodded, and after kissing Shelley for what felt like a long time, followed Sarah into the pub. Once inside, Sarah grabbed his hand and dragged him past the poker machines and into the back wine bar. This was the most private area in the pub, because it was poorly lit and had no pool tables or poker machines. Apart from a handful of lonely drunks and the barmaid, Sarah and Jamie were the only ones there. Sarah pushed him into a booth in the corner furthest from the door and slid in beside him.

'This is better, heh?'

He shrugged. 'Better for what?'

'For us. No one can see us in here.'

'Right. Great.'

Sarah was chilled by his voice. 'What's wrong?'

He tapped the table with his fingertips and did not look at her.

'Jamie? What? Have I done something to upset you?'

Jamie snorted. 'You're unbelievable.'

Sarah was totally lost. Half an hour ago she had been confessing to an unprecedented bout of unasked for monogamy, and he had been all cute and warm and glassy eyed. What had turned him so cold all of a sudden? She placed her hands over his, stopping his irritating drumming. 'Can you give me a hint?'

He snorted again, shaking off her hands and placing his in his pockets. 'I just watched you get fingered for Christ's sake.'

'Oh, that.'

'Do you know how that makes me feel?'

Sarah put her head on his shoulder. 'Yeah. I'm sorry.'

'You told me you're not sleeping with him anymore.'

'No, I told you that I haven't slept with him lately. I didn't say I wouldn't do it ever again. And I didn't say I wouldn't let him touch me.'

Jamie sighed. 'Do you have to do it in front of me?'

'Do you have to pash on with Shelley in front of *me*?'

'She's my wife.'

'I hate it that she's so pretty, and she's got those big tits, and she gets to sleep with you every night. I *never* get to sleep with you. And you *never* stare at my tits.'

'You're drunk.'

'I told you that. Now are you going to let me give you a proper birthday kiss or what?'

Jamie's lips were stiff, his embrace reluctant, but Sarah persisted, stroking the back of his neck and nibbling on his mouth until she felt his body respond. He kissed her deeply and at length, stopping only when she slipped her hand inside the waistband of his pants. 'Naughty,' he said.

'Come back to my place?'

He sighed. 'I can't. Bianca is home with–'

'Right.' She straightened up.

'Don't be like that.'

Sarah lit a cigarette. 'Like what?'

'You're the one who didn't want to be committed. You're the one who insisted I make a go of it with Shelley.'

'Yes, I know.'

'Unless… This thing between us… Maybe it's time to renegotiate.'

'Meaning what?'

Jamie took her free hand and brought it to his lips. 'You said before that things are changing. I think that you want more, and I *know* I do. I think we should talk about that.'

It was what she'd been thinking, sort of. But hearing him say it, seeing the intensity in his eyes, she froze inside. She could never do it.

'I think we're doing fine as we are.'

Jamie dropped her hand, pressed his lips together and nodded. 'I'll leave her, Sarah. If you'll have me, I'll leave her.'

'No.'

'Sarah, I– '

'*No.*'

His lips began quivering. 'But you said things were changing. You said you wanted things to be different.'

'I'm sorry, Jamie, but I wasn't saying anything like that. Nothing's changed. You misunderstood.'

He nodded again, and looked her full in the face. His eyes reminded her of the homeless man with one leg who begged for metho money outside the steakhouse. If he had stared at her like that for two seconds more she might have caved. But he didn't. 'Excuse me,' he said, and pushed past her, his legs tangling up in hers, his crotch in her face. 'I've got to get Shelley back. Bianca will need feeding.'

'Okay. I'll see you soon?'

'Yeah, whatever,' he said, and was gone.

Sarah headed out to the main bar. She intended to get drunk enough to not care about what had just happened. Drunk enough to not care who she took home to her miserable little flat. Drunk enough to forget how pathetic she was.

The floor surrounding the two-up tables was so packed that she had to hold her cigarette above her head so as not to accidentally burn someone. Even then it was risky, because her outstretched arm was at the level of many people's faces. It was worth the trouble though; the mix of sweat and noise and cigarette smoke was comforting. It reminded her that she was a girl who liked the crush of bodies and the stickiness of strangers. Jamie would hate it in here. He would have an asthma attack.

'Really, Sarah,' a voice said directly into her ear 'it is extremely inconsiderate of you to smoke in such an airless space.'

Sarah knew that voice. Knew it because it had been echoing in her head for eight long years. Knew it because it was the goddamn soundtrack to her life. It sounded like blood rushing in her ears. No, that was real, the blood rushing, pulse slamming, heart thumping. All those sounds were real, and incredibly, so was his voice.

In the split second it took to turn around, she braced herself for the onslaught of seeing him. 'Fuck,' she said, as her internal organs liquefied and her muscles went to jelly. There he was. Standing right in front of her, close enough to touch. 'Fucking hell.'

'No need to curse, Sarah. Why don't you smoke your filthy cancer stick outside?' He jerked his head toward the door.

Sarah stared. His eyes were exactly as she remembered them: so green that strangers suspected contact lenses; so knowing that she felt discovered, revealed, stripped naked in every sense. She said to him once *your eyes are so green*, and he said *not as green as your heart*.

'Come on. Snap out of it.' He walked towards the door, and she followed him but did not feel able to snap out of anything. She could barely breathe.

He stopped walking when they got to the bottom of the outside stairs, so Sarah stopped too. She tried to think of something remarkable to say, but couldn't think of anything except how when he'd said her name before it had sounded as though he was the first person to ever say it out loud. She wanted to go back to that moment so that she could hear him say it again: *Really, Sarah.*

'Well, look at you.' He shook his head as though he was a long lost relation who hadn't seen her since she was three feet tall. He sighed, smiled, ran a hand through his hair. 'Little Sarah Clark.'

'Mr Carr,' she said.

He laughed, revealing small white teeth. 'Are we at school?'

'Oh. Duh.' Sarah slapped her forehead. She felt fourteen.

'It's Daniel, please. And actually, it's not Mr anymore, it's Dr.'

'Oooh! I'm so impressed. *Dr* Carr,' Sarah teased, to cover up the fact that she was, in fact, way too impressed with him. It wasn't the title. Everything about him impressed her, his speech and hair, his bearing and eyes and teeth and clothes. He was so fucking impressive that Sarah wondered why he would want to waste his time talking to her at all. Why was he even here?

He read her mind, as he had always done. He told her he had moved back to Sydney about a year ago, that he lived in Rosehill and was the headmaster of a boys' school in Parramatta.

'Fuck!' she said and they both laughed. 'I thought headmasters were all old and wrinkly.'

'They are.'

'So you can't be one. You're too beautiful.'

He reddened, and for a split second, Sarah saw him as he used to be: red-faced, sweaty, tormented. She saw herself beneath him.

'And you… well, I didn't think you could get any prettier, but…' He touched her upper arm. 'Are you here alone?'

'What?' She stared at his hand. Large and warm and soft. His nails were manicured and perfectly clean. There was no residual, deep down dirt in the cracks and pores of his hand like most of the men around here. How would his skin taste? Like salt or chalk or blood?

'You're here alone?'

'Oh. No, I came with…' Sarah couldn't seem to concentrate on anything except the hand on her arm. There was something she should be noticing or remembering or saying.

'A boyfriend?' His finger tips pressed into the flesh at the top of her arm. She wished she was fatter so there was more for him to dig into. She wished she was flabby so he would grab a handful of her instead of this little pinch.

'Friends. I came with friends.'

'Do you…?' He rubbed his left eye. Sarah wanted to pluck his hand away and suck his fingers, one by one. 'Do you have a boyfriend?'

'No.'

'That's wonderful.'

'Yes, it is. How's your wife?'

'We're divorced.'

'Oh.' A large knot in her stomach began to loosen. She hadn't even known it was there until she felt the relief of its unravelling. 'I don't know what to say. I would tell you how incredibly happy I am, but I suppose that would be inappropriate.'

'No.' Daniel smiled. 'That would be a lovely thing to say.'

'I'm incredibly happy that you are divorced. That you're divorced and you're here.'

'You really are pleased to see me then?' he said, wrinkles springing up around his eyes and across his brow. 'I thought you might hate me.'

She placed her palm on his forehead to flatten out the creases. New creases. Creases caused by events unknown, time unshared. 'I hated you for leaving me.'

He took her hand and held it. Pressed. Released. 'I'm sorry. I thought it would be... I'm sorry, Sarah.'

'It's fine,' Sarah said, and now that he was back, it was.

He looked down at her, his lips apart, the tip of his tongue protruding from between his teeth. 'You have the most beautiful skin I have ever seen. I just want to keep touching it.'

'Since when did you ask for permission?'

He closed his eyes and stroked the flesh of her upper arm. When he looked at her again his eyes were glassy. 'Did I mention how breathtakingly beautiful you are?'

Three men in bowling whites interrupted them. They were friends of Daniel's. Or colleagues. Or something. Sarah couldn't concentrate on what he was saying. He was so respectable and charming, but when he shook hands with the men, Sarah remembered that her first orgasm was courtesy of that very same hand. His voice made her want to close her eyes and take off all her clothes. She felt dizzy, like some *Mills and Boon* heroine who faints every time the handsome, powerfully muscled hero comes close. All the blood in her body had rushed to her genitals, leaving her head filled with air.

Daniel had just said something funny. Sarah knew this because the men were laughing. Sarah felt bad that she hadn't heard what he said, because she didn't remember him as being particularly funny. He was always too earnest to be funny. Maybe he had changed. It had been eight years.

The men patted Daniel's back, nodded at Sarah, and went back to wherever it was they had come from. Daniel turned to her and started explaining who those men were and what they did and why he had to be nice to them. Something about an Old Boy's network and an antiquated school administration system. Fucking hell, thought Sarah, let him keep talking all night, all week, forever.

'You're not listening to a word I'm saying.'

'I am listening. Not really comprehending. Sorry.'

He took both her hands in his. 'Not your fault. I don't think I'm talking sense. I've thought about you every day for so many years, and now you're in front of me I can't make a single sentence come out the way I want it to.'

His hands were hot and smooth and she loved them. She remembered how aroused she would get watching him teach the class, the way he used his hands to make a point, punching the air or drawing little circles with his fingers. She loved that everyone was looking at his hands, and his hands knew the secret of what was under her clothes. And Sarah knew his secrets too. She knew every tendon and freckle and muscle hidden underneath his suit, except back then it hadn't been suits, it had been jeans and t-shirts and a black leather jacket that he sometimes let Sarah wear on the drive home.

She could hardly bear the thought that with age he may have changed in ways that had nothing to do with wardrobe. That maybe there were wrinkles or sunspots she had not seen, or maybe his muscles had slackened or tightened. Had he put on weight? It was hard to tell with all the clothes he was wearing, but his waist looked a little thicker than the one she used to circle with her arms. He could have a new scar somewhere, like the one she had across her back. She wanted to shine a light on him and taste, touch, pinch every part of him.

'I've lost you again,' he said, squeezing her hands harder than was necessary to get her attention. God, she remembered that too. The violence of those hands. The tendency to use more force when less would have worked just fine. The casual cruelty with which he would pinch or jab or scratch. The pleasure he took in making her cry and beg. She remembered that the last time she had seen him he almost killed her. She forgot what excuse she gave her parents for the condition she came home in; she remembered her grief when the last bruise faded and her body was restored to its unloved state.

'Sarah?' He squeezed hard enough to make her wince. 'You're making me very nervous. Say something.'

'You're crushing my hands.'

'Oh!' He dropped her hands, then quickly took them back and ran his fingers over her knuckles. 'I forgot how small your bones are. I'll have to be careful not to break you.'

Too fucking late, Sarah thought. 'Can you drive me home?' she said.

Daniel led her out to the car park. 'I've been trying to find you ever since I got back to Sydney.' He unlocked the door of a silver BMW and guided her into the passenger seat. 'You moved out of home.'

'Yes.'

'And you're not listed in the phone directory.'

'Neither are you.'

He smiled. 'A school principal is the perfect target for prank calls. What's your excuse?'

'I have a thing about privacy.'

'I see,' Daniel said. 'Is that why you're being so reticent?'

'It's not reticence; it's shock. And a bit of terror.'

He didn't speak again until they were on the road. 'Do I scare you?'

Sarah turned to him to answer and found herself slipping into a reverie again. What was it that made her unable to look away? He was not really handsome, not if handsome meant those dark, brooding soap opera types with swollen lips and scowling eyes. When she had first seen him she had thought he looked like Billy Idol, because his hair was blond and spiky and he wore a black leather jacket. That had been a first impression, but when she got up close she realised that he didn't look like Billy Idol at all. He didn't look like anybody. Everyone thought he did though, because he had a face and a body and a way of moving that made people think of movie stars or rock singers.

'God, you've been terrified into silence.'

'Something like that. When we're together I go mental. I lapse into flights of fancy. I don't recognise myself. That scares me.'

'Do you know what scares me?' Daniel glanced over at her, and then looked back at the road. 'Living the rest of my life feeling as miserable as I have these last eight years. Living the rest of my life without the woman I love.'

'Oh.'

All she had ever wanted was for Mr Carr to return to her and confess his despair at being away from her and his need to have her now, always and forever. For him, only him, to say the words that so many men who didn't matter had said. And all she could say was *oh*.

He asked for her address, drove to her flat, walked her to the door and declined her invitation to come in. He didn't kiss her, but he did press his palm to the side of her face for a long time.

'I want to take you out tomorrow night.'

'I have to work.'

Daniel removed his hand. 'I'll pick you up at seven.'

'I really do have to–'

He was walking away. 'Seven o'clock,' he called out over his shoulder.

For eight years, Sarah had lived with an emptiness that couldn't be touched. Not by men or booze or drugs or knowledge or hope. She had lived with it for so long that it had become a personality trait; it was her edge, her toughness, her ability to be intimate and still distant, passionate and still calm. She had built her life around the Daniel Carr shaped hole in the centre of the world. And just like that, the void was filled. Overfilled. Overflowing.

Now a new kind of emptiness had established itself, not in her, but around her. She felt, for the first time in years, physically vulnerable. Her tiny flat was cavernous, her creaky bed enormous, her sofa wanted to swallow her up when she retreated there. No safety or comfort could be found. Every space was vast because he did not fill it. She longed for him to come and enlarge her. She hoped it would happen soon.

Part Three

1

Sarah called in sick and was out the front of her building by six-thirty. Daniel pulled up at six-forty-five. Apart from a polite enquiry about her day, he did not speak to her during the drive. She didn't mind the silence; it allowed her to meditate on his thighs. Sarah knew that underneath the stylishly baggy, beige linen slacks, the muscles were tensing and releasing with every brake and acceleration. She knew that the blond curly hair covering his legs thinned and then stopped midway up the insides of his thighs. The skin there was pale and baby-soft and would respond to her tickling tongue by breaking out in goosebumps. In the ten minutes it took Daniel to drive to Parramatta and find a parking space, Sarah worked herself into a mute frenzy.

'Is Mexican okay?' he asked, putting his hand on the small of her back and guiding her down a back alley.

'Fine,' she said, as if it mattered.

The restaurant was dark and half-empty. They sat in a corner booth next to a photograph of a Chihuahua in a sombrero. Daniel ordered a jug of sangria and a glass of scotch, and then turned to Sarah with a frown.

'Is all that face paint for my benefit?'

'Oh, yeah, I suppose so.'

'You look better without it. Plain girls wear make-up, the beautiful ones don't need to.'

Sarah shrugged and picked up the menu, but as soon as they had ordered she went to the ladies room and rubbed off all her lipstick. When she got back to the table he touched a finger to her lips and smiled.

'So,' said Sarah while they picked at their food. 'Where have you been all these years?'

'Ah, that's a big question. The short answer is I've been up north.' Daniel took a sip of his scotch. Was he nervous or did he always drink Scotch and water with dinner? Sarah ached with not knowing him.

'Why don't you give me the long answer?'

He sipped his drink again. 'Right. I moved to Brisbane, taught English and Modern History at a nightmarishly underfunded city school, completed my dissertation, tutored migrant kids, ran a men's devotion group at the local church, learnt to ski, learnt to speak French, took my family around North America and Western Europe, watched my mother die of breast cancer, moved to Kempsey, set up an out-reach program for disadvantaged teens, won a citizenship award, celebrated my twenty-fifth wedding anniversary, took up jogging, learnt to cook, got divorced, moved to Sydney, secured a position at a prestigious boys college, searched for the girl I have thought about every day for the last eight years, found that girl, sat across from her and drank scotch. The End.'

Sarah realised she had been holding her breath. She stared at the tabletop and breathed deeply for a few seconds. She could not bring herself to look at him.

'Now your turn,' he said.

Sarah looked at her plate. 'School, waitressing, uni, haven't been anywhere. Boring.'

'Hmm, no mention of boyfriends. In all those years – teenage years no less – there were no love affairs, no romances?'

'None worth mentioning. My food's cold.' She pushed the plate away and looked around for an ashtray.

'You can't smoke in here, Sarah.'

'I know. Do you see me smoking?'

'I see you looking for an ashtray, and you're jiggling around like a true addict.'

Sarah froze, realising that her shoulders had indeed been jiggling.

'I love the way you move. I think I'll only ever take you to places where you can't smoke, so I can watch you squirm.' He smiled at her with thin lips, and she had to put her hands on her knees to stop them bouncing up and down. He leant forwards, both hands flat on the table. 'I've made you self-conscious.'

'No, you haven't.'

He leant closer. 'Your face is all red.'

Sarah pressed a hand to her cheek; it was burning. 'It's hot in here.'

He leant further, so he was almost out of his chair, and took her chin in his hands. 'The colour of your face right now is exactly the same as the colour of your face when you orgasm, and your throat flushes like that too.'

Sarah felt droplets of sweat run down her temples. She tried to come up with something witty or cutting to say but all she could think was *I never flush red, in bed or out*. Even when she had won the Cross Country race in year ten, her face had not been red. Jamie had said she was bloodless then, and he said it again last week, after they had made love for hours, in her stuffy flat with all the windows closed.

Sarah tried to look away from his green, green eyes but he held her head firmly, and to pull away would have involved a movement more violent than she felt capable of. She didn't feel capable of anything. She sat dumbly staring into his eyes and feeling the heat from his fingertips spread out from the tip of her chin, up over her cheeks and nose and forehead and down over her throat and chest.

'Where do you work?' Daniel said, releasing her chin and leaning back in his chair.

'Western Steakhouse. It's this greasy dump on the other side of the river,' she said, as though this was a normal, everyday conversation.

'Sounds glamorous. How long have you been doing that?'

'Since I left home.'

'Which was when?'

'About six years ago.'

'You wouldn't have even finished school.' He frowned at her. 'Why did you leave home?'

Sarah dreaded that question even under normal circumstances, which these were not. She usually lied, but couldn't to him. If she told him the truth he would pity her and that would be unbearable. 'That's a hell of a story. Let's save it for later.' She smiled as though it was a treat to look forward to.

Daniel nodded, but looked annoyed. To lighten the mood, Sarah asked him about the French classes he had taken. She asked the question in French and was rewarded by a blinding smile. He was delighted with her and she glowed under his delight. Thinking only of keeping that brightness alive, she told him how after he left Sydney, she had started to meet Alex Knight every day after school, supposedly for French tutoring. She had to stay up half the night studying so her results would reflect the hours she had supposedly spent being tutored but had actually spent getting fucked.

He stared at her for several seconds. When he spoke, his voice was low. 'That is the most appalling thing I've ever heard. I feel ill.'

'What? Why?' She laughed. 'Like you never knew that teenagers spend study time screwing on the backseats of cars.'

'That's not the… You were…' Daniel ran his hands through his hair. 'Alex Knight was the School Captain. He was a Christian

Youth Director! Slimy little shit.' He took a large gulp of scotch. 'Did you realise it was illegal for him to be doing that? Did he?'

'You're kidding?'

'If I had known that a Year Twelve boy was carrying on with an underage girl I–'

'Daniel!' Sarah grabbed his hand, and he stopped ranting to stare at it. 'Alex was seventeen. You were how old?'

'That's not the–'

'How old?'

'Thirty-something.'

'Thirty-eight. So, my second lover was twenty-one years younger than my first, and therefore, a total child as far as I was concerned.' Sarah squeezed his hand. 'He was actually the youngest of all the men I slept with in the year after you left.'

'All the… What are you saying? There were others?'

'Of course.'

'I… Damn.' He rubbed his eyes, sucked air between his teeth. 'How many others?'

He was mad with jealousy. She was elated. 'I've no idea. I lost count.'

'But…'

'But what, Daniel? What's the matter?'

'You were so bright. So clever.' He closed his eyes.

'Funny thing about brains is that men don't tend to notice them when you're wearing a short skirt.'

'Shut up, Sarah.'

Daniel refused to see the dessert menu and less than an hour after they had arrived, they were back in his car and heading for home. Several times Sarah started to speak but he would not allow it. Each time she opened her mouth he took his left hand off the wheel and held it up. 'No,' was all he said.

When they were one street away from her flat, he pulled into the deserted netball court car park. 'Okay, listen.' He turned off the engine and faced her in the dark. 'I am incredibly disturbed by what you've told me tonight.'

'Clearly.' Sarah lit up a smoke.

'Must you smoke in my car?'

'If you don't like it you can take me home. In fact,' Sarah opened the window, pegged the cigarette out onto the asphalt, closed the window again and turned to face him, 'you can take me home anyway. I've had enough.'

'Tell me what I'm supposed to feel, Sarah. I've spent all these years believing you meant it when you told me I was the only man you'd ever love. I ignored the fact that you were an attention starved child who always said and did whatever it was you thought would please me, whether you meant it or not. I ignored the fact that you were too naïve to possibly understand what it means to love someone, and I–'

'Stop it!' Sarah slammed her fists against the dashboard. 'This is bullshit. I meant every word I ever said to you. I *loved* you, Daniel. I loved you so fucking much.'

'If you loved me you wouldn't have run straight into the arms of that boy.'

'I can't believe I'm hearing this from you.' Sarah turned to look at him, tucking her legs up under her body. 'You remember you used to tease me about how horny I was, and I hated that word and would get all demure and say "oh, no, I just missed you," or whatever.' She saw the smile flicker across his face and it gave her the courage to reach out and touch his arm. 'I worried that there was something wrong with me. That normal girls didn't get so wet their lovers laughed to touch them. I worried that you found me sluttish or disgusting, because I was always so hungry for you, for sex. But when I asked you whether it was wrong of me, you quoted John Wilmot at me and–'

'For did you love your pleasure less, you were no match for me.'

'Yes. And those words were such a gift to me. To know that my desire was not something monstrous, that anyone who thought I shouldn't want so much and so often, was not worthy of me.'

'I didn't realise at the time that your desire was non-specific. I assumed that the voracious appetite I so admired was for me only.'

Sarah pressed her lips together. She tasted sweat and became aware that her whole face was damp with it. When she'd left her flat earlier she had shivered in response to the cool night air and cursed herself for wearing such a skimpy summer dress in late April. But now the heat was suffocating. Anger and confusion always made her hot.

'Daniel, please don't misunderstand me. The first time you touched me, you turned me on. I mean that literally. I was barely aware I had a body and then, boom, my body was screaming, dripping and aching and twitching all the time. And you made it okay. You showed me what to do with all that heat and need and how fucking incredible I could feel.' His arm shook beneath her hand. She squeezed it hard. 'Problem was, you left without turning me off.'

'God, Sarah,' he said, his voice shaking with his arm, 'I didn't know. I didn't realise you would… this isn't what I expected from you. I never would've gone if… God, this isn't how I expected you to be.'

Sarah felt the automatic shift and made sure it was pushed into park, then she released the handbrake and climbed up on her knees beside him. The world was all wet. Her cheap polyester dress was sticking to her back and breasts, and the sweat dripped down her legs and pooled behind her knees. Her hair stuck to the back of her neck and forehead and ears and cheeks. Her face was wet and so were her lips. Acutely, she was aware of the wetness between her legs being thicker and hotter. It mixed with the dampness of her sweating thighs and the perspiration dripping from her belly.

Then she was feeling how wet his throat was and his wet, wet mouth was under hers, opening and pulling her in. Mr Carr's mouth. Mr Carr's lips. His tongue and his teeth, sharp and mean and wet, wet, wet. She tasted blood and her body surged with recognition. He was the only man who kissed so it hurt.

Sarah remembered the first time he bit her, when she was fourteen and in his car and he had made her turn over so he could take her from behind. She had found it strange to not be able to see his face while he was inside her, and strange also, the very different sensation she got from the new angle, strange and good. Soon she was gasping and pushing back and up into him and as he came, he bit her shoulder, hard.

'I only want you.' Sarah groped for his fly. 'Always, I wanted you. I wish I'd never–'

Daniel bit her cheek. 'Get in the back,' he said, but didn't wait for her to obey. He lifted her by the hips and half-pushed, half-threw her over the centre console and onto the back seat. He pushed her on to her stomach and pulled her dress up to her hips. Sarah reached behind her back to touch him, but he grabbed her wrists and held them together. Then he told her she was impossible and sunk his teeth deep into the flesh of her right thigh. Sarah cried out, in pain and in desire. Daniel bit her again and again and again until both thighs were soaked in sweat and saliva and spotted with blood. He didn't remove her underwear, didn't let her turn over, didn't allow her to kiss him or touch him. He bit her over and over and over until she was crying so hard she thought she'd choke on her own snot.

And then abruptly, he stopped, climbed into the front and drove her home. She asked – she *begged* – him to come in with her. When he said no she cried some more and asked if she could come to his place instead. Or couldn't they stay out? Couldn't they please–?

'I need to be alone, Sarah. This night has not gone well. Not at all how I planned.'

'Daniel, please, *please*, don't leave me like this. I'm so confused, and I–'

Daniel got out of the car, walked around to her side, opened the door, took her arm and pulled her out. Sarah clung to him, trying to kiss him but succeeding only in slobbering over his unmoving chin. He pushed her away, hard enough that she stumbled backward four or five steps. By the time she had regained her balance he was sliding into his seat.

Then he drove away leaving Sarah shaking and bleeding in the middle of the road. Exactly how he'd left her all those years ago.

2

Jamie knew he had to tread carefully with Sarah. Two days ago she had all but said she loved him, and he had been so elated that he pushed too far, and she freaked out and took it back. He had to remember that Sarah had never made a commitment, that she was terrified of losing her hard-won independence, and that better men than he had failed to win her. Jamie had waited for her for so many years and now that she was almost his, it was vital for him to bite down on his joy and let her take the lead.

He decided to leave her alone for a couple of days so she wouldn't think he was getting clingy. The wisdom of his laid back approach was confirmed when she called him at work on the second day and begged him to come over. *I'm sorry we fought,* she said, *I really need you right now.* He managed to wipe the smile off his face for long enough to convince his boss that he had a monstrous headache and had to go home.

As soon as Sarah opened the door, he knew there was something very wrong with her. He knew this because her face was red, and Sarah's face was never red. She said it was just that it was such a hot day.

'It's not hot, Sarah.' Jamie felt her forehead. She was burning up. 'You must be getting sick. Do you feel sick?'

'I feel fine. Why haven't you kissed me yet?'

Kissing her, Jamie felt hot too. He took off his shirt and then hers. Her stomach and back were as hot as her forehead. 'Why aren't you at uni? You are sick, aren't you?' he asked, but the only answer he received was her tongue in his ear. Moving into the bedroom, he unbuttoned his jeans, took off her bra, kicked his pants off while he kissed her breasts, lay with her on the bed and pulled on the waistband of her tracksuit pants.

'Wait.' She sat up. 'Turn the light off.'

'What? Why?' It was difficult for him to get into the state of mind necessary to be able to perform with Sarah. He had to first forget that he was more than likely the worst lover she'd ever had, and second, he had to forget he had a wife and daughter. He could only manage this advanced state of denial by becoming fully absorbed in how she felt and how she smelt and how she looked. By concentrating on Sarah's physical presence, he got so aroused that not even fear of failure or heavy-duty guilt could stop him. And here he was, hard as a rock and ready to roll, and she had broken into his suspension of disbelief.

'I'd just feel more comfortable with the light off,' she said.

She sounded like Shelley. That was not good. He couldn't do this if he was thinking about Shelley. He had to keep things moving or the guilt would overtake him and they'd never get any-where. Jamie walked the two steps to the light switch, telling himself that he would get back into the mood easily once they were in bed. Besides, there would still be light enough to see her because the window over the bed allowed the sunlight to come in. But as he switched off the light, Sarah pulled the blinds closed. The room was so dark he could barely make out the shape of her on the bed.

'Why can't I look at you?' He groped blindly and found hips still covered in fleecy fabric.

'Sssh. Finish undressing me,' Sarah said, pulling him to her.

Jamie had been worried about nothing. Even blind, there was no mistaking who he was making love to. Sarah was unique in every way, but especially in the way she made him feel. Out in the world Jamie always felt inadequate. He was too small, too thin, too anxious, too passive. He felt terrified that someone would catch on to the fact that he was too weak and hesitant to be a husband and father; at any given moment he was sure he would slip up and expose himself as a fake. But when he was making love to Sarah he felt that everything was as it should be. *Jamie* was as he should be. Nothing was awkward or uncomfortable or frightening. It was Sarah and Jamie, and it was easy and perfect and right.

'Sar?' he said afterwards, when she was lying with her head on his chest. 'You'd tell me if something was wrong wouldn't you?'

'Mmm.'

'Is that a yes?'

Sarah mumbled something into his chest.

'I can't understand you.'

She sighed, lifting her head up enough to plant a kiss on his chin. 'Can't a girl have a few minutes of peace to enjoy the afterglow of her mind-blowing orgasm?'

Jamie knew she was avoiding something, but he couldn't stop smiling anyway. Shelley didn't even have orgasms from intercourse and here was Sarah having mind-blowing ones. He gave her the requested few minutes of silence and then tried again. 'Did you end up staying at the pub till stumps?'

'No, I left not long after you.'

'I hope you didn't walk home alone.'

'Don't stress, Mum.' She touched his face with her fingers, tracing his cheekbone and the ridge of his nose. 'I got a lift.'

'With a bloke?'

'Yes.'

'Was it Mike? Because you said you weren't going to see him anymore.'

Cold air rushed over him as she sat up. 'Don't start, please.'

Jamie sat up and faced her although it was so dark he could not really see her face. 'I'm not starting anything, Sarah. I'm just trying to talk to you and you're being all secretive.'

'I can't do this with you, Jamie, I really can't. Just leave if you're going to be an arsehole.'

Jamie had the sudden realisation that they were fighting. He hadn't seen it coming, but here he was smack bang in the middle of a fight with Sarah. He reached for her arm. 'You've always told me everything, and now you're holding back. I feel like I'm losing you.'

Sarah pulled her arm away. 'I didn't realise you'd won me.'

'You know what I mean.'

'No, I don't.'

Jamie felt sick to the stomach at the coldness in her voice. He was undoubtedly losing her, but everything he said was making the situation worse. He had to pull way, way back before she withdrew from him all together.

'Forget it, Sarah. I'm sorry. Let's go get something to eat, heh?'

'That would be good,' she said, in a marginally warmer tone.

Crisis over, Jamie stood up and turned the light on. He began to get dressed, thinking only of how painful it had been to have her angry with him, and how he would have to be much more careful about what he said in the future.

'Will we go to the pub or–' Jamie looked up from buttoning his shirt and caught sight of Sarah. If he had looked up a second later her tracksuit pants would have been pulled up, but as it was she was bent at the waist with her arse in the air and her pants around her calves. Jamie stared. From the backs of her knees to where the curve of her buttocks met her thighs, her skin was purple. Sarah stared at the floor for a second then slowly straightened up, turning so her back was to the wall. Although he could no longer see the backs of her thighs, he couldn't look away from the space they had just occupied.

'Stop staring.' Sarah pulled up her pants, bent over again and retrieved her bra, then her T-shirt.

Jamie couldn't look away from where those battered bits of flesh had been. No wonder she'd been feverish and distracted. But why didn't she tell him? How could she keep something like this from him? It was horrific to think of her lying beneath him, pretending to be having a good time, when the whole experience must have been agonising for her.

'What happened?' he managed to ask when she was sitting on the edge of the bed pulling on her socks.

'Nothing for you to worry about.'

Nothing for him to… had she really just said it was nothing for him to worry about? He asked her to repeat what she'd said. And yes, that was what it was: *It's nothing you need to worry about.*

He started to cry. 'You being raped and beaten is something I don't need to worry about?'

'Oh, Jesus!' Sarah stood and wrapped her arms around his chest. 'Oh, no,' she said, pulling him down on to the bed. 'Oh, no, Jamie. I can't believe you'd think that. I wasn't… it was nothing like that. Oh, God. I'm sorry to scare you, I didn't want you to…' she kissed his cheek. 'This is why I didn't want you to see. You always think the worst.'

Jamie felt a wave of relief. Then rapidly, disgust. 'You *let* someone do that to you?'

'It looks worse than it is.' Sarah looked at her hands. 'They're just love bites. You know I bruise easily.'

Just love bites. Bruise easily. Not to worry. How comforting. Sarah let someone bite her legs hard enough, and for long enough, to cause blanket bruising. What kind of sicko did that to a girl, with or without permission?

'Was it Mike?'

Sarah shook her head. Her lips were pressed together so hard they were turning white. White lips in a red face. Her colours were all reversed, like on a negative.

'I need to know who did this to you.'

Sarah opened her mouth wide, the colour flooding back into her lips as she stretched them into an O. 'You don't *need* to know anything. I appreciate you were concerned, but now that I have told you there is nothing to be concerned about it is time for you to drop it.'

Jamie tried to drop it. He lasted eight seconds. 'Is this something you enjoy then? Being beaten during sex?'

Sarah walked out of the room. Jamie hit himself in the forehead several times and then followed her. She was sitting at the kitchen table smoking and pretending to read a book.

'I only asked because I thought maybe next time we do it you might want me to slap you around or something. I just think it can't be very satisfying for you to have me trying to be gentle and thinking of your pleasure, when what you really want is a good beating.' Jamie *hated* himself. He sounded like a nagging, hysterical woman. Seeing her purple thighs had tripped some switch in his brain and he didn't know how to switch it off again.

She didn't look up from her book. 'Our sexual encounters are perfectly satisfying to me, Jamie.'

Encounters? She made it sound like an accident. Like they bumped into each other when they were naked and just happened to have sex while they were there. Was that all it meant to her? Was he just another dick to get her off? And if that was what Jamie was then what was this other man? Was the act that resulted in her bruises just another *encounter*?

'I hope you at least used a condom. A bloke who'd do that to a girl is probably–'

'Nope, no condom.' Sarah looked up and smiled before returning to her reading.

Jamie walked over and ripped the book from her hands. Sarah blinked three times, then her face settled back into its placid mask.

'You didn't use a condom?'

'Wasn't necessary. I didn't fuck him.'

'You didn't… what did you do then?'

Sarah took her book back from his hand, opened it, inserted her bookmark and placed it on the table. 'That is none of your business.'

'If you're having unsafe sex then it's my business.'

Sarah laughed without a hint of humour. 'You're quite welcome to slap a rubber on before you risk contamination by screwing me. Better yet, how about we just don't do it at all anymore.'

This was very bad. Not just that she'd said it, but that she'd said it so calmly. Like she didn't care one way or the other. This was so, so bad. He sat in the chair beside her and took her hands. 'If I shut up right now will you forgive me for being such a dickhead?'

Sarah looked over his shoulder. He noticed how red her eyes were, and that the always present under-eye circles were darker than he'd seen them in a long time. He had to literally bite down on his tongue to stop from interrogating her.

'You're not a dickhead.' Sarah returned her gaze to his face. 'What you are is a nagging pain in the bum.'

'I'll stop, I swear.'

'No you won't. You've been nagging me since the day I met you.' She smiled. 'Just stop taking everything so personally, okay?'

He had never felt such immense gratitude. He would be happy forever just on the strength of that smile. 'I'll try.'

'I know you will.' She kissed him then, and all the bitterness of the last half hour dissolved. After that she was normal again, laughing and telling rude jokes and smoking too much. Jamie tried to be normal too, and on the surface he succeeded. But underneath it all his heart was stained purple. Like the circles under her eyes. Like the bruises on her legs.

★

Sarah was sorry she'd asked Jamie to come over. She had thought his presence would be a comfort; that his gentle attention would be the perfect antidote to the memory of Daniel's teeth. Usually when Jamie made love to her she felt warm and peaceful, but today his shy, hesitant kisses and cautious thrusting made her feel smothered and lonely. She wanted to shout at him to not be so careful, so bloody controlled.

She gritted her teeth and concentrated on the stinging of her thighs as they chafed against the sheets. She thought about Daniel's teeth. Daniel's mean, sharp, little teeth. Then she thought about the pink gums they lived in and the lips that hid them. She thought of his wet, red mouth, with its mean, white teeth, and its rough, hot tongue, and how one day soon that cruel, beautiful mouth would kiss and lick and bite her all over. Jamie kept fucking her politely, and Sarah kept thinking about Daniel. After they had both come – Sarah first with her head full of Daniel's mouth, and then Jamie with his mouth full of Sarah's name – she felt that she had stolen something from Jamie, and she knew in that moment that she would never be able to have them both.

She had no idea what she was going to do. Daniel Carr got her so she couldn't think straight. Since he had reappeared in her life, wet heat seeped from every pore and drowned out sense. Last night, she would have done whatever he asked, but he barely asked anything at all. Today, she was sobered by pain and frightened by the strength of her longing. Today, she was profoundly unsure of herself.

For a third of her life she had held him in her mind and heart as the only man she could ever love. Each one of the hundreds of men she had been with was compared to him, and none measured up. Her choice of university course was inspired by a barely admitted fantasy that he would come back and she would impress him with how well-read she was. Even her desire to travel had its seed in his long ago assertion that seeing the world was the best education a person could get.

And yet, she was much more than a self-styled Eliza Doolittle. The intensity of her initiation into sex, and the deep loss she felt when he left her, had forced introspection worthy of a mid-life crisis when she was still a child. It had made her strong and self-aware and independent. And although her sexual precociousness was initially sparked by her need to find a replacement for Daniel, she had realised quickly that she had a real talent for sex. In exploring and expanding that natural talent she had found real joy. Her life was what it was because of him, but it was still very much hers.

Giving in to Daniel would be throwing it all away. Like picking up a needle and plunging it into her arm and saying: Hey, this is it. I want to be a junkie and I want the rest of my days on this earth to be junk filled days and I don't mind if I die or am defiled or destroyed, as long as I feel like this. I am never going to travel to the four corners of the earth or have a family or a career or see my parents again. I am not a ball of fiery potential just waiting to find my niche in the world. I am nothing, and I want nothing except this bliss and this pain and this nothingness, emptiness, love.

And giving herself to Daniel would mean sacrificing Jamie. Was it even *possible* to live without Jamie? Since she was an adolescent he had been there to shelter her from the worst storms and to soften the sharp edges of life. Without friends, without boyfriends, without parents, she had survived just fine because Jamie picked up all the slack. She didn't even know who she was without him. She had no concept of what it would be like to live in a Jamie-free world.

But she had lived without Daniel Carr and didn't like it at all.

He called at three o'clock to tell her he would pick her up at eight. She looked over her shoulder at Jamie, who was pretending not to listen.

'I have to work.'

'Don't you want to see me?'

Jesus! He had a wonderful voice, and if Jamie wasn't in the room she would've told him so. 'I already took last night off. I have to go or they'll–'

'Fine, I'll pick you up. What time do you finish?'

Sarah pressed her hand to her lips. She should tell him to leave her alone; she'd call him when she was free. She should tell him that he had real guts ringing her today after the mess he made out of her legs last night. She should tell him that she couldn't see him anymore because he made her lose every scrap of ambition she'd ever had.

She told him she finished at ten and gave him the address. Conscious of Jamie's ears turning red with effort, she whispered that she couldn't wait to see him. It was a pathetic thing to say and as soon as it was out she wished it back, but he liked it.

'I'll be early then,' he said.

3

Daniel came into the restaurant at nine-thirty, sat at the bar and ordered a scotch. Sarah smiled, her heart lurching as it always did when she set eyes on him. He nodded but did not smile or wave. Sarah didn't care. He was here and he was beautiful.

She finished her shift in a cloud of self-consciousness. She had worked at the steakhouse for six years but having him watch her made everything feel new and complex. It was hard to get her voice, or her gait, or her balance right. It was hard not to giggle and toss her hair. Hard not to feel as though she was just playing a part in the movie where the waitress is rescued from her dull, degrading existence by the handsome older man who spies her from across the room and falls in love with the way her hair falls, just so, over her eyes.

When the clock hit ten, Sarah had her bag over her shoulder and was motioning to Daniel to follow. She did not get changed, or chat to the guys in the kitchen or have a beer with the other waitresses as she usually did after a shift. When they were in the car park she stopped and gave him a kiss, which he received impatiently before pushing her into the car with a grunt. He drove at a frightening speed and ignored every traffic light. He drove so recklessly that Sarah, who had little fear of physical injury, begged him to stop.

He pulled off the road and down a steep dirt track, coming to a screeching halt in the middle of bushland. Sarah could hear water running, which indicated a river, but they had driven too long for this to be the Parramatta River, and if it had been Toongabbie Creek she would've recognised the track.

'Where are we?' She unclasped her seat belt and turned to him.

'Look at you!' Daniel said, and then he was kissing her hard on the lips. Sarah almost lost consciousness such was the force with which he kissed her. Her head was smashed back into the seat, her nose mashed against his cheekbone. He kissed her with his whole face, but when she tried to pull his body onto hers he withdrew.

'I loved watching you at work,' he said, panting. 'I've been hard for forty minutes.'

'Seeing me clearing tables got you hard?'

'Oh, yes. You in that tight little dress and those ugly shoes. And a name badge for God's sake! I had never pictured you like that before. A name badge girl.'

She stared down at the flat white sandshoes. He was right: they were ugly and made her legs look even skinnier and shorter than usual. She should have taken the time to change.

Daniel tugged at her collar. 'I've always had a thing about these dresses. I lost my virginity to a waitress, you know?'

Sarah cleared her throat. 'I didn't know that.'

'All the boys lost it to her; she was the town tramp. I remember pulling her name badge right off once… Paula. I don't think I'd even remember her name if it wasn't for that badge.'

'If you're trying to insult me in some way I'd prefer it if you came straight out with it. I'm extremely bored by middle-aged ramblings about how wild you were when you were a lad.' Sarah sunk into the seat and looked out the window.

'Oh, dear,' he said in the warmest, sweetest voice she had ever heard. 'I've offended you when I meant to compliment you.'

He was good at switching his voice around. It was part of his method of controlling her. Going from hot to cold to sweet to angry to cruel to kind and back again. Sarah was even-tempered by nature and such vacillation disoriented her, which was exactly why he did it: to lower her defences. As if she even had defences when it came to him.

'What I meant to say,' he continued, 'was that even in that ugly outfit, with your hair all lank and your skin all greasy – even looking your worst – which you certainly do – you are still the most desirable woman in the world.'

Sarah kept her face to the window. She knew she looked horrible, and it wasn't as though she wanted false compliments; she just didn't understand why he had to be so intentionally hurtful.

'Oh, my Sarah.' His mouth brushed the back of her neck, her ear, her jawbone. *'My mistress' eyes are nothing like the sun; coral is far more red than her lips' red; If snow be white, why then her breasts are dun.'*

Sarah leant back into him, forgiving him instantly and completely. Shakespeare's sonnets were the background noise to their entire affair. In the public torture of the classroom he would read aloud, and every word seemed to be written by him for her. His favourite was eighteen: *Shall I compare thee to a summer's day? Thou art more lovely and more temperate.* Now, it seemed trite and contrived, but maybe that was just because it had become a cliché, a Hallmark greeting floating over a picture of daffodils and long green grass, and a girl with her face hidden by a large white hat. When Shakespeare wrote it, it was original and crammed with sincerity, and so it had been when Sarah heard it for the first time. When he had looked at her across the classroom and she had felt her cheeks redden as he recited. *He is such a spunk. If only he didn't make us do all this lovey dovey crap* Jess had whispered. Sarah couldn't recall what she said in response but whatever it was she had said it too loudly and he stopped reading, his eyes reproachful. *Something you want to share with the class, Miss Clark?* Sarah had shaken her head, mortified. Mr Carr kept her back after class that day and lectured her on being disruptive. He said she had no respect for him as a teacher. Then he fucked her while she recited the sonnet over and over. *So you never forget* he said.

'What will it take to get you to talk to me again?'

'I don't know if I want to talk to you. I don't know what I want to do with you.'

'How about a drink at my apartment?'

Sarah felt like she would weep. 'Yeah, alright.'

Daniel's apartment was on the fifteenth floor of a near new building in Rosehill. Sarah didn't want to look at anything except Daniel, but she forced herself to be polite about his polished timber floorboards and marble bathroom and extra wide balcony. He was childlike in his excitement as he pointed out the fridge with built in icemaker and the rosewood bookshelves that covered an entire wall of his living room. It was as though he was eighteen and living away from home for the first time. Then Sarah realised that he probably *was* living alone for the first time and felt a surge of protectiveness.

She wrapped her arms around his waist and kissed his neck. 'Can we go to bed now?'

Daniel laughed. 'No, we can't go to bed, Sarah. We hardly know each other.'

'That's crazy talk.' Sarah kissed her way up the side of his neck until she got to his ear. 'No one knows me like you do. I wouldn't have let you do what you did last night if we'd hardly known each other.'

'Firstly, Sarah, you didn't *let* me do that; you didn't have a choice.'

'That's what you think.' Sarah stuck her tongue in his ear.

'And second,' Daniel stepped back from her, his hands remaining on her waist. 'Last night is the perfect example of why we can't go to bed. I have no self-control with you.'

'I'm not asking you to have any.'

'It's very important to me that we do this right. It isn't going to be like last time.'

Sarah pulled him close again, pressing her body against him. 'It will be so much better. I can show *you* some things this time.'

'Jesus, Sarah!' Daniel pushed her and she fell backward onto a coffee table. He didn't seem to notice; he was pulling books off the bookshelf and mumbling to himself. When he turned back to her, he was holding a leather book the size of the yellow pages. He pointed to the lounge beside her. 'Sit.'

Sarah did as he said. 'Is this one of your fantasies? You want me to read you bible stories before we fuck? Or will you read them to me while I–'

Daniel put his hand over her mouth. 'Shut up. I want to show you something, then you can tell me how well we know each other.'

He took his hand away and Sarah poked her tongue out at him but didn't say anything more. He had opened the book on his lap, and Sarah saw that it was not a book at all, but a photo album. He had opened it to a wedding photo; the couple in it looked as happy as Sarah had ever seen anybody look. They were smiling, not at the camera, but at each other and their hands were entwined. He had shoulder length blond hair and wore a pale blue tuxedo; she was in a flowing white dress with a garland of flowers on her head. A banner over their heads said: *Congratulations Danny and Lisa*.

'Danny?'

'I was Danny then.'

They were both silent as Sarah turned the pages over. She could hardly believe he had ever been so smooth and fresh. He looked like a surfer or a beach bum hippy, and she – his wife – was beautiful, despite the flicked hair and blue eye shadow.

'How old were you?'

'Too young.' He squinted, revealing deep furrows around his eyes. 'Barely nineteen.'

Sarah counted back. 'You know you got married four years before I was even born?'

'Fuck,' said Daniel, which made Sarah laugh although there was nothing funny about any of it.

Sarah continued turning the pages. Lisa with very long hair, lying on the beach in a yellow bikini. Daniel on the beach in red Speedos striking a muscle man pose. Lisa in a karate outfit holding a certificate up to the camera. Daniel in his graduation gown, with his arm thrown over Lisa's shoulder. Page after page of the golden couple. Her hair got longer and his got shorter as Sarah flipped the pages.

'Here,' Daniel said, and brushed her hand aside. He flicked through the pages hurriedly. 'My girls. That's Abbey in the red hat and Claire over by the tree. This is in Italy a couple of years ago. It was the last proper holiday I had with them.'

Sarah stared. Two slim, blonde teenagers with brightly coloured ski gear and mocking smiles. The younger one, Claire, looked about sixteen and had Daniel's eyes. They were both very pretty. Sarah felt nothing for them; they had nothing to do with her.

She closed the album and put it aside. 'Okay, I get it. You think I don't know you well enough because I haven't confronted the reality of your life away from me. But you're wrong. I've spent the last eight years of my life confronting the reality that you had a family. I never cared and I don't care now.'

'You really don't understand.'

Sarah clenched her fists. 'Can I smoke?'

'No.'

Sarah sighed. 'Are we going to fuck anytime soon?'

'No.'

'What do you want?'

'I want you to understand that I didn't leave my family for the sake of a quick fuck, or a brief, torrid affair. This isn't a mid-life crisis, or temporary insanity, or a whim. This is my life.' Daniel took her hands, pressing them together between his own. His voice was barely a whisper. 'I have never been a risk taker, Sarah. When I made love to you it was the first time I had ever broken the law. It was the first time I had been unfaithful to my wife. After being with you I always felt sick for a day just thinking about my daughters, and Lisa, and my job, and God.'

'Stop acting so fucking superior. So you're old. So you sacrificed shit. Boo hoo!' Sarah pulled her hands away from him and grabbed her cigarettes from her bag. She ignored his narrowed eyes and lit one, feeling better immediately. 'You, Mr-Kind-Religious-Family-Man, got yourself an eager, adoring, obedient little sex slave for a couple of months. Then you fucked off and lived your Kind-Religious-Family-Man life for eight years. While you were having international holidays, and skiing, and fucking your wife, I was back here growing up. I'm not a fourteen-year-old virgin anymore. I've been around the block more times than you'd believe. So stop this melodramatic bullshit. You want me or you don't. Anything else we'll figure out as we go along.'

Daniel stared at her for a full ten seconds. Then he took the cigarette from her hand, walked to the window and tossed it out. When he turned back to her he was smiling. 'You're incredible. I mean…' He came over and knelt at her feet. 'You are *incredible*, Sarah. You keep blowing me away with how beautiful, and smart and gutsy you are. How am I supposed to keep a level head?'

'You're not. The level head is for the rest of the world; with me you get to go crazy.'

'I know you think I'm being absurd, but I have to know you feel the way I do before I can let this happen. Resisting you when you're so available to me is the hardest thing I've ever done in my life, please don't make it harder.'

'I don't get it.' She shrugged, and he, infuriatingly, gorgeously, shrugged back at her.

'I have to show you something else,' he said, returning to the bookshelf.

'If it isn't your cock then I'm not interested'

'Stop talking like that or I'll call you a taxi.' He handed her a crumpled, yellowing envelope. 'Have a look.'

Sarah rolled her eyes, but she took the envelope and pulled out the small pile of photos it contained. The first was an official school photo of fourteen-year-old Sarah in her navy pleated skirt, white shirt and navy blazer, with her long hair plaited on either side of her head. Next were two blurry shots of Sarah playing soccer in her sports uniform. In one shot her arms were in the air, celebrating victory, in the other she was running towards the camera, frowning at her unseen opponent. Next was a photo of Sarah at the school swimming carnival. The photo was almost identical to one that Jamie had in his wallet, except Jamie had been cut out of this one so that only his hand was visible, resting on Sarah's wet shoulder. Jesus, what would *he* say about all this?

She picked up the final photo and winced. When Sarah was on the yearbook committee, Mr Carr had been the supervising teacher and had wanted some pictures of the team at work to put on the inside cover. Sarah and the other four on the committee had struck up some silly poses, tongues sticking out and eyes squeezed shut. He must have taken a whole roll of film and they all thought they were so funny, crossing their eyes and doing bunny ears over each others heads. The photo in Sarah's hand was not one of the silly shots that she remembered being taken. It was of Sarah sitting alone at the editing table, her hair falling loose over one shoulder. She was concentrating on the clippings laid out before her, unaware that a camera was aimed at her, angled so that a triangle of pink underwear was visible between her skinny, unselfconsciously splayed legs.

She put the photos on the floor in front of her. 'These were taken before we… This is sick, Daniel.'

'I know. When Lisa caught me with them she went crazy, threatened to call the police. I told her the truth that I loved you, but it only made her angrier. I suppose under all her ranting about abuse and exploitation she may have been feeling common jealousy.'

'So she kicked you out?'

Daniel shook his head. 'No, she was extremely reasonable. She offered separate bedrooms and psychiatric treatment, and I gratefully accepted. The psychiatrist was more helpful than I could've imagined. I told him all about you, about the affair and the photos and the fantasising, everything. Then he asked me if I was willing to commit myself to moving on from those memories. He said if I was serious about saving my marriage, then I had to be serious about putting the past behind me. I realised I didn't want to do that at all. I went home and told Lisa that I was leaving her to come and find you. The girls sided with her, understandably. They both said as far as they were concerned they had no father.'

'Daniel…' Sarah understood a little more now. She understood that he had given up more than she had ever had. She understood, but it only made her want him more urgently. She ran her hands over his face, through his hair, down his neck and over his shoulders. 'I love you, and I do understand what you've given up. But the past is past, we can be together now.'

He moved out of her reach. 'It's important to me that we do this right. If you love me, you'll let me do this right. You'll wait.'

She sighed and stared at the photos spread out in front of her. 'So did you take these to jerk off to or what?'

'I thought it might help get it out of my system so I wouldn't have to... But it didn't work. I kept... I went to my minister and told him that I was obsessed with another woman. That I was tempted to commit adultery. He told me to pray for forgiveness and to pay more attention to my wife.'

'Did you?' The thought of him with anyone else made her skin prickle. And she was so pretty, his wife, much prettier than Sarah.

'I tried. It didn't work. Every time Lisa and I made love I was thinking about you. It just made me feel worse, because she wasn't you and I was unsatisfied, and I felt ashamed for betraying her, even mentally. I loved her, and I was so angry about what I was feeling. I kept thinking it was a phase, a mid-life crisis or something. But it didn't pass. It got stronger and stronger. Until the photos weren't enough anymore.'

'How long were you doing this before you made a move on me?'

'I don't know. A few months.'

'I'm trying to decide what I would have done at the time, had I known what you were doing. I think I would have been disgusted.'

'I certainly was.'

'I wasn't disgusted when you touched me. And that was a hell of a surprise.'

'God, I was terrified that day. If we'd been caught, worse, if you'd run screaming...' Daniel slid over and kissed her cheek, his lips lingered for a moment then kissed a line up her cheekbone to her forehead. 'I was just so overwhelmed. You were right there, right beside me, I could smell your hair and... oh...' He pushed his face into her hair. She waited in silence for him to continue. 'I was crazed. I had worked myself into such a frenzy, over such an extended period of time that it felt inevitable. One minute I was listening to you talk–'

'Shakespeare wasn't it?' Sarah stroked the back of his head, getting lost in his memory. She could smell the chalk on his hands and hear the tennis ball thumping the classroom window.

'Yes. You were talking and I was thinking about how your skin would feel. I was looking at your knee and it was so close, and I was thinking that I could just reach out, just extend my hand the smallest distance, and then I'd know. I'd know what your skin felt like and that would be enough.'

'And so you did,' Sarah whispered.

'And you did not run screaming,' Daniel whispered back.

'Although, if I had known you were a wanking, stalking, pervert I would never have let you touch me.'

'But you know now. And you are letting me touch you.'

'Now it's too late. I'm already touched.'

Daniel looked into her face. 'I haven't had a single moment of peace since that day.'

'Me neither. I've been so restless all this time. I find ways to zonk myself out so I can have that oblivion. I drink much too much; I have sex until I'm numb; I take muscle relaxants. If I do all three, then sometimes I can sleep all night, or at the very least, my mind goes blank for a few hours.' Sarah couldn't stop herself from leaning forward and kissing Daniel on the lips. 'Lots of times I've fallen asleep only to dream of you. When I wake up I feel like everything is wrong. I feel like my skin is too tight.'

'God, I know, Sarah, darling, I know.'

She couldn't bear it anymore. She threw her body at him, covered his mouth with hers. He struggled for a second then groaned and pushed her onto her back. His hands were all over her, all at once. In her hair, on her neck, her thighs, pushing her dress up over her hips. He was a scavenging, hungry beast, gnashing his teeth and clawing at her like she was a dead thing. He made noises that came from his chest and the back of his throat.

She struggled against his weight, freeing her arm enough to reach down and unzip his pants. He went on, tearing at her neck with his teeth, scratching her belly with his nails. She took hold of his cock and he began thrusting into her hand. 'I love you, Daniel,' she said over and over, while he fucked her hand and tore at her body.

Then he lifted his head, looked into her eyes and slapped her hard across the face. 'Dear God, Sarah! Why won't you let me do this right? Why won't you let me treat you with respect?'

Sarah knew that he could not see how ridiculous his question was. He didn't see that biting her legs and slapping her face was less respectful than a mutually satisfying screw. She didn't know why that intrigued her when any sane person would be disturbed. She could see the twisted logic, the distorted morality, the dangerous self-justification; it's just that she didn't mind.

'I don't want respect. I want you to fuck me.'

He opened his mouth wide, as if to roar, but the sound that came out was an injured whimpering. He rolled off her and on to the floor. 'Shit.' He was panting and clutching his chest. Pitiful wounded beast. 'We're not doing this, Sarah. Not like this.'

Sarah sat up. Her hands were shaking. 'You're a bastard, you know that?'

'It isn't going to be like this.' He did not look at her.

'Fine.' Sarah stood up and put herself together again. She watched him the entire time, afraid that he would never look at her again. 'Tell me how it's going to be.'

'You're going to stop sleeping around, stop dressing like a tart, and stop acting as though I'm a novel distraction from your real life. I am going to get answers for all my questions about you.'

'And then what? Then we can have sex?'

'When I see that you're ready to commit yourself properly, you'll come and live with me.'

Sarah laughed. 'Will I?'

'Yes.' He seemed to notice for the first time that his deflating penis was outside of his pants. He made another noise from his throat, like an animal dying slowly on a country road. 'Until then there will be no more touching; it's too difficult.'

Sarah considered him. He was old, pathetic, crumpled, mean. He'd been back in her life for three days, and was ordering her around already. He put conditions on her that were arbitrary and nonsensical. He was contradictory and cruel. She wanted to hate him. She wanted to tell him to shove his rules and orders up his dirty old man arse. No, she didn't. She wanted to do everything he said, twice as well as he told her to, then he would be delighted with her, and he would love her and touch her forever.

'Okay,' Sarah said. 'I'll play.'

4

When Jamie came over a few days later, Sarah knew she had to tell him about Daniel. It would be impossible to spend the day with him and stay silent about something so huge. But before she could even consider talking to him, she needed to get off. Sexual frustration was a new sensation and one she did not like at all. If Daniel wanted to play some bizarre waiting game then that was his prerogative but there was no way Sarah was giving up her greatest pleasure.

'This is a nice welcome,' Jamie said, as she pushed him against the wall.

'I missed you.' Sarah untucked his T-shirt and slid her hands up over his belly and chest. 'It feels like a long time since I've seen you.'

'It's always too long for me.' Jamie pulled his T-shirt over his head and threw it on the floor. 'I think about you all the time, you know that?'

'I know. Me too.' But even as she said it she was thinking about Daniel.

Sarah knew that Jamie had come from nappies and feedings and whingeing, and would not be anywhere near as aroused as she was. She led him to the sofa, finished undressing him, and took him in her mouth. She tried to stop thinking about Daniel, but couldn't. She let her mind go, imagining this was Daniel in her mouth, under her hands. She was driving him crazy, making him weep with how good she was at this. Making him regret every day she had spent perfecting her techniques on other men.

She was jolted by a hand on her forehead. 'Stop.'

She looked up, breathless. Jamie's eyes were half-closed, his skin ruddy. 'Come here.'

Sarah took off her clothes, keeping her eyes on the erection that could belong to anyone. The dick was what she had to have. It didn't matter who she was thinking about, or wanting, or missing. She just needed to have that thing inside her, needed her feverish, awkward body to be invaded. She needed to be fucked back to normality.

But it did matter. For the first time ever, it mattered who she was with, and her body knew it mattered and wouldn't cooperate at all. Jamie was a real trooper. Sarah couldn't imagine what he was thinking as he endured countless position adjustments, three location changes, and long periods of determined panting broken up by frustrated directives. Maybe he was thinking about work, or Shelley, or something else that would slow him down. Sarah really was very impressed with his stamina and control, but it was futile. Daniel Carr had trapped her orgasm inside her, and only he could get it out.

'Just go ahead and finish,' Sarah said, defeated and sore.

'What's wrong, Sar? What am I doing wrong?'

Sarah told him he was wonderful, that the problem was with her. His jaw stiffened. 'We'll try something else.' They tried three more positions, at various speeds. Sarah told him again that it just wasn't going to happen.

'Fine.' He withdrew.

'No,' she said, pulling him back towards her. 'You finish, it's okay.'

'Let me go down on you.'

'Jamie, no.' Sarah considered oral sex as something to give, not receive. She had explained it to him before, how it made her feel as though she was a saucer of milk being lapped up by a greedy kitten. How passivity felt like dying.

'Please, Sar. Let me try.' Jamie knelt on the floor between her legs and rubbed the insides of her thighs. His cock was pointing at her, red and angry. 'If you hate it I'll stop. Please?'

Sarah rolled her eyes. 'Whatever.'

Jamie pushed his sweat soaked fringe off his forehead and disappeared between her thighs. Sarah was immediately uncomfortable and tried to wriggle away, but he grabbed her hips with both hands and held her still. After a couple of minutes she was wondering if she had been too hasty in excluding this act from her sex life. Another few minutes and Sarah found herself gasping for air and clawing at Jamie's shoulders. She remembered him telling her that Shelley was very bossy in bed, and that she only ever came from being tongued. Sarah said a silent thankyou to Shelley, and then lost all control of her thought processes. For a brief, blissful time she forgot Daniel, and the fast shrinking possibility of her independent life.

They slept through the afternoon, curled up in each other on the living room floor. Sarah woke to see him opening his eyes, blinking at her and smiling in a disoriented, dreamy way. She smiled back, sat up and lit a cigarette. She could not put it off any longer.

'I need to tell you something.'

He held onto her waist and pulled himself to a seated position. 'Yeah?'

'It's about the bloke I went out with the other night.'

Jamie's face hardened. 'The biter?'

'Yeah. Well, I think he might be...'

'A psycho?'

'...more than a passing thing. I think things could become serious.'

Jamie looked right at her. His expression did not change one little bit.

'Anyway, I wanted you to know.'

Jamie stared at her for a full five seconds. 'Right.' He picked up her cigarettes and lit one. That was a very bad sign. 'Well, this is a shock.'

'I know.'

'I mean, I've been trying to win you for all these years. Not just me. Heaps of men have tried to win you over. We've all been so stupid, running around after you, treating you kindly, showing you respect, never once suspecting what you really wanted in a man was the willingness to beat the crap out of you.' He drew back on the cigarette as though he was a pack a day man. His voice was deadly calm. 'I just wish you'd told me earlier, Sarah. Would've saved us both a lot of trouble, wouldn't it? I kept thinking I was doing something wrong, and it turns out I was. I wasn't hurting you enough.'

'That isn't it.'

'No. It's just that I'm not who you want.'

Sarah pressed her lips together because she could not lie and she could not twist the knife in his guts. She got them both a beer. Jamie drained his in less than a minute. Sarah got him another and another cigarette. When she handed them to him she saw a flicker of warmth in his eyes. It was enough to prove that he hadn't been entirely frozen by her.

'I wish you wouldn't be so hostile,' she said.

'How am I supposed to be?'

'You could be supportive. You could be my friend.'

He snorted. 'You want me to congratulate you?'

'Look, Jamie. This may not be what you want to hear, but I assure you it is the greatest compliment I've ever given. I value you as a friend a million times more than I value you as a lover. As a lover you are part of a very large and not particularly prestigious group, as a friend you're it. You're my one and only.'

Jamie's mask cracked. He bit his lip, swiped at his eyes. 'But I'm not, am I? Now you have someone else who is more than a lover.'

'I don't know *what* he is yet. But he isn't you.' Sarah put her head on his shoulder; he shrugged his arm around her. 'And besides, you have someone else too. You got married, you have a kid, and a family and a whole… You have this whole life, and I have nothing except dreams and work and sex. Maybe I want to belong to someone.'

'I just… I suppose I feel that you belong to me. These last few months I've felt that we're a real couple. We hang out together, we're best friends, we can practically finish each others sentences. And we make love. I mean, what's the difference between what we have and a full-blown relationship?'

'You tell me. You're the one who goes home to a full-blown relationship every night.'

They lapsed into silence again. Sarah had wanted to get it all out at once, but Jamie was so upset at the news that there was someone, that she thought telling him who that someone was would send him over the edge. Besides, it wasn't like her relationship with Daniel was speeding ahead. If things continued the way they had been, then it would be a hundred years before he had sex with her. Sarah decided that publicly naming Daniel Carr as the love of her life could wait until he'd at least gotten over himself and fucked her.

During the long silence, Jamie dressed himself and Sarah sat below him and watched. When he sat on the sofa to tie his shoe laces she got to her knees and repeatedly kissed his arms and hands. He swatted at her and giggled, and she tied his laces for him while he stroked her hair.

'So,' he said, taking both her hands, 'who is this remarkably fortunate man?'

Shit. Her plan to not tell him depended on him not asking. She couldn't, *couldn't*, lie to him. Shit.

'You can meet him soon. I promise.'

'That'll be fun.' Jamie brought her hands to his mouth and kissed each one in turn. 'What's his name?'

Shit. Shit. Shit. Sarah cleared her throat. 'Daniel.'

Jamie was quiet for a while. Sarah hoped desperately that he wouldn't remember, that he wouldn't make the connection. She held her breath until he spoke again.

'Daniel who?'

Sarah climbed up beside him on the sofa and lifted his arm up around her shoulders. She wrapped her own arm around his waist and squeezed. 'Carr,' she said softly.

Another extended, airless pause. Then, 'I suppose Carr is a pretty common name, but still, it's a freaky coincidence.'

'Jamie.' Sarah tasted his name as she said it. It tasted like salt. 'It isn't a coincidence.'

The arm around her shoulders stiffened. It felt like he was going to stay that way forever. Sarah was held so tight to him that she couldn't turn her head to see his face. She could imagine it though, frozen and hard like the rest of him.

'Sarah,' Jamie said, his bicep pulsing against Sarah's neck. 'Tell me that was a joke.'

'He's come back for me.' Sarah felt as though she'd swallowed a mouthful of sea water. The salt in her mouth and her gut made her queasy. She wished she could see his face. She thought about how she had felt when Daniel showed her the photos he'd jerked off to for eight years. She wondered if such a sad, creepy pervert could possibly be worth smashing Jamie over. But it didn't matter if it was worth it; it just *was*.

Jamie slid his arm out from behind her. He stood up, walked to the window and put his fist through it. The glass was old and dirty; it broke in lethal looking shards, each one big enough to go straight through a person's heart. Jamie picked up his jacket and wrapped it around his bleeding hand. Then he picked up his keys and wallet from the coffee table and walked out the door.

5

After Jamie smashed Sarah's window, he went home and had a fight with Shelley. She asked him the perfectly reasonable question of what the hell had happened to his hand, but even knowing it was a perfectly reasonable question Jamie could not possibly answer her in a reasonable way. He told her to stop harassing him. He told her that he was sick of her always nagging him and looking at him with suspicion. He told her that just because they were married it didn't mean he had to tell her what he was doing every second of the day. Attack is the best form of defence.

Shelley pointed out that asking why he was bleeding all over the kitchen floor was hardly nagging. She said that she didn't want to know what he was doing every second of the day; just what he was doing at the time of his injury. Jamie swore at her and went outside.

It's impossible to win an argument when you know you're in the wrong. It's impossible to tell your kind, concerned, endlessly patient wife that the reason you're a bloody mess is that the woman you adore, the woman who is more precious to you than your own flesh and blood, the woman you've spent your life trying to make happy, is in love with another man. How could he possibly tell Shelley that he wanted to die because Sarah loved someone else as much as Jamie loved Sarah? Not just someone else. Not just another man. Sarah loved a cruel, sadistic, manipulative criminal. Sarah loved the man whose damage Jamie had spent the last eight years trying to undo.

Shelley came to him after an hour or so. She sat beside him and unwrapped his clumsily bound hand. 'I don't think it needs stitches,' she said, touching her fingertips to the jagged line of dried blood. 'It's stopped bleeding.'

'I'm sorry,' Jamie said. 'I was at Sarah's.'

'I know. She called.'

His stomach muscles clenched up. 'What did she...?'

'She wanted to see if you'd got home alright. She was worried about you.'

Sarah was worried about him. Well, that was something, wasn't it? It wasn't much, but it wasn't indifference, which was what he'd imagined she'd felt.

'What happened? She said you had an argument?'

Sarah said they'd had an argument. That was an interesting way of looking at it. An argument. Implying that there was a difference of opinion, that viewpoints could be voiced and solutions negotiated. Calling it an argument diminished it, made it something that could be sorted out and gotten over. Sarah and Jamie were just arguing.

'Can't you tell me, please?'

'Yeah, it's... she's seeing this bloke and he... he's no good for her.'

'So what? Sarah is always with some loser.'

'This is different,' Jamie said, trying hard not to cry. 'He hurts her.'

'Oh.' Shelley stroked Jamie's hand, carefully avoiding the cut. 'Like, physically hurts her?'

Jamie didn't know how to explain Sarah's bruises. He could describe them in intimate detail, but then Shelley would want to know how he knew, and he could hardly tell her that today he had fucked Sarah for three hours and that whenever he felt himself going over the edge, he changed position so that he could see her beaten up thighs. So while Sarah couldn't come because she was thinking about the man who'd done that to her, Jamie was holding his orgasm off by thinking about the same thing.

'She has bruises,' he said.

'Bruises? Shit. I can't imagine Sarah putting up with that. What does she say about it?'

'She says she loves him.' Jamie started to cry.

'Oh, shit.' Shelley kissed his cheek, stroked his head, held him tight to her breasts. 'I'm sorry, sweetie. I'm sorry. It'll be okay.'

Jamie knew that letting his wife comfort him over his broken heart wasn't right. But then, what was?

After a while, Bianca woke up and started hollering. Together they changed her nappy, and then Shelley sat on the bed to feed Bianca and Jamie lay on one side and watched them.

'I can't believe we made her,' Jamie said, stroking the wispy hair that tried to cover Bianca's still soft skull. 'I can't believe she's ours.'

'I can't believe it either. I can't believe I have this little girl, and I can't believe I have you. I thank God every day for you both.'

'Yeah, right. I'm such a blessing.'

Shelley put her hand over his, both of them holding Bianca's head. 'Blessings, both of you.'

Later that night, Jamie told Shelley about Mr Carr. After listening to him ranting about what that monster had done to Sarah, Shelley made them both a cup of tea and then started in on why Jamie was wrong about it all.

Firstly, what had happened could not really be considered sexual abuse. Fourteen-year-old Sarah was no innocent child. She used to annoy everyone in Media Studies with her rants about child slavery in African diamond mines, paedophile priests, infant clitoridectomies in Somalia and a thousand other injustices. She was always going on about giving a voice to the voiceless, and defending those who can't defend themselves and empowering the abused and downtrodden. So, given that, is it fair to say that, if anything, her bias lay towards exposing men who did what Mr Carr had done? That is, if Mr Carr had assaulted her, or even used his position of power to manipulate her, then wouldn't she have taken great pleasure in bringing him to justice on behalf of all the abused girls who were not as strong and brave as she?

'Maybe she was too afraid to,' Jamie said, grasping, and knowing that he was grasping, 'Maybe she was scared he'd get violent.'

Shelley didn't buy it. She used to go to the same church as Mr Carr. He taught Sunday school and helped run the Friday night youth group. His daughters boasted about how their dad was a big softy and they could get away with anything. At school, he was the same. He never raised his voice or thumped the desk when the class misbehaved. When he supervised sport he always emphasised the need to play fair and respect boundaries. He was a volunteer counsellor for the student help line. In short, he was one of the gentlest, kindest, least intimidating men she had ever met. 'He's as capable of violent sex abuse as you are,' she said.

Jamie met her eyes. 'Maybe I am. Is it so hard to imagine?'

'Yes, it is. You are gentle to a fault. That's why I love you.'

He held up his bandaged hand. 'Not so gentle sometimes.'

Shelley looked away. 'Right, yes, you're right.' She sipped her tea, keeping her eyes on the far wall. 'It's her then. She inspires violence. She turns decent men into animals.'

'Shelley!' He reached across the table and grabbed her chin, turning it so she was facing him. 'Don't you dare blame her. And don't you dare compare me with him!'

'Why not? She clearly makes both of you crazy.'

Jamie felt like slapping her. He resisted, but held her chin hard. 'If you saw what he'd done to her... the damage that he... He's a fucking animal. Her thighs look as though they've been through a meat grinder. Bites and bruises from her knees to her hips! If you'd seen it, you would've been angry enough to break a window too.'

Shelley reached up and removed his hand. 'I guess I'll have to take your word for it,' she said, standing and turning her back on him. 'Since I can't imagine I'll be in a position to examine Sarah's thighs in the near future. But then, why would I be?'

Jamie let her go. There was nothing more to say.

He sat up most of the night thinking it through. Shelley had made some valid arguments, but she was missing the point. Yes, Sarah was precocious, and yes, Mr Carr had some good characteristics, but there was no excuse for a man in his position taking advantage of a girl who thinks she's more grown up than she is. A teacher having sex with an under-age student is wrong in all kinds of ways, and nothing makes it right.

But so what? She loved him. Whatever he was, whatever he did, Sarah loved him and had always loved him. She had always said *he's the one, Jamie, the only one I need, I dream about him, I yearn for him.* She'd said it when she was fourteen with a freshly squashed heart; she'd said it when she was sixteen and newly homeless; then at eighteen when she was screwing celebrities and turning down millionaires; and she'd said it less than a month ago when she was naked and kissing Jamie's chest. *If it hadn't been for Him, I would think this was as good as it gets.* She had meant it as a compliment.

It *was* a compliment. To be second out of a field of thousands, to be first runner-up to a god. Especially a god who had not appeared for worship for eight long years. A god who had abandoned the most faithful of his flock in her time of desperate need.

Sarah had suffered for her belief and devotion. While Daniel Carr was enjoying himself under the Queensland sun, Sarah was caught in a storm, thrashing herself against rocks, trying to break herself open. While the love of her life was playing with his kids at the beach, Sarah was working double shifts at a sleazy restaurant so she could afford to live in a derelict building. While he was teaching English to a fresh batch of adoring teenagers, Sarah was popping pills and losing time and having abortions. And while he was teaching Sunday school, Sarah was getting buggered by strangers in car parks and alleyways.

And while all this was going on, Jamie was holding on tight, riding it out, keeping her alive, waiting for his time to come. It had never occurred to him that he was doing it all for Daniel Carr's benefit, taking care of Sarah so she would be in good condition when he came back to claim her. And if he had known, it wouldn't have made a scrap of difference. Jamie took care of her because he loved her, and he loved her because he couldn't not. If she had never so much as kissed him, never even *spoken* to him, he would still have done everything in his power to make her happy and safe.

Nothing could never change that.

6

Daniel took Sarah to Parramatta Park, because it was a clear warm day, and because he hadn't been to the park since he'd returned to Sydney over a year ago, and because he wanted them to only see each other in public for the time being. Sarah dressed as demurely as she could without going to plain ugly. Dark blue jeans, a pale blue twin set, sneakers. She plaited her hair and tied it with a blue ribbon that she bought specially.

They sat side by side, but not touching, on a bench facing the river. Sarah had promised to tell him everything he wanted to know. She was eager to get it all out, not because she liked talking about her miserable life, but because the sooner they got all the catching up, getting to know each other stuff out of the way, the sooner Daniel would touch her.

'How many men have you been with?' he wanted to know.

'Many.'

'Sarah, you promised to be honest with me.'

She sighed. 'I am. I don't know how many. Hundreds.'

Daniel stared at her, clearly waiting for her to tell him she was joking. She stared back, refusing to let him make her ashamed. 'I see,' he said. 'How many of them did you love?'

'None.'

He squinted. 'None?'

'Just you.'

His face softened and for a moment she thought he might kiss her, but he only nodded and carried on with his questioning. 'Are you sleeping with anyone at the moment?'

'Yeah, just… just Jamie. It's actually pretty serious and… okay, I do love him, but not in the way… not *in love* love. I've known him forever and… It's complicated.'

Daniel closed his eyes. 'Explain it to me.'

'He's my best friend and I pretty much owe him my life. There's a line from Dickinson: "I felt it shelter to speak to you." That's how I feel about Jamie. But he got this silly girl pregnant and married her, but he's in love with me, and, well, I'm in love with *you*. I told him about you and he…' Sarah cringed at the memory. 'He did not handle it well.'

'I want you to stop sleeping with him.'

'You can't expect me to–'

'Goodbye, Sarah.' Daniel stood up. 'Call me when you're ready to take this seriously.'

'Daniel, no!' She grabbed his arm and tugged on it. 'I'll stop, I promise. I'm sorry.'

He sat down, brushing her hand off his arm. 'Anyone else I should know about?'

She shook her head.

'Good girl. Now, I want to know about your family.'

Sarah squeezed her hands together. 'My mum is an economics professor. My dad is an actuary working approximately five hundred hours a week for an insurance company, calculating the statistical probability of not paying out a single claim and still avoiding legal action. Kelly is three years older than me. Last I heard she was doing Law at UNSW.'

Sarah lit a cigarette and Daniel slid across to the far end of the bench. It made her want to kick him when he did things like that. Although, she wanted to kick him anyway just to be touching him.

'I met your mother at parent-teacher night. She was gorgeous, like you, but so brusque, so–'

'Evil?'

Daniel laughed. 'I remember thinking something like that. I was raving about how wonderful you were and–'

'Were we screwing then?'

'No, we weren't *screwing*.' Daniel scrunched his face up to show his distaste. He had a filthy mouth but couldn't abide what he called *tacky* words. Screwing, prick, tits and snatch were off limits. Fucking her cunt with his cock was somehow much classier. 'I was infatuated with you though. I think I came on a bit strong, telling your mum how fantastic you were.'

'You told her I was fantastic?' Sarah ground her cigarette out with her foot and slid across to be close to him again.

'Yes, but she talked about you as though you were somebody else's kid. She lectured me on learning styles and intellectual development and on the fact that you had a sharp mind but you were wasting it on reading romantic rubbish.'

'That's my mum.'

Daniel turned his upper body so he was looking Sarah straight in the face. 'I suggested to your mother that it was quite normal for a girl your age to be reading romantic fiction, and she told me that if it was up to her, you would not be wasting your time in a class like mine. If it were up to her you would not be studying wishy-washy concepts like deconstruction and ethnocentrism, nor would you be going on about expression and interpretation. According to her, I should've been teaching you clear, concise composition skills and that was that.'

His voice was glorious, but she wanted him to stop. She wanted him to kiss her and touch her and tell her with his body that she was much, much better than anyone he knew.

'When she left, all I could think about was how vulnerable you were. That a girl as awake to the world as you were, with such a dead hearted mother, would be open to anyone who showed her the slightest bit of affection.'

Sarah's throat closed. She tried to tell him to shut up, but the words were caught in her chest. She coughed to clear her throat, and held up her hand to tell him to be quiet.

'Are you okay?'

'Fine. Can you shut up for a minute, please?'

'Okay.' After a while, he said, 'I just wanted you to know that I understand about your mum. I understand that you must hate her for her coldness. But also, you could look at it the way I do. If she hadn't been so distant and unloving, maybe you wouldn't have been such an easy fuck.'

Something broke in her and tears poured out. Daniel squatted in front of her, face creased with concern. 'I made you cry. I'm sorry.' He handed her a navy handkerchief. 'I had no idea you'd get so upset.'

'Bullshit, Daniel. You're deliberately fucking with my mind. The other night you told me that you couldn't help yourself, that you tried to resist me and couldn't. Now you're telling me that you intentionally took advantage of me. I don't know what to think.'

He was silent for a few minutes, rocking back on his heels and watching Sarah try to regain her calm. When her breathing slowed to normal, he spoke again, looking right into her eyes. 'I fantasised, tried to resist, decided to have at you then changed my mind, then met your mother and changed it back again, then prayed and decided to leave you alone. I went back and forth, and yes, in the end I took advantage of your vulnerability. But if it hadn't been me it would have been someone else, and he more than likely would not have felt anything except opportunistic. I loved you and I still do. I'm just pointing out that having the parents you had made it easier for you to accept me into your life.'

Sarah looked through him and saw his manipulative black heart. The heart that loved her and that she loved back. She lit a cigarette, blowing the smoke directly into his eyes. He flinched, but did not move away.

'Is that why you left home, Sarah? Because your parents were too strict? Because they were cold towards you?'

'No. Strict I could've lived with. At least until I'd finished school.'

'So what happened?'

'I'll tell you,' she said, 'but don't get too excited, I'm not going to cry again.'

'You think I like it when you cry?'

'Yes.'

'Well, maybe a bit,' he said, without a hint of shame. 'But mostly, I want to know what was so terrible that it's stopped you seeing your family for six years.'

'I got raped. My parents didn't approve.' Sarah shrugged, as though her body could convince her brain that there was nothing to get upset about

'Oh, Christ. Darling, I...' Daniel put his hands on her knees, and then, before her brain had registered the pleasure of his touch, he removed them. 'Tell me what happened.'

Sarah ran her tongue along her teeth, like sharpening the blade of a knife. Amazing how satisfying it was to be able to hurt him back. She licked her lips, tasting blood that was not there, but had been and would be again. 'That's the whole story,' she said, 'You can make up the details yourself if you need something to jerk off to.'

'That's harsh, Sarah. Even for you.' He stood up and walked to the edge of the river, his hands deep in his pockets. Sarah was instantly remorseful. He couldn't help hurting her; he wanted to know her so much that he couldn't hold back, couldn't be polite and dishonest with her.

'I'm sorry,' Sarah called out. 'Please come back and sit with me. I'll tell you whatever you want to know.'

Daniel walked back slowly and sat beside her. 'How can we be together if you won't tell me your secrets?'

'I know. I'm sorry. I'll tell you.'

'Everything, okay?'

'Yes.' Sarah looked around and was disappointed that the park was deserted. Sometimes the absence of others made you feel more suffocated than anything else. A public park on a sunny Saturday should be filled with kids and mums and dogs and frisbees. It shouldn't be funeral home quiet, it shouldn't make you feel as though you could scream and scream and nobody but the ducks would hear.

She took a deep breath. 'I was sixteen. There was a party at Jamie's house –'

'Jamie who you're sleeping with now? You knew him back then?'

'Yeah, you did too. Jamie Wilkes. He was in our class. It was actually his brother Brett's party, which was why I wanted to go.'

'You liked Brett?'

'Oh, yeah, Brett's great. I slept with him a couple of times, but mostly we were just really good buddies. The reason I wanted to go to the party was because all his uni mates would be there, so it would be like, a smorgasbord of older men.'

Daniel's face scrunched. 'Were you sleeping with Jamie and his brother at the same time?'

'No! Stop interrupting.'

Daniel nodded and Sarah continued. 'So anyway, all these men are throwing themselves at me, they're handing me drinks and smokes and joints, they're asking me to dance and trying all these lines. I was taking my time, just hanging with Jamie while I decided who to go for, and then Jamie starts cracking on to me. Like, pressing against me and telling me how good I looked and stuff. It was weird at first because he was sweet and everything but he was just little Jamie. Then it stopped being weird and started being exciting, because I had been in his bedroom about a thousand times and the idea of having sex in there was so deviant and dirty. I started fantasising about watching him come all over his Spiderman sheets and of screwing him on the floor, looking up at the glow-in-the-dark stars on his ceiling.

'So I went for it. And it was nothing like I'd thought. It wasn't at all weird; it was amazing. I mean, he was practically a virgin and so it was just a fast, straightforward hump, but it was *Jamie*. My best friend, you know? And the way he looked at me... God, no one has ever looked at me like that. With such adoration.'

'Hang on,' Daniel interrupted, '*I* look at you like that. *I* adore you.'

Sarah felt all choked up inside. 'Can you just let me tell it?'

He was frowning, the lines across his forehead heavier than usual. 'Fine. We'll get back to that later though. I promise you.'

Sarah nodded, knowing that there was so much in this story that he would want to get back to later. She would die before she had ever managed to satisfy Daniel.

'Jamie went to get us some beer and smokes. He'd only be gone a minute when the door opened. I was facing away from the door, fixing up my hair and I said "Oh that was fast" or something and this voice, not Jamie, goes "Hear that mate, she's waiting for us." I turned around and there's these two blokes standing in the doorway. I told them that Jamie had just gone down for beer and I thought they'd get the hint and piss off, but they shut the door and turned off the light and…' Sarah closed her eyes and concentrated on her breathing. She was fine. Fine, fine, fine. She was absolutely fucking fine.

'Sarah? Are you okay?'

She opened her eyes and smiled. 'Fine. So I'm now in the dark, with these two blokes who I vaguely recognise from the party. One of them was really big, steroid big. The other one was just footy player big and okay looking. Under different circumstances I would've done him for sure. But I was worried that if Jamie came back and they were in the room, he would think I had invited them and would be upset. Jamie's insecure about things like that.

'I told them they had to leave. They laughed, and Steroid guy said something about how he felt bad that him and his mate were the only ones out of their crowd that I hadn't fucked. I told him that there was a very good reason for that, and that he was an ugly rude pig and he better stay away from me. He pushed me on to the bed, and I was so surprised that for a second I did nothing. Then I started lashing out, with my fists and feet and I kept telling him to fuck off. He called his mate over and then my arms were pinned over my head, and my legs were being pushed apart. I started to feel a little scared. I kept screaming at them to fuck off and hoping that Jamie would come back before they did anything.'

Sarah stopped and looked at Daniel. His forehead was glistening, and his cheeks were bright pink. He nodded at her to go on.

'Anyway,' she shrugged, 'Jamie didn't get back until after they'd done it. And when he did, he had to fight them, and so Jamie and me both ended up hurt and the next morning–'

'You promised to tell me everything.'

'Was that not clear? Two men raped me and beat Jamie up.'

'That's telling me the result. I want to know what happened.'

Sarah couldn't look at him. 'I need a smoke.'

'Go ahead,' he said, and Sarah couldn't help looking up, because his voice was devoid of the annoyance he always had when she wanted to smoke.

'Right.' Sarah lit up. 'So the bigger guy, Barry, pushed my skirt up and ripped off my underpants. Like, really ripped them off so they were wrecked. Then he… he pushed into me, really hard and it hurt so much that I yelled and then that was bad, because the guy who had my arms punched me in the mouth, which hurt even more than what Barry was doing. I kept yelling even though my mouth was filling up with blood. And then, the bloke who'd hit me put… put it in my mouth and I–'

'Put what in your mouth?'

'You know what! His *thing*.'

'*Thing*, Sarah? Are we in primary school?'

'Fucking hell! Fine!' She could hardly breathe. 'He put his penis in my mouth. He put it in and I bit down, *really* hard. He punched me again and I thought I might choke to death on my blood and teeth, but I didn't care, I was so happy that I had hurt him.

'Barry had finished and I thought, that's it, the worst is over and I am still alive. And then the one I bit told Barry that he wanted to have a proper go at me. I screamed out again, I think I screamed for Jamie but my mouth was all smashed up so I don't know what it sounded like, and then I was being rolled over and there was a hand at the back of my head, pushing my face into the mattress and I knew what they were going to do to me. I stopped trying to breathe and just hoped that I would pass out and not have to feel anything.

'Of course, it's no fun for them if I'm unconscious, so they pulled my hair and punched me some more and poured beer over my head. I was raped again, anally this time, and it was much worse than the other way. Like being ripped open. Despite their best efforts, I did black out a couple of times. I thought I was dying. I hallucinated, I thought my mother was standing over the bed and I called to her, and then I looked again and it was Jamie, except he wasn't just standing there, he was yelling and then I heard glass breaking, and I realised that it wasn't a hallucination and that Jamie had just smashed a bottle over Barry's head.'

Sarah stopped to stub out her cigarette and light another one. She didn't look at Daniel but she could hear him breathing.

'Jamie managed to get them out of the room. He got smashed up though… Poor bloke. He was bawling his eyes out, but once it was over I was completely calm. He kept saying that I was in shock, but I wasn't; I don't think so anyway. I was just amazed that I was still alive, that I felt thirsty, that I wanted a cigarette. Jamie cleaned me up and I felt embarrassed at him seeing me like that and at him touching me, doing everything with one arm while the other one was, like, limp at his side. He was holding a towel between my legs, and he was crying and carrying on and I just felt like, why did they have to go and do that? Why did these arseholes have to come along and ruin a perfectly good night? I was going to give Jamie his first ever blowjob and now my mouth was so smashed up it would be useless. I said that to Jamie and he just *howled*. It was the worst thing I've ever heard in my life and it made me feel like crying, but I couldn't and so I vomited instead, and that gave him something else practical to do so he stopped making all that noise.'

Daniel cleared his throat. 'Did you call the police?'

'Didn't occur to us. I spent the night in Jamie's room, with the door locked, and the next day Jamie and Brett got a bunch together and went and belted the shit out of the guys who did it. They smashed them up really bad, broke bones and all. I was happy. It felt like justice.

'Anyway, Jamie walked me home in the morning. It wasn't far. He wanted to come in with me but I felt bad enough about what I'd put him through. I didn't want to subject him to what I knew would be another ugly scene where he would feel obliged to defend me. Plus, I could see he was hurt badly; I told him to go to the doctor and I'd call him later.

'I walked into the kitchen and the three of them were sitting around the breakfast table, each with a section of the Sunday paper and a bowl of cereal. And I thought, what a perfect little scene. What a perfect little happy family this is and I am this *mess*. I was wearing Jamie's jacket and that covered all the damage to my arms, but my legs and my face were fucked up. I knew, before anyone even looked at me or spoke, I knew that I was no longer part of that scene. Or really, I knew that I had never been part of it, I had always been too messy for them, even without my busted nose and knocked out teeth.

'They all freaked out, but I was cool. I told them what had happened and asked Mum if she would please drive me to the hospital. She said no.'

Daniel whistled. 'She said *no*?'

'She said no. She said that she was so ashamed that she couldn't even look at me. Dad said that I would be going to boarding school. I asked him if going to boarding school made you rape proof and he told me to stop being so melodramatic. Kelly said that it was impossible I had been raped because everybody knew that I didn't say no to anyone. Mum asked me if that was true and I...' Sarah snorted. 'I said it was true that I had a lot of sex, but that I thought an old school feminist like her would know the difference between being sexually permissive and being forced to take it up the arse while you got your face smashed in.'

Daniel laughed in a shocked sort of way. 'I worship you, Sarah. I really do. You are the classiest woman in the world. A Goddess.'

Sarah and Daniel talked all afternoon, sitting on the bench, walking along the water and then lying on their backs and looking at the clouds. She told him how Jamie's mum took her to the hospital and wrote herself in as next of kin and paid all the medical bills, and how Brett and Jamie helped her find a flat and a job and some second hand furniture. She liked it that Daniel called Jamie a hero, and that he said it was noble of her to leave home rather than stay and be degraded by small minded people.

It had been dark for hours by the time he drove her home. She was dizzy from the entirely new experience of speaking what was in her heart and not being met by dismay or disgust. If she had needed reassurance that her attraction to Daniel was more than just sexual, then today had been it. It was more than sexual, but it was still fundamentally physical. Even connecting with him on an emotional level made her skin prickle. Whenever he laughed at something she said, or nodded in a way that denoted complete understanding, her muscles twitched in recognition. She needed him physically, but it wasn't the base lust she felt around other men. It wasn't about getting off; it was about making one beast with two backs.

Before she got out of his car, she asked the question that had been nagging at her for the last few hours. 'Daniel, when I was telling you what happened… when I described what they did to me, how did you feel?'

He furrowed his brow. 'I felt sorry for you.'

Sarah nodded. 'But… what about…?'

'What?'

She closed her eyes and took a deep breath. 'It seemed like you maybe enjoyed it a bit. The way you enjoy it a bit when I cry?'

'Look at me, Sarah.' She did. His eyes were huge and wet. 'I think what they did was despicable. I am heartbroken at the pain you suffered and at the callous treatment you received from your family. However,' he said, touching the back of her hand with his fingertips. 'There is nothing about you that doesn't turn me on. If becoming aroused while you describe your bloodied thighs makes me sick and depraved, then God help me, I'm sick and depraved.'

'That's what I thought.' Sarah opened the car door, bent over and kissed the top of his head. 'God help me for loving you.'

7

Sarah lived for the day Daniel would touch her again. He took her out for dinner or picked her up from work or dropped in for a drink almost every day, but he never so much as kissed her good-night. She started to skip classes because if she skipped work she would be out on the street, and she had to find the time to see him somehow.

Her phone rang constantly. She did not answer. There was no worry about missing a call from Daniel; he never called because he knew if wanted to talk to her he only had to wait five minutes and she'd be ringing him again. She called him in the middle of the day to tell him about the class she had been to, or the book she'd just finished reading; she called in the evening to hear his voice before she went to work; she called him in the middle of the night because if she was losing sleep over him then she wanted him to be awake too.

One night, sleepless, she watched a documentary about the deep ocean. There was a segment about a fish that mated for life, the male attaching himself to the female and surviving by siphoning her blood, giving her in return a constant stream of semen. It was the sexiest thing Sarah had heard in her whole life. She called Daniel and told him about it.

Daniel scoffed. 'The problem with getting your information from the television is that you are fed these sexy little factoids but there isn't any follow through. You know that one thing about this fish and nothing else. If the female fish dies does the male die too, or can he detach himself? If the male fish dies, does the female have to swim forever with a rotting corpse weighing her down? What happens when she conceives? Does the flow stop? Do they–'

'Jesus, Daniel! Who cares?'

'I do. I bet you don't even know what the fish is called?'

'I don't give a stuff. I'm of the instant gratification generation remember? I only want to know the most interesting thing; leave all that other stuff to the scientists. Give me fast, sexy, exotic factoids.'

Daniel laughed. 'You're adorable. Now go to bed, it's late.'

'Not yet. I want to talk some more.'

'About fish?'

'Why not? Anything, I don't care. I just want to hear your voice. Tell me about the ocean.'

He was quiet for a while. Thinking, or perhaps pulling one of his reference books from the shelf in his living room. When he began to speak, his voice was low and husky.

'The ocean,' he said, 'is a whole world in itself: huge plains spread out across the ocean floor, long mountain ranges rise toward the surface, with deep valleys cutting through them. There are active volcanoes, erupting down so deep that we on the surface would never know. It's a trap, the ocean. It's cool and comforting and so you go in farther, you go in deeper. And then you're dead. Water is tricky like that. If you're burnt or hot or aching, it will heal and soothe and calm you. But also, it can freeze you to death or boil your flesh. Crush or suffocate you.' He paused, then: 'Am I boring you?'

'No, please keep going.'

'Okay, Sarah.' Another pause. 'Will you take off your under-pants for me?'

'Of course.' She slid out of her pants and he went on.

'The great white shark has no natural predator. It has wide serrated teeth that cut easily through tough flesh and bone. Some sharks have long pointed teeth as well, so they can hold their prey in place while they cut into it. Their senses are integrated; they can hear and feel all over their body. When sharks have sex, they bite each other almost to death.'

'Daniel, are you reading this?' Sarah said, feeling and hearing him with her whole body, wanting to bite him to death and have his blood mix with hers and float away with the current.

'Sssh. Imagine a crocodile in his swamp, pretending to sleep when he is actually eyeing you off, imagining the look on your face when he pounces from behind and sinks his teeth into your yielding flesh. Crocodiles thrash around when they feed; they go into a death roll. Half your bones would be shattered by the time the beast put you out of your misery by smashing your skull against a rock.'

Sarah was fevered and wanted to be in the ocean with him. In the swamp or the lake or the fucking creek. She needed coolness, wetness, hidden rocks and treasures. She needed thrashing, biting and lack of air. 'What else?' she asked Daniel, whose voice had taken on the qualities he described. Wet and dark. She could hear the fish splashing all around him.

'The blue-ringed octopus is the size of a golf ball. When it bites, you at first feel nauseous. Your vision becomes hazy. Within seconds you are blind. You lose your sense of touch. You cannot speak or swallow. Three minutes later you are paralysed and unable to breath.'

Sarah felt its poison surging through her veins. Three minutes and it would all be over.

'It's the bigger octopuses that are really fascinating. Can you imagine all those tentacles, Sarah? Imagine the sucking and the twisting and at the same time, weeds tangling around your ankles. And all the while, the water is filling your throat and your lungs. You're going to drown and you are glad, you hope it is soon.'

Sarah was blind and dumb. All there was in the world was Daniel's voice and the sound of limbs crashing through water and the sensation of slimy, reptilian creatures swarming over her. The tentacles were inside her and she told Daniel how that felt. She told him about the sucking and the twisting up inside her and how the water was just *gushing*. He was gushing too, he told her, and she said *I am drowning*.

Then everything was quiet. Slowly, Sarah's vision cleared and so did her mind. She was embarrassed to be alone in her kitchen in the middle of the night, with the phone cord wrapped around her waist and her hand sandwiched between her thighs.

'Daniel?' She could hear him breathing, but it seemed like hours before he spoke.

'You had an orgasm, didn't you?'

'Yeah. Didn't you?'

'That turned you on then? Sea creatures?'

Sarah hesitated, trying to interpret his tone. Was he teasing?

'You're too embarrassed to answer me?' He sounded angry.

'I was turned on by *you*. Why are you being weird?'

'You were turned on by the thought of fucking fish. That is disgusting. I feel like I'm going to be sick.'

Sarah wiped her hand on the corner of her T-shirt. 'Stop it. You're making me feel awful.'

'Really, Sarah. I want to throw up. You are one sick little girl.'

'Hey! You were getting off too! I heard you–'

'Is that what you like? You like men to push live animals up your cunt and–'

Sarah hung up and cried and cried and cried.

The next morning there was an envelope under her door. Inside was a handwritten poem:

The Bait by John Donne.

Come live with me and be my love,
And we will some new pleasures prove,
Of golden sands and crystal brooks,
With silken lines and silver hooks.

There will the river whispering run,
Warmed by thine eyes more than the sun.
And there the enamoured fish will stay,
Begging themselves they may betray.

When thou wilt swim in that live bath,
Each fish, which every channel hath,
Will amorously to thee swim,
Gladder to catch thee live, then thou him.

If thou, to be so seen, beest loath,
By sun or moon, thou darkenest both;
And if myself have leave to see,
I need not their light, having thee.

Let others freeze with angling reeds,
And cut their legs with shells and weeds,
Or treacherously poor fish beset
With strangling snare or windowy net;

Let coarse bold hands from slimy nest
The bedded fish in banks out-wrest.
Of curious traitors, sleave-silk flies,
Bewitch poor fishes' wandering eyes.

For thee, thou needest no such deceit,
For thou thyself art thine own bait;
That fish is not catched thereby,
Alas, is wiser far than I.

She was unfamiliar with the piece, but recognised the first lines as coming from Marlowe. It was a parody then, but was that Daniel's point in sending it? To parody the dramatics of their love, the way Donne parodied Marlowe's? She read it through until she had it memorised. There was a message she was supposed to be getting. There was the obvious allusion to their phone conversation, and maybe that was all he meant by it: an acknowledgement of the eroticism of the sea. An apology. But then, did he see himself as the poet and her as the baiter who had caught him while other, wiser men escaped? Therefore, he is a fool? *Thou art thine own bait*: did that mean he saw her seductiveness as inherent, where other women had to *freeze with angling reeds*? Or was Daniel pointing out the brilliance and passion that can be caught up in everyday things? The use of metaphysical conceit to demonstrate that most basic of human experiences? And there was violence in there as well, with strangling snares and shells that cut. Daniel had tangled her up without a word of his own.

She called him and told him that if he was trying to apologise he should just do it, and if he meant something else then he should just come out and say that too.

'I thought my meaning was very clear,' he said.

'Donne never made anything clear, Daniel. My head's been spinning all day trying to figure this out.'

He laughed softly. 'I chose that poem because its theme seemed apposite, but everything I wanted to say is in the first two lines.'

Sarah looked down at the coffee-stained, crumpled piece of paper and re-read the lines although she knew them by heart. 'Do you mean that?' she said, feeling so afraid that he would laugh again or hang up or tell her she was disgusting.

'I don't say things I don't mean.'

'So what you said last night, you meant that too?'

'Yes, I vomited as soon as I hung up. Then I copied out that poem and drove around to your flat. I sat outside your door all night, listening to you crying. I realised that our telephone conversation had been the turning point I've been waiting for. We had bizarre phone sex that made me sick, and afterwards all I wanted was to do it again. I realised that you would let me. If we can make each other ill and make each other cry, and still be desperate to be together... Sarah, *Come live with me and be my love, And we will some new pleasures prove.*'

'Okay, yes, okay.' Sarah was crying again. 'But I need some time. I have to give notice on my flat, I have to talk to my friends, I have to... well, heaps of stuff. I need at least two weeks.'

'You've got one,' Daniel said. 'I'll leave you alone to do whatever you have to do, and in a week, I'll come and get you.'

One week passed and Sarah sorted out nothing. On the day he'd said it, a Saturday, she stared at her walls and smoked. She spent all day thinking about how they were *her* walls, and even if they were yellowed with chipping paint and dirty finger marks, they were hers and no one else had any rights to them at all. At nine-thirty she remembered that the flat was rented and therefore the walls weren't hers; they were her landlord's. After eleven hours of mourning something that didn't exist, Sarah was manic. She dressed in nothing much and hit the skankiest bar in Parramatta.

The place was half full with bikers and wanna-be bikers, loud drunks, nodding junkies, and drug dealers who stayed perfectly sober to ensure they never got taken advantage of. There were few women and none who looked able to walk without assistance. Every person capable of seeing was staring at Sarah with hostility or desire or both. She sat at the bar alongside a biker with a greying ponytail and beard. He did not bother to conceal the fact he was staring at her breasts, nor did he hide his sneer. Sarah ordered a tequila shot. The biker paid. The knuckles of his left hand said F U C K.

'Fuck what?'

He held his right fist in front of her face. L I F E it said.

'*Fuck life*? What is that supposed to mean? You want to be dead? Because that's easy to accomplish if you really want to. Or is fuck a positive word in this context? Like you want to fuck life because you love it so damn much?'

The biker appeared to have not heard her. He nodded at the bartender and another tequila appeared in front of Sarah. She drank it down.

'Thank you. But do you genuinely think I'm going to screw some neanderthal who gets meaningless tough guy phrases tattooed on his big hairy hands just because he buys me a couple of drinks?'

A third drink was placed on the bar. 'Can you speak at all?' Sarah asked. 'You're not like a deaf mute or something?'

'Fucking talkative cunts like you make me wish I was.'

Sarah shivered. 'Well now, that's just rude. I'll be leaving now. Thanks for the drinks.'

She walked out of there fast, shaky with anticipation, nauseous with fear. As she rounded the corner of the pub she heard the door slam and then heavy, unhurried footsteps. She walked slower and did not look back. The footsteps got closer. A hand closed on her neck, and she very nearly came on the spot.

He pushed her up against an industrial sized waste bin, face first. Her lips touched cold metal and under her cheek was something sticky, but warm. The smell of rotting vegetables and cat piss got in her throat and made her dry retch. Something ran over her left foot, and she remembered the giant rats she had seen skittering under the outdoor dumpster at the restaurant.

'Tell me, why would a sweet little girl like you walk into a place like this and start coming on to a bloke like me?'

He held her head firmly, so when she opened her mouth to speak it filled with the bitter taste of whatever had last been spilt down the side of the dumpster. 'I just wanted a quiet drink,' she said, trying to keep her mouth closed. 'I can't help it if some fat old dumbfuck deludes himself that I'm interested in him.'

He pulled her head back and then slammed it into the dumpster. 'You know what I do to smart arses, girl?

Sarah spat blood; it caught on her chin and dribbled on to her chest. 'Fuck them with your hairy little pin dick?'

'You got the first bit right.' She felt the cold night air on the back of her legs as he pulled at her skirt and underpants. He grunted and pushed, and Sarah bit her tongue. She had not been expecting such a violent and complete entry. The tears streamed out of her eyes, and mixed with whatever was on the side of the dumpster. She tasted metal, and dirt, and something that might have once been chilli. She could hear, from the window over their heads, glasses clinking, and a woman yelling that Carlos was a fucking faggot. Metres away, on the other side of the dumpster, the local toughs revved their engines as they dragged each other off at the traffic lights. Above all, she could hear grunting and the smacking of flesh.

He finished and pulled out with as little care as he had entered. 'Happy now?' he said, zipping his pants and gasping for air.

'Ecstatic.' Sarah said.

She pulled up her underwear, wiped her face on her sleeve, and then vomited all over his boots.

On Sunday night, Sarah went to the local Leagues Club where the Under-17s were celebrating the day's win. Her initial target was the coach, a fat, red-faced man with missing front teeth, but he threw up on the bar and was booted out, leaving Sarah alone with ten over-excited sixteen-year-old boys. She woke the next morning with a throbbing head, an aching jaw and red raw thighs. Four pairs of muddy football socks were draped over her bed head and her sheets were stinking and stiff. She wished she could remember how the socks and the stains came to be there, but her memory of the night ended with her being carried into her flat by a blur of boys.

She went to uni but couldn't concentrate, so she spent the morning working out at the uni gym. Around twelve, she passed out and dropped a dumbbell on a beefy bloke's foot. Sarah and the beefy bloke staggered together to the nurse's office where his foot got strapped up, and Sarah was told she was underweight and hypoglycaemic. Then the beefy bloke took Sarah back to his dorm and had sex with her. Sarah fainted again half way through, and the bloke was kind enough to stop and feed her some apple juice so she could continue.

The rest of the week was similarly filled with obsessive behaviour calculated to cancel out thought. During the day, Sarah swam laps, jumped hurdles, scrubbed floors and ceilings, read Sartre's *Nausea* in French, and worked extra shifts at the steakhouse. At night she screwed the worst men she could find. Over the course of the week she had sex with a one-armed door-to-door charity collector, a taxi driver who charged her full fare to drive her home afterwards, and a semi-famous ageing football hero who made her chant his on-field nickname the whole time he screwed her. On the Friday night, wanting to really push the boundaries of compulsive, disgusting sex, she went to a gay bar in North Sydney. By the time she fell into bed at nine o'clock on Saturday morning she had blown two gay men and pulled off a third.

She was frustrated to find that she still thought of Daniel as she drifted off to sleep. The week of manic behaviour had failed to stop her craving that ridiculous old man. She wished there was something she could take, some drug, that would cure her of her need to have him. She had taken everything she could get her hands on, and she still wanted him. She had even resorted to the pills she'd sworn she would never touch, the ones that had nearly killed her.

That was when she was seventeen and hanging with a DJ named Todd who had filthy orange dreadlocks and a body sculpted by God himself. Sarah took the first pill because he slipped it under her tongue while he was kissing her. After Sarah had swallowed the tablet she was able to dance behind his mixing deck for thirty hours straight.

The pills became a must. Her HSC was approaching and the study load combined with waitressing meant that sleep was a rare and brief luxury. She couldn't afford the pills since she was barely making rent, and so not for the first or last time in her life, Sarah became selective about the men she slept with. It was never a straightforward transaction, never prostitution exactly. It was just that instead of choosing the guy with the cutest arse or wildest moves, she chose the guys who would dose her up before she did them.

She started needing the pills just to get out of bed in the morning. She began to let Todd and his grimy, raver mates stay at her flat so that there was always someone around to get her buzzing. It got to the point where Sarah had to kick someone out of her bed most nights and sometimes she was too tired and so just slept alongside the body of a drug fucked stranger.

One night she was up late studying and heard a noise like a cat being strangled, coming from her bedroom. She stumbled into the room, in a rage at being interrupted and at being so fucking exhausted even though she had taken more pills than usual that day. Todd was in bed with a naked bald woman, who had a needle hanging out of her left arm. Sarah closed the door and slept that night on the sofa.

The next day she confessed all to Jamie, who got his brother and father to come around and evict the squatters from her flat. Then Jamie sat next to Sarah for two days while she swore and sweated and vomited. When the worst had passed he cooked for her, and fed her, and when she began to panic he stroked her hair and read her study notes out loud so that she wouldn't get behind in her exam preparations. He even paid her rent for the week that she was too sick to go to work. She swore to him that she would never do such a thing to herself again.

But this week she had tried her hardest to do just that. She had taken the pink pills in the hope they would make her feel like she did back then, which was like she didn't care about anything except more pills. It didn't work of course. Not the pills or the pot or the coke or the booze or the sex could stop her wanting Daniel. She saw now how ridiculous it was to have thought they would. If eight years of losing herself to men and drugs hadn't crushed the desire for Daniel, one more fucked up week wasn't going to do it. The thing to do was accept it. Plunge the needle into her arm. But first, she had to sleep.

Persistent knocking woke her. She stumbled to the front door, still wearing her fag-hag outfit of leather mini-skirt and gold bra. Daniel was standing on her doorstep, his eyes bright and his face flushed. He grabbed her by the shoulders and kissed her hard, her back up against the door frame, his whole body pressed into hers.

'God, you feel wonderful,' he murmured into her throat. 'Are you ready to go?'

Sarah stepped away and wiped her mouth, trying to pull herself together. He was staring at her. 'Did you just get in?'

'I don't know. What time is it?' She still felt fuzzy from all the shit she had taken last night. It was so good to see him, but it was such an effort not to pass out.

Daniel pushed her inside and closed the front door. His eyes scanned the room, then returned to her and narrowed. 'Did you wear that out?'

Sarah struck what she thought was a sexy pose. 'You like?

'It's appalling. And you've spilt something on your top.'

Sarah looked down and laughed. 'Oh, look at that, will you? I didn't notice that before. That's what you get for giving blowjobs in dark alleyways, huh?'

His fist struck the underside of her chin, and she went flying through the hallway and landed on the kitchen floor. She sat up carefully, registering pain in her left hip and elbow. Daniel was standing over her. Sarah took his outstretched hand, but when she was halfway up, he let go and she went crashing onto the kitchen tiles. She pulled herself to her knees and looked up at him just in time to see his shoe make contact with her right shoulder. She fell again and this time she stayed down, crying into the floor.

Daniel nudged her with his foot. 'Get up.'

'Fuck you.'

He kicked her in the ribs. 'Up.'

Sarah sat up, leaning against the kitchen bench for balance. Daniel squatted in front of her and took her chin in his hands. 'Are you on drugs?' he said, sounding like he was her father or something. Sounding like he was her goddamn *teacher*.

'Sure,' she said. 'Isn't everybody?'

Daniel shook her head in his hands. 'What have you taken?'

'Just, um, just some E, and, ah, uppers, and, oh, lots of vodka, some pot.'

'Are you straight enough to talk to me?'

'Why would I want to talk to you? You're a fucking psycho bully. You like beating me up, that's all.' Sarah started to cry. 'You say all this shit, like you love me, like you care about me, but then you hurt me and make me cry, and leave me alone for a whole week.'

'Who did you give a blowjob to?'

'Aren't you listening? I've had it with you! I'm not answering your stupid questions anymore. You can fuck off.'

Daniel leant forward and softly kissed her lips. Then he took out a handkerchief and wiped her face. She cried harder, but he kept kissing her and wiping her nose until she had exhausted herself. Then he guided her head down on to his lap and stroked her hair.

'I'm sorry. You're not in any state to talk to me at the moment. You're clearly still under the influence of something, and it's unreasonable of me to expect you to talk sense.'

'It's unreasonable to expect anything when you've just beaten the shit out of me.'

He rubbed her hair. 'Don't exaggerate. I barely touched you. You've obviously taken something that heightens sensation. Just lie here and calm down a minute.'

Sarah lay quietly. It was true she was high still, and she was sleep deprived and probably suffering from adrenal exhaustion from all the stress, but she wasn't delusional. He had belted her around, and she had not exaggerated that.

After a little while, he told her to go and clean herself up. When she came back out, showered and dressed in pyjamas, he presented her with a cup of coffee and a plate of vegemite toast. 'You look like you haven't eaten for a week.'

Sarah took his offerings and sat on the floor. She was too sore to sit straight in a wooden chair. He sat beside her and took a finger of toast from the plate.

'I'm not ready to go with you,' Sarah said, when his mouth was full.

He swallowed and smiled at her. 'I won't take no for an answer.'

'I'm not saying no. I'm saying that it isn't going to happen today. I have stuff to sort out.'

'I can't allow that, Sarah. This week has been a new kind of hell. I hated being apart from you, but I comforted myself with the thought that you were preparing to be with me. Now I find you've been running around doing God knows what with God knows who.'

'I never promised to be chaste. You volunteered for abstinence; I didn't.'

'I never said that. I said I wouldn't sleep with you until you moved in with me, and in the meantime, *you* had to stop sleeping around. I've been going at it like you wouldn't believe.'

She put down the half-eaten slice of toast. 'Are you saying that to hurt me?'

'No, if I wanted to hurt you I'd do this.' Daniel pinched her on the inside of the elbow where it really stung.

She pulled her arm away. 'Did you have sex last night?'

'Yes.'

Sarah recoiled as though he had pinched her again. 'Who with?'

He shook his head at her. His forehead was creased and between his eyebrows there were three deep vertical furrows. Sometimes he looked at her as though she was still a student, young and bright and so in awe of him that she would take whatever he said as law. Sometimes she felt like she was. Well, Mr Carr, of course you can kiss me, and of course, you can touch me there, if you'd like. And yes, Sir, if you say that it is true it is, and what you say is right must surely be, and I always thought that it would be wrong to let a man open my veins with his teeth and bleed me dry, but if you say that I should then I will.

'Answer me. Who are you fucking?' She forced herself to hold his gaze.

'A young woman named Tricia,' he said. 'Among others.'

'Among…' Sarah pressed her hand to her throbbing right temple. 'How many others?'

'There are a few I choose from. Depends what mood I'm in and who's available. And how much I'm willing to spend.'

Vomit rose in her throat. She swallowed it down. 'You've been fucking prostitutes?'

'Yes, Sarah.'

'This whole time you've been–' Sarah got to her feet, stumbled to the bathroom, and vomited into the toilet. The small bit of toast she had eaten came up undigested. She drank some water straight from the tap, vomited it back into the sink, had another drink, washed her face and returned to Daniel.

He was sitting cross-legged, looking up at her. 'Are you okay?'

'Just hungover.' Sarah sat down and lit a smoke to get rid of the sour taste in her mouth. 'So you have to pay for it, huh?'

'I choose to. I don't want to spend months wining and dining a woman just to get one night of sex.' Daniel smiled conspiratorially. 'It's only a convenience until I have my girl with me.'

Sarah watched him through the smoke. He was so goddamn calm. He was so fucking sure of himself. She had to maintain the shred of dignity she had left. 'So,' she said, in the most casual tone she could muster, 'what do you do with them?'

'I have sex with them.'

'Just straight sex?'

He laughed. 'Whatever that is.'

'What are they like?'

'They're normal women, just doing their job.'

'What do they look like? The one last night, what did she look like?'

'Bleached blonde, nice body, younger than me, but older than she claimed to be.'

Sarah's façade of indifference was dissolving. She fought to keep her voice in control and to keep her hands still. 'Nice body? What does that mean? Big tits and long legs?'

'It doesn't matter, Sarah.'

'It does matter that you choose whores who look like your wife. It's really *telling* that you choose ones who look nothing like me.'

He stood up and walked to the window over the sofa. 'I'll start requesting scrawny, ugly brunettes if it will make you feel better.'

Sarah ignored his insult. 'I insist that you stop.'

'You don't get to insist anything.' He slammed his fist into the boarded up window, then turned back to face her. 'You think you have the power, but you don't. I can take you any time I choose, just pick you up and carry you home and tie you up. You'll see no one but me forever, until you die.'

'Go ahead. Here I am. Take me.'

Daniel turned back to the window, leaning his forehead against the chipboard. Sarah had meant what she said; she genuinely wished he would abduct her. She wanted the choice to be taken out of her hands. She wanted to feel the total freedom of being owned.

'I hoped I wouldn't have to. I hoped you'd come voluntarily, that you'd want to come.'

'I do want to.' Sarah went to him, kissing the back of his freshly shaved neck. 'The thing is, I've managed to make this life. It's not all that great, but it's mine. Like the song, you know, I've done it *my way*.'

'The Sex Pistols version, I assume?'

'There's another version?'

'I love you.'

'I love you. Why is this so hard? Why can't we just be together? Why can't we just... why can't we stop all this talking and just be happy?'

'I don't want you to be happy with anything except me.' Daniel turned around. He was crying. 'I want you to give up your little life. I want you to have nothing. I want you to be completely helpless. I want you to be scared and broken and shaking with fear.'

Sarah was crying too. 'You're so fucking romantic.'

'Little Sarah Clark.' Daniel ran his neat nails down the side of throat. 'I think we've both had enough of this tension, this struggle. Tell me now, are you going to come and live with me? Are you going to be mine?'

'I've told you yes. I just need–'

'No.' His nails dug in. 'No more waiting.'

Sarah looked into his eyes and wished he would be a little gentler on her, a little weaker. She knew he wished she would be harder, stronger. That was almost funny because every man who had ever been involved with Sarah had told her she was not soft enough. She didn't know if Daniel brought out her softness, or if he was so hard that she just seemed weak in comparison.

'I have to see Jamie.'

'I understand. I'll come back tonight.' Daniel kissed her forehead and was gone.

9

On a Saturday morning, three weeks after Jamie had last seen Sarah, Mike called and asked him to come to the pub. He said they needed to talk about Sarah. Jamie didn't want to talk about Sarah; he wanted to talk *to* Sarah, but since she had stopped answering her phone he decided that talking about her to Mike would have to do.

'What I want to know,' Mike said when they were seated in a booth with a couple of beers, 'is what have I done to piss her off?'

'I don't think you've done anything to piss her off.'

'Well why the hell won't she see me? Why isn't she answering her phone?'

'She won't see or talk to anyone except the bloke she's in love with.'

Mike stared at him for several seconds. Then he took a drink of beer, lit a cigarette, drank some more, and then scratched his nose. 'What bloke?'

'This old fucker. She's serious about him. True love and all that.'

Mike looked dejected. 'When did this happen?'

'When she was a kid.'

'What?'

Jamie shrugged. 'Nothing. I think it was my birthday. I think she went home with him on my birthday.'

'Right, so that was… that's only a month ago. I've been fucking her for six months; she can't just ditch me for some blow in.'

Jamie laughed. 'Right, you have seniority.'

Mike frowned as though he knew he was being made fun of but he wasn't sure how. 'Well, yeah, I do. Both of us screw around, but all the others are one-nighters. Six months is a long time for us. Me and Sarah have something special; we made a commitment.'

Jamie stopped laughing. Something was very wrong. He'd been expecting Mike to talk about how horny he was, or how angry he was that Sarah hadn't even given him a good excuse. He expected bitching and complaining. Mike was genuinely distressed. And what the fuck did he mean by a *commitment*?

'Um, what kind of commitment?'

Mike leant across the table. 'A few months ago Jess went on this training seminar for work and Sarah came to stay with me. We had two days together and it was…' Mike raked his fingers through his hair. 'Jamie, man, it was the best fucking weekend of my life. We did it in every room of the house, we did it in every position known to man and then invented some new ones. She let me do things that I've only ever done with a highly paid professional.' He stopped to sip his beer. 'We talked about how cool it was to find someone else who's into freaky stuff. When you're just picking up a stranger for casual sex you can't very well ask them to… well, anyway, we agreed that what we had was special and that from then on we would be body fluid monogamous.'

Jamie's tongue was stuck to the roof of his mouth. If he moved it he would be able to open his mouth, and then he would scream and scream and not be able to stop. He kept it there and raised his eyebrows questioningly at Mike.

'You know,' Mike said, scratching his neck, 'we agreed to stop using condoms on the condition that we would always use them with other people. I know it sounds tacky, but it wasn't. It was… I hate saying it, but it was really romantic. You have to have a lot of trust in someone to not use protection these days. Me and Sarah have that trust, man.'

Jamie stared at Mike's face and neck. He had been scratching the whole time he talked and now his skin was streaked with red. For Mike, Sarah was a plague of crawling, burrowing insects. The infestation had entered via his genitals and nested under his skin, eating at his gut, blocking his airways, nibbling the edges of his heart. The poor bugger could claw at himself until his flesh was red raw, he could scrape his skin right off, and he wouldn't be able to get her out, because she went so deep. She got into the very core of you. Once she was in, you couldn't get rid of her without a hell of a lot of damage to the supporting structure.

'Well I'm not taking it. If she wants to end it then fine, but she has to at least tell me herself. I shouldn't have to hear this shit from you.' Mike rubbed his hand over his nose six or seven times. 'I'm just gonna go over to her place and demand that she talks to me. I'm not gonna take this shit.'

'She won't listen. You should see this bloke. He's about a hundred, and he's really smooth, really fucking... cold. Sarah's out of her mind about him.'

Mike sniffed, rubbed his nose, scratched his neck. 'You've met him?'

Jamie snorted. 'Yeah. He was my year nine English teacher. *Our* year nine English teacher'

Mike stared at Jamie. 'You shitting me?'

'Ask Jess. Ask her about Mr Carr. She'll tell you about how he suddenly pissed off part way through the year. And how right around that time Sarah stopped eating, and started drinking and smoking and fucking everything in pants.'

Mike didn't believe him. Jamie told him the whole story, or at least as much of the story as he knew. By the end, Mike was plotting Daniel Carr's murder. Jamie didn't care about causing trouble or invading Sarah's privacy or protecting her honour. She was in danger, and since Jamie had been banned – on threat of divorce – from seeing Sarah alone, and since Sarah would not answer her phone and talk to him, Mike was possibly the best chance Jamie had of rescuing Sarah from herself.

'Let's go. We'll bang on her door until she lets us in,' Mike said.

Jamie had considered doing the same thing about a million times. The reason he didn't was that he didn't – at this time – want to be divorced. Also, there was a certain danger in turning up at Sarah's uninvited; last time Mike did it he got a naked giant and a broken nose. He gave Mike this last reason, and not a hint of the first.

'So what?' Mike said. 'It's not going to be a calm conversation anyway is it?'

Jamie wavered. His need to see her was like a burn, but he didn't want to piss her off. Turning up uninvited would piss her off, and turning up uninvited with Mike would piss her off even more. Also, Mike would assert his right to touch her and Jamie would have to sit quietly and watch Mike's hands go all the places that *his* hands should be going.

'We could try and call her again,' Jamie suggested.

Mike thumped the table with both fists, drained his beer and picked up his car keys. 'Fuck that. We'll just go and talk to her.'

'I'll try one more time.'

Mike thumped the table again, but did not argue. He bit his lip and scratched his arm with his keys as he watched Jamie dial.

Jamie was not expecting her to answer; it was more a stalling tactic. He had rushed into giving Mike all the information, thinking it was best to build an army of defence against old Mr Carr, but already he was doubting the wisdom of that move. There was Shelley to consider, although if went to see Sarah with Mike he would not *really* be breaking his promise. But if he went to see Sarah with Mike, there would be no way to talk to her properly.

And she would hate Jamie for involving Mike in all this. Jamie hated himself for involving Mike in all this. Except he needed him to… oh, fuck. It was never-ending.

'Hello?' Sarah's voice, husky and a little anxious.

Jamie nearly dropped the phone. His stomach turned to soup.

'Daniel?' she said.

Oh God. 'It's me, Sar.'

A beat. 'Hi, you. How've you been?'

'I've been worried about you. You okay?' Jamie was going to just burst. Mike was gesturing wildly. Jamie turned away and looked out over the car park.

'Yeah. I was going to call you. It's funny you called, because I was going to call you in like, five minutes.'

'I've been calling all week, Sarah.'

'Oh.' He heard the click of her lighter. 'Look, can you come over? I need to see you.'

'Now?' Jamie said, forgetting Shelley and Mike and everything else that didn't matter. Remembering soft skin, blue eyes, ticklish feet. 'I can come right now.'

'Now would be perfect.'

'On my way.' Jamie hung up, elated at his success.

'Well done, my friend.' Mike punched Jamie in the arm.

Jamie hit himself in the head with the phone repeatedly. When he'd finished he had to run to catch up with Mike who was already climbing into his car.

Although it was past midday, Sarah answered the door in her pink flannelette pyjamas. The bags under her eyes were worse than Jamie had ever seen them. Sallow skin, chapped lips, a tan bruise over her right eyebrow. She was messy and unbelievably, overwhelmingly pretty.

'What's he doing here?' Sarah said, peering over Jamie's shoulder. 'Mike, what are you doing here?'

Mike stepped forward, nudging Jamie aside. 'Can't you even pretend to be happy to see me?'

She grabbed Jamie's hand and pulled him close. She smelt sour, like she'd been sick. Jamie kissed her forehead, cradling the back of her precious head. She whimpered, which was so strange, then gripped him harder. 'Why'd you bring him? I needed to talk to you alone.'

'Can you please not talk about me as though I'm not standing right here?'

Sarah sighed, releasing Jamie and turning to Mike. 'I need to talk to Jamie alone.'

'Why are you giving me the brush off?'

'I really don't have time to explain.'

'Make time. I deserve an explanation.'

Sarah turned to Jamie and pulled a face, then went to Mike and put her hands on his shoulders. She was so short that her arms were stretched to their full length. 'You're right. We do need to talk, and I promise we will, but not now. Right now I need to talk to Jamie alone.'

Mike lifted Sarah's hands off his shoulders and brought them together, pressed between his own. He bent and kissed her lips. Sarah kissed him back, pressing herself into him. This was exactly what Jamie had hoped to avoid: being a witness to the touching reunion between the lovers.

'Please, Mike?' she said in her *fuck me* voice. 'Leave us alone for a couple of hours, okay? When you come back I'll give you my full attention.'

Mike nodded, touching her face in a way that could only be described as tender. 'Promise you won't brush me off again?'

'Promise.'

'Alright, babe.' Mike kissed her again, then came over to Jamie and slapped him on the back. 'I'll head back to the pub. Be back in a couple of hours.' He opened the door then turned back with a grin. 'Be good, kids.'

Sarah and Jamie stood staring at each other until they heard Mike's engine kicking over. Then Jamie wrapped his arms around her and started crying.

'Oh, heh! Oh, don't cry. Come on, Jamie, please.' Sarah kissed his neck and face. He couldn't stop sobbing. She was just so... God, there were no words. She was *everything*. 'Stop this nonsense.' She pulled away and wiped his face off with her pyjama sleeve. 'Come and talk to me.'

He sat with her on the sofa. The sofa he had found for her at a garage sale and helped her carry home. The sofa he had drunk a thousand beers and had a million conversations and not enough sex on. Sarah's sofa. Sarah's flat. Sarah's smile and Sarah's hands turning his over.

'Didn't need stitches?' she said.

Jamie shook his head, turning toward the window and noticing it had a board across it. He wondered if Sarah had done that herself or if *he* had done it for her.

'Do you know how mental I've been going?' Jamie said.

'I'm sorry. If it makes you feel any better, I've been going mental too.'

'The only thing that would make me feel better is hearing you say that you've broken up with old *whatsisname*.'

Sarah bit her lip. She looked so tired, poor darling. God only knew what that monster had been doing to her.

'I hoped you might have gotten a bit used to the idea,' she said.

'I'll never be used to it. He's bad for you.'

Sarah's eyes flashed. 'You're wrong. When I'm not with him, it's bad. I feel bad. I love him. Why can't you be happy for me?'

'I just can't.'

'Try!' Sarah squeezed his hands. 'You're being so selfish, Jamie. You have a whole family. I've never had anyone. Now I do, and you're all angry and mean.'

He *was* angry and mean. But not with Sarah so much as every one in the world who wasn't Sarah. Shelley especially had been copping it. Despite her superhuman tolerance, they were fighting all the time. Just yesterday she had asked why he was so grumpy when she was the one with cracked nipples and swollen ankles and no sleep. Jamie reminded her that he also got up several times a night to soothe the baby and he had to go to work for eight hours every day. Then he said that her cracked nipples and swollen ankles were no treat for him either. Shelley cried for an hour after that one, and Jamie tried to work out what the fuck was wrong with him. He realised that no matter how hard he tried to be a good husband, the fact was that he looked at Shelley and didn't see what he wanted to see, which was Sarah.

He couldn't help thinking that if Shelley had not fallen pregnant then he wouldn't have had to marry her and then he would've been able to marry Sarah. It wasn't logical, because a) Sarah had only shown an interest in him after he moved in with Shelley, and therefore may have never started sleeping with him in the first place if Shelley hadn't got pregnant; b) Sarah didn't want to get married; and c) even if Sarah did want get married it would never be to Jamie, because she didn't love him *in that way*. He used to take comfort in the fact that Sarah didn't love anyone *in that way*, but that comfort was gone because now she did, and Jamie was frozen out and haunted by a train of thought that he knew was ridiculous but which wouldn't stop. He hated Shelley, and he hated himself, and he hated Daniel Carr, and sometimes he even hated Bianca. He never hated Sarah but he was aware that he certainly should.

'I'm moving into his place,' Sarah said in the kind of mock-cheerful voice that people used when they were telling you bad news but wanted you to think it was good.

'When?'

She mumbled something that sounded like 'today.' 'When?' he asked again.

She spoke more clearly. 'Today.'

'Today.' Jamie stared at her fingers. Her nails were bitten to the quick, like his. But Sarah had never been a nail biter; she always trimmed and filed them so there was a perfect white moon at each tip.

'Well, tonight.'

'Tonight?'

'Yeah, so… I have to pack, I have to be ready.'

'You have to be ready.' Jamie continued to stare at those ragged fingernails. They were the nails of an anxious, frustrated, impotent person. The nails of a person just hanging on.

'Stop repeating everything I say!'

Jamie looked up. 'I didn't realise I was.'

'Yeah, well…' Sarah half-smiled into his eyes. 'You okay?'

'Sure. Why wouldn't I be?'

Sarah kissed him then. Soft, sweet, so gentle, so warm. For so many years of his life he'd dreamt of kisses like this. He'd watched her sitting in class and he'd thought about her touching his chin and leaning in with her lips parted. He'd watched her playing soccer and running the Cross Country and swimming in the carnival and had imagined what her natural, joyous athleticism would mean to a boy she loved. He'd seen men grope and pull and prod her, and he imagined how differently he would treat her. He swore that if he had her, he would never treat her roughly. If he ever got that lucky, he would never, ever hurt her, not even in an act of passion.

Fast forward through his dreamy aching teens, and now he was a man, and he'd had Sarah many times. Many times in many ways and he had still never hurt her, although he understood what drove men to do that. Sarah controlled men with her too-soft hair and her clever lips and her insatiable cunt. She made her men feel simultaneously grateful and exploited. And she was so cavalier, so damn *haughty*, that you wanted to make her take you seriously. There was an instinctual need to show her that she had met her match, that you were a stronger, better man, the likes of which she had never come across; you were a man who could make *her* beg *you*. When you had her in your arms you wanted to know that behind the armour of her technique, underneath the roar of her shameless mouth, she was in awe of you. It was a strong, strong drive, and Jamie felt it now like he'd felt it every time she'd touched him.

But he was different to other men. He had been privileged enough to know her when she was brave and sweet and well-fed. He had known her before she'd been screwed, and that made all the difference. It was why he would never hurt her, why he would never let his lust, or his vanity, take control. He would always kiss her like this – *exactly like this now* – because whatever that animal had tricked her into thinking, real love was not selfish and cruel. Real love should draw no blood from the loved and buckets from the lover.

'Why do you have to go?' Jamie asked, still kissing her.

'It's just the way it is.'

Jamie started to cry again and it was like she didn't notice, except, he knew she did. She just wasn't the type of girl to draw attention to pain. She just kept right on kissing him, rubbing his lower back, then the skin above his waistband. Rubbing and kissing, ignoring the hot wet tears that were sticking her eyelashes to his cheeks.

'Where is he taking you?'

'Not far.'

Jamie kept crying, taking off her shirt and pants, helping her with his, kissing her softly in between the unbuttoning and the sleeve pulling and the underwear peeling.

'I'll still be able to see you, won't I?'

Sarah answered with a gasp. She had wriggled her way under him and without really meaning to, Jamie had pushed inside her. He briefly worried that this was the last time he would ever make love to her, but the thought slipped away rapidly. The world was Sarah's flesh clenching his. Everything that wasn't her was incomprehensible, but he intuited that the answers lay somewhere at the end. Surely this unspeakable urge had a purpose beyond physical satiation. Surely there had to be the meaning of life or the secret to inner peace or the key to her heart waiting for him at the end.

There was no revelation. There was just the too brief feeling of peace, and then there was Sarah, as unfathomable as always, smiling up at him, stroking his shoulder blades and his back. He asked if she wanted him to get off and she said *never*.

'Sar, what I asked before, about still being able to see you...'

'Nothing in the world could stop me seeing my Jamie-boy,' she said, but her body had tensed beneath him, and her tone was all wrong. It was that mock-cheerfulness again.

'So nothing will change?'

Silence. Sad eyed, stiff-armed silence.

'Sar?'

'No, things will change. What's the point otherwise?'

Jamie felt himself shrinking out of her. He tried to press back in but it was too late. He would never again be inside Sarah Clark's body. He realised it didn't matter all that much, not compared to the prospect of never seeing her at all. He would gladly give up sex forever if it meant he could talk to her at least every second day.

'So no more of this stuff?'

'No more of this stuff.' Sarah tickled his back. 'One of the few things about my life I'll miss.'

'Sure.'

'It's true. In fact, all of the things I'll miss are all of the things I do with you.' Her eyes widened, moistened, blinked. 'Do you have any idea how important you are to me? When I think about not having you, I can hardly breathe. You look at me with that hang-dog face, all rejected and sorry for yourself, and I don't think you understand that giving you up is the hardest, worst, most painful thing I've ever had to do and am ever likely to do.'

Jamie climbed off her, pushing away the warmth of her flattery and processing the cold message beneath. *Giving you up Not having you All the things I'll miss…*

'I'm never going to see you again, am I?' he said, picking up his clothing, putting his physical self back together.

'Never say never,' Sarah said, and laughed horribly.

'This was a goodbye fuck?'

'I thought you knew that.'

Jamie forced himself to look at her. She was still naked, sprawled out shamelessly. She was lighting a cigarette, as she always did. As he would never see her do again.

'I thought it was a goodbye to fucking fuck. I didn't know it was a goodbye everything, have a nice life fuck. I had no idea you were that insane. I had no idea you were going to give up ten years of friendship over a crazy old man who belts the crap out of you.'

She flinched, then shook her head as if to clear it away. 'We'll see each other, Jamie. It'll just be less often. It'll be twice as sweet for being twice as rare.'

He thought for a minute that he would scream. He turned away and reached for his shoes, glad for the concentration required to untangle the hastily untied laces. 'Okay, Sarah. Just write down the phone number and address and I'll call you in a couple of days. Maybe me and Shell can come over for dinner once you've settled in.'

'Jamie, I don't think–'

'Yeah, I don't think Shelley would want to hang out with a middle aged teacher either. I'll just come around and we'll have a drink or something.'

Sarah touched his shoulder but he kept his eyes on his feet. 'I think it's better if I call you. I don't think Daniel will–'

'Yeah, alright, cool. You'll call me whenever.' His shoes were on. He had no more reasons to be sitting here. 'I'll catch you later then. Thanks for the root.' He stood up.

'Jamie!' Sarah jumped in front of him, naked and wild-eyed. 'How can you be so calm?'

'I don't know. How can you be so cruel?'

Sarah reached for him but he stepped out of her way. If she touched him, he would shatter.

'I can't let you leave like this.'

'Why not? It's not forever is it? I mean, we'll see each other all the time. You're going to call me.' Jamie started walking. Step after step after step.

'Yes, yes, I am, Jamie. You know I love you, right? You know I'm going to call you as soon as I can?' Her voice already sounded far away. She was already a memory. Less than that, she was a memory of a dream he had once. A nice dream, while it lasted.

10

Sarah showered with the water as hot as she could stand it. Her hangover was worse than it had been this morning, the places Daniel had hit and kicked her were beginning to throb, and on top of all that, she could not stop shaking. The hot water was supposed to calm her, but it just made her sicker and shakier. She got out of the shower, threw up nothing, splashed her face with cold water and got dressed.

She was drinking coffee and trembling, trying to get it together enough to start packing, when Mike returned. 'Bloody hell, I've missed you,' he said, putting his arms around her. 'What's wrong, babe? You cold or something?'

Sarah ducked out of his embrace. 'I'm fine. I don't have much time though, so –'

'I see.' Mike sat down on the sofa so he was looking up at her. 'What's going on?'

'With what?'

'With us.'

'Oh, well, nothing. We used to fuck and now we don't.'

His face crumpled up for a second, then quickly smoothed out. 'Jamie said you've hooked up with someone.'

She sighed and sat down beside him. 'Yeah.'

'Is it true he's your old teacher?'

She nodded and Mike clicked his tongue. A habit that made Sarah want to cut it off. Mike lit a smoke and offered it to Sarah; she waved it away and got one for herself.

'Jamie said he slaps you around.'

'J–' Sarah's throat closed over. She cleared it with a painful cough and tried again. 'He finds it hard to be objective. He takes everything the wrong way.'

'Who does? Jamie?'

'Yeah.'

Mike squinted at her through the smoke. 'You're being evasive, Sarah. Does this bloke belt you up, or what?'

'No.'

Mike's eyes screwed up so tightly that they almost disappeared and his bottom lip trembled like a naughty child. 'I suppose you got that bruise on your forehead from walking into a door?'

Sarah resisted the urge to cover the bruise with her hand. 'I have no idea how I got it. I've had a hell of a week.'

'Yeah, sure, whatever.' Mike leant across her to stub his cigarette out in the overflowing ashtray. 'So you're full on with this fella and that means we're done?'

'Yes.'

Mike scratched his neck hard enough for pink streaks to appear. 'You suddenly believe in monogamy?'

'Not at all. I'll continue to fuck whomever I like, whenever I like. It's just that my first choice for who has always been him, and once I'm living with him the when will be all the bloody time, and therefore, I don't see where I'd find the time, or have the need, to fuck you or anyone else.'

'You've gone mental.'

'Call it that if you want. I love him. He's everything I've ever wanted.'

'Great, I'm really fucking happy for you.'

Sarah reached for his hand, pulling it away from his throat. She was afraid he'd gouge a hole otherwise. His hand was hot and sticky, his face mottled red and white. Sarah was aware for the first time that the man sitting across from her had feelings.

'I'm sorry, Mike, but I really have a lot to do. I have to pack and call the real estate and–'

To Sarah's astonishment, Mike's eyes filled with tears. He squeezed his eyes shut, but the tears trickled out from under his lids, some getting caught on his lashes before breaking free again and soaking into the stubble on his jaw. Sarah was sure that if she saw one more man crying today she would murder him.

'Mike…' She had no words to comfort him with. She didn't even *like* him. The only thing they'd ever had in common was a penchant for rough sex. Fully clothed, vulnerable, *weeping,* Sarah just wanted him gone.

'What if I left Jess?' he said, pressing his eyes with the backs of his hands.

'That's a ridiculous thing to say. Pull yourself together.'

He looked at her in a way that made her skin crawl. 'I think I love you, Sarah. I didn't mean to, but I do. I can't believe you're going to–'

Suffocated by his need, Sarah did the only thing she could think of to ease the unbearable intensity. She climbed onto his lap and kissed him. Kissed him as though they were long lost lovers meeting in the middle of a war zone, as though she didn't love Daniel, as though she wasn't aching for Jamie, as though her body and soul weren't worn ragged from a week filled with dodgy sex and nail-biting longing. She kissed him until his emotions subsided and his dick was running the show again.

Mike insisted on a final fuck, and Sarah decided it could only make her feel better. Having Mike slam into her while he shouted obscenities was soothing after the trauma of Jamie's brown eyes asking something of her that she couldn't give.

Sarah had always known instinctively that sex with someone you love is infinitely more painful than even the most physically testing sex with a man you couldn't care less about. But she was suddenly seeing a new and terrifying implication to this rather pedestrian observation. If sex with someone she loved made her feel injured and afraid, and sex with someone dominant and perverse caused her to lose all control of her body, then what the hell was going to happen when Daniel Carr finally fucked her?

It would be like it was back at school, except more so, because this time there would be no legal or moral or social barriers holding them back. There would be no reason to stop. She remembered again the day in the hotel room, how she thought she was going to die in there and didn't care at all so long as he kept doing things to her. That had been eight hours. She tried to imagine what she would be like after two days alone in a room with Daniel. After a week with him she would surely be nothing but a pile of sticky dust. Maybe that was what Jamie sensed. Maybe that was why he'd looked at her like she was already dead.

There was a heavy drumming on the door.

Mike opened his eyes but kept thrusting. Sarah held her breath. The bashing at the door continued. He stopped moving. 'That your door?'

'Sssh.' Sarah said, pressing her hands into Mike's arse to keep him still.

'Sarah!' Daniel's voice called out. 'Open the door.'

Sarah's arms fell to her sides. 'Oh, God. It's him. Mike it's–'

'He can bloody well wait.' Mike started thrusting again.

'You do realise,' Daniel yelled, 'that a person standing on the nature strip can see directly into your living room window?'

'Oh, God,' Sarah said.

'Fuck!' Mike got off her. 'Fucking hell. This is fucking unreal. Unbelievable, just fucking unbelievable. What kind of sick bastard spies on two people fucking? Fucking creep.' Mike pulled on his shorts, yelling abuse in the direction of the door.

Sarah's insides turned to liquid. She was unable to move to stop Mike from walking away and opening the door. It was so bad, so bad and she could not move or speak, only wrap her naked arms around her naked body and wait for him to come and do what he would.

Daniel entered the room. His face was blank. Hovering behind him, Mike was scarlet. 'You can't just walk in and–'

'Get dressed.' Daniel's voice was so calm and quiet that Sarah wondered if she would survive the night. She got up and began to pull on her underwear.

'Who the fuck do you think you are?' Mike said.

'You better go, Mike. I'm sorry.'

'I'm not leaving you alone with this prick.'

Daniel glanced at Mike for half a second before his gaze returned to Sarah. 'He wants to protect you from me. How cute.'

'You're an arsehole, mate.' Mike sat down on the sofa and crossed his arms across his chest. 'I'm not going anywhere.'

Daniel shrugged and turned back to Sarah. 'Let's hurry up and pack your things so we can go.'

'Daniel, I–'

He silenced her with a look, the way teachers are trained to do, grabbed her arm and nodded down the hallway. 'Let's go.'

'Stop telling her what to do!' Mike stood up. 'She's not a fucking child. Sarah? You gonna listen to him?'

Daniel rolled his eyes at Sarah. 'I understand about Jamie, he's been a good friend to you. But this–' he gestured to Mike. 'Why would you let this pretty boy have a poke at you?'

'Yeah, well, he's a friend too, okay? I wanted to say goodbye.'

Daniel looked over at Mike and snorted. 'I hope you don't have too many more friends to farewell. You'll be exhausted before I even get you home.'

'Hey!' Mike was scratching his arms like a junkie. 'Sarah? What's he talking about?'

'Oh.' Daniel smiled, ruffling Sarah's already ruffled hair. 'I assumed he knew about Jamie. I saw them arrive together and thought they were taking it in turns. I thought they must've had an agreement.'

Sarah pulled a face at Daniel, to show him that she did not appreciate his behaviour. He smiled, adorably. Sarah went all mushy and leant up to kiss him. She had missed him in the hours since he'd been gone. That is, the hours he had not been gone at all but had been lurking around the building spying on her. She missed him and loved him and was happy he was claiming her at last. She kissed him, tangling her fingers through his hair.

'Sarah!' Mike stamped his foot. 'Are you screwing Jamie? Is that what this fucker is saying? Is it? Are you?'

'Yeah. I mean, I *was*,' Sarah said into Daniel's eyes. She was going home with him. She was finally, finally going to have him. Why was she still standing here when she could be in his bed? *Their* bed.

'You rotten little slut. You're just completely fucking heartless.'

Daniel laughed, brushing her hair off her forehead. Then he was kissing her hard on the lips and in the background Mike was yelling. The kiss went on and on until she couldn't breathe anymore. Just when she was certain she was going to faint, Daniel released her. Mike was gone.

Part Four

1

Daniel didn't talk in the car. Sarah didn't talk either. She was wondering what he would do to her when they got home. Home. Daniel's home. The home of Daniel and Sarah, not Daniel and Lisa, or Daniel and his family. They were on their way to his home, and he was going to let Sarah stay there, and no one would ever take him away. He was angry with her, but he still wanted her to live in his home, and for that Sarah would happily withstand anything.

He told her to shower and watched to make sure she scrubbed every inch of herself. He did not touch her at all, except to guide her from the shower to the bed and then to fasten her ankles and wrists to the bedposts with red satin ribbons. He left her hair out, dripping wet across the pillow. When he was finished, he stood back and nodded in satisfaction.

'You are so beautiful, my Sarah.' He undressed, not taking his eyes off her.

'You don't have to do this. I want to be here. I'm ready to be here. You don't have to tie me up.'

'Just for a little while, darling.'

'Is this a punishment? For Mike?' Sarah was emboldened by her immobility. It was exciting to be restrained, unable to do what she should, which was fight or run. It was liberating to be excused from action and responsibility and decision.

'I would have thought that being desperate enough to open your legs for a skinny kid like him would have been punishment enough.' Naked, Daniel knelt beside her so that his erection was poking her ear. 'I could see him doing it to you, Sarah. I could see his scrawny back rising and falling in the window and I could see your ankles kicking around. I stood right outside and watched, and I felt sad that you had sunk so low.'

Sarah turned her head to catch him between her lips but he put his hand on her forehead and forced her to lie straight, staring at the ceiling. He straddled her chest, and holding her head in place with his left hand, he worked his right hand up and down his shaft. She struggled against her restraints, and they cut into her flesh; if he noticed he did not react.

'What amazed me was not that you did it, but that you did it so rapidly. It was mere hours since I'd seen you, and only half an hour since poor little Jamie had done his best. You just got straight into it, and I admit that turns me on.' He leant against her forehead harder as his strokes became faster, his knees dug into her ribs. 'I stood outside and watched those kids pounding away and I thought about how silly it was that I've been paying for sex and you've been juggling multiple lovers.' His voice was growing shaky, his breathing irregular. 'We can only satisfy each other can't we, darling? *Oh Christ.* We have only ever been satisfied with each other and – *ah* – we can both whittle our genitals away to nothing by fucking everything that moves, and – *oh oh oh God* – it will never be enough if we're not together. *Oh, dear God!*'

He seemed to be bracing his entire body weight against her forehead, and Sarah was afraid that he might lose control and crush her skull. She told him this, and he did lose control, pressing her head deep into the mattress, calling out to God again and spilling over her face.

Time passed. He cleaned her up and fed her some scotch, but would not let her have any water. He sat on her chest and smoked a cigarette. When she asked for a drag he told her that she could have one when they were done. He did not say when that would be. When she complained of a headache he gave her two small white capsules, washed down with scotch straight from the bottle, and when she said her leg was cramping he massaged it. He talked about his wife and his daughters and his hookers. He did not want Sarah to talk and she did not mind. He masturbated continuously, stopping only to drink or smoke or feed Sarah tablets and alcohol. Each time he came *on* her, never *in* her, and was careful to clean up afterwards. Then he would lie beside her and sleep for a while, his arm covering her chest and his legs bent up and over hers. Sarah slept a bit, but never well. She kept being woken by the sound of his voice or the vibrations of the bed as he crouched over her and tortured her with his ever-renewable, untouchable passion.

As time went on she begged him to enter her, to kiss her or let her kiss him. She couldn't bear the closeness without the closure. Blood dribbled down her inner arms from her efforts to free herself. He licked the blood off, and wiped away her tears, and fed her scotch, but he wouldn't let her touch him, and he wouldn't let her go.

When she had to go to the toilet, he untied her and carried her there and waited right outside the door so he could carry her back to the bed and bind her again. She asked him to tie the ribbons looser this time; he pulled them tighter. She passed out.

And then she was waking up and he was kissing her face.

'Do you love me?' He hovered over her, like a wave cresting.

'So much.'

'Porphyria worshipped me; surprise made my heart swell, and still it grew while I debated what to do. That moment she was mine, mine, fair, perfectly pure and good: I found a thing to do with all her hair.'

'Are you going to strangle me?'

'Not if you don't panic.' His hand closed around her throat and Sarah tried to speak but couldn't. He released his grip. 'If you struggle you will choke. It's that simple. Now be a good girl and lie still.'

He put his hand to her throat again and Sarah closed her eyes and felt the serenity of the lack of oxygen, here under the deep green sea. He entered her body and it was so good to feel him swimming with her. She fought to retain consciousness and concentrate on the sensations flowing through her thighs and the words that he was kissing into her hair. It was hard to understand him though; it was hard to keep her mind focussed on what he was saying. She kept drifting away with the tide, and his sharp words would drag her back and force her to hold on. She tried to hold on like he told her to, to grip him hard as though his cock was the branch overhanging the rapids and if she held tight she wouldn't drown. If she wrapped herself around it and squeezed it hard enough she would be saved. Her limbs were paralysed and so she held on from the inside, knowing as she did that it was a trick and she was drowning much more quickly by drawing him in further.

Then she knew she was dying, because when she forced her eyes open, there was only blackness and she could no longer hear Daniel's voice guiding her. She could see blackness and hear it too, the *whoosh* of nothingness that was not just around her, but in her and through her. She was nothing, floating in nothing, hearing nothing. Then in a rush of light, she was everything, feeling everything, hearing everything. She was being sliced in two, and as her body opened all the way down, Daniel screamed and fell into her and Sarah screamed too, because the light was too bright and the heat was too hot and the spasms wouldn't stop even after he climbed out of her and let her breathe again. It was as though he had pressed his hot strangler's fingers directly to her nerve endings, and her body was in shock because it was not designed to be touched without skin. When the convulsions stopped, he untied her, and she lay in a ball between his legs and slept the deep sleep of the guiltless.

Sarah woke up on Daniel's kitchen floor. Daniel was snoring beside her, his left leg sprawled out over her stomach, bruising her ribs. She felt fresh love bursting from the place that was so full that it hurt to have more love crowding its way in. She gently lifted his leg and slid out from underneath him. He grunted and rolled onto his side.

It was difficult to know how they had ended up on the kitchen floor, because events were so blurred in her mind. Her last clear memory was of dying and being reborn and then there were only a few sharp, violent images that seemed to be part of some weird, drug-fucked dream. She stepped over his sleeping body with difficulty. Everything hurt.

Sarah found the coffee and started the percolator, hoping that the noise and the scent would wake him gently. When she opened the fridge the memory came back: they had been hungry and come in here to eat. Something distracted them – they distracted each other – and who knew how long ago that was now, but Sarah was light-headed with hunger. She found a packet of croissants in the freezer and threw it in the microwave.

'What's my girl doing?'

Sarah turned and smiled at him, causing her dry, cracked lips to sting. Bleary eyed and messy haired, Daniel stretched out his arms and legs and raised himself off the floor to stretch his back. There was a loud crack and he groaned.

'I'm cracking up,' he said, standing up and twisting his head one way and then the other. Crack and then crack. 'Coffee! You are a prize!' He wrapped his arms around her and kissed her lightly. Her lips hurt but she kissed him back, hard.

'I'm making croissants.'

Daniel smiled and looked around the kitchen. The microwave pinged and he laughed. 'In there? They'll be awful and soggy.'

Sarah pulled out the plate. The croissants were awful and soggy, but he just laughed more and helped her pile them with butter and jam. They carried the coffee and the pastry mess onto his back balcony, wrapping themselves in tablecloths from the cupboard on the way.

'What time do you think it is?' Sarah asked, looking at the dark sky, and unlit windows of the building opposite.

Daniel shrugged and craned his head backwards to see the clock inside. 'Ten past four. Bloody hell, we must have slept there for hours. No wonder my back hurts.'

Sarah remembered that the clock in his bedroom had shown six-forty-six when he had first tied her up. 'Daniel, what day is it?'

He laughed and flaky pastry flew out of his mouth and landed on Sarah's lap. She stared at it for a moment feeling disoriented and confused. Everything was hot and shimmery and smelt like his skin and sounded like his laugh.

'Tuesday, space cadet.'

'Oh.' Sarah noticed that he had jam on his chin and she reached out and wiped it off with her finger. 'What happened to Sunday and Monday?'

Daniel caught her hand and put her jam covered finger to his lips, sucking it for longer than was necessary to clean it. 'We demolished them.'

Sarah went back inside to get her cigarettes and as she limped through the apartment searching for them, she shuddered. It was like a crime scene. A burgundy velvet cushion had been ripped open, its guts leaking out onto the living room floor. The cream carpet was stained in several places. On the hallway wall, close to the skirting board, there was a bloodied mark the size and shape of Sarah's hand. In the bathroom, the mirror was broken, as was the shower door which had shattered into a million tiny pieces so unlike the long, shiny shards on the sink. There was no blood in the bathroom, just an overpowering smell of vomit. She found her cigarettes in the bedroom and sat on the bed to smoke one.

Shaking off the tablecloth, Sarah examined her body for evidence of what had taken place. Black bruising on her inner thighs faded into a greyish mess above her knees, and childish scabs and grazes covered from there to her ankles. Her stomach was sore but looked okay. Her ribs were bruised and the skin was broken on the left side. Her breasts were covered in purple and black splotches, and when she leant forward and checked in the mirror, she found that love bites ran up the right side of her throat to her ear. There were black fingermarks on her throat and she touched them reverently, awed by what he had done and what she had endured.

'I thought you'd deserted me.' Daniel sat naked on the edge of the bed and took a cigarette from the crumpled packet.

'Never. Since when do you smoke?' Sarah asked him, thinking that he smoked elegantly.

'I find myself with strange desires lately. Things that I never needed or wanted in my life have suddenly become essential.' He lay across the bed with his head on her stomach. Sarah noticed that his body was relatively undamaged. A small bruise here and there but nowhere near as beaten up as Sarah was.

'What did you do to me?' she asked, stroking his forehead.

Daniel blew smoke up into her face. 'What do you mean?'

'I can't remember much.'

'Ah, I thought maybe you wouldn't. That's a shame. We had a good time.'

'Of that I have no doubt,' Sarah said. 'What I can remember is thinking that I was dying and then having what I think is termed a spinal orgasm. Man, it was like I had an extra set of nerve endings. What the hell was that?'

Daniel handed her the smoking butt, and she stubbed it out while he rolled onto his side so he was looking up into her face. 'You've had some wild days, yes?'

'Mmm, I suppose.'

'Ever used poppers? Nitrate?'

'Yeah. This DJ I used to see was into that shit. Made me want to climb the walls, and not in a good way. But I was speeding all the time back then and I don't think it was a good mix.'

'Jesus, Sarah.' Daniel frowned, his eyebrows knitted together. 'Anyway, what you experienced was the non-chemical equivalent of inhaling nitrate at the moment of climax. I restricted your oxygen supply and the cerebral cortex went to sleep and stopped inhibiting the areas of the brain which stimulate sensation.'

'You strangled me to make me come harder?'

'Basically.'

'Oh.' Sarah touched the tender flesh on her neck, glancing back at the mirror to see again the black marks his fingers had left.

'Don't just say "oh". You're supposed to be terribly impressed. It cost me a lot of money to learn that technique. It's considered a specialty.'

'What if I'd died?'

Daniel bared his teeth and spoke from the back of his throat. 'I would have cut my throat and slowly bled to death over your corpse.'

Sarah lifted his head and slid down to lie alongside him. He covered her with his limbs. She had to fight off his tongue so she could speak. 'If I thought you were joking I would say that's really sick. But I know you mean it and I almost want you to do it. I almost want you to bleed to death over my still warm body. I want them to break the door down and find you on top of me with your throat open and mine squeezed closed, and my hair stiff with your dried up blood. When they separate us, my hair will be pulled out by the roots and stick in your wound, and then there will be part of me inside you forever. Our cells will decompose together.'

Daniel covered her face with kisses. 'You're evil. You make me want to do the most terrible things. Look what I've done to you!'

'What *did* you do to me? I can't remember much after the lack of oxygen thing. I mean, I remember bits, but it's blurry.'

Daniel sat up and reached for the smokes, lighting them one each. 'I plied you with scotch and tranquillisers and then I violated you for two days.'

'You don't need to drug me or tie me up.'

'But it's so much fun. Your skin breaks too easily though. I hardly have to try to make you bleed.'

'I haven't even had a chance to hurt you. I resent your undamaged skin.' Sarah held her smouldering cigarette over his thigh. 'May I?'

'It's no good if you ask permission, Sarah.'

She pushed the cigarette into his flesh and held her breath, while inches away, his cock stiffened. Apart from his erection, Daniel did not react at all. Sarah pulled the cigarette away, leaving a patch of bald, red skin and the smell of burnt hair. His skin was thick; she would have to get tougher. She should have held it at least to a count of five. No, she should have pushed it in until he jerked his leg back, tears filling his eyes and a quiver in his voice.

'You really get off on pain?' she asked, bending to kiss the burnt skin.

'It's not my pain that does it; it's your discomfort. I like it when you are scared but you go ahead anyway, because you trust me that much. I love the shock of discovery on your face when you experience something for the first time.'

Sarah remembered all her firsts with him, a whole lifetime ago. She felt sad that so much time had been wasted, when this was where she was meant to be all along.

2

The days that followed were exploration and discovery. A blur of limbs and whispered words and shadows. For Sarah, it was like finding out what her body was for. Her arms existed to hold her weight up over Daniel, her hands to grab, to squeeze, to stroke and pummel. Her throat existed to roar and howl.

Daniel told her, one night that could have been a morning, that he had planned this for years. Her complete supplication to him was all he ever wanted. Her virginity had been surrendered, at last.

'You took that years ago,' Sarah reminded him.

'You were a virgin back then in the modern sense of the word. But you were not a true virgin, in the classical sense. This time, I have you.'

'Classical sense? Like a sacrificial virgin?' Sarah liked the way that sounded and offered herself to him again. He took her, slowly, because it was difficult to move. Hours later, unable to force heavy limbs into further action, Daniel continued as though nothing had interrupted them.

'The word virgin comes from the Greek and Latin man and woman. It means androgyne, or a person who is whole unto themselves. In ancient times, it was used to describe a woman, or a goddess like Diana, who was on her own. A woman who refused to belong to a man.'

'Like me.'

Daniel rolled over, crushing her. 'You, a virgin, with all your men.'

Sarah tried to smile, but could not manage that as well as talking. Her jaw ached. 'Irony.'

'History. I own you now.' Daniel was inside her again, but he was still. She drifted.

They barely slept. When the smell and stickiness of semen and blood and sweat became overpowering, they stumbled to the shower and blindly, weakly, swiped the bar of soap over each other. Sarah's arms were heavy, her back and neck ached. Daniel complained that his bones hurt and that his knees were wrecked. They collapsed together in bed, on the floor, the sofa, the balcony, but they could never sleep or rest for long before the stirring began in them both. It stopped feeling good and became a painful compulsion. Sarah was an addict all over again. Spaced out, nodding off, she took him again and again, just to feel normal.

'Shit. Daniel, what about work?' It was light outside, and she had woken up feeling as though she was not where she should be.

'What?' His eyes were closed. His hand was resting over her nose and left cheek.

'I have to call work. I have to–'

'I called. I said there'd been a family emergency and you'd be interstate until further notice. You don't need to worry.'

'What about your job?'

'I'm on leave. Four weeks.'

Sarah moved his hand away and tried to sit up. It was too hard. She sank back into the mattress. 'What did you…?'

Daniel opened his eyes a slit. They were more red than green. 'Personal leave. I told them– God, I'm starving. We should get up. Eat something.'

'What did you tell them?'

Daniel's lips barely moved. Sarah knew it was a smile. 'I told them I had a personal crisis to attend to. I suppose everyone thinks I've cracked up.'

Sarah rolled to the side, her head landing on his chest. 'If they could see you now they would be justified in thinking that. You look terrible. Like you've been living in a cardboard box, drinking metho and eating dirt for a year.'

'And you look like the six week old corpse of a crack addict who died from syphilis.'

'Fuck you.'

'Please.'

Somehow, she managed it.

Sarah started bleeding and was scared, then fascinated. She hadn't had a period since she was sixteen. The appearance of the blood reminded her that she had not been taking her pills and forced a pause in the uncontrolled depravity. She made Daniel go out to the chemist for her, and she waited in the shower until he came back. He was embarrassed and awkward, a middle aged man with a black eye and scratched cheeks offering her five boxes of tampons, because he wasn't sure which were the right ones to get.

He wore black linen pants and a dark green polo neck T-shirt. He said that outside it was sunny, but cool. How long since he had worn clothes? Sarah wouldn't let him take them off. She dressed in thick, grey socks, pink undies and singlet, a navy blue tracksuit. After being naked for a week, being covered was torturously sexy. The cotton of her underwear brushed against her like tentative fingertips, the elastic of her socks grabbed at her ankles.

Daniel had bought fresh bread and ham while he was out, and they stood at the kitchen bench and crammed hastily made sandwiches into their mouths. Their long ignored appetites stimulated, they went through the kitchen in a frenzy, scoffing stale biscuits and half-defrosted cheesecake. Then they drank red wine until Sarah vomited and Daniel put her to bed.

She dreamt about Jamie and woke up sobbing, calling his name. Daniel was disturbed at hearing Jamie's name called out with longing; he sat up and smoked, his face dark and frightening. Sarah swore that it had been a crazy, confused nothing dream, a collage of meaningless images that her drunken brain had thrown up. She told him about last night's dream in which a rabbit plague had forced everyone in Sydney to stay inside until the authorities could take care of the problem. Sarah – dream Sarah – had gone out anyway and been smothered to death by bunnies. Daniel laughed then and called her a mental case.

It was a lie she had given him, because today's dream had been startlingly vivid, and as coherent as any she had ever had. She had watched Jamie looping a rope around his neck with the other end attached to a ceiling fan. She had screamed and screamed at him to get down, to stop, she was sorry and she had been blind and selfish and stupid, and please, please, please, get down from there. Jamie looked at her with blank eyes and kicked the chair out from under himself. The sound of his neck breaking had woken her up.

Despite her assurances and tales about rabbits Daniel was agitated. He took off all his clothes and sat cross-legged on the bed, looking down at Sarah. He poked her in the ear, and in the throat and then in the stomach. She smiled and let him slap her face and pinch her cheeks. Even when he pulled her hair so hard that the skin on her forehead stung, she did not react. He was like a child, prodding and pushing and teasing a small animal. And like a child, he was not doing it out of cruelty, but out of curiosity. He wanted to see how far he could go before she fought back.

Without a reaction from Sarah he got tired of his game and tried to strip her. She said no, and then when he kept trying anyway, she punched his face. This excited him; he sat back away from her and started stroking himself. He asked her to tell him about Jamie. Specifically, he wanted to know what they had done together in bed. She tried but choked on the words, and instead told him stories about all the men she hadn't loved, starting right after Daniel first moved away. She didn't even get to her sixteenth birthday before he sighed and made a mess of himself.

'You are truly depraved,' Sarah said.

'You make me depraved.' Daniel pressed his hand and arm to Sarah's mouth. He kept talking while she cleaned him with her tongue. 'I feel perverted just being around you, and then you tell me that you've done all these terrible, wanton things. You're just a baby and you've had more lovers than I have in my life. You're... what are you thinking? You have to tell me everything you're thinking, *everything*.'

Sarah was sweating inside her fleecy suit. She was not as romantic as he was, she couldn't tell him that she was thinking about whether Jamie would ever talk to her again. She supposed that Daniel would consider her thoughts, and her dishonesty about them, as signs that she loved him less. Maybe she did. Or maybe, she just wanted to keep something for herself. A lifeboat to climb into when Daniel overwhelmed her.

'I was thinking that you might be the reincarnation of the Marquis de Sade,' she said.

'Oh, yes?' Sarah could see he was intrigued by the evocation of such a fiend into their bed.

'I read a book about him when I was seventeen, and I showed some bits to Jamie and Jess, and they freaked. They thought he was like, Satan, or something. I remember, even then, I thought of you when I read it. He got off on the thought of corrupting a much young lover and said that you have to do violence to the object of your desire so when it surrenders the pleasure is greater.'

Daniel lay down beside Sarah and put his hand up her top, scratching tight circles around her belly button. 'Why were you reading stuff like that when you were seventeen? When I was that age I was reading detective comics.'

'This bloke I met at a Goth club thought that if I read it I might be more open to "ingesting his solidified essence". I took the book and ran away.'

'And you call me depraved!'

'There was a story about a man who locked a woman in a dungeon and didn't feed her. He watched her constantly, examining her body as she passed through the stages of starvation, and he played with himself over her, but it wasn't until she was dead that he allowed himself to come. That sounds like something you'd do.'

Daniel traced a ring of fire on her belly. 'I would *not* do that. You've got me all wrong.'

'Do I?'

'I am offended by the comparison. I'm not a bad person, Sarah, not at all. Ask the School Board or the Church fundraising committee. Ask any of the parents of my students. They'll all vouch for me.'

'Ah, but that's just a cover. Like how Ted Bundy wore a cast on his arm, or how the killer in midday movies is always dressed as a deliveryman. Women trust you because you are quiet and reserved and you look as though you would be horrified at even the thought of sexual relations outside of a marriage sanctioned by God. A hedonistic, hooker fucking, sex fiend disguised as a gentle, God-fearing headmaster.'

'It isn't a disguise, Sarah. That's who I am.'

'Bullshit, it's an act. Out in the real world you play this respectable middle-aged man, then you come inside with me and lock the doors and you turn into a monster. But nobody would suspect would they? I never did, when you were my teacher. I used to think you were so handsome and that you probably went home and had married sex under the covers every Saturday night. I thought you were such a nice man, Mr Carr.'

'*Dr* Carr, thank you, Miss Clark.' He poked his finger hard into her navel. 'You know, that *is* what I was like. Until you.'

'Right, little girl me corrupted you. You big creep.'

'You did. The way I love you, the way I want you, your presence and your body and your laugh, make me want to find new ways to be with you. I want to peel back your skin and see what's underneath. Not just see, but taste and feel and smell what is under your skin.'

Daniel kissed her in an unexpectedly tender way. His gentle mouth was at odds with the cruel fingernail sticking into her belly. She ignored the discomfort of it and kissed him back. After a few moments he began to moan, but still did not remove his hand from her stomach. Sarah kissed him harder and he responded by humping her fleece-covered thigh.

'Oh, right,' Sarah said, breaking off the kiss. 'I'm the depraved one, like I'm making you rub your dick against my leg. Why don't you admit that you're a kinky freak?'

Daniel stopped rubbing against her. He lay beside her with his hand flat on her stomach, and smiled in a way that made him look very old, and very sweet. 'I used to think I was having kinky sex if Lisa and I did it in the morning instead of at bedtime. Then I made love to a tiny schoolgirl on a winter afternoon and everything changed. A whole world of possibilities opened up. There isn't a place or an action or a time that would seem wrong with you.'

'I love you.'

Daniel poked her belly button.

'Why do you keep doing that?'

He laughed and poked harder. Sarah started to cry. Not from physical pain of any kind – he was only poking her navel after all – but from the realisation that he would always get his own way no matter how clever Sarah thought she was.

Poke.

'Stop poking me! Why are you being so mean?'

'If you don't like what I'm doing, you should stop me.' Daniel jabbed her again.

He had won. She slapped his hand out of the way and got on top of him, forcing his arms down with her knees. He let her think she had him for about half a second, and then he rolled her over and twisted her arms behind her back. He told her that he liked it when she fought back and she tried to tell him that she wasn't playing, but he talked over the top of her. She said something that was sort of *stop* and nearly *please*, but came out sounding like a whimper. He slapped her face and told her to stop being a baby. He said *tell me what you want.* She couldn't speak. He slapped her again and said *you have to say it or I won't know.* He slapped her until she couldn't do anything but squeal and then, just to really shake her up, he got off her and sat on the side of the bed without touching her at all.

'Please,' Sarah said.

'Please what?' He sounded very, very far away.

Please what? She was going to black out. Please touch me. Please leave me alone. Please, Daniel, Please. Please do that thing you do that makes me forget, so I don't feel bad, please don't be so mean, please knock me out again, or kill me, or kiss me. Please don't make me hurt. Her voice, when she spoke again, was clear and loud.

'Please let me call Jamie.'

He stared at her until she caved in and closed her eyes. Then he got up and went away.

Sarah waited in the bedroom for several minutes, and when he didn't return, she got up and went to find him. The apartment was empty. She took the elevator down to the car park and confirmed that his car was gone. In the lift on the way back up, a woman in a sun hat asked if Sarah was okay. Sarah's voice wouldn't work, so she just nodded and coughed and the woman looked away.

Back inside, Sarah realised why the woman had been concerned. Her hair was a black tangle, individual strands sticking up as if glued or gelled. Her face was sickly pale with red blotches, yellow bruises and purple bags. She was wearing the pink singlet and navy pants and her arms were black and blue. She looked like a junkie or a rock star. Where was that healthy, mysterious glow that was supposed to come when you were in love?

Daniel was gone.

Sarah showered and shaved her legs, underarms and bikini line; it was disgusting how prickly she was. She washed and conditioned her hair, combed out all the knots and carefully plaited it, tying the end with a red ribbon. There was Dettol under the sink and Sarah splashed it all over her body, gritting her teeth at the pain as it fizzed up on the million cuts and abrasions.

The apartment was trashed. Sarah spent an hour and a half cleaning, and then had to shower again because she felt all dirty. She made the bed with clean sheets and even picked some camellias from the balcony pot and put them in a vase on the dining table.

Daniel was still gone. It had been hours.

She smoked three cigarettes, then picked up the phone and dialled Jamie's number. Shelley answered, called her a whore and hung up. Sarah drank two large glasses of Wild Turkey, straight up, and smoked, watching the front door. Then she called Jamie again. Shelley told her that if she called again she would take out a restraining order. Sarah had another drink and made another call.

'About fucking time!'

'Don't yell at me, Mike.'

She could hear him exhaling, trying to get his breathing under control. 'I've been so worried. Are you okay?'

'I'm fine. Have you seen Jamie?'

'Where are you?'

'I'm at Daniel's. How's Jamie?'

'Sarah, baby, I miss you, and I'm worried because that bloke is a fucking psycho. Just let me see you. *Please*.'

'I really need to know how Jamie is.'

He sighed. 'He's shattered, Sarah. What did you expect? He totally cracked up, and he's seeing a psychiatrist like, every day. And he's on these drugs that make him sleep all the time.'

Sarah forced the words out. 'Can you make sure he knows that I love him?'

'No, Sarah, I fucking won't.'

She started to cry and beg, but then the front door opened. Daniel's legs, and Daniel's hands holding so many white roses that she could not see his head. She hung up the phone and Daniel's roses rained down over her tears.

Daniel reacted to Sarah's sorrow with what she at first thought was compassion. She had been afraid of his anger when he found out she was missing Jamie, but his voice stayed low and sweet. He showered her with roses and kisses and soothing words. He showered her with understanding. It was only hours later, after she had cried her heart out to him and confessed the secrets of her soul, that she realised he was tricking her.

'Poor darling,' he said. 'You're so conflicted.'

Sarah couldn't respond. She was underneath him, crushed by him. She had cried so much that her throat ached and her eyes were swollen shut. His calmness was a gift. A gift like the roses he had brought her. The roses that surrounded them on the kitchen floor.

'I think,' Daniel went on, 'that you should leave.'

'No,' Sarah croaked, her eyes filling with fresh tears.

'Yes, Sarah. I think it's best. If you're thinking about Jamie so much, you should go and be with him. If you don't want to be here, if you don't want to be with me, then I won't keep you.'

'No.'

'No? No what, Sarah? I didn't even ask you a fucking question! What is *no*?'

'No, I don't want to leave. Just, no to everything you're saying. I'm not conflicted. I love you. I don't want to leave; I'm not going to leave. Ever.' It hurt her to say, but once she had forced the words out she felt better. Daniel's kisses started again and he supported his weight on his elbows so that the pressure on her ribs and chest was relieved.

'Okay, Sarah, okay,' he said. 'But if I ever, *ever*, find out that you have seen Jamie, or spoken to him, then that will be the end.'

'The end of what?'

Daniel got up onto his knees, one leg on either side of hers. He picked up a rose and held it up in front of him, hovering over Sarah's chest. In one sharp movement he stabbed himself in the throat with the thorn. Hard enough that a pin prick of blood appeared and began to swell. He dropped the rose on to Sarah's stomach and closed his eyes.

'You'll stab me with a rose thorn?' Sarah tried for flippancy, part of her still holding on to her inherent dislike of dramatics. A bigger part of her – the part that knew it was more than dramatics with him – won out. Her words sounded weak and afraid.

'I won't lay a finger on you, my darling. I'll drive you over to Jamie's house. I'll wish you both well. And then–' He held up a finger and drew it sharply across his throat. The small spot of blood spread, giving his throat the appearance of being cut.

Sarah knew she would never leave him. Not because she was afraid he would kill himself – that threat was more irritating than frightening – but because even when he was being a manipulative, cruel, psychotic bastard; even when he had a dirty streak of blood across his throat; even when he was threatening her and his face was ugly with cruelty; *even then*, she wanted him and loved him and couldn't stop herself from telling him this. Even when he pressed the rose thorns into her body and slammed her head into the floor and called her a fickle little fool, she couldn't say anything except *Yes*.

3

The intensity of the first two weeks could not be sustained. Physically, they were both wrecked. They stood in front of the mirror on the Monday of the third week and pointed out each other's injuries with awe. Sarah was more visibly damaged than Daniel, but he assured her that his bones were aching more than she could imagine. Daniel promised Sarah he would go easy on her for a while, to allow the abrasions and bruises to heal properly; Sarah promised Daniel she would let him sleep for more than three hours at a time, and that she would stop expecting acrobatics every time they made love.

Sarah was worried about what she would do when Daniel went back to work. Not only was she unemployed, but she had missed too much uni to finish the semester and would have to wait until next year to re-enrol.

Daniel was pleased. 'You can be my slave.'

'Just what I've always wanted,' Sarah said, and they both knew she was not being at all sarcastic.

On Daniel's first day back at work, Sarah called him fifteen times. When he got home, she was waiting for him at the front door, naked and holding a glass of scotch. He closed the door, locked it, put his keys and briefcase on the front table, hung his jacket on the hook by the door. Without looking at her, he took the offered drink and finished it in two large gulps. His glass deposited on the table, he turned to Sarah and looked her up and down. His face was very red.

'Aren't you going to ask me how my day was?'

'I don't much care. I'm just glad you're back.' She stepped towards him but was stopped by his outstretched hand.

'My day, Sarah, was absolutely fucking awful. It was the worst fucking day of my life.' He closed his eyes and unbuckled his belt. 'Do you know why it was so goddamn fucking terrible?' He looked at her, sliding his belt from its loops. 'Because I was required to concentrate on budgets and disciplinary procedure while some silly, selfish, thoughtless little brat kept ringing me with half-hourly updates on the state of her cunt.'

Sarah held his gaze, but was conscious of the belt swishing and snapping at his side. 'I missed you.'

'Yes, I know. You told me at least twenty times already.'

Sarah braced herself. 'And you've not told me once, you bastard, oh!' The leather cut across her stomach; she fell to her knees. 'You should be grateful I love you so much. You should think yourself lucky, I... ugh.' This time he brought the belt down on her shoulders. She went to stand up, but he pushed her to her back and belted her hard between the legs.

Hot, blinding pain shot up through her groin into her stomach. She started to cry and he knelt beside her, the belt resting across her thighs. 'Did that hurt?'

'Of course it hurt.'

'Every time you called me today, it was like you were whipping my cock, and me in a room full of people, unable to do anything to relieve the agony.' He lifted the belt and struck her across the front of her thighs. 'It was really very thoughtless of you.'

'But you did miss me? That's why you were in agony.'

'Yes, Sarah.' He belted her across the hips. 'Being apart from you caused me enormous pain and your constant phone calls increased my suffering. Does that make you happy?'

She shook her head. Daniel pushed her thighs apart, lifted the belt and brought it down hard. 'I think it does, Sarah. I think you enjoy tormenting me.' Again, she shook her head, and again he whipped her. 'Say something.'

She dug her nails into her palms, distracting herself from the searing pain between her legs. She was thrilled at his rage, at this proof of his continued obsession, but she needed so badly to be making love to him that she did not want to prolong his fury. *'Being your slave,'* she whispered, *'what should I do but tend upon the hours and times of your desire?'*

'Oh, Sarah.' Daniel bent his head and kissed her burning cunt. 'Continue, please.'

'I have no precious time at all to spend, Nor services to do till you require, nor dare I chide the world-without-end-hour, whilst I, my sovereign, watch the clock for you, nor think the bitterness of absence sour. That's all I can remember. No! Don't stop, please, no, okay, okay, ah *O, let me suffer, being at your beck, th'imprisoned absence of your liberty; and patience, tame to sufferance, bide each check without accusing you of injury.'*

Daniel sat up, wiping his mouth with the back of his hand. 'You're mixing your sonnets, Sarah. Not good enough.'

'I'll learn them properly. I'll spend all tomorrow studying. And I won't bother you at work, I promise. But please, please, please, Daniel, will you take me to bed now?'

He looked at her for a long moment. 'All right then. But I will test you tomorrow. You can count on it.'

Sarah studied her Shakespeare and did not call Daniel at work, but still he arrived home in an awful temper. It took her almost an hour to get him to touch her, and then once he started he wouldn't stop. Before going to sleep he bound her wrists together over her head and tied her left leg to his right one, so he could be secure in the knowledge she would be by his side all night long. Although she did not sleep at all due to the extreme discomfort of the pose, she had a wonderful night, listening to his breathing, remembering a time when the lack of him had kept her awake.

Some days he had to work late and when he finally got home, he all but tore her apart in his frenzy; other days he was early home and bursting to tell her how much he missed her. On several occasions, he was late for work because he could not let her go, twice he cried as he was leaving; often he wrote her a list of tasks to complete that day and warned her that there would be consequences for unfinished chores.

She liked his lists; along with *Change bed linen* and *Clean bathroom* he would write *Have a midday nap* or *Eat a bar of chocolate*. Sometimes he wrote *Do whatever makes you smile*. Once she purposely ignored his daily instructions, hoping he would punish her with his body, but it turned out the penalty for disobedience was to be barred from touching him for twenty-four hours. She always did as he asked after that.

When Daniel was at work, Sarah experienced a loneliness of such intensity she almost wished he had never returned. Before he'd come back into her life she spent most of her time alone at her flat and never felt so bad about it. It was disconcerting that being in love felt lonelier than aloneness. It was disconcerting that every time she felt lonely she thought about Jamie. Most disconcerting of all was the fact that she had left messages for Jamie with every member of his family, every friend of his she could remember the name of, and with the receptionist at his work, and he had not called her back. She thought about sending him a letter, but he clearly wanted to be left alone.

After three months, she accepted that Jamie was not going to fill the hollow that appeared in her chest every time Daniel left for work, and that was as it should be. Jamie was of the past, and the past had been no good anyway. She had Daniel now and he was everything, and if she had everything then there was nothing to miss.

In the evenings, they took turns choosing books from Daniel's extensive collection to read to each other. Sometimes it was like being back in his classroom, except now they both drank red wine and smoked while they talked, and when, inevitably, the book in question was discarded so love could be made, they could make as much noise as they liked.

Sarah enjoyed provoking him by flaunting the knowledge she had gained and opinions she'd formed since he left her. *Wuthering Heights* was contentious: Daniel believed that it was the greatest love story ever written; Sarah was outraged.

'That stupid Catherine wouldn't know true love if it slapped her across the face, which I wish it would because that girl has a slapping coming to her. She says that she and Heathcliff share a soul or some such crap, but then she runs off and marries that Linton dweeb. If you want to talk great gothic love stories, *Jane Eyre* is where it's at. Here's a girl whose identity, whose very right to exist has been attacked her whole life, yet she not only retains her sense of self but she does so while winning the love of a difficult, dominant man. Far more romantic than stupid Catherine letting Heathcliff influence her to the point where she says she *is* him.'

'But the love between Catherine and Heathcliff is unconditional,' Daniel argued. 'Jane can only give herself to Rochester once he's been punished for his past. He's blinded and burnt, humbled – pious even. But Catherine knows Heathcliff is a beast and loves him for it. She doesn't want him de-clawed.'

Sarah had to concede that his argument was a compelling one, but the discussion had been so much fun she intentionally picked texts which she knew they would disagree on. She argued bitterly against *Heart of Darkness,* which Daniel considered a masterpiece, and horrified him by declaring Sylvia Plath a more accomplished poet than Ted Hughes. For that, he tied her to a chair and refused to let her up until she had memorised every poem in *Birthday Letters*. A whole day and night he kept her there. She wet herself and begged for cigarettes and wept, but she did not ask to be set free. When he at last released her, she told him she hated Hughes more than ever, and Daniel laughed and called her a silly girl, but she could tell by his eyes that he was proud of her.

Apart from the occasional trip to the shops or to dinner with Daniel, Sarah did not go out. Most days she spoke to no one but Daniel. She felt disconnected from the world and developed an obsession with the news. Everyday she would jog to the Pakistani grocer on the corner and buy the *Telegraph* and the *Herald*, as well as *The Australian*. Each week she read *The Bulletin* and *Time* from cover to cover.

Daniel brought home *Cosmopolitan* as a joke. He said that she was so up on current events that he was beginning to feel stupid; he suggested she spend more time reading up on *How to tell if he's Mr Right or Mr Right Now*. After hitting each other over the head with the rolled up magazine, Sarah and Daniel read it together, cackling at the tips to spice up a dull sex life.

'Oh, apparently we're doing it all wrong,' Daniel said. 'We should be taking more time with foreplay and investing in candles and sensual fabrics.'

'Well, they do say that candlelight is flattering. Helps to conceal unsightly wrinkles.'

'Hmm, we should definitely get some candles then. Your crow's feet are terrible, Sarah.'

Sarah flicked the page over with a disgusted snort. 'I've never understood this sensual crap. I mean, if you want to fuck why not just do it?'

'Some would say that is boring. Anyway, you're hardly a flat on your back, stare at the ceiling covered in a sheet kind of girl. Thank God.'

'That isn't what I mean. Sex should be urgent and aggressive. It should be *raw*. If you know you want someone, why would you bother wasting time lighting candles?'

'Because anticipation can be sweet. The history of our relationship should be proof enough. Don't you value this more because we waited so long for it?'

'Not at all. Don't you mourn the time wasted when we should've been together?'

'God, Sarah, yes. Every minute.'

Sarah came out of the shower one night and found Daniel lying on the bed with the magazine open in front of him. From the doorway, she could see the bold print title of the article: *Get your best ever beach bod!* and the accompanying full page photograph: a close-up of a girl's crotch, barely covered in a transparent white g-string, demonstrating the result of her 'all off' wax. Daniel didn't know Sarah was there, that she could see his narrowed eyes and slack jaw. She silently backed out of the room, wondering if this was how his wife had felt when she'd caught him with Sarah's pictures: revolted by his desire for smooth, young flesh and disgusted at herself for not providing him with what he needed.

The next day, Sarah went to the Sydney salon mentioned in the article and felt nothing but determination as she stripped and had a man called Niki spread hot wax over her entire body.

Back at the apartment, Sarah stood naked in front of the full-length mirror. She didn't recognise herself. It wasn't just the lack of hair; it was the months of staying inside, the months of barely eating and barely sleeping. No breasts to speak of, no hips or thighs. Without curves or hair she looked like a newborn baby or an alien. She was nothing but blue toned skin and too large eyes. She tried to see herself as Daniel would, tried to determine what it was about this vacuity that appealed to him. She thought she looked deformed and creepy. She couldn't understand what it was that made him want this.

That night, she got her answer. Daniel went crazy. He said she presented herself as a challenge to his decency and self-control; that the preparation of her body in this way was the mark of a whore, and so how did she expect him to treat her; that in posing as an adolescent she was begging him to father her, control her, punish her; that she was offering herself as a blank canvas and shouldn't be surprised that he wanted to make an impression on it; that her unnatural smoothness would provoke unnatural violence; that she was cruel to incite him to acts he would regret; that she was contemptible for manipulating his desires in this way; that she was genius in knowing what he needed without being told; that her perception and generosity put him to shame; that she was miraculous, divine, impossibly perfect; that his love for her was beyond description.

The next morning she could barely walk, but she managed to drag herself to the mirror, where she stood smiling at herself until her face ached as much as the rest of her. Yesterday she'd been an arctic landscape: icy blankness, nothingness. Daniel had brought her to life. With teeth and nails, with belts and buckles, with matches and glass, he had given her texture and colour. His darkness, the worst of who he was, was written all over her. She was pleased to be so marked.

4

Then one Friday afternoon, Daniel did not come home from work. Not wanting to aggravate him if it turned out he had only forgotten to let her know about a late meeting, Sarah waited until seven o'clock before calling first his office and then his mobile phone. Both calls went through to his voicemail, as did the hundred or more calls she made during the next four and a half hours.

At eleven-thirty, he walked through the front door, past the living room where she sat sobbing on the floor, and into the bathroom. Sarah ran after him, but the door was locked.

'Where have you been?' she called.

There was no response. She stood and listened to the shower. When the water stopped she tried again. 'Are you okay?'

He opened the door and stepped out. 'Fine.' He walked around her and into the bedroom.

Feeling more panicked than when he was gone, she followed. 'What's wrong?'

He sat on the bed, drying his feet. 'Nothing at all, Sarah.' He did not look at her.

'I've been so worried. I couldn't reach you and I didn't know–'

'I went out for a few quiet drinks. Quiet being the operative word. I simply could not tolerate the idea of coming home and having to listen to your incessant chatter all evening.' He stood up and hung his towel over the bed head. 'So do shut up or I'll be forced to go back to the pub.'

Sarah watched him pull back the covers and climb into bed. This morning he got carried away while saying goodbye and fucked her in the hallway with the front door wide open. When she came she bit him too hard, and he had to change his shirt because of the blood on the collar. Finally leaving, he said *I wonder if I'll ever be able to look at you and not want to eat you up.*

Sarah undressed, turned off the light and slid in beside him. When she tried to kiss him he grunted and curled his body into a ball at the edge of the bed.

'Daniel? Why are you being like this?'

He sighed. 'I told you.'

'You're annoyed by my incessant chattering?'

'Yes, that and your pasty face and bony arse.'

Sarah knew he used insults as a tool to deflect attention from what was truly wrong. This did not make it hurt any less. She took several deep breaths. 'Would you like me to leave?'

'Yes, good idea. Go and annoy one of your other lovers. I'm sure there's at least one among the thousands who will put you up for the night.'

'Okay, that's enough.' Sarah turned on the bedside lamp, climbed over his body and squatted at the bedside, looking up at him. 'Tell me what the fuck is wrong, Daniel, or I really will leave.'

'Fine, Sarah. Come here.' He swung his legs over the edge of the bed and held his hands out to her. Melting, she let him pull her up. She went to kiss him and he laughed, grabbed her around the waist and lifted her off the ground. 'You just don't know when to stop, do you?'

He carried her out of the bedroom, through the hallway, past the kitchen and living room and along the entrance hall. Sarah kicked at him and cried, but he was unmoved. He opened the front door and dropped her. 'Don't–' she started, but the door had closed.

There was only one other apartment on this floor and it was vacant, but she was still in a common area and in clear, humiliating view if anyone should happen to press the wrong button on the elevator. She spent the night huddled against the door, naked and terrified.

When morning came and Daniel opened the door, she was too exhausted to stand or speak. 'Oh, Sarah,' he said, and gathered her in his arms. He carried her to bed, where he cried into her stomach and begged her to forgive him.

'Yesterday,' he explained, 'I was hauled in front of the board and given an official warning. Inappropriate behaviour and unsatisfactory performance, they said. I demanded they specify their complaints.' He sobbed. 'Inattentiveness. Lateness. Unkempt appearance, specifically–' he sobbed again, 'bruises and grazes on my face, giving me the appearance of having "frequent violent altercations."'

'I'm sorry.'

'We have to stop doing what we've been doing. You have to calm down.'

'I'll try.' She was already having trouble. His head on her stomach, his tears, his touch after that long, cold, terrible night were enough to make her want to tear open his chest.

'I never used to be like this. I was married for twenty-five years without receiving a single facial wound. I certainly was never late for work because I couldn't stop licking my wife's arsehole.'

'So it's all my fault?'

He sat up and held her face between his palms. 'Not you, *us*. We're out of control. God, this is why I left in the first place.'

'Yeah, well you're not leaving this time. No fucking way. We will calm down, Daniel. I promise. I won't bite you or scratch you, and I'll make sure you get to bed nice and early so you can concentrate the next day. And I'll keep my arsehole far away from your tongue in the mornings so you'll never be late again.'

'Thank you.' He kissed her lips, ran his hands down her spine. 'How long until I have to be at work again?'

'Forty-nine hours or so.'

Daniel was inside her within seconds.

On Monday morning, Sarah watched him attempt to cover the purple bruise on his cheek and the bloody gouges on his neck with her foundation. 'This can't go on,' he said to his reflection. He left for work without saying goodbye.

Daniel would not let her touch him; he growled and held up his hands if she so much as edged towards him. He spoke hardly at all, and when he did, it was to say *shut up* or *keep away from me*. She kept trying, though, because what else could she do?

The Ancient Greeks believed that at the time of Creation every human being was made up of two separate people, joined together in body, heart and mind. Angry that these creatures were perfectly content within themselves and therefore had no time or deference for the gods, Zeus tore them apart, separating each whole into two halves. Ever since, human beings have been miserable and lonely, wandering the planet searching for their other half. Everybody feels dissatisfied and empty until they find the one person who completes them; once the match is made, they need nothing else. Not work. Not family. Not gods.

Sarah didn't believe in Greek gods anymore than she believed in the Christian one, but the essence of this story seemed to her to be perfectly true. Love was not about happiness or security. It had nothing to do with common interests and shared life goals. Respect, kindness, affection: irrelevant. Love was blood rushing through veins searching out its source. Flesh screaming to be joined with flesh. The bone deep understanding that there wasn't anything else but *this*.

Sarah tried for a week to make Daniel speak to her. She tried poetry, lectures, lingerie, nudity, begging, shouting, screaming and sobbing. He stayed out late every night and locked himself in the bedroom when he was at home. By the end of the week, the marks on his throat and face had faded but he looked to have aged ten years. The strain was showing under his eyes and across his forehead and in the way his shoulders slumped. His physical deterioration heartened her: he was dying without her touch.

Then on Saturday night he did not come home at all. Sarah sat up all night, watching the door, dialling his number, telling herself he would be home any minute. In her mind she saw him passed out in a gutter, smashed up in a car wreck, mugged and beaten, in the arms of a woman who looked like his wife, being stroked by a prostitute with oversized breasts and no front teeth, sitting alone on a park bench, sobbing on the floor of his office, in a jail cell, floating face down in the harbour, extinguished.

At nine o'clock Sunday morning, his key turned in the lock and he stumbled into the apartment. He leant on the doorframe, struggled to get his wallet out of his pocket, dropped his keys, hit his head, swore and burped. Sarah's insides liquefied and she was drowning in what she felt.

He looked up as she ran at him, his face crumpled, as did his legs. He scrunched down into the corner, between the front door and the hall table. Sarah fell on him, and when he tried to push her away she beat him with her fists and ripped the hair from his head. He sobbed at her to leave him and she tore at his cheeks and nose and chin with her fingernails. She spat in his eye, and when he stopped fighting her, she grabbed his dropped keys and gouged at the flesh on his face. Her skull became a weapon, smashing up against his cheekbones and nose. His tears made it easier. His wet face produced a satisfying *Splat* when she slapped it. Her arms ached, her vision blurred, there was blood on her hands and in her mouth. She beat on.

She thought she might kill him and was scared, but could not stop. All week he had frozen her out and now she was melting into an icy sea. Her elbows replaced her bruised hands and slammed fresh blood from his nose. She thrashed at him with her whole body. His eyes were half opened, watching her. She felt as though she was watching herself. Watching her bony elbows fly through the space between them and land on his face. She could hear herself screaming. She was so frightened. She couldn't stop. She ripped open his bloody shirt and stabbed the keys into his stomach with as much force as she was capable of. He didn't flinch. Sarah found the strength to push harder. Her biceps were quivering like a junkie without a fix. Concentrating on her hand she noticed that her knuckles were red raw from scraping against his weekend beard.

In physicality there is honesty. Sarah had always been able to know the truth about a man through his body. The pale circle on the ring finger gave away a cheating husband. The labourer, masquerading as a stockbroker, couldn't hide his sun freckled shoulders or his work worn hands. The bloke who told her he was into extreme sports made her laugh when later she touched his flabby buttocks and saw the moonlight reflecting off his lily white skin. And how many men claimed that they did not care about appearances and then proudly flexed their super sized biceps and mega-crunched abs at her in the bedroom? The surface holds the truth.

In the expression of physicality, in the tearing of the flesh and the intermingling of fluids, there is honesty. Sarah had always known the things that Daniel had never been able to admit out loud. She knew them ever since he pushed himself onto and into her immature body. All the time he had been spewing out justifications and explanations and rationalisations, his true nature was pounding the hell out of her flesh. And now she was showing him, with teeth and claw, that they were the same. One.

His hand closed over hers and it was over.

Freud believed that the sublimation of desires was responsible for civilisation. The basest, most animalistic urges were repressed, and the energy that would otherwise have been wasted in hedonism was harnessed and re-directed. In other words, Daniel told Sarah, instead of having sex, people built cathedrals and cities and nations.

'The world has enough of all those things, don't you think?'

'More than enough.'

5

The last thing Jamie expected at five fifteen on a Friday afternoon was for Sarah Clark to walk through his office door. The only time Sarah Clark ever walked through his door these days was in his dreams, and even then it was never his office door.

She was much thinner than in his dreams and she was wearing more clothing too. She looked different all together. Older, smaller, tireder. Defeated. But he must have been reading her wrong or projecting, because Sarah Clark had never been defeated in her life.

Defeated, old, tired, thin, whatever. She could have snakes for hair and blood pouring from the eyes and she would still be the most beautiful thing he had seen in over a year. He stared at the fortnightly sales sheet on his desk and concentrated on breathing.

'There was no one at the front desk so I just wandered in.' She was standing in the doorway, and he thought she sounded nervous but that was impossible. 'Is it okay that I'm here?' She sounded scared but that was impossible too. Sarah Clark did not get nervous or scared. Jamie thought he must be projecting again. He was fucking terrified.

Thirteen months and twelve days. That bastard must have finished with her. She must have been dumped out on the street and had to come home. He knew she'd given up her job, because he'd gone to the restaurant to find her. He'd tried to find her at the university too. That was over a year ago.

'I guess you're not happy to see me then?' Sarah started to cry.

Jamie's paralysis broke. Sarah in pain caused a reflex reaction much like the mother's instinct to protect her child. He knew he was weak and weedy, a pathetic excuse for a father, a terrible husband, a failure as a man in general, but what he could do and would do with his dying breath, was take care of Sarah.

He wrapped his arms around her, wincing as his fingertips scraped her too prominent spine and his ribs clashed against hers. She felt different than he remembered, and it wasn't his memory failing him. The end of time was when Jamie would forget the way Sarah Clark felt. He remembered *perfectly* how she felt: bony and smooth and warm. And she felt too light, as though a heavy hand would crush her. She had always felt that way, and she felt that way now, but more so. Bonier, smoother, warmer, lighter. That wasn't what made her feel strange to him though. It was something else, something that wasn't to do with the tiny bones and the impossibly pale, always hot skin.

He tried to pull back from her to see her face but she clung tight, quivering like a tiny bird thrown from the nest before its wings were strong enough to support it. She was injured and afraid, and that was why she felt so unfamiliar to him. Jamie had always been aware of how breakable she was, but now, as she shivered in his arms and drenched his shirt with tears and mucus, she was broken.

'Come and sit down.' He tried to step out of her arms but she held fast, so he had to half walk, half stumble backwards with her clinging to him, and then ease her into the chair. Her grip remained tight on his arms. 'Stop crying now. Everything's fine. Come on now.' He pulled one hand free and brushed away some hair that had broken free of her plait and was plastered to her cheek.

'Jamie, oh God. I missed you so much. I needed you and now it's all a mess. I understand why you didn't want to… I know you were mad, but, Jamie, you've been mad before and I've done stupid stuff, but you always helped me. Why didn't you…' Sarah released his arms, burying her face in her hands.

She was verging on hysterical which scared him, because if Sarah was *anything* she was calm and unemotional. 'You have to stop crying, Sarah, I can't understand you.' Jamie stroked her face and then her arms and made what he thought were comforting noises. They were the kind of noises that Shelley always made when he woke up from one of his nightmares. Sarah kept crying and shaking. Jamie wondered if she was on drugs.

She stopped abruptly and stood up, knocking him backwards. 'Enough. If I keep crying like this I'm going to burst a fucking tear duct.' She walked to the window and peered out, wiping her face with her sleeve. Jamie noticed that she was wearing a white cardigan. It was very odd, the kind of hand knitted matinee jacket that they dressed Bianca in when there was a cool breeze outside.

She cleared her throat a few times, leaning her forehead against the glass. 'You must be doing well. Got a view of the river and everything, huh? Must be nice looking at the fast flowing sludge all day.'

'Yep, I saw them drag a body out the other day.'

'You did not.'

'No, I didn't.'

Sarah sat back down at his desk and lit a cigarette.

'This is a non-smoking building, Sarah.'

'Aren't they all? You want me to hang out the window or something?'

He shook his head. 'So how ya been, Sarah Clark?'

'Well, how do I look?'

'Like absolute shit,' he said and Sarah laughed. 'I've missed you, Sar. I've been waiting for that phone call you promised me.'

'What?' She frowned. 'I called you a hundred times!'

'No, you didn't. When did you call?'

She returned to the window, opened it a crack, tapped the ash from her cigarette and then closed it. When she turned back to him, there were tears running down her cheeks again. 'I called all the time, at first anyway. I left messages with Mike, and with your mum, with Brett. I tried to talk to Shelley but she... well, I can't blame her.'

He stood up and walked towards the window. He had to get a better look at her face. 'Sarah, if you called so many times then why have I been going out of my mind worrying about you?'

'Jesus, Jamie, no one told you? What a fucking... what about the messages I left here?'

Jamie felt the nausea returning and focussed on the flashing blue *Car Parking* sign across the street to keep steady. 'Messages?'

She opened the window and threw the cigarette butt out. 'Twenty or so. More probably.'

Jamie sat down and pressed his hands together the way his therapist had shown him to. He was supposed to focus his feelings of panic and anger between his palms and then release them by turning his palms up. *Let it go, Jamie, let it all go.*

'Where did you leave the messages?'

'I left them with that snappy bitch of a receptionist.'

Why would Angie not tell him that Sarah had called? Angie did not even know Sarah. Except she probably did know *about* Sarah, because she went to yoga with Shelley every Tuesday night. Jamie pressed his hands together so hard he thought his wrists might break. 'So you're saying that Shelley knew you were trying to get in touch with me?'

'Shit.' Sarah kicked the wall. 'Yes, she fucking knew.'

Focus the rage. Squeeze it between your palms. It is just a tiny ball. Flatten it. Control it. Thirteen months and twelve days she had been trying to contact him, and everyone he knew had conspired to keep her away. Own the anger; don't let it own you. Thirteen months and twelve days of his life had been wasted in pain and misery.

Out of the corner of his eye, he saw her cross the room and climb onto his desk. He thought she was sitting cross-legged but couldn't be sure, because he was focussing on the despair and betrayal and lost hope being squashed and compressed. He controlled his feelings; they did not control him.

'Are you praying? Have you found God or something?'

'You talked to my mum? You talked to Brett?'

'Yeah, and your dad. What's with that crazy hand business?'

'It's a behavioural therapy thing. I have to squash the bad feelings between my palms and then I can let them go.'

'What a load of shit. Give me your hands.'

It *was* a load of shit. He relaxed his hands and let Sarah take them, one in each of her own. This was much more effective than any of the techniques he had been taught. When Sarah pressed her fingertips into his palms the panic and anger all went away. What did it matter that he had suffered needlessly because of the selfish plotting of his nearest and dearest? What did it matter that over a year of his life had been lived without Sarah when all along she had wanted him, needed him, called for him? It didn't matter one bit, because she was here now, and nothing else had *ever* mattered.

'God, it's good to see you,' Jamie said. 'Not that there's much of you to see. How's that old man treating you?'

She smiled. 'Like a Queen.'

'Great, I'm glad.' Jamie managed to not choke on the words only by pretending that this was one of his nightmares, and that any minute her head would split open and spurt hot blood all over his desk and chair and body.

Sarah's head did not split open. 'Whatever you think of Daniel, you should know that he does love me. He loves me as much as anyone could, Jamie. Even you.'

Jamie had a moment of genuine pity for Daniel Carr, who was in for some serious heartache if he loved Sarah as much as Jamie did. Then he looked up at her blue lips, and any sympathy for the bastard vanished. She looked like a twelve-year-old junkie.

'If he treats you so well then why do you look like death? Why did you turn up here crying and shaking?'

She climbed down off the desk and walked over to the window, lighting another cigarette. For several minutes she stared out into the approaching night and Jamie watched her. She seemed to be considering something. Twice she half turned to Jamie with an open mouth, and both times she pressed her lips together and turned back to the window. Jamie waited because he didn't know what else to do. Probing had never worked with Sarah. It was likely to make her feel pressured, and then she would turn sarcastic or start joking, and he would never know what was wrong.

The more he waited and the longer he examined her, the more his dread grew. She was sallow, scraggy, wasted. Even after the rape she had not looked this bad, so it must be something truly awful that she was working up to telling him. It was possible that she was on the pills again, or something worse. Who could tell what a sick fuck like Daniel Carr would do? Maybe he dealt heroin, or maybe he pimped her out to his jaded intellectual friends. Maybe she was sick. She looked sick. Jamie's heart sped up and he pressed his palms together.

He had seen people on *60 Minutes* looking like concentration camp victims and talking about how it can happen to anyone. And she wasn't just anyone – she was Sarah Clark. Talk about high risk. Jamie looked at her emaciated form leaning heavily against the glass, and he remembered how good it had felt to spurt inside her and feel her fluids mixing with his own. It had seemed so important that there be nothing between them, no barriers to their intimacy. He remembered Mike saying how sharing body fluid was the ultimate vote of trust in this day and age. He saw that Sarah's hand shook as she raised the cigarette to her lips, and he realised there were very few things in this world that would cause Sarah Clark to look scared and weak and to sob and shake.

Actions and consequences and what goes around comes around and you think that these things will never happen to you but this disease does not discriminate and the only safe sex is abstinence and the grim reaper knocks down the pins and there are pretty girls falling down too and love will not protect you and beauty will not protect you and every time you go to bed with someone you are going to bed with their partners and their partners and their partners but Sarah was always careful except when she could tell that a guy was Clean.

'God, Jamie, it's the most terrible thing. I never thought it could happen to me.' She turned and smiled and it was like looking at a corpse. 'I'm love's bitch.'

After Sarah had made her pronouncement, Jamie knelt at her feet, wrapped his arms around her waist and cried. She allowed him the same liberty in this as she had always allowed him. It occurred to him, as he covered the front of her dress in tears and snot, that she had never rejected him physically. It also occurred to him that he had never seen Sarah in a dress except at weddings or parties, and then it would be a tight, sexy number, not a yellow sundress made modest with a prim white cardigan. Things were much worse than he had thought.

'What's with the dress, Sar?' He lifted his wet face to look up at her.

She smiled and then her forehead creased as the smile morphed into a grimace and then back into the original smile. 'Do you like it?'

'Do *you* like it?'

'Daniel bought it for me. *He* likes it.'

Jamie hated the way she was smiling, so he spoke into her stomach. 'Jesus, Sarah. You turn up after so long and you look so bad, I thought you had some fucking disease and you tell me you're so in love and that he loves you, and I don't understand because if he loved you, he would not put you in some stupid little girl's outfit and he would make sure you ate and didn't smoke so much and he wouldn't make you cry.'

Jamie knew he was babbling. What did it matter? All the therapy and the anti-depressants and anxiety suppressors and relaxation tapes only worked when Sarah was not around. It was easy to keep his shit together when she had disappeared off the face of the earth. Or was believed to have disappeared off the face of the earth. But here she was looking like an extra from *Return of the Living Dead* and he didn't give a fuck if he was babbling or hyperventilating or ruining her stupid fucking dress.

Sarah stroked his hair. 'I know it sounds bad, but all that stuff doesn't matter to me. It never mattered to me what I wore or ate or if my iron levels were high enough. If I ever had a half-normal existence it was because you nagged me into it.'

'And that was a bad thing?' Jamie said, as a stabbing sensation shot down his left side. He wondered if it was possible to have a stroke at twenty-four.

'No, it was a wonderful thing. I always felt loved, even when I knew I didn't deserve to be. I wouldn't have made it out of my teens if it wasn't for you.'

The stabbing sensation eased off into a dull ache. 'But…?'

'But…' Sarah sighed. Her hand fell from Jamie's hair, landing lightly on his shoulder. She coughed, sighed again, then continued. 'I was never the fragile creature you thought I was. I loved you for taking care of me, but I always felt… cloistered. I've always had this need to… push things as far as they'll go. Push myself. You always stopped me right when I got to the edge. Daniel doesn't stop me. He binds my hands and feet and throws me right over.'

'Oh.' Jamie wondered if he was being dense. Firstly, how the hell was what she just said a compliment, to Jamie or to Daniel? She made it sound as though she had a choice between a nurse-maid and a psychopath. And all that aside, if she loved the psycho-path and the psychopath loved her back, then why the hell was she weeping on the nursemaid's shoulder? Why wasn't she off with the psychopath having nails driven through her palms or something?

'Is it true that you freaked out when I left?' Sarah said.

Freaked out was one way to put it. Another way would be totally, utterly and completely lost his will to live. No need to make Sarah feel bad about it though. 'I was pretty upset.'

'I didn't know how you felt, Jamie. I'm sorry.'

The pain in his side flared up again. 'Sarah, you knew that I loved you. I told you all the time.'

'I thought you meant you liked hanging out with me and you liked fucking me, and you didn't want me to hang out with or fuck any other blokes. I thought that's what you meant when you said you loved me. I didn't know… I didn't understand how hard it is to walk around all day feeling like half of your body is missing.'

'So, um… so now you understand about love because… because of *him*?'

Sarah recommenced stroking Jamie's hair, but it wasn't comforting anymore. It felt as though she was doing it to soothe herself, the way people fingered worry beads or chewed their nails. The way he pressed his palms together. It felt to Jamie that she was disconnected from him in a way she never had been before. For the first time since she'd arrived, it occurred to him that maybe her absence had been more than a blip in their relationship. Something had been damaged, and just having her here, having her skin touching his, was not enough to fix it.

'The thing I never understood about love is that it can't be quelled, like lust can. With love, if you follow its call, if you give in to it, it just gets worse. The more you have, the deeper you go, the more you need.' Sarah's voice broke and she paused to blink the tears away. 'When Daniel's not with me, I have this agonising need to talk to him. So I call him and as soon as I hear his voice, I have to see him. When I see him, I need to touch him. Then I touch him and it isn't enough, so we make love. And then, where do you go? Because it still isn't enough. It is less than *nothing* to be in his bed. I feel like I'm starving.'

Jamie leapt up and grabbed her shoulders. 'Sarah! You *are* starving. You're really scaring me. You need to get a grip on reality or you're going to fucking die.'

She smiled without teeth. Calmly, as though she understood, she agreed, she accepted. She smiled in that resigned way and kept talking in a voice that was distorted by too much smoke and alcohol, and not enough water and sleep. 'We tried. For a little while everything was normal. Well, not normal the way I used to be, when you knew me before. But normal the way you and Shelley are. We played house, lived as though we were part of the world. But when we're together something happens. It's like… *synergy?* There's too much power, too much energy flying around. I can't even explain to you what it feels like to love someone so much.'

Her eyes were the saddest thing Jamie had ever seen but that didn't stop him wanting to slap her. Did she actually think he had stopped loving her? Or was she so selfish she didn't care? Probably she was so locked up in that extra-special, extra-thick Sarah bubble that it didn't even occur to her that bursting so dramatically into his life would be at all difficult for him. She was not so changed by love to think of anyone except herself.

The phone rang and Jamie went to answer it, knowing it would be Shelley wanting to know why he was still at the office at – he glanced at his watch – shit, at six-forty-five on a Friday night. Jamie was ashamed at how easily he lied to Shelley, but relieved his voice sounded so calm. He talked to her for a few minutes, promised to get home as soon as the damn computers came back on line so he could finish the report, told her he loved her and hung up.

'Do you really love her?' Sarah asked.

'Yeah, I really do. You should see the way she's stuck by me.'

'Do you still love me?'

Jamie sat on the floor and took her hands. 'I will always love you.'

She smiled and slid down off her knees, crossing her obscenely thin calves in front of her. 'You know how you used to say it was different? How you loved Shelley and me in different ways?'

Jamie nodded, amazed that she could talk as though it was ancient history, like it could be discussed and analysed without any immediate or personal pain.

'I understand that now. You love her because she's safe and that was attractive to you because you needed protection from how you felt about me. I feel like that now, I feel like I need to be sheltered from how I feel about Daniel.'

Jamie fought the wave of self-pity. 'Sarah, the situation is not the same at all. Daniel loves you. You didn't love me and that is why I needed protection from you.'

Sarah put her hand on Jamie's knee. 'Who says I didn't love you?'

Jamie's heart stopped for several long seconds and then started again with another painful jolt down his left side. 'Yeah, it was different though, right?'

She nodded and the expression on her face told him that it was so different she couldn't even articulate it. What she felt for Daniel Carr and what she had felt for Jamie were not even in the same category. It was impossible for her to even *imagine* feeling for Jamie the passion, and desire and devotion she felt for that other man.

Jamie covered her hand with his own. 'So you came here because you needed someone to protect you from yourself?'

'I guess so, I… I don't know what I'm doing.' She drew in her breath and the tears flowed. 'My life wasn't supposed to be this way. It wasn't meant to be like this.'

Jamie couldn't have agreed more. When the little dark haired girl had boldly met his eyes across the classroom in year seven Geography and smiled in a way that made his throat hurt, he had known instantly how it was supposed to be. He was supposed to take care of her and make sure she was never hurt or sad or scared. In return she would love him forever and never make *him* hurt or sad or scared. If Jamie had taken better care of her, neither of them would be in this position. It had all gone so wrong.

Sarah had retreated. She had her arms wrapped around her knees and her back against the wall, crying enough to break his heart. If it hadn't already been blown into a million pieces, that is. He watched her and she didn't seem to know he was there; her eyes were opened but focussed on something Jamie couldn't see. He couldn't stand thinking about what she might be seeing, what images danced in her mind when she gazed off like that.

He looked at her legs instead. These legs used to fascinate him because although they were short, they could move really fast. Sarah was always winning races at school against girls with longer, stronger legs. In year eleven she started to wear these tiny black sports shorts that barely covered her arse, and when Mr O'Grady told her off for not wearing the correct sports uniform, she got all teary and said it wasn't easy supporting yourself through school, and if he wanted her to wear the stupid sports uniform he would have to buy it for her himself, or would he prefer her to go without groceries for a few weeks. Mr O'Grady apologised for the misunderstanding and Sarah was allowed to wear the shorts. Jamie knew that the shorts actually cost more than the subsidised school skirt, but Sarah liked the way all the boys, several of the girls and many of the teachers looked at her when she wore the shorts. That was a good memory about Sarah's legs.

A bad memory about Sarah's legs was the mixture of blood and beer and semen that Jamie had wiped off them after she was raped. That was about six months before the sports shorts incident. He remembered gagging as he cleaned her while she lay still and silent, and when he went into the bathroom to rinse the washcloth he had vomited into the sink and the combination of his vomit with the mess coming off the cloth was the most horrible thing he had ever smelt. By morning the bruises had come out and her legs were no longer white at all, they were speckled brown and black and blue and purple, with a red streak here and there. When he walked her home an old lady walking a Shitzu stopped to see if Sarah was okay. When Jamie assured her that they were fine, the old lady looked at Sarah's legs and stared at Jamie in a way that made him glad she wasn't walking an Alsatian.

Another good memory: during his affair with Sarah she had thrilled him with all the different things she did in bed. She loved to give head, to get on top, to have him take her from behind and to do it standing up. None of which was exactly deviant, but you would think so if you were married to Shelley. Jamie and Sarah must have done it in just about every position there was, but the one he liked most of all was when she was below him and she would wrap her legs around his back and squeeze like she was trying to crush his bones.

Today her legs, like the rest of her, were skeletal, and he was sure that if she squeezed him he wouldn't feel a thing. Her skin looked as though it might tear if he rubbed it the wrong way. It was tissue with blue veins showing through, like old people's skin. She had seven bruises that Jamie could see. Most of them were turning yellow already and so must have been at least a few days old, but there was a big blackish splotch on her right shin that looked swollen and fresh. Jamie placed his palm over the bruise and could feel the heat coming off it.

'What are you doing?' she said, startling him.

'Does this hurt?' He pressed the dark spot with the heel of his palm.

'Yeah.'

'How did it happen?'

She stretched out her legs and Jamie's hand slid with the movement and landed on her knee, which was much colder to touch than her bruised shin had been. 'I'm not sure. I find these marks and I can't remember how I got them.' She lifted her skirt and pointed to a red mark at the top of her right inner thigh. 'See this. It's been hurting me like hell, and I can't remember how it happened.'

Jamie pressed the mark with his fingers and she flinched. This was not just some little scratch or bruise. It was an inch long, shiny red, raised up welt. Someone had burnt Sarah's precious flesh and she did not recall this happening. There was something so pitiable about the way she had revealed this to him, as though she wanted him to congratulate her for proving that she too could be scarred by love. It was like the way blokes compared football injuries or mothers showed each other their stretch marks. He was always excluded from those conversations, but this was something he could relate to because Sarah knew about how he broke his arm and ribs once. And that was nothing if not a love related injury.

'Does he hurt you like this a lot?' Jamie did not look at her face. He continued to stroke and press the welt and although it clearly hurt her, she did not stop him.

'Oh, yeah, I suppose. But it isn't… it isn't like I'm some abused woman or anything. We both do it. We both forget that the body has certain limits. We get all… lost in each other. I broke two of his fingers the other day. I didn't realise I was squeezing his hand so hard. He has big hands. Strong fingers, with really… big knuckles and I just… he told the doctor that the car door closed on him and the doctor said that it must have been a heavy door.' Sarah made a choking noise. 'I'm scared of killing him. He left his family for me, before he even knew he could have me. And now… he got fired from his job, his job that he just *loved*. He kept going in late, or not at all, or with… he's given up his whole life for me, and I'm killing him.'

Jamie could see that she was wearing white underpants with daises the exact same colour as her dress. His hand was already on her upper thigh and so it wasn't much of a move to brush a fingertip over the yellow border. Just a millisecond of contact, so swift and light that she couldn't have noticed, but it was enough to make him feel hot all over. He edged his hand over another millimetre, so his palm remained on her thigh, but his fingers hovered over her flowery crotch. He didn't touch, just felt the air above her, and imagined, *remembered*, what she felt like.

As he stared, and hovered, and listened, he was surprised by an erection. It had been months since this had happened without considerable manual effort. Shelley had been good about it, blaming it on the Zoloft he was taking and working tirelessly to bring the sad little fellow to life, but he was rarely able to manage anything past half-mast. If he thought about Sarah and masturbated he could sometimes get really hard, but coming took so long that he couldn't be bothered.

Sarah told him how when Daniel tried to withdraw from the madness of their life together she had gone crazy. On that night, she said, she had broken Daniel's nose, cheekbone, and four of his ribs. She had made a hole in his cheek that had never completely healed. She would've killed him – yes tiny Sarah would've killed him – if he hadn't managed through his drunkenness and despair and concussion to stop her. He didn't hurt her. He just held on to her hand until she calmed down, and then he went to the hospital.

Jamie heard all this but it was beyond him to care. This was not only the first erection in as long as he could remember, it was the most insistent he had ever experienced. He pushed his hand between her thighs and moved her legs apart so he could touch her properly. She looked down at his hand and her face crumpled, but she kept talking and let Jamie stroke her through the daisy pants. He knew she would, because she always let men do whatever they wanted to her.

'When he came out of the hospital, he was different,' Sarah said. 'He said that I had proved to him that resistance was pointless. He said that there was nothing left to protect us from each other anymore. We've crossed the line.'

The anguish in her voice pricked him, and he was disgusted at himself for taking advantage of her. He withdrew his hand, pressing it hard against the other, concentrating on Sarah's swollen eyes. 'That's crap, Sarah,' he said. 'There isn't a line, and even if there is, there's no rule to say you can't cross back and forth as many times as you like.'

She closed her eyes and pressed her lips together, inhaling deeply. Jamie's heart skipped a beat. He recognised that she was gathering her strength, calling up her inner resources. She was hearing him, and thinking it through and preparing herself to do the hard thing. Jamie grabbed her hands. 'He's convinced you that you don't have a choice, but that's not right. You're Sarah Clark! You're stronger than him, stronger than love or passion or... you're the strongest person I know. You can't forfeit your life because you fell for the wrong bloke. Fight this, Sar. You can get over this. I'll help you. You're going to get away from him, and have the life you deserve. I'll give it to you, Sar, I will.'

'That sounds great.' She opened her eyes, bringing his hands to her mouth and planting a dry kiss on his knuckles. 'But the thing is, if I'm away from him, I don't want any kind of life at all. Deserved or not.'

Jamie realised he could never save her. He would never be able to save Sarah Clark from herself, and the harder he tried the more he would fuck himself up. It was futile to be the nice guy. It was her destiny to fuck and be fucked by every single last arsehole in the country, and she had done that and gone back to the start with the very first arsehole who had used her.

Sarah kept on talking. She was glad she had come because she missed him, but also, talking about Daniel had helped her to clarify the situation. After a year with Daniel she had felt trapped and afraid of the future, but now Jamie had offered her an escape and she knew that she didn't want that at all. She wanted relief from the madness of her love affair, that was true, but if that meant not having Daniel at all, well, she would endure the insanity. Endure? No, *embrace.*

Jamie dropped his hands to her thighs, opened her legs wider and knelt between them. She stopped her pathetic rambling. 'Jamie?'

'Lean forward.' She did, and he peeled off her cardigan. Her dress was sleeveless, held up by a bow on each shoulder.

'Jamie?'

'Yeah?' He avoided her eyes while he untied the left shoulder strap.

'What are you doing?'

'I'm listening to you tell me how you're content to throw your life away for an ageing paedophile.' He untied the right bow and ran his hands over her bare shoulders. The dress was flimsy and her breasts were so small that Jamie knew it would fall right down if she moved. The anticipation made him harder.

'I didn't come here for this.'

Jamie discovered that he could not stand anticipation for very long. It must be because he had been waiting for Sarah in one way or another for a decade. That would stretch anyone's patience. He nudged the top of her dress and it slipped easily over her flat chest and came to rest on her lap. There were bite marks covering her breasts and stomach. The picture that came to mind was of Sarah lying naked in the grass while a wild dog savaged her. He felt dizzy.

'Did you hear me, Jamie? I came here to talk to you.'

Sarah's ribs digging into him had always been a turn on but she looked seriously ill now. Jamie wondered if pressing against her might actually injure her. He sat back on his heels and ran his fingers over her ribcage while she stared at him. He realised he must look crazy, squatting between her legs and meditating on her ribs. He realised he *was* crazy.

'You hate talking, Sarah. And I hate listening to all this crap about how much you're getting hurt and how miserable you are but how you really can't leave him. You know how much I love you. I lost it when you went away, I lost my fucking mind, but you come here because *you* feel bad. Because *you* want good old Jamie to make all the bad feelings go away. You expect me to force a smile, wipe the tears from your cheeks, validate your stupidity, give you a friendly hug, and then go home and jerk off into a sock.'

Sarah didn't speak or move. Jamie stood up and walked over to his desk. He removed his tie and shirt, hanging them over the back of his chair. He sat down, being careful not to lean back and crush the shirt, and removed his shoes and socks, placing them neatly next to the chair. Standing up again he took off his trousers and lay them carefully over the seat of the chair, and as Sarah watched, he took off his boxers and placed them on top of the pants. When he was naked he turned to her and beckoned. 'Come here.'

Sarah nodded and stood up, her dress slipping all the way to the floor. She stepped over it without a downward glance and stood in front of Jamie. Her shoulders were stooped, and her arms hung loosely by her sides. 'Do you really want to do this?'

'Yeah, I do.' Jamie lifted her easily and sat her on the desk with her legs dangling. She did not fight him as he pulled off those stupid underpants and threw them in the corner on top of the stupid dress. Sarah's body was completely hairless, and he knew he shouldn't have been surprised. This animal she loved liked her starved and waxed into pre-pubescence while he maimed her. Jamie noticed that her hair was tied back with a yellow ribbon. He pulled it out and hurled it across the room.

'That hurt,' she said, as though having a few strands of hair pulled was more painful then being burnt or bitten or having hot wax poured all over you. 'Why do you want to do this?'

'Because there isn't anything else to do with you, Sarah.'

She stroked his hair and his neck. 'You could talk to me. I miss talking to you, Jamie. You were always saying that I placed too much importance on sex. You once said that you would give up sex if it meant more time talking. Remember?'

'I remember.' Jamie took her hands away from his head, held her arms up, and guided her down onto her back. 'And look where it got me.'

She didn't make a sound when Jamie pushed into her. Her eyes showed shame, helplessness and a sad sort of tenderness. She was his in a way that she never had been before. The knowledge that he could really hurt her had always made him determined not to, but now her vulnerability appalled him; it was disgusting that she would let him do this to her. And it was more revolting still, that she had allowed this to happen to her so many times with so many men. To just lie there and be penetrated like she was *nothing*!

The Zoloft gave him the power to go on and on. The friction was painful for him and was without doubt agonising for her. She lay still, silently staring up at him as he worked harder and harder. There was no indication she was even alive, except for the tears running down her cheeks. He closed his eyes.

'I'm sorry for doing this to you,' she said. 'I'm sorry for making you hate me. I didn't realise. I didn't understand. I love you. I know it's no comfort to you, but I want you to know it anyway.'

'Quiet,' he told her, and she was. He pushed harder, deeper, faster. The muscles in his thighs were burning, and he was going to run out of breath soon, but he knew it was almost over. There was no pleasure in it, just a painful drive for it to be finished. And then it was. He collapsed on to her sharp little body.

After a few minutes his breathing returned to normal, and he propped himself up on his elbows and opened his eyes. She was looking right at him.

'Do you feel better now?' she said.

Jamie saw the creases around her eyes, the yellow tinge to her skin, the cracked lips and the jutting cheekbones as if for the first time. Her eyes were red and teary like they had been since she walked in, but now – *oh, God, he was going to be sick* – now, the tears were because of him. Now *he* was the arsehole, the abuser, the pitiless man who could not see that she needed help and protection, not more fucking. The last thing his poor little Sarah needed was another dick, another careless intruder.

He climbed off her, forgetting he was on the desk and half falling, half stumbling to the floor. He sat with his arms around his knees, his hands pressed together. She was moving behind him but he couldn't bring himself to look up. He didn't want to see her bruised knees or her chewed over breasts or her resolute jaw. For the first time since he'd met her, he didn't want to look at her, or speak to her or touch her. How could he, when the damage he would see was his?

'Jamie?'

He held his breath, focussed on his hands. He heard her sigh and then the click of her lighter. The smell of cigarettes was always the smell of Sarah to him. How many times had he inhaled second-hand smoke while his body recovered from making love to her? His brain had not yet rewired, for he felt the peace and gratefulness that came with the scent of smoke and sex.

'I hurt you,' Jamie said.

'Yeah, well, I'll live.' Her hand closed on his shoulder. Cold, dry hand on his hot, wet skin. Hot and wet from the effort of abusing her. Her voice was unnaturally high. 'I think on the balance of things you still come out on top. You're still the best friend I ever had. I guess you owed me some hurt.'

He couldn't respond. He had nothing left. His shoulder was cold where her hand had been. The smoke was no longer drifting into his eyes. He stared at his hands for a few more seconds and then got up. He stood in the doorway and watched Sarah walking across the reception area. The lift took a long time but she didn't turn and look at him or fidget or anything. She stared straight ahead. The lift came and she stepped inside, and for half a second she looked at him before the doors closed. Her face in that second contained her entire history and was too much to bear.

6

If she returned to Daniel he would know. He would know as soon as he saw her. Without her even getting close enough for him to smell the scent of another man on her skin, Daniel would know she had been touched. He would look at her, and she wouldn't speak or breathe or cry, but he would know. And then he would find Jamie and rip his head off his body.

She couldn't go home, although she ached for him, and she was so, so, sorry – *unbelievably sorry* – that she'd gone to see Jamie in the first place. She couldn't face Daniel's hurt, and his demands and his questions. She couldn't face lying to him. She couldn't face the battle that would inevitably follow if she told him the truth. Couldn't face his wrath. Couldn't allow Jamie to be hurt any more than he already was.

She was directionless. Aware of people and the soft rushing of the river and the busy whir of Church Street on a Friday night, but with no sense of being a part of it.

She had nowhere to go.

When Sarah had nowhere to go she went to Jamie.

She had nowhere to go.

She had been ambushed. Seeking out the safest place she knew she had walked straight into a trap. Jamie had – *what?* Round and round her head, while the wind whipped branches heavy with rain against the windows of the scungy flats in Sorrel Street. While kids on skateboards taunted her from a distance and a truck driver yelled at her to get out of the rain, she wondered what it was that Jamie had done to her. She buried the panic at being alone in the dark, wet night, and walked on, trying to figure out why she felt so destroyed.

When Sarah was eighteen, she had a fling with an Alistair Crowley wanna-be who could only come if Sarah lay perfectly still, with unblinking eyes, pretending to be dead. This was exciting at first, quickly became frustrating, and by the fourth or fifth time, was just boring. It was kind of sick, and kind of degrading, but it never, ever, made her feel this bad. Neither did getting fingered by Mike while he talked to his wife on the phone, blowing Todd while he scored coke out the car window, or pulling off Jess' Uncle Rodger under the dinner table.

So many men and boys and faces and cocks and hands and lips and tongues. Gentle, rough, loving, impersonal, fast, slow, needy, indifferent, handsome, ugly, young, old, sober, wasted, sick, mean, go down, get up, against the wall, under, over, back, front, tied up, hair pulling, bed smashing, window breaking, face slapping, ear licking, eyelash kissing, whispers and shouts and love and hate and *never* did Sarah want to disappear because of how and why and where she had been touched. Because of *who* she'd been touched by.

Jamie had not raped her. She had been raped before and knew what that was. It felt nothing like sex. Even the roughest, cruellest most violent sex, even Daniel sex, felt nothing like rape. Being raped and having sex were as different as being mugged at knifepoint and donating to your favourite feel-good charity. Sarah's rape felt like being robbed and beaten up by a couple of street thugs who she would have given her money to of her own free will, if only they had asked nicely. She had never considered those two mongrels to be sex partners: they were armed bandits.

She thought that what hurt so much about the thing with Jamie was how cold and controlled he had been, not caught up in furious passion at all. She had looked in his eyes, and where she expected to see friendship she saw coldness; where she remembered love, there was bitterness. Her body was unimportant; he had wrecked her inside, and no one else had ever done that to her before. Was there any hurt worse than this?

She had been walking forever. There was a bus stop up ahead, and she sat for a while staring at the road, trying to work out what she should be doing. Part of her wanted to go back to Jamie's office and look into his face and see that she had misread his coldness and his cruelty. Part of her wanted to die. She did not at all want Jamie to die, which is why she could not go home to Daniel.

'Want a lift?'

Sarah focussed on the blur in front of her. A man leant from a car window. Sarah shook her head at his shape. 'Just come for a ride then, eh?' Car doors opened, closed. There were two men, no, three, standing on the path.

'No,' she said, but as she said it she realised that the men were not listening. It was dark and wet, and she had nothing in her but the horror of being touched. It was enough: she ran and ran and ran. She kept running long after she was sure that the men had driven off to find an easier victim. She realised that if she stopped running she would fall down, and she doubted her ability to get back up again.

Three streets away was Jess and Mike's house. They did not like her, she knew, but if she fell down they would help her up. If she asked to stay safe inside until morning, to shower the smell of Jamie's bitterness away before she returned home, they would not like it, but they would say yes.

At the front door, she stopped running, banged three times with her fists and then she fell down.

When Sarah opened her eyes she was looking at photo of Jess and Mike on their wedding day. She was in their bedroom, in their bed, naked. She had a moment of panic at what Daniel would do when he found out she was here, then she remembered everything that had happened and her panic turned to dull despair.

'Jess?' she called, surprised at the huskiness of her own voice. The rain, she remembered and the crying. 'Mike?' She climbed out of the bed and looked around for her clothes.

'At last.' Mike stood in the doorway. 'I thought you were going to sleep all day.'

Sarah glanced at the bedside clock. Twelve past eleven. 'My clothes?'

Mike glanced down at her body and cringed. 'In the wash. You'll have to put something of mine on until they dry.'

'Something of Jess' would be–'

'Jess moved out.'

'Oh.' Sarah wondered why Mike wouldn't look at her for more than a second. Not that she minded; if he touched her sexually she would scream and never stop.

'Have a shower,' he said, handing her a towel. 'Then we'll sort you out.'

She would have laughed if she'd had the energy. The lowest point of her life – rock fucking bottom – and this was who she had to help her out. Mike Leyton, professional cad. She walked past his down-turned eyes to reach the bathroom, and thought that life would never surprise her again.

Sarah found Mike in the kitchen. She sat next to him and he filled a mug with steaming black coffee, looked into her eyes and took her hand. 'What's going on with you, Sarah? You got an eating disorder or something?'

She closed her eyes and took a gulp of the coffee. It burnt her tongue and the roof of her mouth, but was soothing going down her throat. 'Nothing as glamorous as that, unfortunately.'

'What were you doing passed out on my front porch?'

'Seeking asylum at the home of my oldest friend.'

He looked at her over the top of his coffee mug. 'Jess hasn't lived here for months.'

'She finally caught you, huh?'

Mike nodded, lighting a cigarette. Sarah grabbed the pack from him and lit herself one. She didn't know what had happened to her cigarettes. Probably got ruined in all the rain. Or maybe she'd left them in Jamie's office. Yes, that was it. She could see them in her mind, the blue and white packet sitting on top of his blotter, the red lighter beside it.

'It turns out that I really miss her. Don't know what you've got till it's gone and all that.'

'Ah, so that's why you haven't tried to ravage me. You're love-sick.'

Mike took a drag of his cigarette. He looked into her eyes, winced, and looked down at the table. The silence dragged on. Sarah felt icy fingers on her spine. If there was one thing she had liked about Mike back in the old days – apart from the sex – it was his straight talking. Evasiveness and awkward silences were not his style.

'Heh,' she said, showing him her palms, 'I'm not having a go at you. I appreciate it that you haven't tried to jump my bones, really I do, and I think it's sweet that you have all this loyalty for Jess, even if it did take you–'

'Sarah!' Mike grabbed her wrists. 'That isn't it! Jesus!' He swallowed hard, as though there was something stuck in his throat. His hands fell away from her wrists as he looked back into her eyes. Looked at her as though it hurt him. 'Have you looked at yourself in a mirror lately?'

She turned her head against his disgust. 'Oh. I forgot you like curves.'

'No, Sarah, that's not…' Mike covered his eyes and sighed. 'I didn't recognise you when I first saw you. I was about to call the police to come collect the bashed up ten-year old lying on my doorstep. I'm scared to touch you in case you break in two. I wouldn't have undressed you except your clothes were soaked and filthy and I had to try and dry you… you were shivering and…' Mike swallowed again, his eyes closing for a second. 'What's happened to you? Did that old man do this to you?'

'No. Well, I don't know. If you mean the bruises and stuff, then yeah, Daniel did that, but that's not why I'm here. He's not the reason I'm… I went to Jamie's office.'

Mike's coffee cup crashed to the table. They watched in silence as the coffee soaked into the pale blue tablecloth. If Jess ever came back she would go off her head about the stain.

'What happened?' Mike leant across the mess to pick up his cigarettes.

She pressed her knees together until it hurt. 'It wasn't good. He misunderstood me, he…' Sarah took the smoke from Mike's hand and drew back on it. 'He seemed very confused.'

Mike reclaimed his cigarette. 'You do that to people, Sarah. You cross all these lines, and break all these boundaries and people don't know what to do. And Jamie… God, the poor bugger has never been the same since you left. His brain probably short circuited when you appeared out of nowhere.' Mike handed the smoke to Sarah. 'Did he hurt you?'

Sarah nodded.

'Does he know he hurt you?' he asked, and Sarah nodded again, wondering if she would ever be able to think of Jamie again without thinking of the pain when he ripped the yellow ribbon from her hair.

The phone rang. Mike glanced at it, then shrugged and turned back to Sarah. He stroked her cheek with his fingertips. 'Poor Sarah,' he said over the insistent trilling. 'Poor kid.'

The phone stopped and Sarah realised her shoulders had been all tensed up. She relaxed them, closed her eyes, let her head rest against Mike's arm, breathed in the scent of his aftershave. She had a crazy thought that the unanswered call had been Daniel, that he had somehow found out where she was and he was calling to tell her–

The phone started up again.

'God, alright!' Mike carefully lifted Sarah's head off his arm, patting her lightly as he stood up and reached for the phone. Sarah watched him and thought that surely it was Daniel, because only he would be so persistent calling and calling until he was answered. Only he could fill a room with tension and a sense of urgency without even being there.

There was a crash, louder and denser sounding than when Mike had dropped his cup. Loud and dense like the sound of a ninety-kilogram adult male falling to his knees on timber floorboards. Then a small *clack* as the phone receiver landed beside him. Then Mike was screaming the exact same words that had been screaming through Sarah's brain since last night.

'Jamie,' Mike howled. 'No, Jamie. No, no, no, no, no.'

7

She barely survived the funeral. Several times she fell and was sorry that Mike was there to catch her. There were animals scratching and clawing inside her; she wanted to smash herself open and let them out. When she saw the damn box he was in, she felt sure that she was supposed to break it open with her skull, but she was stopped by people who did not understand that Jamie would want her to do it. 'Can't you control her,' someone said, and Mike held her tighter and kissed her forehead which made the scratching worse. Someone told Mike to take her home, which felt unfair because there was a kid howling much louder than she was, but she was too tired to struggle.

Mike drove her back to his place, seated her at the kitchen table and went out for a couple of bottles of bourbon and some more cigarettes. When he returned, he told her he didn't know what to do except get drunk and say what was true, and Sarah wondered why she had never noticed how wise Mike was.

'A few years ago,' she said, shortly after the second bottle was opened, 'this bloke got carried away – it was New Year's – we were both out of our minds, and he somehow managed to put my head through a shower screen. My face was all swollen, red, black, purple, for a week. Five days, I went to work like that. One eye closed over completely. Five fucking days and not one person asked if I was okay. Then another week with yellow bruising, weeping eyes. Nothing.' She drank deeply from the bottle. 'Jamie comes back from his family holiday. My face is almost totally better. He takes–' She drank again. 'He took one look at me. At this tiny little cut under my eye, this faint yellow bruise on my cheek... He fucking cried.'

'I've never seen a bloke so soft on a girl as he was on you.'

'Too soft.' *The stupid bastard.*

They drank to the point of illness and passed out together in Mike's double bed. When they woke they lay side by side, holding hands and looking at the ceiling.

'When are you going to go back to your old man?' Mike asked.

'Do you want me gone?' Sarah asked.

'You can stay as long as you like, but I don't think you should. Life goes on. You can't just hide from it forever, no matter how sad you are.'

She rolled on to her side and looked at him. His eyes were bloodshot from all the booze and crying. 'I'll go home soon,' she said. 'When I feel a bit stronger.'

'I think you should at least call him. Let him know where you are, that you're okay.'

'If I tell him where I am, he'll come here and he'll kill you.'

'This is who you want to spend your life with?'

'Want to? No. I don't want to spend my life with him anymore than Jamie wanted to... sometimes you're fucked either way, it's just a matter of how and how fast.'

'God!' Mike turned to her. His distress was clear; it bled out of the corners of his eyes and into the lines of his face. 'You say these big, huge, heartbreaking things, and you're so calm. Not a tear, not a quiver in your voice. Like everything that happens is as dull as everything else. You're like a robot.'

'Would you feel better if I cried? Would it make you happy?'

A sigh. 'What has my happiness ever had to do with you, Sarah?'

Sarah almost did cry then. Instead, she pulled him to her and kissed him.

Sex had always been her cure all, and even though Daniel chided her for it, and Jamie had catastrophically used it against her, she still felt there was value in it. Loneliness and fear and loss were not intellectual states that could be healed through talk or analysis. They were physical conditions and could only be soothed by physical means.

The loss of Jamie manifested itself as a sensation of bareness. Even weighed down under blankets Sarah felt too exposed. There was too much air on her skin. Air that rushed in through the Jamie shaped hole in the world. Mike's body shut off the air for a little while and made her feel something that wasn't pain. It was good that it was Mike, because he knew why she could hardly move, why her legs and arms stayed locked around him, why she whimpered when he stopped cradling her neck. He knew without her having to explain, because he knew Jamie, and he knew what the cold, relentless wind of missing him was like.

They clung together and whispered things to each other, both nonsensical and important. Sarah remembered something of Mallarmé's and said the words into Mike's ear and he moaned as though he understood her. Afterwards, he asked her what she had said.

'*La chair est triste, helas, et j'ai lu tous les livres,*' Sarah repeated, holding him as tightly as she could. 'The flesh is sad, alas, and I have read all the books.'

'Amen,' Mike said.

Sarah woke early and dressed in the clothes Mike had washed and dried for her. She shook him awake.

'You leaving?' He squinted up with half-closed, crusty eyes.

She nodded and he sat up, rubbing his face. 'Will I see you again?'

Sarah sat beside him and took his hand. 'I don't know.'

He turned her hand over and pressed the inside of her knuckles. 'Take care of yourself.'

'You too.' She pecked his cheek, gave his hands a final squeeze and walked calmly out of his bedroom. Door closed behind her, she started to run.

She found Daniel on the sofa, naked, except for a pair of black socks. Stubble covered his cheeks, coarse and almost white. There was a packet of salted peanuts wedged under his left thigh. His eyes were closed. One arm was twisted at the elbow, pointing over his head to the back wall. The other arm hung over the edge of the sofa, his fingertips skimming the floor.

'Daniel?'

He didn't stir.

On the floor, a photo of Sarah was lying in a pool of vomit. The stomach acid had eaten away at Sarah's face, leaving her a torso with just the swirly shadow of a head. Next to that, an ashtray with a cigarette butt balanced perfectly on the rim. A bottle of vodka, empty, and a bottle of scotch, two-thirds gone.

Sarah stepped over them, and picked up his hand. 'Daniel?' She understood for the first time what it was to have your heart in your mouth. Hers was blocking her windpipe and pressing up into her palate. It was pushing up against her teeth.

His hand was limp and cold. Breathing, concentrating on breathing, Sarah remembered to use her index finger, not her thumb, to touch his wrist. Her heart had left her mouth and filled her ears with its desperate pounding. Her hand was shaking too much to be of use. He is just trying to give me a scare, she thought. And then: *maybe that was all Jamie had wanted to do.* Sarah pressed hard on Daniel's wrist, then harder, then gave it up and pulled on his whole arm.

The cold white arm jerked, then pulled away and tucked itself into the body.

Sarah felt everything rising up inside her. All those things that Mike had said, the things he thought she should cry over, the things he thought she couldn't cry over and didn't care about, all came rushing out. She had thought she was numb but that wasn't right, she had just been anaesthetised, and now it had worn off and the wounds were screaming.

Some hours later, she stopped crying enough to raise her head. Her eyes met his and he moaned in relief and sorrow. Sarah answered in kind. Their bodies merged and more time passed.

'You love me,' Daniel said, and Sarah didn't answer because it wasn't a question. It had never been a question and answering yes or no wouldn't make it one.

Time then, to accept certain realities. This pathetic old man smelling of piss and vomit, being the first one. The reality of him was both uglier and sweeter than she had previously admitted. More vile, and more human. But no less hers than he had ever been.

'Someone died,' she told him.

'Not you though. Not me.'

'No,' Sarah said. 'Not fair is it?'

'Never has been.'

The other reality was harder to face and more important. For the twenty seconds that Sarah thought Daniel dead, she had felt fear and repulsion and regret, but also, she had known in some deep, unexamined corner of herself that she could live without him. She knew that this dark, messy, inexplicably beautiful entanglement was a choice. It was not fated, and she could leave anytime she liked. If she were to stay, she would have to do so knowing that a life with him was but one option out of a million.

But then, life is a constant withering of possibilities. Some are stolen with the lives of people you love. Others are let go, with regret and reluctance and deep, deep sorrow. But there is compensation for lives unlived in the intoxicating joy of knowing that the life you have – right here, right now – is the one you have chosen. There is power in that, and hope.

Other Serpent's Tail books of interest

One Hundred Strokes of the Brush Before Bed

Melissa P.
Translated by Lawrence Venuti

'A very elegantly written memoir... Her reflections on the power of sensual memory are particularly poignant, to the point of Proustian... This is a beautiful book, serious in its intent *Sunday Independent*

'The sex diary of Melissa P shows she is experienced – and wise – beyond her years... [a] combination of candour and intelligence, and Melissa's compelling mix of aggression and passivity' *GQ*

'A frank and vivid account of sexual rites of passage' *Telegraph*

'A blistering bestselling Italian debut' *The List*

'Melissa's candour regarding her extreme experience offers an apprehension, however fleeting, of modern adolescence' *The Times*

'A warm and erotic book, packed with intense and shocking sexual experiences' *Diva*

An immediate bestseller, *One Hundred Strokes of the Brush Before Bed* is the candid diary of a beautiful Sicilian teenager who embarks upon a quest for love but instead enters a world of eroticism and sadomasochism.

Melissa writes: 'I want love, Diary. I want to feel my heart melt, want to see my icy stalactites shatter and plunge into a river of passion and beauty.' She searches for love through lonely-hearts columns, internet chat rooms and even with her math tutor but the men she meets only want sex. With the pain of unrequited love comes the excitement caused by her discovery of the sexual power she has over men (and other women). Her sex life comes to define her clandestine identity, revealed only in her diary entries. When first published, it was assumed that a teenager could not write such a novel and Melissa was forced to reveal her identity to her shocked family and to the world.

girls

Nic Kelman

girls is a journey into the most forbidden corners of male desire and a brilliantly provocative novel about lust, obsession and power.

A wealthy father of two deserts his family in order to spend the night in a college girl's dorm room. A CEO visiting his friends' villa feigns a sprained ankle in order to have sex with their teenage daughter. A businessman in Korea has the best sexual experience of his life with a young woman whose true age he never learns. Juxtaposing philosophical asides and travelling deep inside the most forbidden corners of male desire, *girls* is a perverse novel whose honest insights are both breathtaking and shocking.

'*girls* recalls the territory of Brett Easton Ellis, and in particular *American Psycho*... *girls* is alive with challenging ideas about a society in which teenage girlhood bombards all of us... Like the French novelist Michel Houllebecq, Kelman is not afraid to risk opprobrium to ask what it says about relations between men and women that every town in the West now seems to contain a lapdancing club... it is still gripping to see a light shone so unsparingly into the mind of that beleagured, frightened figure – the 21st-century male' *Daily Telegraph*

'This book is a most uncomfortable study of human desire... scalpel-sharp prose' *Time Out* Book of the Week

'*girls* is bleakly beautiful, razor-sharp and brutally honest' *City Life*

'A cleverly written critique of the valueless nature of a society in which everything has a price. Combining a brilliant nastiness with a tragic sense of dehumanisation, this is a truly shocking work' *Big Issue*

'Raw as Selby Jr or Buwowksi and as powerful in its depiction of male mid-life crisis as any novel by John Updike, Philip Roth or Richard Yates, *girls* is too sick to read on, too compelling not to, brilliant, voyeuristic portrait of despairing male libido' *Uncut*

'Echoing *Lolita*, Kelman paints a disturbing composite portrait of men who approach sex with young women as a kind of rejuvenating sacrament...[and] insightfully portrays male fear and desire' *New York Times Book Review*